No Port in a A Storm

Storm

LEGENDS & LEGACIES BOOK TWO

CAL BLACK

BEARBERRY

BEARBERRY STUDIO

Published by Bearberry Studio 2023

Copyright © 2023 by Cal Black

Cover by Cal Black

First edition

For Mia, who's been there through the dark days and the bright.
For Mom, who's been there for all of it.
For the fellow survivors, who have wondered 'why me?' when better people are gone.

FOREWORD

While there are obvious parallels and inspiration taken from our world, it's important to note that the world presented in Legends & Legacies is intentionally more optimistic than our history. The portrayal of slavery within this book is far kinder than the reality many slaves faced in Caribbean and American plantations. I strongly recommend learning about the San Domingue uprising and the conditions that lead to it, to better understand the inhumane treatment so many people suffered. We must face the dark truths of our collective history if we are to learn from them.

Please note this book mentions slavery, abuse, torture, war, survivor's guilt, generational trauma, and (fantastical) racism. A full list of content warnings can be found at Bearberrystudio.com.

THE STORY SO FAR

MILDRED BERRY AND HER friend Ryan Collins rob a train for much-needed ammunition to keep their town safe and fed, however their plan goes to hell when a dragon attacks the locomotive and derails the train. Millie notices the ammunition crates belong to Frederic Rousseau, war hero of the Amelior Union.

Isaiah Willard, the youngest brother of the Willard gang, stumbles on the women and tries to rob them of the cargo. To keep the robbery secret, Millie kills him. The eldest Willard, Jeb, finds Isaiah's body and vows revenge.

Gilbert Goldman is a banker who handles Frederic Rousseau's finances (which are mostly debts). When the train disappears, Rousseau demands Gilbert pay out the insurance claim or find the cargo. Hiring his longtime friend, Detective Hal Stratton, Gilbert sets out to investigate the crash.

His arrival in Scorched Bluffs is met with hostility, but Millie agrees to bring the men to the wreck site where she plans to eliminate them. A storm blows in, trapping Gil, Hal and Millie in the train's wreckage. Millie discovers

Rousseau sent them, and believes it is for her, as she knows a secret about Rousseau that would ruin his life.

The dragon returns, seeking shelter from the storm. Millie distracts it long enough for the three to make an escape, only for Gilbert to get shot by one of the Willards who has been hired to kill him and Hal. Millie pretends to kill the city men to get the Willards to leave. While recovering from their wounds, she tells Hal and Gilbert the secret about Rousseau: she served under him during the civil war, and won the decisive victory at Marigot city. Rousseau took credit for the battle and kept Millie prisoner for years until he sent her to kill a family to settle his debts. Instead of killing anyone, Millie saves her target, revealing that Sheriff Ryan is actually the lone survivor of the Colfield family, the owners of the rail company they stole from.

Gilbert correctly guesses that Millie is the so-called 'Bayou Butcher', the story spun by Frederic to cover up the sacrifice. Millie admits as much, finally accepting that she can't keep hiding from her past. The man who hired the Willards to kill Gilbert is revealed to be Rousseau himself, and the moment he hears about a ghostly elf, he plans to attack Millie's town and eliminate any witnesses.

Millie prepares for the battle, only to get blindsided by Gilbert, who proposes a marriage to protect their daughters. Whoever survives protects the other's family. Millie agrees, and the two are married by the local medicine woman.

The sound of gunfire and smoke from the shootout attracts the dragon. In the chaos, Fred spots Gilbert and shoots him in the hip before fleeing. Millie and her friends kill the dragon, but are too late to catch Fred. Ryan calls in a favour with her family's company, and an express train takes them to the city.

Rousseau has taken Gilbert's father and daughter hostage, expecting Gilbert to be the one who followed him. Millie, keeping her promise to the banker, surrenders to Fred in exchange for the release of the Goldman family. In a confrontation with Rousseau, Millie disarms him and escapes with the Goldmans. Millie lets Rousseau live so he can be held accountable. Ryan (Rhiannon) takes her family home back from her uncle, who had hired Rousseau to kill her family. Gilbert returns from Scorched Bluffs with Millie's daughters, and a still-healing injury that has left him with a permanent limp.

Also By

Legends & Legacies
No Land for Heroes
No Port in a Storm
No Legend Lives Forever (2024)

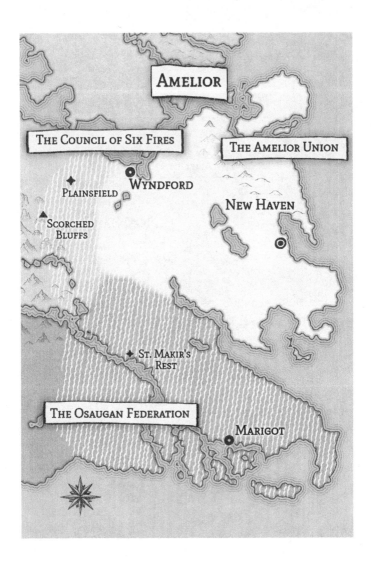

A storm is brewin' down in the bayou,
Rattlin' these bones of sugar cane.
Yes, a storm is brewin' down in the bayou,
A storm of fire, and long held pain.

The war drums are ready, fires are lit,
We're fightin' for our tomorrows,
A pound for flesh, but two for blood,
We gonna paint those masters scarlet,
Let 'em weep and wail their sorrows,
Drownin' in that black bayou mud.

Oh, a storm is brewin' down in the bayou,
Our voices thunder, tears as rain,
Yes, a storm is brewin' down in the bayou,
Won't stop till we break these chains.
— Marigot Folk Song

1

RATTLING CAGES

MILLIE

IN THE DEAD HOURS of the night, Wyndford was as quiet as it ever got. The yowl of a street cat clashed with the clatter of cartwheels on cobbles, making the ghostly elf perched on the roof of a tenement building wince. Mildred Berry flicked her ears to shake out the sharpness of the noise and turned her focus back to the building next to her.

The Wyndford City Jail was built out of the same granite as the rest of the city, a four-storey block of a building in the centre of the city. It had a steady business for the first hour she'd watched, drunk after drunk was escorted through its doors. Some went quietly, others singing or shouting. A fog rolled in off the lake during the second hour, muffling the sharp edges of the city. A lucky break for her. The fog would help to obscure her in an already dark night: a few of the officers she had were elven, and their eyes could see in the darkness just as clearly as her own.

A narrow alleyway separated the roof of the jail from Millie's perch, littered with trash and squabbling rats. Once upon a time, Millie wouldn't have hesitated at the distance. She'd have leapt across it with the confidence that only came with young joints and the sense of invulnerability that got people killed. Instead, tonight she had a length of sturdy rope in hand and a plan.

Rising to her feet, Millie spun the loop of rope a few times to build momentum and released it, sending the lasso across the empty space and hooking it onto one of the jail's chimneys. Pulling the rope taut, she tied off her end onto one chimney on the tenement. She'd checked it over for any weakness, but the grout of the brick was sturdy and the bricks whole. It might not hold a full-grown human man, but a petite elf? Not a problem.

Pulling her newsboy cap low to cover her hair, Millie climbed onto the rope, arms held out to either side to keep her balanced. Her moccasins' thin soles let her feel the hemp rope as though she were barefoot. Millie tested her weight on the rope, and while she felt it sag slightly under her, it held. Carefully and quickly, she put one foot in front of the other until she reached the jail's rooftop. She crouched once she'd made it, ears perked for any sounds of commotion.

Somewhere in the jail, a drunk man was singing, his voice faint and surprisingly on key. Millie raised her eyebrows as she realised he was singing an old Union marching song, something she hadn't heard since the war. Either that was a good sign, or it meant exactly nothing.

Creeping across the roof, Millie found the trapdoor that led down into the jail's interior. She made out the runes and sigils of an alarm, and a magical lock, but there didn't seem to be a mechanical one. Then again, most jails were built to be difficult to break out of, not to break into.

She placed the flat of her hand on the runes and watched the faint glimmer of magic die. Most of the time, the way magic reacted around Millie made life difficult, so she was happy to use the strange effect to her advantage whenever she could. Lifting the trapdoor carefully, Millie heard the clink of a hook and eye latch. Pulling out a small knife, she slid it along the crack between the trapdoor and its frame until she caught the hook. With a little wiggle, she freed it from the loop of metal that had held the trapdoor in place.

Opening the trapdoor just enough to peer inside, Millie took stock of the situation. There was a ladder that led down to the attic, with bundles of cloth, dried rations, and more stored inside. She eased herself down, moving slowly and quietly down the ladder. The attic was dusty from disuse, and Millie pulled her shirt up over her nose to keep from sneezing. She crossed the floor, following the nails in the floorboards that told her there was a crossbeam underfoot. The floor wouldn't creak where it was supported, nor was it as likely to give way if a plank was rotten.

The man she was looking for was below, and the thought made her heart race. Millie could kill him tonight and end the cycle of suffering that he'd put her and so many others through. She wanted to do it, to make sure Frederic Rousseau would never hurt another person and give herself peace of mind.

How often had Millie waited for him, locked in a half-flooded cell in the Marigot jail? Crumbling brick walls that let the water in whenever it rained, it was a far cry from the dusty, dry Wyndford building. Her last stay in Marigot had been shortly before the war turned hot, and Millie remembered the feeling of rough scales coiling around her ankle as a palemouth viper soaked up her body heat underwater.

Millie blinked, realising that this was the first time that Fred was in a real cell. Every time she'd been tossed into the rat-filled bowels of the centuries-old fort that served as the Marigot jail, Fred had been put up in an inn across the street until he sobered up enough to retrieve his property.

Closing her eyes, Millie let herself remember what those nights were like. Rats were attracted to the smell of food and drink in her hair, or the blood that seeped from the cuts she'd sustained in the inevitable brawl Fred would start.

The rats attracted the vipers, who were far more palatable. The trick was to snap its neck before the snake realised you'd grabbed it. Its head tried to bite you even after you'd killed it and the snake started to stink badly enough to chase away the remaining rats. Marigot Jail didn't feed its prisoners the way Wyndford did. You had to catch your supper if you wanted to eat.

The stink of snake musk was only a memory now, though Millie could smell Fred through the dust of the attic. The rotten smell of old drink mixed with the regular prison smells of piss and unwashed bodies. Crouching by a floorboard, Millie used her knife to pry up the nails that held it down. Pulling the plank up, she peeked down to spot a familiar blond head buried in bandaged hands.

So he wasn't asleep, good.

Slipping through the space the removed board gave her, Millie climbed down the door of an empty cell until she was face to face with the man she'd spent so long hiding from. The sounds of the jail were quieter once she was inside. Someone was still singing, but it was muffled by the layers of stone and wood between them.

Frederic Fucking Rousseau looked up from his cot, his eyes searching the darkness of the otherwise empty cell-block. Lionel, Fred's ever-loyal servant, lay in the far corner of the cell, deeply asleep.

"Mil?" Fred asked in a whisper. "I know it's you."

There was no one to stop her if she sank the knife into his throat. She could do it, step up close to the bars and just—

"Have you come to gloat, then?" he asked, voice raspy. He smiled as she stepped into the light, and Millie crossed her arms instead of lunging at him like her instinct screamed to do. "The healer says I won't be able to walk again without using a cane."

"Are you saying I should have shot you in the head?" she asked, sinking her emotions deep into her belly. Away from the surface, away from him. The night she'd shot him in the ankle, she'd been too exhausted and shaken to keep her composure. He had kidnapped a little girl, and wanted to take Millie back. The thought of it still made her stomach churn.

"I was wondering what had made you go soft," Fred said, rheumy blue eyes fixing her in place. He was stone sober, she realised. Maybe for the first time in years. "But I've had a lot of time to think, Mil. I think you know deep down that I'm the only one who'll love you for what you are." He smiled again, but the expression was soft and sad.

"You're wrong," she started. This wasn't going right. She was supposed to have the upper hand, but a sober Fred was a dangerous Fred. It was so easy to underestimate Fred when he was sober. He still looked like a drunk, swollen and ruddy-faced, but somehow the drink had left his mind in pristine form despite the years of abuse.

"Am I?" He sniffed, and pushed himself up to stand on his good leg, using the bars of his cell for support as he hobbled closer. "I learned my lesson. You marked me the way I marked you. I shouldn't have forgotten who you are. I shouldn't have given so much of myself up to the drink. But you saved me by sending me here."

The blood drained slowly from her, leaving Millie cold despite the layers she wore. He was up to something, and she wasn't sure what he was getting at just yet.

"You think I shot you in the ankle to teach you a lesson?" she asked, her whisper getting dangerously close to a hiss. He was right, though. Millie had wanted to hurt him, to make him feel just a sliver of all the suffering he'd inflicted on her and her friend Rhiannon over the years. To leave him with a permanent reminder of what he'd done. He'd arranged the killing of the whole Colfield family, sending Millie and other assassins to eliminate any other claims to the family's fortune so that Rhiannon's uncle could inherit the whole thing. Millie reminded herself of why she was there. Rhiannon didn't know, but it was for her benefit that Fred wouldn't die tonight.

"Why did you come then, Mil?" Fred asked, resting his head against the bars. "If it wasn't to gloat, then why are you here?"

"I'm going to testify," Millie said, straightening her shoulders. "About what you did to the Colfields."

Fred looked through the bars at her, his brow knit slightly in confusion.

"And then what?" he asked. "They'll arrest you for Marigot. Or are you going to 'testify' against me for that, too?"

"Yes," she breathed. "About all of it."

Fred pushed himself up straight, grunting as his fresh scars pulled on healing muscle. Rhiannon's dog had savaged his arm, and the scars that peeked out from under his bandages were an angry red. It looked like a vishap had gotten at him.

"Well, if you're going to tell the *truth*," Fred whispered, his eyes fixed on hers. "You'll hang right next to me. I appreciate the romantic gesture, Mil. Together, we face death, just like old times. Us against the world."

Millie's hands gripped fistfuls of her shirt and it took every shred of composure she had left to stay rooted where she was, and not launch herself at the man on the other side of the cell door. Why had she come here? What was the real reason? It was hard to remember with his words bouncing around inside her head.

"If you plead guilty and testify against Harrold Colfield, they won't hang you." Millie took a deep breath, forcing her heartbeat to slow and her hands to still. "Rhiannon Colfield will arrive later today to make you an official offer."

Fred listened, eyebrows raised.

"And what life would there be for me? A known coward, left to rot in a cell until I die from sobriety?" He cleared his throat and shook his head slowly, eyes slipping from Millie to focus on the ground between them. "I'm surprised you haven't tried to talk her out of it."

"I tried," Millie said, and scowled at the smile that appeared on his face. "But she's a kind woman, Fred. Even after everything you did to her—"

"That we did," he corrected.

"Don't try that on me," Millie hissed. "I kept her safe for years. I taught her how to survive. I might have hurt a lot of people in the past, but I did right by her."

They watched each other in the weak moonlight, filtered through the fog outside.

"I never meant for you to take the fall for that," he whispered.

"But you did in Marigot," she countered. "You didn't even hesitate back then. The 'Butcher of the Bayou' was too perfect of an excuse for that fucking ritual we found O'Leary doing. Couldn't let a human be caught performing sacrificial magic, now could we?"

Fred's face fell, and if she were less familiar with his moods, Millie might have thought the grief there was genuine. Maybe it still was, but that meant nothing. It was easy to grieve a mistake when you weren't the one whose life had been ruined.

"That was an order," he said, rubbing his face with his newly scarred hand. "It came down from top brass. I hid you so you wouldn't be pilloried. What was I supposed to do, Mil? They would have labelled you a traitor, a heretic."

"You were supposed to set me free, Fred." Her voice was harsh, and Millie had to pull herself back from breaking out of her whisper. She wanted to yell at him, scream it until his ears bled. Instead she swivelled an ear toward the door "You were supposed to set us all free after, not kill everyone off one by one. Not keep me in a fucking cellar for three years."

Fred's shoulders sagged, and he eased himself back onto the cot, his injured leg stretched out in front of him.

"You're right," he said. He smiled at her, looking as tired and sad as she felt. Neither of them were young like they had been during the war. It had drained them both, leaving them broken and grim. "Better late than never, right?" he said, running a hand through his hair. "I'll tell your friend I'll testify. But I need you to promise me something."

"I don't need to do *anything*," Millie hissed.

"Well, then please promise me you won't forget. Once a master, always a master. I know that better than anyone. Your friend might act like she's grateful, but she's back in society now. She's the wealthiest woman this side of New Haven, and she's going to forget you the same way I forgot who you were to me."

Even after all these years, Fred's words could knock the air from her. Millie grit her teeth, refusing to let him see just how deeply that had cut. Rhiannon wasn't like that, she wasn't like Fred at all.

"No masters," Fred said. "No kings. Remember?"

"You don't get to say that," Millie snapped. She spun on her heel and climbed up the cell door to the hole she'd made in the ceiling. His words chased her up into the attic, and she wasn't fast enough to escape them.

"Don't let her make the same mistakes I did, Mil. You deserve better than that."

2

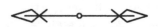

RETRIBUTION

THE RED HAND

THE PERSON WHO WENT by The Red Hand watched the pale elf emerge from the jail and cross her rope back to the building she'd used to surveil the police officers. Deep in the shadows of a tenement across the street, the Hand lowered the spyglass from their eye and checked that their hood was still drawn low over their face.

Curious. What had happened in the jail that made her less careful on the elf's exit? She hadn't checked for any witnesses other than a quick glance down the alleyway.

The rope was severed on the jail's side, though the figure hadn't seen how the elf had managed it. She didn't have her axes with her, and no gunshot echoed through the sleepy Wyndford streets. Magic, perhaps? Raising the spyglass to their eye once again, they watched the Bayou Butcher quickly pull her rope up, coiling it around her forearm and hand before tying it off. The clothes she wore were plain, a child's shirt and breeches that made her look like an underfed youth, but her skin practically glowed in the night's fog.

The Hand didn't need to follow the Butcher to know where she was going, but they would trail her back to the banker's home the same as they had every night since her arrival in Wyndford.

The children had been a surprise, but any doubt that Mildred Berry was the Bayou Butcher had evaporated the first night she had snuck out of the home to case the city jail. The Hand moved quietly, descending from their own perch, feeling clumsy compared to the silent movement of the elf. They had lost her those first few nights. She'd disappear behind a building and be gone when the Hand reached it, or the clatter of a late-night carriage passing by covered her scramble up a building where they did not yet dare to follow.

The years since the war had done little to slow her, it seemed. The Hand smiled under their hood as they slipped out from their hiding spot to follow the pale elf home. It was a relief that the elf had not gone soft like the captain had. It would have soured what the figure had planned.

Ten years ago, the elf had murdered someone dear to the Hand. Eight years ago, she had burned Marigot down, uncaring who was caught up in the flames. But soon, the Bayou Butcher would face the consequences she'd evaded for so long.

3

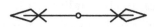

Long Lost, Now Found

Nathalie

Nathalie Wolfe was perched on the edge of the carriage's bench, hands clasped tightly in her lap. Holding herself rigid, she didn't allow herself to crane her neck and gawp at the Colfield Manor as it came into view. A grand old building, built from local granite as grey as Wyndford's morning sky.

There had been a time when the Colfield estate had been a place of wonder for Nathie, when it meant summers visiting the lakeshore, splashing in the waves with her cousins and building sandcastles that Nathie would invent tragic backstories for. There was always a dramatic betrayal among the family, a love lost, and then ended with the ghosts of isolated widows haunting the halls of the misshapen sand piles.

She had never intended for her stories to be anything but flights of fancy, but sometimes Nathie wondered if her stories had prophesied what befell the family years later. Nathie had lost her parents to sickness and war, only to lose her dearest cousins in a massacre only years later. In time, Nathie even became the mournful widow of her own stories. Wealthy, reclusive, and more than half mad with grief.

What she hadn't known, and couldn't have known, back during those summers was that all injuries healed in time. Even grief, though its scars never disappeared. A second husband came and went, though Nathie didn't miss that one nearly so much. But there was also her son, precious and dear, lighting up her heart and home. It was a shattered life, but one that Nathalie had been slowly piecing back together when a telegram had arrived from the Stratton Detective Agency.

Rhiannon Colfield was alive.

The news came as a shock, even though it was what Nathie had prayed for. Her baby cousin, so gentle and sweet, had survived the massacre that took her parents and elder brothers. When the Colfield police department didn't find Rhiannon's body, Nathie had been certain that her favourite cousin had been taken for ransom. She had hired the Strattons to find Rhiannon, and to let Nathie know as soon as the letter arrived, demanding funds for Rhi's safe return.

The letter never came. There was no lock of dark hair sent in an envelope, no shakily penned letter in Rhi's handwriting. Nothing for over five years. Nathie hadn't realised she'd given up hope until the Strattons' telegram arrived a week ago.

In her lap, Nathie worried at the cuticle on her thumb, watching through the window as the carriage approached her cousin's manor. Nathie was no Colfield, or she would have fought the dreadful Harrold for the deeds to this home. Rhiannon's mother and Nathie's were sisters, twins. Their daughters could easily have passed as sisters themselves. Both had long, dark hair like their mothers and porcelain-pale skin. The major difference, aside from disposition, was their eyes. Rhiannon had pale hazel eyes shaped like a rising sun, while Nathie's were wide, blue, and deep-set. Sullen, just like she was.

She frowned. Could Rhiannon still smile so widely that her eyes scrunched up into slits? Did she still try to maintain her composure until she dissolved into mad giggles? After losing her family, how could she?

The carriage arrived at the manor's front entrance. Nathie clenched her hands so tightly that her knuckles turned white. A last, desperate urge gripped her to tell the cab driver to turn around and take her back to the hotel where she was staying and return with a letter instead.

"We've arrived, Ma'am," the cabbie said. A polite older elf, the man clearly had some orcish relative that had passed down a faint green hue to his skin. The thick moustache he wore hid any sign of tusks. Not that Nathalie would have treated him any differently. He climbed down from his perch and opened the door for her like a proper gentleman. Nathie smoothed away the last of her doubts and smiled at the elf as he offered a gloved hand to help her down.

Taking it, Nathie descended onto the cobbled drive of the Colfield estate for the first time in over a decade. Closing her eyes, she took a deep breath and frowned. It didn't smell like she remembered. The warm smell of the stable was still there, as was the faint scent of the rose garden she knew was in the back lawn, but there was something else that tinged the air.

The sharp report of a rifle split the lazy afternoon, and Nathie ducked. Had someone come to eliminate Rhiannon at Harrold's request? Gathering up her skirts, Nathie dashed for the door and shoved it open.

The cabbie was calling after her, but she needed to make sure her cousin was safe. Nathie couldn't lose Rhi as soon as she'd found her. In a panic, she threaded her way past the servants and out onto the back landing, snatching up a brass candlestick on the way by. It was far from efficient, but it would have to do.

Bursting outside in a flurry of black skirts, Nathie held the candlestick ready to bring down onto the skulls of whatever blaggards Harrold had hired this time.

It was immediately shot from her hand, the candlestick's reverberation stinging Nathie's palm as a parting kiss. Clutching her hand to her chest, Nathie hissed and looked up to see how many there were.

Two women stared back at her, one tall and looking breathtakingly familiar. The other was someone that Nathie could never forget. Paler than the dead, an elf with lilac eyes held a rifle trained on Nathalie, a wisp of smoke drifting from its muzzle. Between them, a huge Moorlander mastiff got to its feet, lips peeling back from his teeth in a warning snarl.

"Who the hell are you?" the elf asked, voice cold.

Nathie stared back, eyes wide and wild as she took in the tiny woman who had just shot at her.

Silver-white hair was cut short in the Ogausan style, cropped close to the skin along either side of her head and longer in a braided strip down the centre. The elf had been dressed up in a grey skirt that was far too well made for her station, and had stripped off the walking suit jacket, leaving her in a blouse she'd rolled up to her elbows. She would have looked utterly pathetic if it weren't for the hardness in her eyes and the way scars covered her arms.

She was small, even for an elf... but it was unmistakable. This was the Bayou Butcher, the Ghost of Marigot, the woman that had destroyed Nathie's life.

"Nathalie?" Rhiannon's breathless question shook Nathie from her stupor. She wanted to sweep forward and pull her cousin into a hug, but the elf still had a rifle levelled at her, and Nathie wasn't about to do something stupid and die right after finally finding Rhiannon. The dog's snarl faded, and he looked up at his mistress, tail wagging.

Freed from the pull of the albino elf, Nathie looked at her cousin for the first time in nearly ten years. She was beautiful, tall and strong, her dark hair pulled up into a pile on her head and... she was dressed much the same as the elf, her blouse revealing strong shoulders and tanned, muscular arms. Hardly the build of the proper young lady that Rhiannon had been as a little girl. Wherever she had been, Rhiannon had hardened in her years away.

Heat welled up in Nathie's throat. She choked it down, barely able to blink back the tears threatening to spill onto her cheeks.

"Where have you been?" she whispered, pressing one hand to her mouth. If only Rhiannon had come to her, Nathie would have kept her safe from the world until she was ready to face it.

"You know her?" the elf asked.

"She's my cousin," Rhiannon whispered. Whatever held the women in place broke. Rhiannon pushed the barrel of the elf's rifle down and closed the distance between Nathie and herself.

Nathie met her, sweeping her little cousin up into a big hug, and realised with delayed shock that Rhiannon was now the taller of the two. The emotions no longer could be held back, and a gasping sob wrung itself from her throat as Nathalie finally held her cousin again. Her fingers were greedy, digging into Rhi's shoulders as though if she didn't hold on tight enough, Rhiannon might once again disappear.

"Where have you *been?*" she repeated, barely able to form the words. "I looked for you. I looked everywhere for you." Doubt crept in, twisting around Nathie's words even as she spoke them. Clearly, she had not searched hard enough or long enough after Rhiannon had gone missing. At the time, Nathie had felt she was doing everything she could, but she had barely been hanging on to her sanity back then. How much had she missed while caught in one of her fugues?

A canine huff announced the mastiff, and Nathie glanced down to see him lean his head against her cousin's hip, giant eyes fixed on her. Good boy, she thought. At least Rhiannon hadn't been truly alone for all those years.

"It wasn't safe," Rhiannon whispered, and while her voice was steady, Nathalie could feel the tremble in her shoulders. "No one was safe."

The doubt was squashed by indignation, and Nathie pulled herself back to stare into her cousin's eyes, wiping away some tears on Rhiannon's cheek with a gentle thumb. The gesture was so familiar that it almost took Nathie back to the summers when life had still held promise. Wiping away her darling cousin's tears after Rhiannon had tripped and scraped her knee while playing tag.

"Who told you that?" she asked, her voice sharper than she'd meant it to be. Nathie frowned in concern. "I would have kept you safe, Rhi. You know I would never hurt you. I would have destroyed anyone who came after you. Anyone who even thought of coming after you."

"About that," the elf said, clearing her throat from where she stood. Nathie shot her a glare, indicating that her interruption was not wanted. No doubt the elf had been the one who sowed paranoia in Rhiannon's mind. Hadn't she done enough damage to Nathie's family? Now she had poisoned Rhiannon's thoughts, making her not able to trust her own cousin.

"How do we know you're not just another Harrold?" The elf raised an eyebrow, resting the rifle against her shoulder in a casual threat.

"How dare you," Nathie whispered, holding Rhiannon tightly. She wanted to stride over to the elf and knock her down with a well-placed slap. Instead, out of consideration for her cousin, she clenched her jaw and forced herself to ease her grip on Rhiannon. A deep breath helped hold the anger back, but only just.

"I would never hurt my cousin," Nathie hissed through bared teeth. "How dare you, of all people, suggest otherwise?" This was dangerous, she knew. Provoking the Bayou Butcher could end with a bullet in her breast, but the wrong-headed insult of being called untrustworthy by a woman who had killed *children*.

"Millie, go home," Rhiannon said quietly. "Nathie isn't Harrold. It's going to be a long day. I'll come by this evening to see you and the girls."

Rhiannon's words might have been quiet, but Nathie watched with a dark glee as they shattered the elf's aggressive posture. The Butcher blinked those strange eyes of hers and slowly looked away from Nathie to fix on Rhiannon. Pressing her lips together in a smile, Nathie let go of her cousin's shoulders and took Rhiannon's hand in hers. She watched the elf's eyes flick down at the gesture, and the smallest of frowns appeared on that unnaturally pale brow.

Nathie waited, biting the inside of her lip as she prepared for the onslaught of the infamous Butcher's temper.

"Fine," the elf said, fixing her eyes back on Nathie. They watched each other for a moment. The anger that Nathie had expected simmered behind lilac eyes, but there was another emotion that tempered it. What it was, Nathie couldn't say. She didn't know enough about the elf's mannerisms yet, but that would change.

"Fyo, you make sure Ry doesn't get into trouble, alright?" the elf told the mastiff. Much to Nathie's regret, the dog sat up straighter and gave an affirmative whuff. Moorlanders were supposed to be trained to only accept commands from their masters, yet here was Rhiannon's listening to an elf, of all things.

"She will be fine," Nathie said, a bit of an edge creeping back into her voice.

The Bayou Butcher nodded to Rhiannon, picked up her jacket, and departed.

"Did you have to be rude?" Rhiannon asked softly once they were alone. "She saved my life, you know."

Nathie smiled, but she could feel that her sadness leaked through the attempt at joviality. Giving Rhiannon's hand a gentle squeeze, Nathie turned to study her cousin. How, even through sadness, she was resilient and compassionate enough to think about a war criminal's feelings.

"My darling Rhi," Nathalie Wolfe said. "That elf killed my father and would have killed me without a second thought. She might have saved you, but you cannot trust her."

Rhiannon's back straightened, and her hand went cold in Nathie's. She opened her mouth to protest, but Nathie shook her head to forestall it.

"I watched her do it during the war. She shot him in cold blood."

"But your father was a Unionist," Rhiannon whispered. "She only hurt people she had to."

Nathie battled to keep her smile in place, but as tears welled up in her eyes, she gave it up. Instead, she pulled Rhiannon into a tight hug, pressing her nose into her cousin's hair. Propriety demanded she be reserved and mourn in private, but Rhiannon was family. She was the only family Nathie had left other than her son.

She would die before letting the elf take her cousin from her, too.

"Sweet darling Rhiannon," Nathie whispered. "She's a killer and killers lie."

4

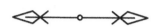

BANKING ON BUSINESS

GILBERT

GOLDMAN NATIONAL BANK HAD the bones for growth. Gilbert had made sure of that when he'd planned out its first five years of business. He'd accounted for shortages, for a fluctuating market, he'd even accounted for his largest client, Frederic Rousseau, losing a significant amount of money. What he had not accounted for, however, was becoming the personal bank of the wealthiest heiress in the West.

Rhiannon Colfield had completely upended his plans just as easily as her short, angry friend had. But where Mildred had become a surprise wife, Rhiannon had changed the course of his bank and single-handedly ensured his family would never go hungry. The Colfields were old money, but had made shrewd business decisions when they moved to the new world. Investing first in shipbuilding and then in rail, they would have been the wealthiest family in all of Amelior if they didn't invest a significant portion of their money back into the community.

The Wyndford hospital? Funded and built by the Colfields. The sewage system that kept the slums relatively clean? Paid for by the Colfields. When he was younger, Gilbert had thought it was nothing but a smart business strategy: take care of your customers and they would choose you over a competitor every time. That was how the Colfields did business... until the Bayou Butcher had massacred the entire family, leaving a distant uncle as the sole inheritor.

Gilbert sipped his coffee, reviewing the notes he had been making for Rhiannon's investment strategy. That uncle, Harrold Colfield, had soured much of the city on the family name, but now the prodigal daughter had come home to return the family to its former glory. Breathless headlines in the city's papers announced that the very Butcher that had killed her family had saved the heiress.

Gilbert looked down at his cup. His secretary had prepared his coffee as she always did: cream and a spoonful of sugar to take the bite out of the brew. But what he'd remembered as delicious now tasted too heavy and too sweet.

"Is everything alright, Mister Goldman?"

Looking up from his cup, Gilbert smiled at the severe-looking woman who stood in front of his desk. Tabea's slightly pointed ears were made prominent by the way she slicked her dark hair back into a tight topknot. She watched him through narrow eyes, her hazel irises barely glinting from under pinched monolids. He'd never thought to ask if she was part arroyan, but now after meeting more of them he couldn't help but pick up on the slight hitch on Tabea's T's. Like she was overcompensating the pronunciation. He almost wanted to ask her if she had any family from the Empire, but the last arroyan he'd met could call down thunderstorms from blue skies.

Perhaps it was best to leave some questions unasked.

"It's fine," Gilbert said, feeling a cool shiver creep up his neck. When had he gone and surrounded himself with scary women? He smiled at his secretary and took a long sip, murmuring his appreciation after.

Tabea didn't look convinced.

"There wasn't much sugar out west, I'm afraid," Gilbert said smoothly. "I just have to get re-accustomed to city tastes."

"Yes," Tabea said with a dangerous chill in her voice. "I noticed you seem to have taken quite a liking to frontier tastes. Such as their women."

Gil set his coffee down on his desk, away from the papers he'd been reviewing. Leaning on one forearm, he squinted at his secretary. They'd worked together for years, she'd left their previous bank to found this one. Tabea had never expressed more than a clinical interest in him or his bachelordom. So where was this coming from?

"Tabea, do you have a problem with me being married?" he asked carefully. Tabea was an exceptional secretary. Not only did she frighten most clients into behaving, but she was also as sharp as any auditor and caught half of their mistakes before the reports hit Gilbert's desk. He might be able to afford to replace her now that Rhiannon's money was being transferred over to their coffers, but that didn't mean he *wanted* to.

Tabea kicked the door to his office closed, and Gilbert winced at the loud bang the solid oak door made as it struck home.

"First you run off on a fool's errand," Tabea said, counting his sins off on her fingers. "Leaving me and your father worried you'd die out in that godless land." Sin number two. "*Then* you got shot, and came back married to some woman you'd just met." Sins three and four. Instead of counting off sin number five, Tabea slammed her now-open palm onto his desk, making his coffee cup jump. Gilbert reached out and steadied it to prevent any spills.

"Not only that, but the woman you married is the one and only Bayou Butcher, the single most reviled, hated, feared person in the whole damn Union. Did you even know who she really was when you exchanged vows?" Tabea had raised her voice, but only slightly.

Gilbert sat up straight in his chair, hands held up in self-defence. If he had learned one thing over the last few weeks, it was that the best thing to do with angry women capable of shooting you was to let them finish speaking.

"I did, yes," he said, once he was certain his secretary had finished. He cleared his throat lightly and picked up his coffee again. "That was part of why I suggested marriage in the first place. I didn't plan on us both surviving the day, but the vows would protect the girls. Both hers and Sarah."

Tabea leaned on the hand she'd slammed on his desk, eyes boring into him.

"So you married her *because* she's the most reviled person in the country... Am I understanding that correctly?" Tabea eased back, some of the anger fading back into her usual neutral expression.

"Yes ma'am," Gilbert said. He let his hands sag slightly. He knew he wasn't out of danger yet, but at least Tabea was giving him some breathing room. "I figured if Rousseau was going to kill me, I wanted the meanest son of a bitch out there keeping the rest of my family safe." He coughed, realising his slip of the tongue. "Daughter of a bitch, I suppose. Either way, I figured only one of us would survive Fred. Probably her." Turning his palms up to the ceiling, Gilbert shrugged.

"But turns out we both lived, and now here we are. It was her who landed Miss Colfield as a client for us, actually. Those two are—" he paused, trying to think of a way to explain it. "*Exceptionally* close after what Rousseau put them both through. More like sisters than friends."

Tabea's internal struggle manifested in a slight purse of her lips as she considered the benefits of having her boss married to the Butcher compared to the obvious draw- backs. She eased her hand off the desk and rubbed the red flesh of her palm with her thumb. The closest thing she gave to her approval was a tight nod.

"You didn't think I was jealous, did you?" she asked, voice flat. "Even though you haven't even brought her to the bank to introduce us?"

Gilbert pressed his lips together and shook his head. Somehow, he was certain Tabea would not appreciate knowing he had considered, albeit briefly and with great confusion, that she had been jealous.

"No, Ma'am. I'll bring her by tomorrow morning. She should see the bank anyways."

"Good. There will be no further issues so long as your wife doesn't harm you or the bank," Tabea said, tucking her hands together like a prim schoolmarm.

A polite cough from the other side of the office door ended the conversation.

"Ah, yes," Tabea said, adjusting her spectacles. "Mister Whistenhowler is here to take you to lunch." She pressed her lips together tight. "He did *not* have an appointment." Showing up without an appointment was the only sin worse than murder, as far as she was concerned.

The Whistenhowlers were Inglic nobility, and Charlie, youngest of the Whistenhowler's three adult sons, had been a drinking buddy of Rousseau's. Gilbert knew him casually, but Charlie had never bought Gil so much as a drink. Why invite him out to lunch now? Charlie might not be the primary heir to the fortune, but the man would still stand to inherit a significant sum and shares of his family's companies.

"I'd better not keep him waiting." Gilbert leaned on his desk and pushed himself to his feet. The twinge of scar tissue in his hip protested, but not as sharply as it did when he first staggered out of bed. Gilbert let himself smile as he thought of the scene he'd left behind in that bed: one small, grumpy Bayou Butcher who had been pinned by three sleepy little girls. There were worse ways to wake up every morning.

The marriage's duration was tenuous, so Gilbert was determined to enjoy the illusion of domestic bliss while he had it. Eventually, he and Mildred would need to talk about what to do about the situation, but it was surprisingly difficult to get a private conversation in when there were three little girls instead of just one.

Tabea opened his office door to let Charlie in. Gilbert set aside thoughts of the marriage and widened his smile at the man waiting there. Dressed in an expensive wool suit and a crisp cotton shirt, Charlie tipped his hat toward Tabea before striding over to Gilbert, hand outstretched to shake. Gilbert shifted his cane to his left hand and gripped

Charle's offered one firmly. Whistenhowler's hand was soft, his carefully manicured nails buffed to a sheen.

"Messiah's grace, Gil," Charlie said, clasping Gilbert's hand with both of his. "I would not have pegged you as one to seek out adventure, but what an adventure you had! You'll have to tell me about it over lunch." Charlie's grey eyes sparked with curiosity, and the much shorter man's enthusiasm was contagious. He held out a hand, offering to help Gilbert walk, but Gil waved him off. His cane worked well enough.

The walk to the gentlemen's club wasn't far, and after a few minutes of walking, the tension in Gilbert's hip eased, lengthening his stride. He listened to Charlie chatter about the latest Wyndford gossip and enjoyed the cool breeze that swept uptown from the docks. It was refreshing in the lingering summer heat. The gossip was also more interesting than the usual trysts and faux pas'. Wyndford was absolutely consumed by the return of the Bayou Butcher, and the news that the Hero of Amelior Union, Frederic Rousseau, was jailed instead. Not only that, but the two had served side by side during the civil war. Everyone loved a downfall, it seemed.

"What's she look like?" Charlie asked as they reached the club. This early in the day, it was moderately busy. The day-drinking elite were nursing hangovers with the hair of the dog that bit them. Metaphorically, of course, the only person who'd been bitten by a dog recently was Rousseau himself. Gilbert suppressed a chuckle as he realised this was the same club that Rousseau had frequented for years, until he could no longer afford the monthly fee, and resorted to drinking at home.

"Hm?" Gilbert asked, distracted by the cathartic thought of a painfully sober Frederic. "Do you mean Mildred?"

He smiled at the doorman and tipped his hat as the man showed them to Charlie's usual table. The club was panelled with dark wood, though at noon the shutters were opened wide to allow Wyndford's meagre sunlight to illuminate the room. It smelled of expensive cigars, quality whiskey, and delicious food.

Gil had long hoped to join, and he realised with a surprise that he might be able to. With the Colfield fortune funding his bank, he could set aside a little money for small luxuries like this. The club's luncheons were second best in the city. Not even Charlie could afford the club that hosted men like the Colfields.

"'Mildred'?" Charlie asked with a laugh, pulling off his suit jacket and taking a seat at his table. "The Bayou Butcher's name is 'Mildred'? By the Wheel, that's nearly as bad as being named *Prudence*. Mother would disown me if I ever called her that." Gilbert smiled, easing himself down into his own chair. He grunted softly as his hip adjusted to the new position.

"Mildred would do much worse if anyone called her prudent," Gilbert said, hooking the handle of his cane over the arm of his chair. "She might not be what the legends say she is, but she's the one they're about, that's certain."

Charlie leaned over the table, eyes hungry for more. They flicked back and forth, making Gil feel as though he was more of a book to be read than a man. It was unnerving, and Gil wracked his brain, trying to remember if Charlie had always been this attentive. He'd always hung on Rousseau's every word, but the man seemed far more intense than he had the last time they'd all gone out drinking.

"Did she threaten to kill you?" Charlie asked.

"She did, repeatedly." Gilbert thought about the first time he'd met the pale elf. Mildred had pulled a gun on him, and while Gilbert had thought it was excessive, her actions had made more sense after he learned she knew Rousseau. Now, he was impressed she hadn't just shot him on the spot. "However, after getting to know each other, she ended up saving my life instead of taking it. Our dear friend Frederic was the one who tried to kill me." Gilbert took a sip of the ice water a server placed in front of each of them. It was so cold it made his teeth hurt.

"And... you married her?" Charlie asked, agog. "Why in the Messiah's name would you do that? Did she threaten you? Surely she's monstrous, her nature leaking out into her features." Gilbert frowned slightly, watching Charlie lick the corner of his lips. "What's being with her like?"

"It was a Six Fires ceremony. I'm not certain it will hold up in Amelian courts," Gilbert said. Charlie's behaviour almost made Gilbert miss Rousseau, a feat he would have thought impossible mere minutes ago. "And she's just a woman, Whistenhowler. A damn good fighter, but no more a monster than anyone else." Gilbert certainly wasn't going to answer the last question. Between his hip and the three little girls who were plagued by nightmares, there hadn't exactly been time to talk to his new wife, let alone have sex.

Charlie bit his lower lip and nodded. He motioned Gilbert closer, and with great reluctance, Gil complied.

"She's close with Rhiannon Colfield, right?" Charlie asked, his eyes darting about the room. He didn't want anyone else listening, and Gilbert was certain he knew why. Miss Rhiannon was the most eligible young woman in the west. Charlie thought he had a lead on a personal introduction.

"You'd like me to introduce you?" Gilbert asked, arching an eyebrow.

"Mother says we'd make a great match, but no. I'm a third son. I have little to offer the last Colfield," Charlie said with a small sigh. "I'm just curious how they ended up in the same town, of all places."

"Mhm," Gilbert said, leaning back in his chair. He certainly wasn't going to explain the connection. That was Rhiannon's business. "Well, if you have an invitation to her soirée tomorrow, you can always ask the lady herself."

Charlie burst into a grin and smacked the table out of sheer excitement.

"That's an excellent idea! Thank you, Gil. I can't wait to hear it from the Butcher herself."

Gilbert frowned. That wasn't what he'd meant at all. Mildred would not be happy about this.

THE BEST PART OF Gilbert's day was when he stepped into his home and a flock of nightgown clad little girls raced toward him to hug his legs, followed by a fox-red fluff ball puppy. The redhead, Rasha, was the first to reach him, followed by his own Sarah with dark curls and a big smile. The third was a little elf with white hair and tanned skin, holding back until Gilbert motioned for her to join her sister. Or was it sisters, now? Ears flapping, Fenna hurried over and threw her arms around both Sarah and his leg.

"Look at all these freshly washed Berries," Gilbert said, setting his cane aside to scoop the little girls up one by one to kiss their cheeks. "Were you ladies good for Mister Arnaud and Tata Avrom while your momma was out?"

The redhead and the little blond looked at each other, then back at Gilbert.

"We *tried*," Rasha said. "The rules are different. Tata is really nice. He read us books!" Her eyes were as big as saucers. Rasha held her hands up as far apart as they could go. "You have so many books! Momma said it's a lie... a lie-" She looked at Sarah for help with the word.

"Library," his daughter said, getting her 'r' almost right.

"Yeah! A Libwawy," Rasha said, copying Sarah's pronunciation exactly. The puppy, Freckle, barked in agreement.

"Where is your momma?" Gil asked, ushering the girls out of the front hall. It took some doing. Fenna wouldn't go until she was holding someone's hand, and Rasha was weaving in and around the other two, too excited to focus on walking forward. The puppy seemed to be everywhere at once, unsure which little girl to follow. After the strange conversations he'd had that day, Gilbert basked in the domestic chaos.

"She and Mister Arnaud are in the kitchen," Sarah said, her face growing serious. "They're fighting."

"I think Mister Arnaud dropped the sugar," Fenna whispered. Rasha nodded solemnly.

Gilbert strained his ears and caught the murmur of voices, but they didn't seem sharp enough to be an argument.

Scooping Sarah up and settling her on his good hip, Gil herded the other two girls toward the kitchen.

"Missus Goldman you can't-"

"I told you not to call me that. Call me Millie," Gilbert's temporary wife said, stirring a pot of something on the stove.

"I will *not*," Arnaud said, with an audible sniff. "I pride myself on having a professional relationship with my employers. I will not address you as some sort of... peer." A distinguished half-orc, Arnaud's minty hair had escaped its normal pompadour, and the poor man looked frazzled. Spotting Gilbert, Arnaud gestured in horror at the tiny woman who had invaded *his* kitchen.

"Mister Goldman, please get your wife under control."

The kitchen went quiet, save for three little gasps in chorus. At the stove, Millie's ears dropped low and lay flat against her skull. Gently, Gil bent down and set his little girl back down next to the two small elves.

"Sarah, darling, why don't you, Rasha, and Fenna get into bed and pick which story you want me to read for you? I'll be up as soon as I save Mister Arnaud from their momma." He smiled and tucked a curl behind one of her ears. Sarah, old enough to feel the discomfort in the room, nodded and grabbed a hand of each little elf, pulling them out of the kitchen after her. Freckle followed, tail wagging so hard he nearly fell over.

"'Under control'?" Mildred Berry-turned-Goldman asked as soon as the girls were gone. She turned away from the stove, a wooden spoon clenched tightly in one hand. She looked at Arnaud, then Gilbert, daring him to so much as try to get her 'under control'. Gilbert was quite happy being alive and did no such thing.

"Arnaud," Gilbert said, placing one hand on Arnaud's shoulder. "I understand things have been incredibly stressful. I believe you deserve the night off. Why don't you go enjoy yourself?" he suggested gently, guiding his steward toward the door of the kitchen.

"She is using *my stove*," the orcish man protested. He was as tall as Gilbert, and if he wanted to, Gil was certain that Arnaud could overpower him. Not that strength would help the steward against the little elf, though. Gil had seen her take down men twice her size.

"Mildred is *Missus* Millie Goldman right now, so she's allowed to use the stove," Gilbert said soothingly. "I'm certain she's used many stoves without blowing any up." He paused, thinking of his wife's reputation. Glancing over his shoulder at her, he lifted an eyebrow for confirmation.

"The only stoves that I blew up were blown up on purpose," she said, arms crossed. But her ears had lifted off her skull, a good sign.

"See? I doubt she wants to explode this one, so it'll be fine." Arnaud muttered another weak protest, but Gilbert slipped a banknote into his hand and nudged him the rest of the way out the door. "Your long overdue bonus!" He called down the hall, then closed the door before the man could step back into his kitchen. He slipped his cane under the knob, keeping Arnaud out.

"I apologise for that," Gilbert said, glancing back over at his wife. "He gets particular about the kitchen. I don't expect that his comment was anything more than an attempt to regain control over the stove." Gilbert sniffed the air, smelling something earthy and sweet. The kitchen door rattled, but the cane held firm.

"This didn't have anything to do with sugar, did it?" Gilbert asked. He blinked in surprise as Mildred bristled.

"No," she snapped. "I didn't steal any sugar."

Gil held his hands up in surrender.

"No stealing, Fenna just thought Arnaud 'dropped the sugar'. I wasn't sure if that was literal or a euphemism for being a jerk."

Mildred visibly deflated, even her ears drooped as she glanced past him to the kitchen door. Pressing her lips together, she shook her head.

"No, she means actually dropping sugar," she said with a tired sigh. "Sugar costs so much. Back in town, the girls spilled some, and I reacted badly. It was during a lean period, hunting was poor and we were surviving mostly on bone and root stews. I regret losing my temper, but they still think wasting sugar is the worst thing a person can do."

"I'm certain they'll grow out of it," Gil said, hobbling over, leaning on the counter for support. "With Sarah, it's ink instead of sugar. She still gets upset if anyone mentions it." He sniffed the air, curious. "What are you making?"

"Roughleaf tea," Mildred said, rubbing her shoulder. She didn't look convinced that her daughters would forgive her, but the change in topic seemed welcome. "It helps me fall asleep. Ryan was supposed to be by." she paused, and Gilbert watched her ears flick backward in annoyance. It was terribly endearing. "Sorry, *Rhiannon Colfield* was supposed to visit, but she never came by." Her ears drooped, and Millie turned back to the stove, stirring the tea she was making.

"That doesn't sound like her," Gilbert said, leaning against the counter nearest to the iron stove. It was too tall for her, and he noticed that Millie had found one of Sarah's footstools to use. He decided not to comment on her resourcefulness. "Something important must have come up for her to miss a visit to your girls."

He watched Millie scowl down into the pot, its liquid amber. It smelled quite good; he had to admit.

"It wasn't just that. She was supposed to talk to Fred today, and let me know what happened. This isn't like her," Millie said, pressing her lips together.

Gilbert lifted an eyebrow.

"Why in God's name would she want to go speak with that asshole?" he asked, dropping the volume of his voice in case any little ears were listening at the kitchen door.

Mildred looked up at him, a faint smile touching her face. She looked tired, Gil realised. She'd been sneaking out most nights, and he'd pretended not to notice since she always came back before dawn and without any blood stains. Not even the Ghost of Marigot could escape from a bed with three sleeping little girls and their parents without notice. Eventually, the girls would stop having nightmares and Gil would get his bed back but between the three of them, it would be a while.

"That's where you've been going?" he asked.

"No," she said with a sigh. "Only sort of. I had to—" the words caught in her throat, and Gilbert watched as Mildred took a deep breath and closed her eyes. She squared her shoulders before opening them, and when she looked at him, Gilbert was surprised to see guilt there.

"Rhiannon is going to offer him a deal. If Fred testifies against her uncle, he won't face the noose. I went to tell him to take the offer."

Gilbert blinked and shook his head slightly, certain he had heard that wrong.

"I thought you wanted him dead," he said, frowning slightly. "Why talk to him at all?"

She smiled sadly at him.

"Rhiannon. She needs this, and without Fred, the case isn't very strong. Harrold might not get the family money, but he'd get part of West-Colfield Rail. If Harrold hangs, it's hers; if he doesn't, she'll have to work with the man who killed her family."

Gil studied her, the gentle droop of her ears, the crinkle under her eyes.

"Do you think something happened at the jail?" he asked. "I would think that discussion would be even more reason for her to come by."

"Not at the jail," Mildred said with a heavy sigh. "Her cousin showed up, wide-eyed and howling like a banshee. I thought she was going to attack Ry, so I shot the candlestick out of her hand." She stirred the tea, her frown only deepening. "I didn't know she even had a cousin."

"Well, given that it was Rhiannon's uncle that tried to have her killed, I would argue that was a reasonable reaction to an unknown cousin brandishing a candlestick," Gilbert said. He smiled when she looked up at him in surprise. Gil shrugged. "You know how much you mean to her, Millie. I'm sure Rhiannon is just soothing upset nerves. If her cousin is anything like the more dramatic women of Wyndford's high society, it's a wonder she didn't faint dead away when you shot at her."

"I didn't shoot *at her*," the elf grumbled. "That's the first time you called me Millie. No 'Deputy' anymore?"

"Are you a deputy?" Gil asked, tilting his head. "You told Arnaud you'd like to be called Millie. If that's too familiar—"

"No, no, it's..." she hesitated, and finally moved the pot off the stove, flipping down the burner's iron cover to keep the heat in. "It's nice. And I meant I shot at the candlestick. If I'd shot at *her*—"

"You'd have hit her," Gilbert answered for her. "I'm sure tomorrow night Rhiannon will be back to normal. But right now, would you care to join me in reading some bedtime stories?" He held his arm out to her, crooked at the elbow.

He watched a small smile flicker at the corners of her lips. Pouring the tea into a mug, the Butcher took his arm. It was easy to forget how short she was. Mildred Berry projected such a large and spiky presence to keep people away that when she let you in, she was just... tiny. Still spiky and sharp, but tiny.

"The cousin's trouble," she said, helping Gil back to where he'd left his cane. "I don't know how yet, but there was a look in her eye. It set all the hairs on my neck on end."

Gil looked down at her. Was that what truly bothered her? Or was it that Ryan had sent her away? He'd make his own opinion after the soirée, tomorrow. No doubt this new cousin would be in attendance. He gave his wife's hand a little squeeze of reassurance.

"If she is, we'll sort her out."

5

LOST SUMMERS

RHIANNON

RHIANNON INVITED NATHALIE AND her little family to stay at the manor. Getting her cousin and Nathie's son Owen and his nanny settled made for a busy afternoon, a distraction which she was grateful for. The morning's confrontation between Millie and her cousin had left Rhiannon unsettled.

Fyodor was happy to have a new pair of friends to chase around the garden. Nathalie's Norlund Lophund, appropriately named Agnar, outran both Fyodor and Owen, but would tumble tail over snout every time he tried to make a sharp turn. It sent everyone into fits of giggles, and before long, the boy had collapsed into the grass, with Fyodor cautiously sniffing at him and licking at his face, which sent Owen into further giggles.

Rhiannon wasn't sure if Millie really had killed Uncle Wolfe, but even if she hadn't, it was a shame she and Nathie had gotten off to such a poor start. Owen was a few years older than Fenna and Rasha, but the two little girls would be good company for him. The last children that had run around the lawns playing with pups were Rhiannon and Nathalie themselves, who were now familiar strangers trying to figure each other out.

Now, as Owen had a bath to wash off all the dirt and grass before bed, Rhiannon and Nathalie had a moment to themselves and a pot of tea to smooth over any awkwardness.

"You're good with him," Nathie said, the first to speak. "Were there children out in your town?"

Rhiannon cupped her hands around the fine china out of habit, and at Nathie's raised eyebrow, remembered that ladies drank by holding the delicate handle, pinky raised. Cheeks getting warm, Rhiannon adjusted her grip on the cup and blew off the steam before taking a sip.

"Two. Millie's girls often needed someone to look after them while she was out hunting. Fyodor adored them, so it usually wasn't too much trouble."

She watched her cousin's face freeze over into a pleasant smile.

"Oh, I didn't realise the Butcher had reproduced." Nathalie's smile wavered at the corners. "How lovely."

"The girls are lovely," Rhiannon said. "When they're not catching snakes."

There was a flicker of horror on Nathalie's face at the mention of the little Berrys' favourite pastime. Rhiannon wasn't about to go into detail, but she'd always marvelled at how many dangerous critters those two showed up with. It was a wonder that the town only burnt down twice, really.

"Owen's caught a few, back home," Nathie said. "Luckily just grass snakes, nothing dangerous, though I can't say the nanny was ever pleased when he gave them to her as gifts."

Rhiannon chuckled at the thought. The poor woman must be worth her weight in gold to have put up with that.

"Are they... like her?" Nathie asked. "Violent?"

Rhiannon shook her head. "Fenna, the blonde, she's the sweetest child you'll ever meet. Very shy at first, but a real darling if she thinks your feelings are hurt. Rasha, the redhead, is more bold. Adventurous and a bit too eager to explore on her own. But they're only four, they're not violent at all." She looked down at her tea, milky and warm.

"I don't think Millie was violent at four either," Rhiannon said. "What she's told me about Marigot, it sounds like it was a dangerous place to grow up. She couldn't help that any more than I could help that I grew up in four-poster beds and with etiquette lessons."

"You always excelled at those," Nathalie said with a pretend huff of annoyance. "I never understood why there needed to be an escargot fork *and* a seafood fork. What person in their right mind would eat snails by choice?" She made a face.

Rhiannon smiled and sipped her tea, thinking of the lean times out at Scorched Bluffs. The place had been too arid for snails, but they'd eaten everything else that wasn't poisonous or too big to bring down. Dirt turkey, snake, lizards and hares. Rhiannon had learned that if she got hungry enough, she'd eat anything.

"I'm holding a soirée as a way of proving I'm neither dead nor an imposter," she said, changing the topic. "I'd love it if you would come. I could use someone next to me to help remind me which fork is used for what. I'm dreadfully out of practice."

Nathalie's eyes sparkled, and she reached out to take Rhiannon's hand.

"Anything you need," she said. "Point out the unwanted suitors and I'll glare at them so sharply, they'll hide in a corner until next season."

Rhiannon must have let her annoyance show, because Nathalie laughed and covered her mouth until she regained control over herself.

"Oh darling," she wheezed, dabbing tears from her eyes with a linen napkin. "That many already?"

"The letters started coming in as soon as news broke that I was back," Rhiannon muttered into her cup. "I haven't heard of some of these names before, and some are older than Father is." She caught herself, but the slip hurt deeply just the same.

"As old as he was," she corrected herself quietly, feeling a fresh twist of pain in her heart. Rhiannon rubbed her temple. They'd all died over five years ago, but it had been easier to hold the pain at bay when she hadn't been surrounded by memories every day.

"It doesn't get much easier," Nathalie said with a deep sigh. "I still can't go to the farm my father loved so much without feeling like I'm drowning. Now the house sits there, empty, while the workers live in the old slave dormitories."

Rhiannon's eyebrows shot up.

"Oh, don't look at me like that," Nathalie said. "Papa treated them well. They didn't live in squalor sleeping on the dirt as they did with other families. After the war, I made sure to modernise the buildings so that our workers have the best living facilities available to them." Her cousin looked down at the cup of tea in her hand and took another sip. "It's better than redecorating the manor I can't live in anymore."

"That makes sense," Rhiannon said, her chest aching. "I don't think I could change much here. It's been almost the same since Grandfather owned it. I suppose I might update a few of the smaller rooms, but mostly I'm just grateful that Harrold didn't destroy it all."

Grief's grip on her heart didn't ease, and Rhiannon felt like she was slowly being crushed from within. Finishing her tea in a single gulp, she stood, placing the napkin on the table.

"I'm sorry," she whispered, her voice hoarse. "I think I'm going to turn in a bit early tonight." She smiled at her cousin, not wanting Nathie to think she had caused the sudden fit of emotion. "If you need anything, just ask Murphy or one of the maids."

Nathie made to speak, but instead of saying a thing, she set her tea and napkin down and stood, pulling Rhiannon into a hug.

"I understand," her cousin whispered. Nathie released Rhiannon and stepped back, placing her hands on Rhi's shoulders. "I'll be here in the morning. Just know that you're not alone, not anymore." Nathalie returned the sad smile and let go.

"Thank you."

The words barely made it past Rhiannon's throat, as thick as it was. With a departing nod, Rhiannon headed for her room. At her hip, Fyodor whined. He always knew when something was wrong and he was usually the only one who could make her feel better. Brushing her hand over the mastiff's head, Rhiannon bit her lip. There was no easy way to feel better from grief, though.

Opening the door to her room, Rhiannon stepped inside and held the door for her dog to follow. Her room was much the same as it had been when she'd fled from it years ago. The bed, the vanity, and the trunk at the foot of the bed were all the same, but Harrold had removed every trace of her from the room. Murphy and the rest of the staff had stored it in the attic, unwilling to throw out memories of the family they loved so much.

Her girlhood fit into a chest that still sat waiting by the wardrobe for her to go through. Rhiannon hadn't been brave enough to touch it yet. Just being in the house was hard enough. Her first night back, she could have sworn she'd heard the muffled voices of her father and mother discussing the cost of iron. When she'd poked her head out of her room, the only soul she'd seen was a startled maid who apologised for being up so late.

Rhiannon had barely slept since.

"I'm glad Nathalie's here," she said to Fyodor, unbuttoning the bodice of her dress. She'd forgotten how much fussier dresses were compared to her old shirt. But the buttons were so much smaller and were made for a maid to help the lady get dressed, even if Rhiannon refused the help. "It's too big a house for just us, don't you think?"

The mastiff perked his ears and tilted his head with a soft whine.

"I don't know, Fyo. You know Millie. Surely she had some reason to kill Uncle TK." Rhiannon thought about her friend, remembering how easily she had shot the outlaw Isaiah Willard for stumbling into the wrong place at the wrong time. That hadn't been during a war, and Millie herself had told Rhiannon she'd done terrible things back then. Rhiannon had never asked for details, but now, as doubt twisted in her belly, she was certain she should have.

"At least," she said hesitantly, a frown spreading across her brow. "I hope she had a reason."

6

Opportunity Knocks

The Red Hand

No pale elf was perched on the tenement building that night. Whatever business the Butcher had with the Wyndford City Jail had been concluded the night before.

The Red Hand had briefly considered copying the elf's methods but settled on a far more efficient plan. They waited by the side door in the alley, hood pulled low against any prying eyes. At the given hour, the door opened and a broad-shouldered guard tilted his head to motion the Hand inside. Waiting in the hall was a second guard, notably thinner than the first.

"Up this way, sir," the smaller guard said in a low voice, "You keep between us and no one will notice." The Hand felt a tingle of magic as they took their place, following the guard up the back service stairwell. They noted each door was locked and reinforced against any escape attempts. How lucky for them that the guards held all the keys that the Hand needed.

Reaching the top floor of the jail, the guard in front unlocked the door and lead the way to the cell block where Rousseau was kept. Two guards that weren't on the Hand's payroll stood on either side of the cellblock door, looking bored.

"It's not shift change yet, is it?" one asked, knitting their brow at the trio's arrival.

"Nah, the 'hero' owes my friend some money. Just here to collect," the guard in front of the Hand said.

"There'll be compensation for your time," the Hand added. "Doubly so if this is kept quiet. It wouldn't do to be associated with your prisoner these days. You're welcome to come with me to ensure his safety, if you'd like." They pulled a shiny gold coin from their pocket and set it dancing through their fingers before making it disappear once more.

The two stationed guards looked at each other, then nodded.

"Alright, if we supervise, there ain't no harm in getting your money back. Rousseau seems to own half of the city. At least you aren't here to break his legs."

"His legs are safe with me, my friend," the Hand said with a chuckle, and waved the notion away.

One guard unlocked the door, and stepped into the cell block, hanging his lantern up so it illuminated the space. Four cells, though only one was occupied. The Hand looked around as they stepped inside, curious to see if the elf had left any sign of her presence. He found none.

"Visitor," the guard on duty said. He didn't get any further. Clasping a gloved hand over the man's mouth, the Hand stuck their knife into the guard's throat. Behind them, they heard the second on-duty guard gurgle as the Hand's taller guard slit his throat.

"That's quite an entrance," Rousseau said, hobbling to lean against the bars of his jail cell. The Hand smiled, letting the dying guard fall to the floor, the knife staying in their hand.

Frederic Rousseau had seen better days and seen far worse ones. The sobriety in his eyes was shocking after a decade of drinking. The way the former war hero reacted and covered his surprise at the Hand's arrival was both impressive and concerning. They had been certain the old alcoholic had scrambled his brain with whiskey, yet here he was, annoyingly coherent.

"I favour the dramatic," the Hand said, wiping their knife on the sleeve of their black coat. "We can discuss performances at another time, however. Our time here is short. I come with an offer, Frederic. One that I think you'll find unable to pass up."

Rousseau's lackey lifted his head in the cell, but knew better than to interrupt when his betters were talking.

"I'm listening," Frederic said, lifting his eyebrows.

"Come with me back to Marigot, and your past sins will be forgiven," the Red Hand said, motioning for the paid guards to unlock the cell door. "Stay, and you hang."

Frederic frowned. It wasn't much of a choice, the Hand knew. Certain death compared to returning to a city that the Captain had betrayed during the Civil war. Marigot would want Frederic dead, but the Hand could protect him from those other dangers... if properly motivated.

"Fine. What's in Marigot?"

The cell door opened, and the Hand smiled, holding out their hand to shake on the agreement. Frederic took it, unbothered by the blood on the glove. It made sense.

The man had enough blood on his hands that a little more wouldn't bother him.

The taller guard stepped forward, pulling a garrotte from his pocket. It sang with magic, making the hairs on the back of the Hand's neck stand on end. They grabbed Frederic's hand with both of theirs, holding it steady while the man tried to pull himself free.

"What are you—"

It was over in just a moment. The garrotte was wrapped around Rousseau's wrist and with a sharp pull, the enchanted wire sliced through meat and bone like butter. In a well-choreographed move, the mage stepped in and grabbed the bloody stump of Rousseau's arm, his hand glowing orange as he sealed the wound with a fire spell. A gesture from the mage and the disgraced hero choked on his scream, stifling the sound to a sad wheeze.

"Kill the servant," the Hand said, extracting Rousseau's severed one from his grip. Shaking it to drain the appendage of blood, they stepped back to let the other two get to work. "We'll need all three bodies."

7

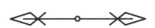

LIKE A CAT IN BOOTS

MILLIE

THERE WAS AN ALIEN version of Millie staring back at her through the silvered mirror she held. This was the reflection that a naïve little elven girl used to dream about. Silver hair curled and pinned along the top and side of her head, hiding half of her sheared scalp. The other half was downy and soft, freshly washed and glowing in the last rays of sunset that streamed through the window. Kohl had been artfully applied to her lashes to make them less jarring to society, but had the same effect that Millie's old warpaint had: it focused attention on how large and pale her eyes were. Lilac, flashing red when the sun's dying light caught them at a certain angle.

She looked beautiful, and it made her feel sick.

"Is this satisfactory?" The low arroyan woman asked, her dark hair pinned back into a severe bun. Tabea's arrival earlier that afternoon had been a surprise, but one Millie ended up grateful for. Gilbert's secretary had arrived with dangerous-looking metal irons to curl hair, and worked with a spartan efficiency that impressed Millie.

Tabea could pass as an elf, but after living in a town with a high arroyan who had fully manifested horns and tail, the tells of an arroyan were easier to spot. Tabea's canines were longer than an elf's, and present on the top and lower jaw, unlike orcish tusks that only grew on the lower jaw. Arroyans had pointed ears, but they were shorter than Millie's, and were fixed in place.

Tabea must have reasons for passing as an elf, and Millie wasn't about to press for them. The world could be unkind to anyone, but there were fanatics who thought arroyans were demon-kin. Even if, according to Grannie Whitewing, demons were just spirits that didn't align with the endless cycle of sin and forgiveness the Church of the Wheel preached about. Millie knew who she trusted between the church and her great aunt, and it wasn't the one who broke people on wheels.

All at once, Millie found herself homesick for her little town. Sweetpea, her high arroyan friend, would be making jokes in her bakery while the smell of fresh bread wafted out from her oven. Fyodor would be flopped in front of it, soaking up the heat in the chill evening while the girls played at Millie's feet, ears perked to listen to the song Millie strummed on her battered guitar. Even for Eyota and Grannie, who would be discussing where the next Ghost Eye camp should be.

Instead, she was tight-laced in the latest style of corset and had to have Tabea's help to get dressed into the yellow silk monstrosity that was carefully laid out on Gilbert's bed.

"Is it *not* satisfactory, then?" Tabea asked, sharp eyes catching the small swoop of Millie's ears as she looked toward the dress.

Shit.

"No, your work is fine. I mean, it's good," Millie said, watching Tabea's sleek eyebrows twitch downward into a frown. "Excellent, even. I'm just not looking forward to *that*." she flicked an ear toward the dress. It was beautiful, and just the thought of having to wear it constricted Millie's breath more than the corset ever could.

"You don't like yellow?" Tabea asked, her voice was impressively neutral. No doubt Millie was getting on her nerves. If the situation was reversed, Millie knew she would not handle these doubts so patiently.

"I don't like someone who is fond of yellow." The Rousseau family colours were canary yellow and royal blue. Blue had made the cool undertones in Millie's skin stand out, so Fred had often chosen to dress her up in yellow. At least the dress on Gilbert's bed was buttery, instead of bright.

"It's also so expensive," she muttered, ears drooping again. Surely, Tabea would understand this concern, even if the Goldmans didn't. "If I damage it, or stain it, I don't think I could ever repay what it cost—"

"Mrs Goldman," Tabea said, reaching out and pressing a warm hand to Millie's forearm. Millie twitched at the name. "I don't think you would be required to repay it. Miss Colfield can afford to replace a dress like that without batting an eye."

Somehow, that was worse. Millie took as deep a breath as the corset allowed and nodded grimly. She had faced down Fred twice now, she could put on a frilly dress for Rhiannon. It was just fabric. It wasn't the product of hours of labour as seamstresses slaved over ribbons and ruffles.

"Okay," Millie said, standing. She squared her shoulders and set her jaw. She could do this. One last fancy evening for Rhiannon.

THE DOOR TO THE bedroom creaked open as Tabea finished buttoning Millie's bodice closed. Turning to look over her shoulder, the elf spotted two curious little faces whose ears immediately started to wiggle in confusion. Rasha's mouth fell open at the luxury of the dress, but Fenna burst into tears.

"Shh," Millie said, stepping forward to scoop up her daughter. Tabea intercepted her and swatted her out of the way.

"Don't you dare get tear stains on that silk," the arroyan said, and reached for the crying elf. Millie didn't have time to warn her, and winced in sympathy as Tabea received a swift kick in the shins. Still sobbing, Fenna took off down the hall, shouting for 'Papa' with Rasha hot on her heels.

"She's strong," Tabea said, rubbing her shin. "And she found my leg through my skirt. Did you teach her that?"

Millie snorted, pulling on the stupid fancy little gloves she'd been given that ended up at her wrist. They were incredibly soft leather, and would wear through in a single day's ride. They felt lovely, though. Much better than the silk skirts that rustled loudly with every movement.

"No," Millie said, joining Tabea at the doorway to peer down the hall. "That's just Fenna. She's shy around strangers. I'm just glad she didn't have any salamanders nearby." Tabea stared at her in confusion, which Millie ignored.

Gilbert stood at the bottom of the stairs, holding Fenna, who had buried her face into the fancy wool scarf he had draped around his neck. Something in Millie's belly twisted at the sight. Nerves, no doubt. He looked comfortable in his fancy suit, the white tie at his throat was even and the black suit jacket fit him perfectly. Asshole. Why did he get to be comfortable?

He glanced up and caught her staring. Pressing her lips together, Millie's ears grew hot in embarrassment, but she refused to dart back into the bedroom. He might laugh at her, but she had made fun of his fancy clothes often enough that she would deserve it.

"I'm sorry," she said, hobbling down the stairs in her skirts. At least the slippers she had to wear were thin, letting her feel the floor through their soles. She preferred them to the fiddly boots that had too many buttons instead of sensible laces.

"I think I frightened her," Millie said, dying inside at the sight of her little girl's teary face. Fenna had always been sensitive, able to tell when her mother or sister was sad. "It's just Mama, Fen. I'm okay, see?" she murmured. Gilbert was looking at her strangely, and Millie ducked her head, feeling ashamed. She didn't want to be wearing any of this. She would, for Rhiannon, but it felt wrong. Just like everything else about this city beyond the Goldman home felt wrong.

"I'll take her," Avrom said, appearing from his study with the two other girls in tow. "We've got a whole pile of stories to read that Sarah has chosen." Fenna sniffed, and leaned out toward the old man, allowing him to take her off his son. He peered out from under his unruly eyebrows at Millie, then harrumphed.

"You look like a cat in boots," he muttered. "Good God, woman, the dress won't kill you."

"*Tata*," Gilbert said, the sharpness in his voice surprised Millie. Normally the two men bickered lovingly. This was the first time she'd heard any kind of heat in it.

"It's okay," Millie said, glancing up at her husband-for-now. She felt her ears get warm, and she tucked them back against her head as though that might hide their colour from him. It had been so long since she'd needed to keep them under control, she'd nearly forgotten how to do so.

"I know. I look ridiculous."

"Only because I'm used to seeing you splattered with blood," Gilbert said, draping a cloak around her shoulders. "I suggested Tabea allow you to wear some to the party, but she said that it would be an incredible faux pas, even for the Bayou Butcher." He kept a straight face, but Millie caught the way his eyes crinkled up at the corners.

It was a joke, but one that rang with more truth than Millie would ever admit. Instead, she shot Gilbert a ghost of a smile in thanks. If he wasn't taking this too seriously, he would be less likely to get upset when she inevitably ruined the evening.

He offered his arm to her, and she took it, grateful for the physical anchor when everything else that night felt so wildly wrong. The cabbie waiting for them outside was a familiar one, the older elf man tipping his hat toward her. He'd been the same cabbie that she'd seen outside Rhiannon's home the other day, though he'd dressed up a little for the evening's work. No doubt he would ferry fancy people back and forth to the soirée all evening.

"What's your name?" she asked, catching the driver by surprise. He'd been in the middle of opening the carriage door for them, and he pulled a bit too hard. The door hit the driver in the shoulder and the man winced, rubbing at his collarbone on that side.

"Sorry!" Millie said, feeling Gilbert usher her forward. "I just—"

"She's particular about drivers," Gilbert said, practically lifting Millie into the carriage. They weren't even at the stupid party yet and already she was ruining the evening. "You don't need to answer if you're not comfortable with it, but it will make requesting your services easier in the future."

"Not at all, sir," the cabbie said, his voice gruffer than Millie expected. "Naveed Bobbins, if you need me. I just wasn't expecting the Butcher to ask who I was. It's quite a shock, it is."

Oh.

Millie swallowed her further apologies and tucked herself into the corner of the carriage as far from the door as she could. Staring down at the fancy gloves on her hands, she focused on her breathing. The corset constricted her, forcing her to breathe using her shoulders instead of her belly. She'd been so focused on the ridiculous clothes that she'd forgotten that tonight she wouldn't be able to just disappear when the discussion turned to her past.

What was it that Fred had said back at the jail? '*Once a master, always a master. Your friend might act like she's grateful, but she's back in society now. She's the wealthiest woman this side of New Haven, and she's going to forget you.'*

Five years on, and he still knew exactly what to say to get under her skin. Rhiannon wasn't like him. She was just distracted by her cousin's arrival and the upcoming trial. It was why Millie had even agreed to go to the stupid soirée: to support her friend, not to parade around as a curio.

The stories of the Bayou Butcher were terrible, a bogeyman in the night that wasn't real to anyone who hadn't been around Marigot during the war. But Millie was a living, breathing person who had faced the realities of war, and had no intention of humouring the men and women too rich to get their hands bloody.

Gilbert climbed into the carriage with a grunt, wincing as he sat next to her.

"Sorry," she mumbled, unable to make eye contact. Instead, she fiddled with the button on her glove's wrist. It was made of mother-of-pearl and the gleam in the gloom reminded her of her revolvers that had been destroyed in the explosion at Fred's home. It was both a comforting and a sickening thought.

"It's fine," Gilbert said, taking her hand and giving it a reassuring squeeze. Millie wasn't sure if it was to calm her, or to prevent her from pulling the button off.

"You know, I'm not actually Avrom's son by blood."

Millie looked up at him in surprise, her ears perking. Gilbert was nearly a head taller than his father, and had eyebrows only half as wild, but she hadn't considered that he might be adopted.

"Shocking, I know," he said, flashing her a grin before he continued. "I spent my early years on the street, stealing from people that look like we do now. I used to only steal half what someone carried. See, a mark would notice a missing purse long before they realised they had fewer bank notes than they expected to. It's a person's nature to second guess themselves. Maybe they had spent more than they thought? It worked out well for me until I stole from Avrom."

"He noticed," Millie said. It wasn't a question. The old man was sharp as a tack, and Millie had been caught out more than once since her arrival, sneaking an extra cookie to the girls after bedtime.

"He noticed," Gilbert agreed with a chuckle. "He'd been watching me for a while, and noticed I only took half each time. Instead of turning me in, he offered to put me through school and give me a place to stay. I thought I'd take him up on the offer, then steal everything I could. Instead, I ended up liking the old man, and he adopted me shortly after." He cleared his throat and looked over at her, his face serious.

"But once he took me in, everything changed," Gilbert said. "My old mates wouldn't talk to me. They thought I'd abandoned them. Even the help Avrom hired to get me used to my new life treated me like I hadn't just been sleeping in an alleyway a month before. The stable boy wouldn't talk to me, because I wasn't like him anymore. I was lifted out of that social class, and I felt lost. I didn't fit in with the boys at school when I first attended. I hoarded food at first, certain I'd be kicked back out onto the street."

Millie frowned, listening to the story. She could see the obvious parallels between it and her current situation, but she didn't like them. Not one bit.

"It's different," she argued. But was it? "I'm an adult, I'm this terrifying story people tell their children about, and my friend is..." she trailed off, struggling to describe the unique status Rhiannon had walked into. Wealth, fame, social elite, and the darling of Amelior.

"And your friend is Rhiannon Colfield, and she's no longer just Sheriff Collins, no matter how much you wish she was," Gilbert said quietly. "Rhiannon won't abandon you, but high society won't see you as her equal."

Millie's frown turned into a scowl, and she looked away from him, pulling her hand free to wrap her arms around herself.

"I know that," she said through gritted teeth. "This isn't my first time being the elf companion of someone important."

"That's not what I meant," Gilbert said. He huffed, but she refused to look at him to see if he was annoyed or calm. She was barely holding her emotions in check, and if she saw pity on his face, it would shatter whatever composure she had left.

"I meant you were lifted to somewhere new by Rhiannon, the way Avrom lifted me out of the street," he said. "The rules have changed, and asking people their names can make them feel uncomfortable because that usually only happens when someone wants to get them in trouble."

Millie's ears sank, and she thought about all the times she'd faced that problem. Only in Marigot, the humans hadn't asked for your name, but who you belonged to. How often had she gotten into trouble while running Fred's errands and had to tell some asshole rich human who she belonged to?

"Naveed isn't afraid of you, by the way. He fought for the Union during the war until some weird elf won the battle of Marigot for them."

Gilbert was trying to make her feel better, but the anecdote just made Millie feel worse.

"I should have known better," she muttered, plucking at the button on her glove again. "It was like that during the war. I was a sergeant. The privates and corporals would talk to me, but it was different. I was different. Only a few—" she had to stop and take a shaky breath to keep from falling apart. "Only a few treated me the same as they used to, outside of combat."

She watched the massive houses of the Gold district pass by, each safe behind wrought-iron gates that kept Wyndford's less desirable citizens at bay. Like her. Like Gilbert.

"Thank you," she said, as the cab rolled past the empty lot where Frederic Rousseau's manor had once stood. Millie had set it on fire while rescuing Gilbert's family, and seeing the scorched foundations made her feel a little less out of place. Looking back at Gilbert, she took his hand and gave it a gentle squeeze, echoing his earlier gesture.

"I'm sorry I assumed you were born into wealth and an asshole," she added.

"It's alright, you were half right, I *am* an asshole," he said. "I was thinking, if tonight gets to be too much, let me know. I'll make an excuse that my hip is bothering me and we can leave." Gilbert made a face and shifted on the cab's bench. "It won't be a lie," he added.

They rode the rest of the way to Rhiannon's home in silence. It would be the last quiet either of them would get for a few hours, and Millie was grateful that she had at least one ally for what was to come. She would have preferred to disappear and spend time with Fyodor, but Rhiannon would need his support tonight. Maybe after the party things would get better.

Torches lined the driveway up to the main entrance, where staff in neatly pressed and well-fitting suits helped guests from their cabs and carriages. They glittered in the torchlight, draped in jewels and silks that far outdid what Millie had been laced into. Suddenly, the ruffles along the hem of her dress and the strange bustle no longer seemed as overwhelming.

Naveed helped her and Gilbert descend from his cab, and she shot the driver an apologetic look before Gilbert swept her away toward the hell that awaited.

"Did Fred ever tell you about the rainbow balls?" she asked her husband, though she couldn't look at him. There were too many strangers, too many people who could ruin her life if she so much as sneezed in their direction. While Millie knew the layout of the manor well by now, she couldn't help but look for the avenues of escape, just in case.

"The *what* balls?" Gilbert asked, making a strange, strangled sound. "Are you sure that's an appropriate discussion for where we are?"

"Rich humans would attend these events that were all fancy, bringing their inhuman mistresses and paramours for a night of drinking, dancing and ...everything else." Her ears swept back and low as she remembered how those nights had smelled. Sweat, sex, and alcohol. Once upon a time, it had been thrilling. Now the memories turned her stomach.

"Ah, rainbow because of skin colours," Gilbert said, and Millie risked a glance at him, unwilling to ask what he'd thought she meant. The tips of his ears were a touch pink, and Millie almost stopped in her tracks.

"Are you blushing?" she asked. Gilbert tugged at her hand, his ears only getting brighter. Reluctantly, Millie let him lead her down the hall to the Colfield ballroom.

"No," he muttered, his eyes strangely fixed on the couples ahead of them. "I just wasn't certain where this story was going."

"Well," Millie said, no longer certain herself. Strains of fancy people's music wafted through the hall, playing a song that Millie had never heard before. "The people here might have more money, but the music is better back home."

Home. The word stuck in her throat like a fishbone. Marigot hadn't been home in nearly a decade, and she'd been a stupid, young thing back then. Being around fancy people was getting to her, and she'd just arrived. The sooner she could escape this party, the better.

"Mister and Missus Gilbert Goldman," the servant at the door of the ballroom announced. Somewhere, someone dropped a glass that shattered, but the dizzying swirl of dancers and glittering guests made it impossible for Millie to pinpoint where the sound had come from. Dozens of faces turned to stare at them, and conversation rose as the guests gossiped about the Bayou Butcher.

In the thick of it all, laughing and looking perfectly at ease, stood Rhiannon in a beautiful blue gown. Next to her, dressed in red silk shot with black, was her cousin. Nathalie turned her severe eyes toward Millie and the smile that graced her face sent a chill down the elf's spine.

That was the smile of a viper.

8

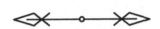

UNWANTED ATTENTION

GILBERT

GILBERT HAD VISITED THE Colfield manor a handful of times since Rhiannon forcefully recovered it from her uncle, and was familiar with the simple statements of wealth, but tonight it positively dripped with luxury. Large bouquets of exotic flowers filled gilt Zhinquan vases, while crystal chandeliers scattered the candlelight across dancers that swirled in silk. It was everything Gilbert ever dreamed of, the kind of money that meant he would never have to worry about Sarah going hungry. Nor would he need to worry about providing for the chaotic little elves that had adopted her as a sister so quickly.

Feeling a small hand tighten on his arm, Gilbert looked down at Millie and was struck again by the transformation. When they'd met, she was scruffy, sunburnt, and wearing threadbare clothes. Tonight, she was dressed in silks, her hair glowing in the soft light of the chandeliers, and could put any of the beauties of Wyndford to shame. She was also clearly hating every second, which made Gilbert's chest strangely tight.

The grumpy elf had put up with the pampering and fancy dress for Rhiannon's sake, but Gilbert wondered what it cost her. Sarah had told him that Fred had put Millie in a fancy dress the night the elf had rescued his family. Millie had mentioned the rainbow balls they'd held in Marigot, and Gilbert knew Fred used to enjoy showing off his girl of the month back when they'd been on good terms. Frederic had been right about one thing though, none of the past flames could compare to the woman who'd gotten away from the miserable bastard.

"That's her," Millie said, shaking his arm gently to get his attention. "The cousin."

Gilbert scanned the crowd and spotted a woman staring at them with piercing eyes. She looked like Rhiannon, with whom she had linked arms, but her features were sharper. The smile on her severe lips was gloating, and the gleam in her eyes reminded Gilbert of the way the elf on his arm had looked back on the frontier, splattered red, axes in hand.

"Ah," he said, glancing from said cousin back to Millie. "I see what you mean, but we should still greet Rhiannon, even if it means entering that woman's striking range."

He watched Millie's ears flick down and back, giving away her irritation while her face remained impressively impassive. Out on the frontier, he'd gotten shot too frequently to figure out what the different ear gestures meant. It was only after spending time with Millie and her little girls at his home, Gilbert had learned how to decipher what mood matched which ear posture. It was terribly adorable, and when the party was over and his wife was in a less stabby mood, he'd ask why the settler elves didn't emote the same way.

Or maybe they did, but not around humans. The thought was sour with truth. Rousseau was the man who had used people's tells against them in cards, at least until he was too drunk to notice when he tipped his hand toward his opponents. Then, Gilbert would move some numbers around and rescue Rousseau from his debtors.

The drunk bastard deserved to die penniless.

Gilbert shrugged the thought of Rousseau away, realising that Rhiannon's cousin had left the heiress's side and was approaching them. Gilbert straightened, giving Millie's hand a light squeeze where it nestled in the crook of his elbow. She was holding on tight enough to crease the wool of his suit and make his fingertips tingle with pins and needles.

"Ah, is this Mister 'Bayou Butcher'?" the evil version of Rhiannon asked, with a smile that displayed a sharpness of canine that made Millie's earlier comparison to a viper remarkably accurate.

"No," Millie said sharply.

"Yes," Gilbert said, applying his most charming smile. He could feel the glare his wife shot him, but he knew this game. He had played it on the streets as 'flinch', and again in boarding school, and it was one of Fred's favourites. Your opponent would say something meant to get a rise out of you and you had to return the volley or risk getting punched if you showed an emotional reaction.

"Gilbert Goldman," he said, reaching out to take the woman's hand and bowing over it. His hip protested, but he kept his smile in place as he straightened. "You must be Miss Rhiannon's cousin. My wife told me you'd met."

The wife who'd slipped her hand free of his arm the moment he reached for the cousin's hand. Gilbert could feel the wariness radiating off the short elf. Rhiannon's cousin could, too, if the predatory spark in her eye was anything to go by.

"Nathalie Wolfe," she said, her dark blue eyes still fixed on Mildred. "And indeed, we have met. Your wife shot at me, thinking I was a savage brigand like herself, no doubt. I took offence then, but if I'd known she preferred tall individuals with dark hair, I might have asked her to kiss the bruise better, instead. She's rather fetching, isn't she?"

The air around Gilbert changed, and he glanced down at Millie from the corner of his eye. The tips of her ears had gone red, but they were pressed flat against her scalp. Not a good sign.

"Don't use that word in front of me ever again," Millie said quietly, lips peeled back from her teeth. "Gil, I'll find you when you're done with her." The elf turned on her heel and melted into the crowd, weaving her way through it with surprising ease. As short as she was, her telltale hair disappeared into the gathered humans easily.

Gilbert frowned, glancing around the room. Was she the only elven guest? She was.

"Perhaps you could enlighten me," Ms. Wolfe said, taking the spot on Gilbert's arm that had been occupied by his wife only a moment before. Her predatory affectation had dropped, leaving behind a small frown of confusion on her dark brow. "Which word triggered that reaction?"

"Savage," Gil said with a light sigh.

"But she is, is she not?" Wolfe asked, looking up at him. "Her actions during the war were nothing if not savage. How else would I describe the killing of civilians? Of killing children?"

Her question left a foul taste in Gil's mouth. A few weeks ago, he had challenged Millie on those same actions, using similar language. It felt different coming from someone else, less defensible.

"It's a slur used against Six Fire people out on the frontier." He ran his thumb over the handle of his cane. The smooth brass warmed to the temperature of his skin. "Usually by the idiots who think they can push the clans off their land."

"Well, that's silly," Nathalie said, nostrils flaring as she exhaled sharply. "The Union bans land expansion beyond the treatied borders. Why, the Union overlaps with several nations, and neither the Six Fires, nor the Osauga has had any conflict with us since the war."

Gil watched as the woman's eyes widened slightly, but he wasn't certain what it was that she had let slip. The Osauga Nation was on the east coast, he knew, but they'd been too far south for him to be familiar with their customs. He knew they ran the most efficient trading network in the new world, and that if you really needed to ship something somewhere quickly, you paid an arm and a leg to the seven runners.

"Then, I should apologise," Ms. Wolfe said, turning her culpability into a sharp smile. "Do enjoy the evening, won't you? I'll find your wife and set things right."

Gilbert had no intention of letting this woman find Millie before he did, but he didn't want to lead Ms. Wolfe right to Millie, either. So he smiled and tilted his head toward Rhiannon's cousin in a goodbye.

"Of course, have a good evening, Ms. Wolfe." Gilbert said, letting her extract her hand from his arm and resisting the urge to shake off the lingering chill of her hand. Millie's touch had been so hot he could feel it heat his skin through his suit, but Wolfe's had been cold enough to sap away any lingering heat the elf had left behind.

Glancing over at the heiress, Gil frowned slightly as Rhiannon quickly looked away, turning to speak to someone so her back was turned to him. Millie was right, something was off about Rhiannon. Why hadn't the heiress greeted the friend that had dedicated years to keeping her alive? Who'd helped her regain her lost status as the surviving Colfield? Gil was certain it had something to do with the venomous cousin, but untangling that web was best left to sober minds in private.

What Gilbert needed was a drink. Then he needed to find his murderous wife before she stabbed anyone, even if they deserved it.

"Gil, my boy!" Charlie announced himself, a grin on his boyish face. He swept a pair of champagne flutes from the tray of an elven server and handed one to Gilbert. "You lucky dog! You survived a meeting with the blackest widow in Amelior." Wonderful, exactly who he did not want to see right now. Their last conversation still itched at the back of his mind. Gilbert plastered a smile on his face and took the offered glass. Charlie lifted his own in silent cheers and took a sip.

"Ms. Wolfe, you mean?" he asked, deciding to take Whistenhowler's bait. If Charlie knew something about Rhiannon's cousin, Gil planned to find out for Millie's sake. "I'd assumed she was a widow, but I can't say I know the details." Mirroring Charlie was second nature, the habit long-established from Gilbert's time with Frederic. The wealthy assholes liked it when you did things after their lead.

At least the wine was superb, since the company was not. No doubt a single bottle of the sparkling white would bankrupt most households. A creeping twinge of guilt nestled in the pit of Gil's stomach as he thought about all the small cabins in Scorched Buffs that had burnt down.

"I heard she's prowling for husband number four," Charlie said in a low voice, wiggling his eyebrows. "Each richer than the last, and each dead under suspicious circumstances." Gil looked out across the crowd to see the black widow herself had returned to Rhiannon's side, and was speaking with the Wyndford Mayor, who looked to be equal parts charmed and afraid.

"You're still single," Gil joked. "She's quite a handsome woman, Charlie."

Whistenhowler snorted into his champagne and downed half the glass in a single go.

"I'd prefer to live long enough to see my children born, thank you," he said, almost primly. "Speaking of wives, I saw you come in with the Butcher," Charlie said, nudging Gilbert with an elbow. "Messiah's grace, what a striking woman." He let out a low whistle. "I thought the stories exaggerated how pale the Ghost was, but if I saw her in the middle of the night, I might think she was undead myself!"

Gilbert made a noncommittal sound in his throat and took another sip of wine. He preferred talking about Rhiannon's killer cousin.

"Terribly small, though," Charlie continued. "How'd she kill anyone, let alone take down dear old Fred?" and Gil choked, mid-sip. He swallowed the wine before he made an embarrassment of himself.

"Well, Charlie," Gilbert managed, clearing his throat. It was difficult not to laugh at the suggestion that the Bayou

Butcher struggled to bring down anyone. "She carries a gun, which doesn't care how big someone is." He watched his friend's face fall slightly.

"Oh, so she doesn't use the axes like in the stories?"

"No," Gilbert said, thinking back to the shootout in Scorched Bluffs and the bloody swath Millie had cut through Fred's men. "She uses the axes." He hesitated, watching Charlie's face. A strange gleam had returned to his eyes, and Gil sighed.

"Would you like me to introduce you to my wife?" He asked, hoping the man would decline. Instead, Whistenhowler's face lit up like a boy at midwinter's feast. "We'll need to find her first," Gil warned. "And she might not like you."

"Of course, of course," Charlie said, finishing his champagne and switching the empty glass out for a full one. "I saw her heading toward the gardens. She should be easy to spot, pale as she is."

Well, Mildred might be angry at him for introducing her to another of Rousseau's friends, but at least Charlie had seen which direction she had gone.

Making his way through the crowd took longer than Gil liked and his hip had started to ache something fierce by the time they reached the stone terrace that overlooked the Colfield lawn and gardens. Torches and braziers had been placed to illuminate the terrace, and to keep the chill of the late summer evening at bay.

A pair of older men sat at a table, enjoying some cigars. Chixian, based on the spicy flavour of the smoke, a style no longer imported by the Union. No longer officially imported, at least. Gilbert remembered when Rousseau threw a fit about not being able to find any, though that clearly had been a cash flow problem rather than one of supply.

Squinting out at the garden, Gilbert looked for the pale figure of Mildred among the perfectly manicured topiaries and rose bushes. It was a shame that Miss Sweetpea had returned to Scorched Bluffs. He could have used the mage's eyesight spell at the moment.

"I think I saw her there," Charlie said, gesturing at a gazebo covered in a climbing plant whose pale blooms had closed with the fall of night. Gilbert reached out, catching Charlie's arm before the other man could rush off without him.

"I'd best go get her alone," Gilbert said, patting Charlie's arm lightly. "She tends to be a bit... stabby if you catch her off guard." Charlie's face lit up, and he nodded eagerly. The way Whistenhowler was acting would have been amusing if it were centred on anyone but the infamously grumpy elf who was already on edge. The last thing Mildred needed tonight was to stab someone important and wealthy. Although Gilbert was certain that Charlie would deserve it.

"Oh, oh, of course," he stammered, smoothing the jacket of his suit against his front. "'Stabby.'" he said, making quotation marks with his fingers. "Of course she would be 'stabby'."

Gilbert smiled tightly at the man and left him on the terrace. Walking on the grass was a bit more difficult than walking on the parquet floor of the Colfield ballroom. The elegant tip of his cane sank into the manicured lawn if he leaned on it too heavily. Feeling Charlie's eyes on his back, Gilbert took a deep breath and tucked the cane under his arm, limping forward under his own power. It cost him, and by the time he reached the gazebo, the muscles in Gilbert's lower back had knotted up and threatened to steal his breath.

"I apologise for earlier," he said, half collapsing against the gazebo's wooden post and looking back at where Charlie waited, illuminated by the terrace's braziers. With a grimace, he rubbed at the knotted muscles, trying to get them to release his spine from their chokehold.

"Do you mean it?"

The voice that answered was dulcet and sweet, and it certainly did not belong to his wife. Gilbert's blood ran cold and for a moment, he felt like he had been pulled outside himself. He hadn't heard that voice in years. Once, he would have done anything to hear it again... but that had been a different time and he had been a different man, then.

Gilbert looked up at the night sky, as though searching for the God who kept putting him through these trials.

"This isn't funny," he told God, wherever they were.

"What isn't? My word, Gil, you're hurt!" Bianca Montalto cooed. Gilbert heard her cross the wooden platform toward him. Her steps were light, and the faint floral musk of her perfume brought back too many memories for the way the night was going.

"Yes, your fiancé 's thug shot me," Gilbert said, finally looking over at her. "It was all in the news, didn't you hear?"

Bianca was as beautiful as ever, her pale skin gleaming in the night while luminous grey eyes watched him from behind dark lashes. It was her eyes that caught his breath, so like their daughter's. In Bianca, Gilbert could see the woman Sarah might become. The resemblance was almost enough to forget that Bianca had left an infant at his doorstep, and not once inquired about her wellbeing.

No, Sarah might look like her mother, but Gilbert would ensure she was nothing like her.

"*Ex*-fiancé," Bianca said, pouting prettily. She reached up to place a hand on his chest, but hesitated, and instead wrapped her arms around herself as though she were cold. Perhaps she was, if she'd been hiding in the garden all evening. She was dressed in fine silk, the quality of which was only matched by a few other women at the party, of which Miss Rhiannon was one. The Montaltos were wealthy and respected, but they had invested in both sides of the War and lost a significant amount of respect and wealth. Bianca's brother had attended school with Gilbert and Hal, and introduced them to the devil herself one winter break.

"I had no idea he wanted to hurt you, Gil. I would never have stood for it." It would be easy to believe her, and part of him wanted to.

"Well, he did," Gilbert said, pushing himself off the post of the gazebo and brushing past her. The gazebo had a few benches in it, and if he didn't sit soon, his hip would seize up completely. Then they'd have to get Fyodor to drag him out of the garden in the morning. "He wanted me dead, and he killed his entire family. So, I suppose your taste in men has only gotten worse since we last spoke, hm?"

Easing himself onto the bench, Gilbert grunted, but refused to let the true pain show.

"I hardly knew all that when I accepted his proposal," Bianca said with a huff. She turned and moved to join him on the bench. Gilbert stopped her with a twirl of his cane.

"Ah, no. You can sit over there while we have this conversation," he said, pointing at the bench opposite his with the tip of his cane. "But this will be our *last* conversation."

They watched each other for a moment, and Gil smiled to himself as the softness melted away from Bianca. She lifted her chin and set her jaw, then stomped over to the other bench and sat down. With a prim sniff, she adjusted her skirts and placed her hands on her lap.

"Alright," she said, eyes flashing in the darkness. "Let's talk. I didn't know Harry wanted to hurt you. I would have stopped him if I'd known. Despite everything, you're still important to me."

"Despite everything? You left our daughter—"

"Gilbert, someone might hear!" Bianca hissed, half off her bench and looking wildly around them.

"Right, a Montalto can't have a child out of wedlock because the scandal would further destroy the family name," Gilbert drawled. "I'm sure Daddy Montalto is pleased you decided to marry a family massacrer instead of a banker. Well done." More venom slipped into his voice than he would have liked. Bianca had a way of getting under his skin, even now.

"You're one to talk," Bianca snapped. "You married the Bayou Butcher, of all people! How many families did she kill? She killed some of my third cousins, you know!"

"At least she's honest about it," Gilbert said. "And your third cousins were slavers. Your father disowned them once he finally realised which direction the war was going. I think it's a bit much to pretend you care how they died."

He leaned forward, resting his hands on his cane. He studied Bianca in the darkness, the way her eyes gleamed in what little light reached them from the party.

"You're right to be afraid of her, you know," he said. "She was furious when she heard how I ended up a single father to little Sarah. She loves that little girl, and she would have killed half of Wyndford to get Sarah to safety the night Rousseau took her."

Bianca seemed taken aback, but she ruined whatever empathy might have stirred in Gilbert's heart with her next question.

"You named her 'Sarah'?" Bianca asked, voice dripping with disgust. "What an ugly name for an ugly little thing."

Gilbert had never hit a woman who hadn't hit him first, but he was on his feet and halfway across the platform to Bianca before he could stop himself. He stepped back purposefully, hating the way Bianca could still provoke him.

"I know you're hiding in the garden because you weren't invited tonight," Gilbert whispered, his voice flat and cold. "I can ruin your family if I choose to. The richest woman in Wyndford is at that party, as is the most dangerous. Both would love a reason to drag you out by the hair. You've made some powerful enemies, Bee." He used the old pet name as a knife, cutting through the remnants of whatever warmth he'd once felt for her.

"You wouldn't—"

Gilbert smiled.

"When it comes to my daughter, I would make the Butcher look like a saint." He straightened and bit the side of his cheek to keep from grunting in pain. The night had not been kind to his hip, and as soon as he returned to the manor, he was going to see about getting a drop of laudanum to ease the pain.

"Now," he said, brushing off a few stray specks of dust from his suit. "Never contact me or my family again, or I'll let my wife know where you live. Go hunt for a husband elsewhere."

He left her there and started slowly back toward the terrace. Charlie and the other men had disappeared, leaving the space empty. As much as Gilbert would have liked to take a seat in the night air and wait until he and Millie could leave the party, he didn't want to risk Bianca growing a spine and following him.

And so, back into the soirée he went.

9

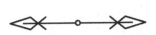

MISSTEPS AND MEMORIES

NATHALIE

THIS SOIRÉE WAS SUPPOSED to be a shining achievement: a moment to bask in the discomfort of a monster, watching it flounder and drown in the social maelstrom of high society. Instead, Nathie's schadenfreude was soured by her misstep. She had called the Butcher savage, fully intending it to be insulting. However, it hadn't been meant as a slur. The short elf had slaughtered dozens of people during the war and after, uncaring about their allegiance or age. What other word would suit a woman like that? And yet, to hear it was a slur hurled at innocent elves on the western frontier made her heart sick. They did not deserve to be lumped in with the likes of the Butcher.

The men talking to her and Rhiannon said something that was meant to be a joke, so Nathie laughed politely. She smiled over at her cousin, noticing the faint creases at the corners of her lips that meant Rhiannon was humouring the men more than they humoured her.

Since her arrival the other day, Rhiannon had been cool and distant, lost in her thoughts so frequently that Nathie had joked that she'd picked up some of their grandmother's sullen temperament after all. Instead of laughing, Rhiannon frowned and mumbled in agreement. She was putting up a good front with the strangers of the soirée, but Nathie knew better.

She knew how costly wearing a mask could be.

How would Rhiannon, once the most patient little girl in the whole world, react when she learned her cousin had used a terrible slur? Even if it was out of ignorance?

"Did I offend?" one man asked, prompting Nathie to realise she'd let her smile lapse into a frown.

"Oh, not at all," she said, smoothing her brow back into a neutral expression. "I thought of something that requires my attention. I apologise, but I must step away." Rhiannon lifted her eyebrows in a silent question. It would be best if she didn't join Nathie when finding the elf. Patting her cousin's arm to reassure her all was well, Nathie excused herself from the conversation.

Freed from the discussion on increasing the taxation rate on iron, Nathie scanned the soirée for white hair that didn't belong to portly old men or their distinguished and long-suffering wives. It should have been easy to spot the elf among human guests, but to Nathie's annoyance, the little beast was nowhere in sight.

Snatching a glass of wine from a servant, she stalked through the guests, pleased that they parted before her like so many minnows before a shark. Back home, she'd be one predator among many. Wyndford seemed to be quite complacent in comparison, with one short exception.

Reaching the far end of the ballroom, Nathie frowned as she reached the linen-covered tables laden with drinks and candles and noticed that the guests seated there did not include the elf. It seemed the giant banker who had married her was also missing. No stranger to being a new-lywed, Nathie rolled her eyes to herself and motioned one of Rhiannon's staff over from where they were posted by the door, ready to refresh any glasses of wine.

The young man was partially elven, but only the very tips of his ears gave his heritage away. In the candlelit ballroom, his brown eyes remained as dark as any other human's. He swallowed visibly as he hurried over, pitcher at the ready.

"Oh, not the wine, darling," Nathie said with what she hoped was a reassuring smile. "Have you seen where the Butcher's gone off to? I'm afraid I need to speak with her."

"Oh, Mrs. Millie, Madam?" the man asked, regaining his composure with remarkable speed for someone so young. Rhiannon's staff were simply excellent, and Nathie made a note to commend her cousin on keeping such a fine household. However, at the mention of the Butcher's name, so freely used, Nathie felt a tiny muscle in her eye twitch.

"Yes, 'Mrs. Millie'," she echoed. "Have you seen where she's gone? Perhaps with her giant husband?"

"Mrs. Millie went to the kitchen to ask for some cof-fee, Madam. Should I fetch her for you?" The server asked, suppressing a smile at the description of Rhian-non's banker. He might be discreet, but the flush along the boy's neck to his ears gave his admiration away. Poor thing was smitten.

"No, no, I'll go find her myself. I have an apology to make." The word caught in Nathie's throat, and she forced it down with a gulp of wine. Handing her now empty glass to the server, she slipped out of the ballroom into the cool calm of the hallway. A few other guests had sought refuge in the hall, chatting quietly about the miraculous survival of Rhiannon, and how well she looked.

Walking past with measured steps, Nathie's ears strained to pick up specifics, but the moment guests spotted her, they stopped talking until she had safely passed. Rhiannon wasn't the only celebrity in the family.

Once safely away from the guests, Nathie could walk at a quicker pace, her slippers silent on the well-kept floorboards.

The main kitchen wasn't far, though Nathie hadn't entered it since she'd been a child. Her brusque air faltered as a memory surfaced of sneaking out of bed late at night for something tasty, only to get caught by Rhiannon's father. Rather than reprimand her, he shared in her illicit snack before sending her off to bed with a cup of warmed milk. It was so vivid she could remember the taste of the gingersnap cookie, and the smell of the kitchen, kept warm by the large iron hob stove.

The tenderness cut at her heart, and Nathie had to stagger to a stop, bracing herself against the wall to catch her breath before sobs ripped it away from her. Uncle Alfred had deserved to live to see how beautiful and strong his daughter had become, and Nathie deserved to have her own father do the same. He'd been equally kind, with her mother joking that she'd had to go find herself a version of her sister's doting husband.

The man behind Alfred's death would face justice soon, but Nathie's own family remained unanswered. Steeling herself, she blinked away the tears seeding her lashes, and Nathie smoothed down the bodice of her dress with a sharp tug.

The door to the main kitchen swung open, and a trio of servers emerged, carrying trays of mouth-watering duck tartelettes, reminding Nathie she hadn't eaten since breakfast that morning. Stepping aside to let the servers by, Nathie plucked one tartelette as they passed. The flaky crust was still warm, planned to arrive at the ballroom and be the perfect temperature for taking an immediate bite. Nathie blew the steam from the little tart and had popped it into her mouth when the elf emerged from the kitchen, a cup of what looked to be coffee in hand.

The rich flavours of duck and caramelised onion soured on Nathie's tongue, and she chewed viciously, forcing the snack down with as much grace as she could.

The elf tried to skirt around her, but Nathie put out an arm, blocking the way. Immediately, the short woman's demeanour changed. Her long ears flicked back and a dangerous gleam in those lilac eyes told Nathie that no matter how harmless she looked, Mildred Goldman was a killer.

"You'd better move that arm," the elf said in a quiet, even voice.

"I will, once you hear me out," Nathie answered. She sniffed and drew herself up to perfect posture, practically looming over the other woman. "Your husband has told me I have made a terrible mistake and I would like to apologise for it."

"I don't need—" the butcher started. She stopped, wiggling an ear to clear it of some imagined blockage. "Excuse me, what?"

Nathie took a deep breath and cleared her throat. Her hands brushed away imaginary crumbs from her skirts.

"Earlier I used a word that holds implications I was not aware of—"

"Yeah," the elf said, eying her like Nathie was about to erupt into flame. From the heat spreading along the back of her neck, Nathie felt like it was a growing possibility. "You called me a savage."

"I'd meant to call you savage," Nathie said. She sniffed again and looked at the elf directly. Her father had raised her to own her mistakes. She would not throw away his lessons, even in the face of the woman who had killed him. "I could not think of a better word to describe your actions during the war. However, I did not intend to insult the good people of the Six Fires Council, nor your heritage."

They watched each other in the hallway, the silence only broken by a server who emerged from the kitchen, spotted the two of them, and turned right back around without saying a word.

"Alright," the elf said, caution painfully obvious on her face. "I accept your apology. I'm sorry I shot at you the other afternoon. You came running out of the house holding a weapon, and I don't trust that Harry would give up the family fortune without a fight."

The reversal was unexpected, and Nathie found herself taken aback by the elf's willingness to admit she was wrong. Where was the heartless butcher of ten years ago? Back then, she had killed Nathie's father without so much as blinking. There had been no apology that night.

"I... well," she stammered, "It was a *candlestick*, not a sword."

"You can still kill someone with a candlestick," the elf said, bringing the cup of coffee to her lip. She blew the steam from the dark liquid and took a sip, visibly relaxing.

"Have you?" Nathie asked, tilting her head. "Killed someone with a candlestick? I've only used poison and steel myself." She was rewarded with a choking sound as Mildred sputtered into her coffee, turning to the wall to avoid spitting any onto either of their silk dresses. Leaning against the beautiful wallpaper, Nathie watched the elf pull a handkerchief out and hurriedly wipe down the stray coffee droplets before they could stain the paper further.

"You didn't answer my question," Nathie said, letting her voice slip into something close to a purr. "Have you killed anyone with a candlestick?"

She watched the elf's ears flush red and smirked as the Butcher of the Bayou struggled to regain her composure. If she couldn't kill the elf right away, Nathie fully intended to make her squirm until Rhiannon came to her senses.

"Maybe," the elf mumbled into her cup, keeping it up by her lips. "Probably. I don't remember everything."

The floor felt like it dropped out beneath her, and Nathie was struck by sudden vertigo that made her glad she was leaning against the wall. How could the elf not remember? Did she not remember Nathie's father, who begged her to take what she wanted and leave? Did she not remember the man she'd mutilated that night?

Nathie remembered. She couldn't possibly forget.

"You don't remember," her voice sounded far away, her mask doing what she'd trained it to do when she had to retreat to her emotions. Her face smiled of it's own accord and Nathie flicked a fingertip along the butcher's jaw. "My word, you really are a Butcher, aren't you? The war was just another day in the abattoir. "

The flush on those pointed ears had spread to the elf's cheeks now. But even as distanced as Nathie felt, she could see how the other woman's eyes creased with an emotion too dangerous to call out. Guilt? Shame? Regret?

"War does things to people," the elf said, taking a step to the side, moving away from Nathie's reach. "You can pretend you'd be different, that you wouldn't do what I've done..." Pale eyes searched Nathie's face, and she wondered what the elf found there. "But you'd do anything to survive," the Butcher whispered. "I recognize a killer when I see one."

She left, then. Nathie let her go, still working through the revelation that the elf didn't remember all the murders, even one that would have surely stood out because of an unconventional weapon. Her parting words mattered little. Nathie knew what she was capable of. When it came to her family, Nathie would do anything to keep them safe.

Adjusting her gloves, Nathie pushed herself off the wall and headed into the kitchen. She was famished, and food always tastes best when pilfered.

10

Rousseau Means Red

Millie

Rhiannon's cousin was weird as hell.

Coffee clutched in hand, Millie hurried out to the terrace to put distance between her and the crazy woman who swung between hating Millie and flirting with her. There was no way to get Rhiannon alone tonight to ask her what was going on, and her behaviour was baffling. What had the cousin said to make her friend so distant?

Stepping out into the evening air, Millie closed her eyes and took a deep breath to calm her nerves. Instead of the familiar scent of flowers and dirt, she got a lungful of cigar smoke and musky cologne. A scent that was also familiar, but far less welcome.

Dancers wearing every colour swirled around the dance-floor, giant hoop skirts swishing in time to the music as the wealthy men of Marigot revelled with their inhuman mistresses. Fred had bought her a new dress for the season, a canary yellow thing of cotton that made Millie look like a lemon cake. She stood at his shoulder, hands tucked behind her back as he sat at the poker table, smoking his favourite

brand of cigar. Chixian, laced with cocoa leaves and import-
ed from the Nahuatl empire to the south.

"What do you think about the rumours?" Patrick O'Leary
asked as he shuffled the cards to deal a new hand. "You think
New Haven will push for abolition? Or is this more bluster?"

Still as a statue, Millie kept her eyes on Fred's hand. But
in her chest, her heart raced.

"They seem serious about it this time," Comte Gallois said,
swirling his glass of spiced rum before taking a sip. "The
Caliphates are offering to open trade again if Parliament
outlaws it, as though the bastards weren't the ones selling
them to us for a hundred years." The men at the table
laughed, all except Fred. He glanced back at her, his blue eyes
dark with worry.

"Mrs. Butcher?"

The name yanked Millie back to the present, knocking
the breath from her lungs. Someone gently touched her
arm, and she flinched away, the coffee spilling onto her
beautiful, expensive silk dress. The old men with their
cigars burst out laughing, their already ruddy faces turning
bright red.

"I'm so sorry," the man stammered, pulling out a handkerchief and reaching out to dab at the growing stain. "I
didn't mean to startle you," he kept talking, but Millie
couldn't understand any of it. The dress that cost more
than she could ever hope to repay was ruined. She'd ruined
it, and Rhiannon was going to be so disappointed, and
Nathalie would be so smug.

"You can dress an elf in the best finery, but they'll never be
human," Clem told her, helping Millie put her hair up for
the very first outing at the rainbow ball. "Remember that,
Millie. We will always be decorations to them, never people."

The man kept touching her, patting awkwardly at the skirt, and he smelled like Fred used to, before the stink of alcohol was the only cologne he wore. Millie staggered back, mumbling an apology through rapid breaths. The corset, comfortable enough all night, suddenly was crushing her ribs. She couldn't breathe, and she needed to get out of it.

"Gilbert's in the garden, he went—"

Desperate, Millie glanced over to the gazebo where the man was pointing, but saw Gilbert standing close to another woman. Of course, she would find no help there.

Her heart hammered against her chest; her hands trembled, risking another spill of the coffee. Millie shoved the coffee cup at the man who kept touching her and fled deep into the Colfield manor.

No ONE CAME LOOKING to see where she'd gone off to, for which Millie had been thankful. Once she'd regained control of herself, she'd headed straight to the laundry, found one of Rhiannon's laundresses, and talked her way into borrowing a maid uniform to change into. The silken dress was left as collateral while they attempted to clean it. Millie tried very hard not to think about the cost of replacing it should the stain be permanent. Any time she considered that possibility, she felt sick.

The maid uniform was good quality wool, but it might as well have been a hug with how it felt to pull on something that wouldn't beggar half the city if she stained it. It was a little large, but a few hairpins along the waistband held the skirt in place, and the buttoned cuffs kept the sleeves from hanging down beyond her fingertips. Without the crisp white apron, Millie looked like any other elf in Wyndford, albeit one with a cushy job.

"Thank you," she said, straightening her hair. She was still wearing the slippers, but the maid's dress was so long it swept the floor, hiding the fancy shoes.

The laundress looked up from the buttery silk dress and held out a small bundle toward her. "Found this in the skirts, ma'am. Thought you might want it."

Curious, Millie took the bundle and turned it over in her hand. It was made from dark wool, sewn shut with a red thread in a series of Xs. The blood drained from Millie's face and fingertips as she ran her thumb over the stitches. The little pouch was a gris-gris. A spell bundled into a little sachet that could be placed near a target to influence nearby spirits.

Every gris-gris was different. The components of a spell might be similar between practitioners, but the way those components were combined and the personalization that fuelled the spells they held were unique. A clip of hair, a drop of piss or spit, and the gris-gris would call spirits to weave subtle magic around the target. And there was always a target, whether the spell was made with goodwill in mind or harm. They were also unique to Marigot and its swamp, a result of the magical traditions clashing together to produce something new. However, most that Millie had seen were made from white cloth, not dark.

"Ma'am?" The Laundress prompted. She looked uncomfortable, fiddling with the hem of her apron.

Millie remembered what Gilbert had said in the carriage. While she felt more comfortable in the servant rooms, she knew she was no longer welcome there. Instead of making the poor woman any more nervous, Millie slipped the gris-gris into the pocket of her borrowed dress and smiled at her.

"Thank you, I thought I'd lost this," she lied. "If you find any others, can you set them aside for me? I'll pick them up in a few days when I return for the dress."

"Of course, Ma'am."

Millie nodded to the woman and left her alone, heading up the servants' stairs. She wouldn't be able to return to the party dressed like a maid, a realisation that made her wish she had spilled water on her dress an hour ago. Then she could have left before Rhiannon's weird cousin confronted her. Millie's thoughts trailed off as she fingered the small pouch in her pocket. Had it been the cousin who had placed the gris-gris in the dress?

As much as Millie wanted to blame the crazy woman, the press of guests at the party made it possible for almost anyone to have planted the little spell. Until she could find out what it did, she wouldn't be able to narrow down who had placed it. Whoever they were, they had wasted their money. Gris-gris spells snuffed out if Millie got too close. Back in Marigot, Fred used to joke that she was his own little gris-gris, keeping him safe from the influence of others.

The once-warm memory made her feel sick. It had been from what had been both a better time and a worse one. She needed fresh air, away from the stink of cigars and money. As she emerged from the manor near the carriage house, she found it. The familiar smell of horses and hay greeted her, along with the smell of well-oiled tack. Leave it to rich people to rename a stable to something fancy. The building looked fancier than most buildings in Wyndford, with its own weathervane stuck on top.

"Deputy?"

Allan Duncan, the extremely ordinary marshal who normally was terrified of her, waved from the driveway. He hopped down from a buggy and jogged over, the brass buttons on his Wyndford metropolitan police uniform gleaming in the light of the manor's lanterns.

"Duncan?" she asked, confused. He should be out on the prairie, chasing down the drunk sheriff of Plainfield. When had he arrived in Wyndford, and what spirit had possessed him to join the cops here?

"I normally don't say this, but boy, am I glad to see you," Allan said, pulling his hat off to run a meaty hand through his ginger hair. "We have a problem, and the fancy people won't let me in to talk to Ry." Marshall Duncan was normally a bit snarky, a bit awkward, but looking at him now, Millie could see that his jaw was set and his brows were knit in concern.

"What happened?" she asked. "I could get her for you." But to her surprise, Allan shook his head.

"Rousseau is missing." Allan took a deep breath. "It's best if you come with me to the Jail and see it for yourself. Ry can wait, this can't."

THE WARDEN MET THEM in the hall, face still puffy from sleep. He'd dressed, but the collar of his nightshirt poked out from under his suit jacket.

"Ah, Sergeant, thank the Messiah, you found her."

"How—" Millie asked, but realised that she was not the 'sergeant' mentioned. Glancing up at Allan, she saw him square his shoulders and nod in acknowledgement. Ears burning in private embarrassment, she cleared her throat to pretend she hadn't said a thing.

"Duncan said Fred is missing," Millie said, willing the flush on her ears to fade. When it didn't, she flicked one in annoyance. "What happened? Where are the guards?" Guards wouldn't have mattered if someone had used the same way to break into the jail as she had, though. The thought twisted in Millie's gut. Had someone watched her the night she'd paid Fred a visit and learned how to get into the jail? Shit.

"Well, we had two posted at the cellblock, as always. It prevents corruption, you see. The other cell blocks are less of an issue, but the men we hold here are often more ...persuasive." The warden said, wringing a handkerchief between his hands. The cotton had creased into tight wrinkles, with only the monogrammed corner safe from the man's anxiety. "Corruption had been a problem when I first took over the jail. I instituted the double guard system and had the guards rotated out after three days to avoid temptation."

"You mean the guards used to take bribes." Millie didn't see a point in beating around the bush. Cops always had a price, didn't they? Glancing at Allan from the corner of her eye, Millie wondered what the former marshal's price was. She imagined it was quite dear, with dark hair and light hazel eyes that disappeared when their owner smiled.

"Regardless," the warden said, beads of sweat forming at his temples. "The guards are both accounted for. They're inside."

The warden unlocked the heavy cellblock door and pushed it open for Millie to enter.

The metallic smell of blood flooded Millie's nose as she stepped inside. Two nights ago, she'd slipped into the cell block and Fred had played her like a damn fiddle. Tonight, Millie walked into a bloodbath.

Red splashed out of Fred's cell onto the stone floor, with a long smear leading to what could only be described as the 'centrepiece' of the cellblock. The bodies of both guards and Fred's steward Lionel were laid out in a triangle, face up, each with one arm outstretched toward the triangle's epicentre, fingers almost touching the disembodied hand that had been carefully placed there. A hand wearing a familiar signet ring on its meaty pinky.

When she made to walk closer, Allan reached out to catch her arm.

"The wall," he whispered. "Look at the wall, Berry."

Painted in block letters, a message was spelled out in blood on the far wall. She'd been so focused on the display of bodies that she had completely missed it.

The Bayou wants its Butcher back.

"Well," Millie breathed, the gris-gris burning a hole in her pocket. "Shit."

11

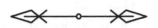

A Bitter Aftertaste

Gilbert

Gilbert desperately wanted to leave. The soirée had started poorly, gotten worse, and he had no interest in what would surely be a terrible finale. Rather than wander the floor with the pain radiating from his hip, Gil had stationed himself at a table by the dance floor. Mildred could disappear when she wanted to, and it would be easiest to let her find him so they could both leave. He was certain she wouldn't argue.

A server set down a glass of wine in front of him, and Gilbert thanked the young man absently. Rhiannon was whirling around to a merry waltz in the arms of the Mayor's nephew, and her evil cousin chatted on the sidelines, charming or terrifying some of the local bachelors. At this distance, it was hard to tell.

"There you are, my boy!" Gil looked up to see a harried Charlie hurrying over. His pompadour was slightly askew, and from the rattled expression he wore, it wasn't from a sly tryst in the side rooms.

"You look like you ran into Mildred," Gil said, taking a sip of wine. It was fruity and light, an excellent choice for a celebration of life. He also wished it was plain coffee. "That wasn't her in the garden, by the way."

"I know," Charlie said, gracelessly. He collapsed into the chair next to Gilbert and leaned over, eyes glittering. "I ran into her shortly after you went to look. Will you apologise to her for me?"

Gilbert looked the man over. He was clearly upset, but he didn't seem to have any open wounds, and he hadn't been limping when he came over to the table. It didn't seem like Millie had taken too much offence to whatever Charlie had said.

"What did you do?" He asked, reluctant to actually find out.

"I only tried to introduce myself, but she flinched, and the coffee she had spilled, I'll pay for the dress," Charlie stammered. "I tried to sop up the worst of it, but she pushed me away and left. I haven't seen her since. I've been looking for her to apologise."

Gilbert let the explanation aerate, and he took another small sip of the excellent wine. It would suit a picnic better, he thought. He should invite Millie and the girls out to one to help make up for this disastrous evening. Leading up to the soirée, she had been so uncomfortable with the cost of the dress, even though it was being paid for by Rhiannon. None of the other guests would understand the sheer panic of ruining something worth more than the home you grew up in, but Gilbert did.

"She didn't yell at you?" he asked, doubtfully. None of this sounded right, other than the drink being coffee. "Hit you?"

Charlie paled and shook his head. "Would she have done that?" he asked, voice low.

"Without hesitation," Gilbert said, adjusting himself in the chair. His back and hip were well past complaining now. They were screaming at him, and his wife had run off and all he wanted to do was go home and lie down in his own bed. "Charlie, why are you so interested in my wife?"

The other man swallowed audibly.

"I—I just—I heard the stories and, well. I mean," Gilbert watched as Whistenhowler struggled to come up with an answer, the man's face getting progressively redder. "Axes."

"Forget I asked," Gilbert said, picking up his cane and pushing himself to his feet with a grunt. "She'll have gone home. I'll let her know about your offer, but otherwise, leave her alone, Charlie." Gil sighed, draining the last of the wine and setting the empty glass on the table. "She's been through enough."

Gil half-expected Whistenhowler to argue, but the man let him leave without comment. It would be too much to hope Charlie might learn from his experience with Millie, but the man had been a close friend of Rousseau's until the latter's arrest. Reluctantly, Gil had to admit he'd counted Rousseau as a friend once, too. A drunk, annoying, belligerent friend, but a friend nonetheless.

Well, if Gilbert had come to his senses, maybe there was still hope for Charlie.

Emerging into the evening, Gil was surprised to find Naveed the cabbie hurrying over to him, one hand holding his bowler down so it didn't fall off.

"Mister Goldman! The—your wife, she left with another man. I wasn't sure if I should come find you, or send you word." Naveed whispered urgently. Gilbert blinked, then blinked again as he tried to understand what the cabbie had told him.

"Are you sure?" he asked the man gently. "And no one was bleeding? She wasn't holding him hostage?" Any other cabbie might have been shocked by these questions, but Naveed had fought in the war and heard about Mildred's exploits. He didn't bat an eye.

"No, no blood, sir," Naveed said, offering his shoulder to Gil as they walked back to the cab where Naveed's horse stood dozing. "It was a police officer. She had changed into a maid's dress, but I know it was her."

"She willingly left with a police officer *and* no one was bleeding?" Gil asked with a laugh. "That doesn't sound like her." Except, there was one person who might cause a situation where Millie did exactly what Naveed said she had. Something had happened with Rousseau.

"Change of plan, my good man," Gil said, appreciating Naveed's help as he climbed into the cab. "I'll double your fee for the night, but we need to go to the Wyndford City Jail. I imagine she'll want to head home after she's finished."

GILBERT FELT TERRIBLY OVERDRESSED as he walked into the jail, especially when a jumpy guard greeted him at the door with a raised billy club.

"I have one of those too," Gilbert said, lifting his cane and waggling it at the guard. "But I don't go around waving it around in people's faces. Tsk, rude."

The guard flushed bright red, but before he could bungle the situation any more than he had, a familiar face poked itself out of an office down the hall, one ear perked. Gilbert smiled at his wife and waved. Her perfect curls had gotten a bit mussed, but she still looked beautiful as she stared at him and the guard in confusion.

"Let him in," she said, using her deputy voice. The red-faced guard squared his shoulders and puffed out his chest, ready to argue.

A second familiar face poked out overtop Millie's, though this one was a surprise. Marshal Alan had cleaned up a bit since they'd last seen each other, but the last Gilbert knew, Allan was still working out on the Frontier.

"She said let him in, Thompson," the once-marshal said, doing a remarkable impression of the deputy voice. 'Thompson' drained of colour and snapped to attention.

"Absolutely, Sergeant."

Gil watched as Millie and Alan both nodded in acknowledgement, only for his wife's ears to turn pink. Ah, yes. She had been a sergeant in the war. It must be strange hearing that title used for someone else.

"Wonderful," Gil said, limping his way down the hall. Mildred emerged from the office and ducked under his arm to help. His pride was bruised, but between walking on the grass and the carriage ride, his hip had grown too stiff to walk comfortably. He would need to stretch it carefully once they got home, or he'd be bedbound the next day.

"Why's the marshal here?" he murmured, glancing down at Mildred. She looked up at him and shrugged, her ears still hanging low. Something had definitely happened, but he waited until they'd entered the warden's office to ask anything more.

Sitting at his desk, the warden was grim-faced, and had a bottle of whiskey out that he had poured into a few short glasses. Wooden chairs had been pulled to the other side of the desk, and there were a few footprints in red on the floor that led into the room. One set was small, no doubt belonging to his wife.

"Warden, this is Gilbert Goldman," Mildred said as she helped Gil to a chair. "He was Rousseau's banker, and I trust him."

"I'd hope so," Allan muttered, closing the door behind them. "You married him."

The warden watched them, the poor man dying inside as Mildred glared at Allan. Instead of saying anything, the warden poured another finger of whiskey into his glass, then one for Gilbert. He leaned over, revealing a tuft of his nightshirt collar that poked up from under his suit collar.

"So, what happened?" Gil asked, taking the offered glass and sniffing it. Much better than the stuff Rousseau used to drink, but several grades below the quality of what had been served at Rhiannon's party. With a relief he didn't want to examine too closely, he took a sip and looked over at Mildred.

The elf sank into the other chair, all spite draining from her. She reached out, and to Gilbert's great surprise, picked up one of the whiskey glasses and took a drink. Screwing up her face at the taste, she fanned the water from her eyes before answering.

"Rousseau is gone," she said, voice weak from the strength of the drink. "I don't know if he was abducted for ransom, or if someone else who has a grudge took him for revenge. He's gone, and they killed Lionel and two guards to leave a message." She breathed out a sigh and stared down at the whiskey in her hand. Gil knew she hated the stuff, which meant that this was not as simple as an escape.

"Why would someone abduct him?" Gil asked. He was familiar with 'Lenny', Frederic's loyal servant, who always seemed far more capable than the captain himself. "Did they leave a note?"

"Sort of," Alan said, as grim as Millie. "They left his hand behind, wearing a Rousseau crest signet ring. As mad as that man could get, I don't think he'd cut his own hand off just to spite Mrs. Berry."

That was true. The thing Frederic Rousseau loved most of all was Frederic Rousseau. Despite his obsession with Millie, cutting off his own hand seemed a touch drastic for the disgraced war hero.

"They also left a message on the wall," Millie said. "'The Bayou wants its Butcher back'." She grimaced and downed the rest of her whiskey. She sputtered and coughed, and Gil reached out to rub her back. To his great surprise, Millie didn't knock his hand away.

"So someone wants us to think whoever did this was from Marigot?" Gil asked, glancing at Allan. The warden seemed content to mope and drink, so Gil let him. Rousseau was the highest-profile prisoner held in the jail since it had been built. Eventually, news would leak that Rousseau had escaped. When that happened, someone would have to pay, and Gil would bet his bank that the warden would have to take the fall.

"No," Mildred said with another sigh. She reached up and rubbed her face, smearing some of the kohl that lined her eyes. "They *are* from Marigot. Fred's hand was left in the centre of a ternaire. It's a triangle used in conjure magic. Three sacrifices laid out end to end, with an object in the centre."

The warden recoiled, eyes going wide in horror. He made the sign of the wheel over himself with a shaking hand, and it took Gilbert a moment to remember that sacrificial magic was deemed heretical by the Rota Sanctum. To followers of the wheel, sacrifices were the worst form of disrespect against the cycle of death and rebirth that the Messiah had gifted them. To Carpenters like Gil, sacrifices were just weird.

"The sacrifices aren't usually people," Mildred said, watching the warden's reaction. "It can be fruit, cloth, anything."

"Well, this one *was* made of people," Alan muttered. "Which is disgusting. So you're saying that was a spell?"

"Was it?" The warden asked. The poor man's worst day of his life just kept getting more awful. Gil felt a small pang of pity for him. "A spell? Was. It. A. Spell?"

Millie shrugged, rubbing the back of her neck.

"I don't know. It seems more like a message," she said. "What with the big words on the wall and everything. Whoever left it really wanted us to know they were from Marigot. Even if it was magic, the object in the middle, Fred's hand, was the target. We should be fine."

Gilbert cleared his throat before the warden could respond. The poor man looked like he was about to piss himself. Back in Scorched Bluffs, the local rancher, Annie, had mentioned to him that Millie made magic stop working. When they were alone, he planned to ask her what really had happened on that cellblock.

"Right," he said. His hip was nearly unbearable now. The whiskey hadn't helped a bit. "I think this needs to be carefully discussed after a good night's sleep. I have a friend—"

"Hal?" Mildred interrupted. Gilbert nodded in her direction, not missing a beat.

"Hal. He's a Stratton detective and discreet. He should be able to help us cover more ground."

"I must protest," the warden stammered. "We do not need the assistance of the Strattons. This is an internal problem and must be handled with the utmost discretion."

Mildred stood and placed her hands on the warden's desk, leaning over it to stare the man down.

"You said no one noticed anyone coming in or out. You either have corrupt guards, or careless ones," she said. "The Stratton will help, or so help me, I will find every secret you've buried in this place and make sure that every Wyndford socialite hears about what really happens in the city jail they're so proud of."

The office was quiet. The warden was sweating again, and Allan didn't look particularly inclined to step in to help, which meant that Mildred had hit on something true with her threat. Gil pushed himself to his feet with the help of his cane and the warden's desk, setting his unfinished glass of whiskey down and leaving it. He'd had enough for the night.

"I think the warden agrees, darling," he said, the word slipping out. Mildred's ears flew up, and she looked over at him in surprise at the term of affection. He held out his arm to her to play it off as normal in front of the two others. "Let's go get some rest and discuss this at home, alright?"

To his surprise, Allan replied before she could.

"I think that's an excellent idea. I'll go inform Ry. She'll need to know." With a nod in their direction and a warning glare at the warden, the marshal excused himself and left the office.

"At least you're not the only one who still calls her that," Gilbert said quietly to Mildred, and he saw a flicker of a sad smile cross her face. Releasing the warden's desk, she stepped under Gil's offered arm and wrapped one arm around his back to help relieve the pressure on his hip.

"Old habits can be hard to break," she agreed. She was deceptively strong for her slight frame, and Gil was grateful for it as they hobbled out to where Naveed waited with his cab. Gil would have to ask if the man wanted a job. A steward would help relieve Arnaud from his least favourite tasks, and a good driver was hard to come by these days.

"I thought you'd still be at the party," Mildred said once they were settled in the cab. "Isn't that your thing? Rich people with too much money?"

Gil smiled. It was his thing, especially the 'too much money' part.

"You know," he said. "It was a terrible party. I was ambushed by Sarah's mother when I went looking for you. An acquaintance of mine is uncomfortably interested in you and your axes, and that cousin of Rhiannon's is absolutely dreadful. The wine was good, but I'd much rather have spent the evening at home with a nice cup of tea and the three gremlins who want too many bedtime stories."

Next to him, she relaxed.

"I saw you in the garden, but I didn't realise the woman with you was Sarah's mother," she said, resting her head against his shoulder. "It's probably a good thing. I might have stabbed her with one of those fancy food forks."

"She would have deserved it." Gil said with a laugh and wrapped his arm around her shoulders. He told himself it was in case she was cold. Under it, Millie stilled and Gil glanced down, concerned he had overstepped.

"There's something in your pocket," Millie whispered, reaching into the jacket pocket of his suit. She pulled out a small bit of cloth sewn into a square sachet, so light he hadn't noticed it was there at all. Immediately, the pain in his hip eased to a low throb.

"Do you know who gave this to you?" Millie asked, looking up at him. Her ears were down, and her eyes were wide. She almost looked afraid. "Or who could have slipped it into your pocket?"

Gil shook his head. "The party was rather crowded. It could have been anyone," he admitted. Millie had faced down a damn greater dragon without so much as blinking, but the bit of fabric had her shaken. It was unnerving. "I take it this isn't a token of someone's admiration?"

"This is a gris-gris," she said, her voice so quiet it was almost lost in the clatter of the cab as it rolled over Wyndford's cobblestones. "The ternaire was more of a message than a spell, but this is real conjure. Someone wanted to influence you."

A chill ran down Gilbert's spine. His hip had been nearly unbearable all night, but the moment Millie had pulled the little pouch from his pocket, the discomfort eased. It still ached, but nowhere near as badly. Someone didn't want to influence him, they wanted to hurt him.

"Why didn't I feel it, the way I felt Annie's magic back at the ranch?" he asked, remembering how he'd tasted metal and gotten a headache just from being near an orcish spell.

"It's a different magic," Millie said, glancing at Gilbert. "Annie uses old orcish spellsongs out on the ranch since there's not many humans around, but in Marigot it would be–" she paused and frowned. "It *was* dangerous to do any magic that risked a master feeling ill. Conjure is more like, you make the spell the way you might write a letter, and ask for spirits to do something for you. If the spirits accept the offerings, the spell becomes active. If they don't, it doesn't. Since it's the spirits doing the work, humans don't get sick."

Gilbert frowned down at the small square bundle in Millie's hand. He placed his hand over it, wrapping his fingers around hers.

"You still got rid of the spell, though," he said, feeling only the familiar scratch of wool. His hip remained blissfully quiet.

"Not on purpose," she said, looking sheepish. "I've been told that when I touch or get near a conjure spell, it's like the whole letter gets burnt. Even if the spell was active, the connection to the spirit dissolves, and any effects fade. I don't really know why it does that to other kinds of magic, it just does."

"When we were back in Scorched Bluffs, Miss Sweetpea could cast spells around you during the shootout. Is her magic different?" Gilbert had never bothered studying magical theory. He did his magic with numbers. He'd never needed to understand how this all worked. Now, he wished he'd paid at least a little attention during the few lectures he'd had to sit through in school.

"Sweetpea is Sweetpea," Millie said with a shrug. "She can cast around me, but most people struggle to." She leaned forward, peering out the cab's window to watch the homes of Gilbert's neighbourhood roll past. "I wish she was here," Millie admitted. "Someone put a gris-gris on me, too. Whoever took Fred wants something from us, and I know shit about magic."

"Well," Gilbert said, tucking a stray curl behind her long ear. "So much for getting any sleep tonight."

12

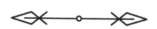

WHERE YOU BELONG

NATHALIE

DESPITE HER EARLIER FAUX pas, Nathie felt Rhiannon's soirée was a success. The Butcher had left without causing a scene, and her banker husband had followed, leaving Nathie free to enjoy the usual social game of manoeuvring among the social elite. She'd been chatting to Rhiannon about the success of the evening when Rhi's butler arrived at her side and whispered something into her ear.

Before her eyes, Rhiannon transformed from composed lady to bright-eyed ingénue. Colour touched her cheeks and her hazel eyes opened wide. Just like that, Nathie was looking at the cheerful girl she remembered from her childhood. The transformation felt bittersweet. As glad as she was that Rhiannon hadn't lost her spark, she couldn't help but wonder why it took this secret news to reignite it.

"Who is this? Has a suitor come calling?" Nathie asked, leaning in to nudge her cousin. There were plenty of suitors at the soirée, but Rhiannon had been politely distant with all of them.

"What?" Rhiannon asked, cheeks flushing. She fanned a hand in Nathie's direction to dispel any notions of courting, which only made Nathie more curious. "Oh no, nothing like that. A friend from out west, but I need to speak with him right away. Something's happened."

"Well, let's go speak with him," Nathie said, motioning for Rhiannon to take the lead. "I want to meet this friend of yours." Hopefully, it would be someone who was not a mass murderer. There could only be so many of those out on the frontier, and Nathie had always thought her cousin's taste was better than that.

A handsome man waited in the foyer, dressed in the indigo wool uniform of the Wyndford city police. Spotting Rhiannon, the man reached up to smooth down his short red hair. Tanned and broad-shouldered, the man looked at them with a tentative smile. Nathie felt a warmth spread up her neck as she realised the police officer wasn't smiling at her, but at her cousin, who had rushed over to pull him into a warm, undignified hug.

"Well then," Nathie said to herself, watching the police officer's tan face light up with a hot flush. This hardly looked like two friends meeting after an absence.

"Nathalie, this is Marshal Alan Duncan," Rhiannon said, turning her body toward Nathie but keeping her eyes fixed on the officer. "He was a wonderful help in Scorched Bluffs."

"It's just 'Sergeant', these days," Mister Duncan said, rubbing the back of his neck. "But, I wanted to s—" he cut himself off and cleared his throat to try again. "I wanted to see the city you talked about. With some of the changes going on in the territory, I thought it was the right time to come. I was going to visit you, but I hadn't gotten up the nerve to..." he trailed off, looking around at the manor, and Nathie watched him wilt in the face of the grandeur.

"Well, a friend of my cousin's is a friend of mine," she said, striding over to shake his hand the way a man would. In the absence of Uncle Edmund or Auntie Eleanor, Nathie was happy to step into the role of a protective family member. "Nathalie Wolfe."

"Cousin?" Duncan asked, taking Nathie's hand with a firm grip.

"From my mother's side of the family," Rhiannon explained. "Nathie and her son are the other family I have, other than my uncle."

Nathie smiled, internally sizing up the man. He seemed properly concerned, but unlike certain other 'friends' of Rhiannon's, he hadn't tried to shoot her.

"You said there was a problem?" Nathie prompted, realising the two had forgotten the reason Duncan had arrived in the first place.

The boyish shyness faded before her eyes, and Duncan nodded. He fiddled with his hat nervously, running a calloused thumb over the brim. Hands like that could crush a man, but he held the hat so carefully that Nathie wondered if he would hold her cousin's hand with as much care.

"There was a problem at the jail," Duncan said, dropping his voice so he wouldn't be overheard. "Rousseau is gone."

The air was sucked from the room.

"Oh, did the elf kill him?" Nathie asked flippantly, sounding far away from herself. If her earlier confrontation with the elf had ended in her going on a rampage through the jail, Nathie was going to kick herself. Years of planning all gone awry because a bleached elf couldn't control herself. Without Fred or the elf, the case against Harrold would fall apart, making Rhiannon the one who would suffer. Nathie wouldn't allow that to happen.

"How could she?" Rhiannon asked, glancing at Nathie for the first time since they'd entered the foyer. "She's here," her cousin said. Then paused, frowning in concern. "Isn't she?"

"No, ma'am," Duncan said, saving Nathie the trouble. "I actually met Mrs. Berry when I first arrived to speak with you over an hour ago. She came with me to examine the situation. Gilbert joined us there. I suppose he heard that she'd left with me." Duncan's brow knit, and he shook his head slightly. "I don't know how Rousseau got out, but he did. He had help, but we don't know who was involved yet. We only know that they're targeting Berry."

He dipped his head in apology.

"Ry, she's going to need your help with this," he said quietly. "I've never seen her shaken before."

Nathie watched her cousin's face. The confliction of feelings was bare to them, a surprise given how reserved and calm Rhiannon had been since Nathie had arrived. Guilt, concern, and reluctance, all there as Rhi thought over the news.

"Ry?" Duncan asked, growing concerned.

"I need to go talk to her," Rhiannon said, glancing over at Nathie. "Are you alright to wrap up the evening here?"

"Absolutely not," Nathie said with a small huff. "I'm going with you. My personal feelings about Berry are just that, personal. Finding where Rousseau has escaped to is far more important than being upset that she shot at me."

Rhiannon shot Nathie a warning look, but she ignored it. She wasn't about to open up about the truth in front of a police officer, even if it was one who seemed completely besotted with her cousin. Let the man think she was insulted that she'd been shot at, for the time being. It would be safer for everyone.

Duncan's eyebrows shot up.

"Oh, did you surprise her too?" he asked. He ran a hand over his hair again, as though to check that it hadn't wandered out of place. "She shot my hat clean off my head the first time we met."

Nathie sighed, rolling her eyes at her cousin.

"Of course she did."

THE GOLDMAN RESIDENCE WAS a modest townhome, but kept in good order. The shutters were freshly painted, and the brass knocker on the door was polished to a shine. Marching past Rhiannon and Officer Duncan, Nathie reached for the knocker.

"Nathie wait-" Rhiannon said, but Nathie held up a hand to stall complaints and knocked with three sharp raps.

"If she doesn't want to see me, she'll have to get over it," she said over her shoulder to Rhiannon, who was cringing. Perhaps the elf had a bad temper, but surely—

The door swung open, and an exhausted-looking orcish man glared down at her.

"The children had *just* fallen asleep," the butler said, his Ormani accent thick as he hissed each word through his teeth. "Do you know how hard it is to get three little girls to sleep at the same time?"

"Yeah, it wasn't about Millie," Rhiannon said quietly. From inside, a little girl's voice bellowed, asking who was at the doors.

"I am holding you responsible for this woman," the butler told Rhiannon, tossing his minty hair out of his eyes. "Now, if you will excuse me, I must go warm up some milk. *Again.*"

Without so much as announcing their arrival, the butler turned on his heel and stalked down the hall in a huff. For a moment, Nathie stood there, stunned. In her entire life, she had never experienced such rude behaviour from a servant.

Hesitantly, she stepped inside and looked around at the decor. It was tasteful and well-made, making the best of the small space. A stairwell led up to the second floor, and a ghost flitted into view at the top. No, not a ghost, but a little elven girl in a white nightgown who stared down at her with wide golden eyes that glowed in the dim hallway light.

"Auntie Ry?" A second little girl appeared, this one's hair a riot of red curls that were barely contained in braids. The first little girl shook her head and whispered something to the other, ears wiggling adorably as she did so.

"Shhh, go back to bed, Rasha," Rhiannon said, waving from behind Nathie. "I'll see you tomorrow."

"Go back to bed, you two," the Butcher appeared at the top of the steps in a simple nightshirt and robe that was clearly too large for her. She scooped up the golden-eyed child whose hair matched her own and herded the redhead back out of sight to the tune of much protest. When the Butcher reappeared moments later, the Banker was with her, similarly dressed for bed, with a robe perfectly tailored to fit his large frame.

Nathie felt a twinge of guilt. She wouldn't have minded waking the elf and her husband, but the little girls had been so young, and Owen had been such a terror to get to bed at that age. When Rhiannon had mentioned the Butcher was a mother, Nathie had assumed the child was older, from the years between the end of the war and the massacre of the Colfield family. Instead, those were two little babies, still with soft cheeks and wide eyes.

"Thank you for waking up my girls," the elf said, voice dripping sarcasm. She helped the banker descend the stairs with her ears low. "It's not like they have a hard enough time sleeping these days without some asshole knocking on the door late at night."

"It was my fault. I didn't warn her," Rhiannon said, resting a hand on Nathie's shoulder. "I'm sorry Millie. But Alan told us what happened, and I know how important this is. We came straight here."

Duncan had stayed at the doorway, and tipped his head toward the Goldmans, but didn't seem inclined to go inside.

"I need to return to the station, make sure the investigation doesn't go sideways." It was an excuse, and Nathie knew it. The man was properly afraid of the short elf woman. Hopefully, his caution would rub off on her cousin. As soon as the Colfield murder trial was over, Nathie hoped they never had to see the Butcher again.

Excusing himself again, Duncan left, gently closing the door behind him.

"I didn't realise they were so young. I apologise, Mrs. Goldman," Nathie said. The pair flinched, adding to

Nathie's confusion. Now she regretted avoiding the topic of the woman with Rhiannon. There seemed to be so much more going on than a murderer playing house.

"Well, we might as well talk," the elf said, leading them to the parlour. Goldman eased himself down into a horsehair chair with a grunt, extending his bad leg out in front of him. The elf gestured at the two cousins to sit on the divan.

The half-orc appeared at the doorway with a pair of mugs, and the elf took them both, handing one to Goldman and keeping the other. With a shock, Nathalie realised they weren't going to be offered anything. It was one thing to be a murderer, but there was no need to be a poor hostess.

"Alan said Rousseau escaped," Rhiannon said, worrying at a ruffle of silk on her dress. "Do we know what happened? Have we talked to the witnesses?"

"Well, the witnesses are dead or say they didn't see anything," the elf said, finally settling on a chair. Her feet barely reached the ground. "We don't know anything other than whoever took Fred wasn't really after *him*. They left something behind that suggests they don't care much about his well-being."

Nathie exchanged glances with Rhiannon. The latter's dark with concern.

"Do you think it was Harrold? Frederic can't testify against him if he's dead," Nathie asked, determined to help despite her earlier misstep. "Rhiannon needs his testimony. The word of an elf doesn't carry the same weight in court."

"Fred is all right," the elf said, blowing the steam from her tea. "Seeing as whoever took him left his hand behind as proof. They don't care about him, but they don't want him dead yet."

Rhiannon stared at her for a moment, but Nathie didn't understand what was going on. Was this a riddle? Or was the elf being obtuse on purpose?

"That's not funny, Millie," Rhiannon said, frowning. "Someone left his hand behind?" Ah, not a riddle, a joke in poor taste. One that snuck a small chuckle out of Nathie, much to her surprise.

"Well, I think it's funny," the elf snapped, scowling toward Rhiannon. "And frankly, my opinion is the one that matters tonight. Fred is gone. A message was written on the wall for me in blood and someone's been casting conjure up here. While I love you Ry, this is my call. Not yours. You don't know what Marigot is like."

Nathie cleared her throat politely. Every set of eyes in the room snapped onto her, and Nathie took the moment to smooth her silk skirts and luxuriate in the attention.

"Rhiannon might not, but I do," she said. "I live in Marigot, and it's changed since the war. I know it better than you do, Mildred. I'll go with you to find him, and Rhiannon can stay here where it's safe." Calling the elf by her first name felt awkward and clumsy, but if they were going to work together, Nathie would have to set aside her own feelings for a while.

"There," Rhiannon said, spreading her hands in the air like she was presenting the offer to the elf. "I can't go, but Nathie will. She knows the city, knows who's still around. You said it yourself: most of the people you knew back before the war have died." Rhiannon might have thought she was helping, but at the mention of lost comrades, the elf lost all colour in her face.

"You think staying here is more important?" Mildred asked, voice flat. Her ears had swished back, reminding Nathie of a deeply annoyed cat.

"Millie, don't get like this. You know I can't leave Wyndford until Harrold is convicted. I need to be here for court," Rhiannon said, with a scowl that Nathie was immensely proud of. It seemed Rhi had learned a thing or two from her older cousin, after all.

"Right," Mildred's voice was hollow. "Court. For the money."

"For my family's company," Rhiannon said, an edge creeping into her voice. "I thought you'd understand. You always have before."

The elf stood, setting aside her cup of tea, and shrugged.

"How can I understand? Everyone who I called family 'is dead now'," she said, echoing Rhiannon's words. Her cousin flinched, as if the elf had physically struck her. Nathie had expected Mildred to fly into a rage, but she only sat there, cold and empty. This was much worse. Nathie knew that kind of expression. It was the one she'd worn as she'd watched her second husband die, choking on his own tongue.

"Your cousin is from Marigot and you didn't think to tell me? I've never kept a secret from you, Ry," the elf's voice fell to a whisper. "Never. But your cousin is a master and you can't be bothered to warn me?"

"She wasn't-" Rhiannon started.

"Like hell she wasn't," Millie hissed. Nathie shifted uncomfortably where she sat.

"I asked her not to tell you," she said, in defence of her cousin. Nathie reached out and took Rhi's hand, giving it a supportive squeeze. "Your feelings toward the city are infamous and you shot at me without even knowing where I was from."

"No, you didn't." The elf kept her eyes fixed on Rhiannon's face, and whatever she found there gave up Nathie's attempted white lie. Slipping off the seat, the Butcher left the room, knuckles white from how hard she was holding onto the tea mug.

The banker had been silent, but as his wife left the room, he turned to Nathalie and Rhiannon with half-lidded eyes.

"She deserves better than that, Rhiannon," he said. "Both of you, get out of my house. I'll send you a message when we've decided what we're doing."

"I should go talk to her—" Rhiannon protested, rising to her feet. The banker pushed himself to his feet, towering over her.

"Not tonight," Nathie said, taking her arm and patting it lightly. "As loath as I am to admit it, I agree with Mister Goldman. We all need some rest before cooler heads can prevail. You didn't mean what she heard," she said, steering Rhiannon toward the front door.

"No, but she still said it," Gilbert said from behind them. "That woman has dedicated years of her life to keeping you safe, and you threw that into her face."

With less grace than perhaps was warranted, Nathie opened the door and pulled Rhiannon out through it. Enough damage had been done to her cousin that night, and Nathie wasn't about to stay and let that damage become irreparable.

"It's not only a company," Rhiannon whispered, letting Nathie walk her out to where their carriage was waiting. Her voice hitched and tears were flooding her eyes. "It was my father's, and before that, my grandfather's. It's the family legacy. That's all I have left of them."

Nathie pulled her into a tight hug. There it was. Rhiannon had held herself together so well until tonight. Stroking her cousin's hair, Nathie held her as Rhiannon's stoic composure finally broke.

"You have yourself," she murmured, waiting it out. Nathie knew from experience the tears would only end when Rhiannon had run out of them. "And you, my darling cousin, are the thing your parents would be most proud of. You have grown into such a strong young woman and you came home after such a deep heartbreak. No matter what happens with the company, your parents will be so proud of you. As proud as I am."

Nathie hoped Rhiannon could hear what she was saying. It might take a while for her cousin to believe her, but they had time.

"Don't hurt her," Rhiannon whispered, lifting her face from Nathie's shoulder to look into her eyes. "Please, Nathie. I know she hurt you, but don't take that out on her yet. Wait until you're both back."

Nathie smiled and wiped the tears from one of Rhiannon's cheeks with her thumb.

"Of course," she lied. "Anything for my darling cousin."

13

MILDRED ARGENT

MILLIE

MILLIE SAT ON THE floor of Gilbert's bedroom, tucked into the corner made by the wall and his giant bed. The shelter it offered helped calm her racing heart, even if she knew that no one in the house would shoot at her. Some old instincts were stubborn, and being out in the open in the parlour made the point between her shoulder blades itch. She pressed her cheek against the soft blanket that hung over the side as she stared at the photograph in her hands.

Hal had found it among Fred's things after the battle of Scorched Bluffs and had given it to her once Fred had been arrested. It was supposed to be evidence if she ever had to go to trial for what she'd done to keep Gilbert's family safe, blowing up Fred's Wyndford home and killing some men loyal to him. The safety of a little girl had hung in the balance, and Millie would make the same decisions over again without hesitation.

But the decisions she'd made when the photo was taken, that was different. A hundred choices gone wrong, a hundred mistakes made.

The 43rd company of the Amelior Union Infantry stared back at her from a decade ago. Millie was in the centre next to Fred, both grim and determined. Fred was dressed in his field uniform, hair in disarray and dirt smudged across his square jaw. Her eyes glowed from behind the black warpaint that kept the sun from blinding her during a fight. A roach of horsehair had been sewn into her braid. The tips of it were dyed, and while it looked black in the photograph, it had been a vivid red to match the sash tied around her waist to keep her coat out of the way while fighting. Around her stood the other soldiers, freed slaves from every corner of the old world and some from the new one.

The picture didn't show how muddy the field had been behind them, churned to sludge by their successful attack on the secessionist camp they had captured. It didn't show the way the bodies had disappeared into that mud, stinking before the day was out, or the way the swamp vishaps had swarmed the battlefield that night, their eyes glowing red in the dark as they ate the dead, Union soldiers and secessionists alike.

She'd stood watch that night and the grotesque sounds of that night had kept her up for days, creeping into her dreams whenever she tried to sleep. Even now, she could remember the horrible feast perfectly, while she barely remembered the sound of her soldiers' voices.

Millie ran her fingertips along the edge of the photograph, fighting the heat in her throat. Ten years, but losing her company still felt raw.

Delilah had died opening the gate to downtown Marigot, leaving behind a younger sister. Clem had died to a sniper, her daughter hidden safely out in Laflotte, far from the fighting. Akhun died from artillery, taking a round to the chest the day the photograph was taken. He was missing from the photograph, though Delilah had his knife stuck in her belt to remember him. Of the company, only Remi, the rat-faced bastard, and Millie had survived Fred's final cull. Remi had stayed loyal until he died. Millie had not.

"Your name is Argent now," Frederic said, a hand on either of her small shoulders. His eyes were so clear and blue, Mildred was certain she'd get lost in them. "Mildred Argent, and you belong to me. That means that woman can't touch you anymore, that I'll keep you fed, that you'll have a safe place to sleep."

Food, safety, and freedom from her mother had sounded like heaven.

"What do you need me to do?" she asked, squaring her shoulders as much as possible and trying to look like she was more capable than her eleven years. She even held her ears alert, in case he knew how to read elven body language.

"You are going to learn how to fight," Frederic said, smiling down at her.

"I know how to fight," she said, frowning. That's what had gotten his attention, after all. She'd killed one of his guards. She'd had surprise on her side, and the man had underestimated the tiny elf, but he'd died all the same, leaving her covered in blood and dragged in front of Frederic to answer for the crime. Instead of punishing her, he'd made an offer.

"You do, but I have someone that will teach you how to become the best fighter Marigot has ever seen. And then, when you're done training, you'll become my personal guard."

Her chest puffed out, and Mildred nodded eagerly. She wanted to be the best. She wanted to earn the kindness of clean clothing and food that didn't have maggots in it. The world was cold and cruel, so she would learn how to become just as cold, just as cruel. She would not throw away this one chance at something better.

"Yes, Master Frederic," she breathed. "Anything. I'll do anything."

And so she had.

Some people were not worth being loyal to.

"No more kings, no more masters," Millie whispered again, a tear finally slipping through her lashes to roll down her cheek. No more cane kings, using the bodies of fallen slaves to fertilise the sugarcane. No more masters holding debt over the necks of the poor like a goddamn guillotine. Once a rallying cry, now it sounded hollow. Fred had been both: he'd owned her, his family fortune made on the backs of the slaves that harvested sugarcane, making him a cane king, one of Marigot's untouchable elite. When he promised freedom, she believed him. She'd believed him when he'd promised love. She'd believed him until he had her arrested for a crime she didn't commit.

The world couldn't know that the secessionist general had resorted to human sacrifice in a last-ditch effort to win the war. One man's death was enough to summon a spirit of war that would cut through the city like a scythe, uncaring if its victims wore blue coats or green. Millie had interrupted the ritual, forced O'Leary to surrender, and been blamed for all of it.

A human, a man with such an important reputation, could not be known as a blasphemer. But the Bayou Butcher could, and the legend of Amelior's boogie man was born the night Fred locked her away in his family's cellar to rot. Hope had died down there, right along with whatever scraps of loyalty she'd had left.

Heart aching, Millie grit her teeth. Nathalie was right. She couldn't hide forever. Fred had escaped, and someone was targeting her using conjure. She had to go back to Marigot, if only to wipe out whatever remained of that threat before it reached her daughters. Her free daughters, who didn't know that a slave market smelled like piss and soap, or that the jangle of bells on a slave collar meant they had attempted escape.

Akhun, a fieldworker before the war, had worn a belled collar until Fred freed him to fight. He had never talked about it, instead learning to walk in a way that muffled the awful jangling. After Millie had approached him about freedom in exchange for fighting, Akhun had taught her how to move as quietly as he did. Akhun hadn't hesitated to take her up on Fred's offer, but he had warned her that night that masters never stopped being masters. The power they held over other souls was too heady. They would hunger for it until they were put down.

He'd been right, but at least he had died a free man.

"No more," she whispered, pushing herself up to her feet. It might be ten years late, but she was going to make good on that promise.

If it meant she had to rely on the banker she'd married and Rhiannon's terrible cousin, so be it. Masters would only stop being masters once they were dead, and far too many had survived the war while too few of their slaves had.

A gentle knock on the door made Millie jump, and she scrubbed away the tears on the cuff of her nightshirt.

"May I come in?" Gilbert asked from the other side of the door. "If not, that's—"

Millie crossed the room silently and opened the door for him. He deserved to know her decision, after all. She took a deep breath and squared her shoulders, looking up at his face. The quiet sadness there caught her by surprise, and her breath rushed out in a useless whoosh.

"What's wrong?" she asked, frowning. Had Nathalie said something to him?

Gilbert laughed, but it was humourless.

"You're asking what's wrong with me?" he asked, lifting an eyebrow. "You're the one who was reminded that her friends all died in a war. How are *you* doing?"

She opened her mouth, ready to snap that she was fine. Why wouldn't she be? But the sadness on his face and the gentle way he'd asked left her bare of her normal armour.

"I feel like shit," she admitted, stepping to one side so he could come into his bedroom. "I thought I was over most of this, but tonight everything feels raw."

Gil limped inside, leaning heavily on his cane. She stepped in, tucking herself under his other arm to help him get to the bed. He had a bundle in his hand, and she took it from him until he eased himself down onto the mattress with a deep groan.

She held the bundle out for him, but Gil patted the bed beside him.

"I think," he said slowly, grimacing as he stretched out his bad leg. "It's high time we have that conversation about the marriage."

Millie climbed up next to him, settling the bundle in her lap. Wrapped in buckskin, the contents felt mostly like cloth, but there was a comforting weight to it that suggested it contained something heavier.

"I think you're right," she said, plucking at the string that held the bundle closed. She opened her mouth, then closed it again, unsure what to say or how to say it.

"You are..." Gil started, then shook his head. "You are the best mother I have ever met. Sarah adores you, and even my grouch of a father complains less about you every day. But you're a wild woman, and I mean that as a compliment," he said, glancing her way. "I can see how the city is stifling to you. The party only proved what I already suspected. Asking you to stay here would be asking you to give up everything you've fought for. I refuse to ask you to make that choice."

Her throat was getting tight, and her eyes, hot. She was out of practice hiding her emotions, but since the party, it seemed like she was barely holding on as they battered her towards insanity. Biting the inside of her cheek, Millie looked away from Gilbert, down at the bundle in her lap.

This would be easier if he was the smarmy asshole she'd first thought he was, demanding that she stay. But she liked him, liked his daughter and his father and even the prim chef who yelled every time she broke into his kitchen. She even was fond of the fancy house with its warm fireplaces and soft beds. Gilbert was right though: the city was stifling.

"Back in Scorched Bluffs, I thought I was going to die, so I might as well enjoy my last night alive. Some asshole banker was handsome, and I figured there were worse options." Gilbert chuckled and Millie glanced up at him, ears burning.

"Then we both survived and now I don't know what I want anymore," she admitted, feeling very small. "For years I thought I wanted to hide, to become someone else." She tried to laugh, but only managed a sad huff. "That didn't work out very well, did it?" she asked, looking up at him.

"Not really, no." Gil smiled and took her hand to give it a small squeeze. "If you don't know what you want, you don't have to decide yet. The girls will be safe here while we go to Marigot and get this mess sorted out. Rhiannon might be acting strangely, but she would die to keep them safe."

Millie blinked.

"'We'?" she asked, shaking her ears. Had she heard that right? "You don't... Gil, you don't know Marigot. Last time Fred saw you, he *shot* you."

He winced and shifted his weight on the bed. Something in his hip popped audibly, and Millie cringed in sympathy.

"Thank you for reminding me," he said dryly. "I have no desire to repeat that experience, but hear me out on this, Millie. You know Frederic. I know Frederic. We both know he's shit at cards and gets into debt to powerful people. It's how he ended up in Harrold Colfield's pocket, and I'd bet my bank that he's got even bigger debts down in Marigot."

Millie listened, ears drooped. So far, this all made sense. She didn't like it, but she didn't interrupt him, either.

"Unless Rhiannon's lovely cousin is secretly a financier, there's only one person who we can all trust to search through his affairs to find out who he owed and how much." Gilbert let go of her hand and spread his hands wide, smiling at her with the same smug expression he'd worn when they first met.

Millie scowled, but she knew she was beaten. She could read and write, she could count bullets and bodies, but the maths that banks ran on might as well be magic. It was beyond her, and Gil knew that. Bastard.

"I'm going to guess from the way you're glaring at me that you agree," Gil said, looking quite pleased with himself. He smoothed the lapels of his robe down his chest. "I promise to let you handle the fighting and focus on the paperwork. Now," he reached out and patted the bundle in her lap.

"You can't fight in a pretty dress. I got your measurements from the dressmaker. I was going to offer this as a thank you for saving my family once you'd decided about the marriage, but I think you might as well have it now. Please, don't take this into account when you make your decision, however. This is a gift, regardless of what you decide."

The heat was back in her throat, so Millie focused on untying the string that held it all closed. She unwrapped the buckskin outer layer to reveal a neat pile of clothing topped with a pair of sheathed hatchets, nearly identical to the ones that had been twisted and melted during a fight with a dragon. Picking one up, she tested the weight of it in her hand. The spike at the back of the axe was shorter, curved slightly into a pick.

Slipping the leather sheath off the blade, Millie ran her thumb along its edge. It was unsharpened, but she could solve that easily enough. Something was engraved into the blade, and it took Millie a moment to realise it was a blueberry. A berry for a Berry.

"It was a bit of a rushed order," Gil said, clearing his throat. "But the blacksmith provided a sharpening kit. I hope it's good enough quality, I admit—"

Millie cut him off with a hug, throwing her arms around him, careful to keep the axe's pick clear of him. Gilbert stiffened for a moment, but laughed and tucked her into his arms, resting his chin on the top of her head.

"Thank you," she said. She could hear the thump of his heart where her ear pressed to his chest, and the slowing rhythm was an anchor she desperately needed in the turmoil of the last few days. With every beat, the coil of anxiety that had wrapped around her chest slowly began to unwind.

"You'll have to find guns on your own," he murmured. "The gunsmith was no help and kept trying to sell me some pea shooter that he insisted was safe for a lady's hand. Rhiannon helped to get the axes right, so as much as I'd like to take credit for that, I can't."

"Guns won't be a problem," Millie said, hoping she was right. She still had some old favours to call in. As long as the people that owed her were alive, she could get what she needed in Marigot.

"The rest is clothes, and the buckskin is for a new coat that has nothing to do with an army," Gil said, his voice slipping into the same soothing cadence he used when reading stories to the girls before bed. "But I thought you'd want to make that yourself."

Stifling a yawn, Millie slid the bundle and its contents from her lap to the floor with a quiet thump. The axe in her hand was sheathed and joined the pile. She'd change in the morning, get everything packed and say goodbye to the girls. But for now, she was wrung dry and desperately needed sleep.

"You're a good husband, Gilbert," she said. "Too bad you live in a city."

14

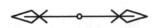

GOODBYES

RHIANNON

THE SOIRÉE GUESTS WERE gone, Nathalie had gone to bed, and Rhiannon could finally breathe again. She'd considered going to sleep, but her thoughts were still churning through the events of that evening. Instead of lying in her childhood bedroom and staring at the ceiling for another long night, Rhiannon went to what had once been her father's study, Fyodor close on her heels.

Opening the heavy door to the study, Rhiannon stepped inside, the oak parquet floor cold under her bare feet. The study was almost the same as it had been when it was her father's. Harrold had changed the portrait that hung over the massive mahogany desk to one of himself, but Rhiannon had pulled it off and replaced it with her father's on her first day of being home. Now, lit only by the lantern in her hand, Rhiannon looked up at the man she missed so much.

The painter had captured the slight curl of his lips that always was the first sign of a smile, and the mischievous crinkle at the corner of his eyes that were so much like her own. He looked so real that more than once since returning home, Rhiannon had found herself about to ask the portrait what he thought of the morning news.

The Rota Sanctum, the holy church of the Wheel, said that her father was still around while he waited to be re-born. That he would never truly be gone. They'd been a faithful family, attending weekly services and donating to city improvements such as hospitals and orphanages. Doing the work of the Messiah for those born less for-tunate. Rhiannon had never had a reason to doubt that they would be born again... until she'd lost everything in a single night. Her parents, her brother and his family, her home, the family company — all of it was ripped away by an uncle who wasn't content with the wealth he had. It was hard to hold faith that her family would be reborn anew, and she might never see them again. Since returning home, Rhiannon had felt their loss deeply. Every time she stepped into the study, she expected to find her father at his desk, and every time she found it empty, the grief cut a fresh wound.

Nathalie helped as best she could, but she was half a stranger. Or maybe it was Rhiannon who had grown es-tranged. It was so hard to tell.

Gilbert's voice echoed in her ears. '*That woman has ded-icated years of her life to keeping you safe, and you just threw that into her face.*'

Rhiannon winced. Gilbert was right. She had phrased that terribly. Yet Millie, of all people, should understand that Colfield Rail was so much more than just a company. It was her family's legacy. This wasn't about Rhiannon's money. It was about the hundreds of workers who de-pended on the company to keep their families fed the same way Scorched Bluffs had depended on her and Millie to provide fresh meat to supplement whatever they could grow in the dusty dirt.

"I made a mess of things," she said, not sure if she was speaking to Fyodor or the portrait. Setting down her lantern on the desk, she sat down on the stuffed chair behind it and wrapped her arms around Fyodor as he sat in front of her and leaned into her.

The big Moorlander was still sulking from being put in her room all evening, but it had been safest for him with all the fatty foods being served at the soirée. After years of eating lean meat out on the Frontier, Rhiannon hadn't wanted him to eat something that upset his stomach. It had seemed so important that morning, but now Rhiannon couldn't help but wonder if she'd saved him from getting poisoned instead.

"I can't lose you too," she told him, cupping his jowly face in her hands and looking into those warm brown eyes. "So no treats from strangers, ok? Just from me and Auntie Nathie." Fyodor whined and licked at her hand. He knew she was unhappy, as he always did.

Kissing his forehead, Rhi released Fyo's face and rubbed his ears just the way he liked. His face split into a dopey smile, leaning his massive head into her hands while one back foot thumped against the floor.

"I don't know what to do," she admitted to her father. She knew what Fyodor would do. Dogs were loyal beyond logic. He had rushed toward a burning building to save Millie, and would charge straight into Marigot's swamp if given the chance. People were more complicated, though. People had their duty to think about, in addition to loyalty. How many times had Millie warned her that blind loyalty led to being blind-sided by the one you trust? Yet here she was, demanding that same loyalty from Rhiannon.

She sighed and rested her cheek on Fyodor's head.

Rhiannon knew what she wanted to do, but she also knew what she needed to do. She had to hope that Millie would forgive her for it when they had Frederic back in custody. Hopefully, the bastard wouldn't hurt anyone else until then.

THE RED HAND WOULDN'T be missed this late at night. The jail had noticed that Rousseau was missing sooner than expected, but the rest of the evening had gone so well that the Hand's mood remained high. They whistled to themself as they walked through dark streets to the safe house where they'd put Rousseau.

Knocking at the door in a pre-arranged rhythm, the Hand smiled under their hood as it swung open to reveal their coconspirator from the jail. They ducked inside the dilapidated apartment, feeling the tingle of a ward wash over their skin. The apartment was sparsely furnished. A pair of stools, a pot of coffee simmering on the wood stove, and a bedroll on the floor were the only signs that someone occupied it. The smell of alcohol was strong, but the Hand was relieved to see that the mage and the muscle were stone cold sober. The only person drunk in the small room was Rousseau, slumped in one corner and hugging a bottle and his wrist to his chest in his drink-induced sleep. Excellent.

"The jail has noticed our friend's departure early, I'm afraid," the Hand said once the door was closed and latched. "I want you to move him tonight. I've arranged for passage on the overnight freight for the three of you."

Perched on the stool by the stove, the mage nodded. The muscle leaned against the door behind the Hand and grunted in agreement.

"What about you?" the muscle asked. "Won't you be missed?"

The Hand grinned.

"My friend, the moment the city realises Rousseau is missing, no one will notice if I get declared the newest Messiah." The Hand pulled out a gris-gris from their pocket and tossed it to the Mage. "Keep that on our drunk friend, and he won't give you any trouble."

The mage nodded, a man of few words. He caught the gris-gris and tucked it away into a pocket.

"I'll find you at the rendezvous," the Hand said, adjusting their hood. "Now, if you'll excuse me, I have some further preparations to make before the sun rises."

THE SMELL OF COFFEE and breakfast woke Rhiannon, and she groaned as tense muscles in her back and a hard surface under her face told her she'd fallen asleep at her father's desk again. Opening her eyes, she blinked the world into focus to see a silver platter set in front of her. Fresh coffee, eggs, toast and bacon waited for her, as did a pair of extremely well-practised puppy eyes as Fyodor rested his chin on the other side of the desk, waiting for her to tell him he could have some of the delicious bacon. A small puddle of drool under his chops suggested he had been waiting for a few minutes.

"Good boy," she told him, straightening and stretching out her back. A few vertebrae popped back into place, and she rolled her neck to loosen it. Plucking a piece of bacon from the plate, she whistled for Fyodor to sit. He did, ears perked and licking his chops.

"Catch," Rhiannon said, and tossed the strip of meat to her dog. Fyodor caught it expertly and immediately hunkered down to eat it, licking every drop of grease from his paws. Picking up a slice of bacon for herself, Rhiannon nibbled on it and pulled over the morning's paper and letters.

The Wyndford Tribune mentioned nothing about Rousseau's escape, much to Rhiannon's relief. She had a feeling that Uncle Harrold was involved, but without proof, she couldn't bring this to court as extra charges.

Wiping the grease from her fingers with a linen napkin, Rhiannon reached for her coffee, already perfectly made with a touch of cream and sugar. The stack of letters was slightly taller than usual, and Rhiannon sorted the usual marriage propositions into their own pile as she did every morning. Most were from potential matchmakers and suitors, hoping to take advantage of Rhiannon's precarious position. The transparent greed left her disgusted, and she placed them in a pile to read later. She stopped as she reached for the last pair of letters, mug resting against her lip. Three envelopes tied together with a bit of string addressed in Millie's handwriting. It was neat and plain, lacking the flourishes found on every other envelope in Rhiannon's pile.

For a moment, Rhiannon considered setting it aside too, until after she'd finished a coffee or two. Instead, she took a single sip and set the mug down, untying the string that held the bundle together. The top letter was labelled 'for today', while the two below had different instructions. One was 'for when you feel alone', and the other was 'the truth'.

The coffee's warmth faded, leaving Rhiannon cold. Since Nathalie had told her that Millie had killed her father, Rhi had been uncertain about what to do about the situation. Not that she didn't believe Nathie, but surely Millie had a reason to do such a thing. There had been a war on, Rousseau ordered many atrocities to be committed, and there were plenty of excuses that would make the act seem less vile in hindsight. Until this letter. Millie herself had said she had never once lied to Rhiannon, and Rhiannon had believed that. Now, with the promise of finding out 'the truth', she was filled with doubts.

"One thing at a time," she murmured to Fyodor, and slipped the two letters with instructions into a drawer of the desk, resting them atop her court papers for the coming trial.

She took another fortifying sip of coffee and opened the 'for today' letter, surprised to see a paragraph from both Millie and Gilbert, the latter's handwriting exquisitely readable. Schoolboy perfect, compared to the simple script of his wife's. She started with Millie's half, blinking at the name the elf had addressed it to.

Ry,

I've decided to go to Marigot. We need Fred for the trial. Your cousin can come if she wants, but she'll need to keep up. Please keep an eye on the girls while I'm gone. Avrom

(Gilbert's father) will take care of them, but I don't know if I'll be coming back. A lot of people in Marigot have a lot of reasons to hate me, and I don't think I blame them for it. But I will haunt the shit out of you if you let anything happen to my children. Keep them safe, please.

Millie

The sentences were clipped and short, but there was no blame or venom from their disagreement the night before. Rhiannon took a deep breath and let it out slowly, relieved that Nathalie wouldn't have to fight with Millie about going. Her cousin could hold her own, but both women needed to remember the real goal was to retrieve Rousseau. Not to squabble.

Gilbert's paragraph followed, chilling in its businesslike tone.

Miss Colfield,

My father will personally take over your accounts while I am away, and you can rest assured that they are in expert hands. Should you have any questions, ask for Avrom Goldman. Unfortunately, we, Goldman National Bank, will be unable to accommodate your cousin's accounts at this point in time.

Gilbert Goldman

At the bottom of the letter, three names were signed in pencil with misshapen letters. Fenna, Rasha, Sarah. One of them, likely Fenna, had included a drawing on the next page of what had to be Freckle. No other dog was that fluffy.

She stared at the drawing, coffee forgotten until it had gone cold. Shaking off her morbid worries, Rhiannon stood and picked up her mug to bring with her. Millie and

Nathie might be away, but there were things Rhiannon could look into while staying in Wyndford.

"Murphy?" she called, slipping out of the office, Fyodor hot on her heels. "Can you request Sergeant Duncan to stop by after his duties? I have some important things to discuss concerning his investigation." She pursed her lips and thought. She had access to funds that she hadn't had in a long time, and three sets of eyes were better than one.

"And can you please arrange an appointment with the head of the Wyndford Stratton Agency, please? I believe I'll need their services."

"At once, miss," her butler said with a small bow. "I expect Mrs. Wolfe will wish to see you before she departs this afternoon."

Rhiannon frowned. So soon? She supposed it made sense. The sooner the group left for Marigot, the sooner they'd catch up with whoever had taken Rousseau.

"Yes, I will. Can you make some more breakfast and bring it to the terrace? I'll eat with her there," Rhiannon said. Then, after a moment's thought, added: "And have the company arrange a locomotive and the family sleeper car for them, at our expense. Nathalie will know best which route to take."

Murphy smiled, a twinkle in his eye that reminded Rhiannon of her father's. The thought hurt, and she covered the pain with a small smile before she turned away and headed to her room to get dressed for the day. There was so much to do.

15

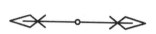

TIME TO GO (HOME)

MILLIE

"But *why do you* hafta go?" Rasha asked for the third time during the brief cab ride to the train station. She was perched on Avrom's lap, across from where Millie sat with Fenna on her knee. Sarah occupied her father's lap next to them, and only Arnaud was free of a little girl passenger. Millie pretended not to notice how he was sulky about it.

"Because a long time ago, Mama used to live there," Millie said, stroking Fenna's hair. They were nearly at the station, and it would be easier to say goodbye in the cab than on a busy platform. This was never how she'd imagined she would tell them about her past. She'd always hoped they would be older, better able to understand. She'd hoped they wouldn't hate her, and that they could ask all the questions they'd wanted. Instead, she had to speak up to be heard over the clatter of the cab wheels on cobblestones. "Mama wasn't a very nice person back then. She was very mean to some people."

"Did they deserve it?" Rasha asked, puffing her chest out and scowling.

Stifling a smile, Millie shrugged. "Some did, but some didn't. When we get angry, sometimes we forget who we're angry at. I was very angry at some very bad people, but I hurt some good people when I shouldn't have. So, just like when I make you three apologise to each other after a fight, it's time Mama goes to apologise to the people she fought back then."

Fenna huffed in her lap and muttered something about a stolen cookie, clearly not having forgiven Rasha for that morning's theft. Sarah had witnessed the argument and still seemed to be concerned that the other two wouldn't make up. Millie knew better, though her golden-eyed girl was prone to holding a grudge, just like her momma.

"But you're coming back, right?" Sarah asked, tiny face serious.

"That's why Papa's going," Gilbert said. "To drag her back once she's said all her sorries." The girls all giggled, but Arnaud and Avrom exchanged a glance that made Millie feel uncomfortable. They were smart men, and the morning had been equally full of adult arguments about the dangers of going to Marigot. In the end, Gilbert and Millie had won out when Millie pointed out that if she didn't go, whoever wanted her to would start targeting the reasons she had stayed in Wyndford. The safety of the girls was paramount.

"Uncle Hal will join us down there once he can," Gilbert added as the cab rolled to a stop in front of Wyndford Central Station. Unfortunately, the Stratton detective had a case to wrap up before he was free to help. The situation made Millie anxious, but there wasn't much any of them could do about it other than adapt.

"Alright gremlins," Millie said, giving each little girl a hug and kiss. No matter how often she had to leave them, saying goodbye made her want to scoop them close and hold on for dear life. Sarah included. "You behave for Tata Avrom and Uncle Arnaud, okay? No stealing cookies or sneaking food to Freckle." She pretended not to see the way Arnaud's shoulders straightened, and he suddenly seemed to have dust in his eyes.

Climbing out of the cab with Naveed's help, Millie helped Gilbert down. At least she was finally dressed comfortably again. Gilbert's gift fit well: the leggings were comfortable and not too long, while the white shirt and wool vest were actually sized to her shoulders, the cuffs small enough to stay on her wrists rather than slip down and make her look like a child playing dress up. She left the buckskin behind, knowing Marigot would be too hot to wear it. In the meantime, she had a wool jacket meant to wear over dresses that would make do.

The moment their parents were out of the cab, three little faces appeared at the cab window to wave goodbye.

"Mama, catch a frog for us!" Fenna pleaded, quickly echoed by the two others. "Or a snake!"

"I will," she said, adjusting her jacket and slinging her cartridge bag over her shoulder. There were plenty of maps and parchment in it to keep her busy on the trip. It was better than staring out the train window for the long ride south. Nathalie might be awful, but she'd been right. Marigot had changed since Millie had last walked its streets. If she could, Millie planned to learn the new lay of the land before returning.

Neither she nor Gilbert had much luggage, and it wasn't long before the cab was pulling away with three arms sticking out the window, waving goodbye.

"Oh, how darling are they?" Nathalie called out from the station's entrance.

Millie closed her eyes and took a deep breath before turning around to greet her. Whatever stories she had told Rhiannon had broken through years of mutual trust, turning a woman who once trusted Millie with her life into an aloof stranger. Though, as much as Millie wanted to shove Nathalie in front of one of the Colfield locomotives, they had to work together until Fred was apprehended. So she turned, trying to maintain a neutral expression on her face.

The neutrality lasted less than a heartbeat. Next to Nathalie stood a human man with sandy blond hair, blue eyes, and a neatly trimmed beard and moustache that did nothing to hide the slight crookedness of his nose. The world dropped away from her, leaving only the man ahead, who lifted a single hand in greeting. Pierre Luc Rousseau.

"You piece of shit!" she hissed, launching herself at Fred's younger brother. Something caught her around the waist, pulling her up short. "Let go," she snapped, looking up at Gilbert, who held her tightly in place. She could break free. They both knew that, but in doing so, she'd wind up hurting him. "You don't understand."

"Save it for later," he whispered, pulling her tight against him. "Save it for Fred."

She wanted to scream, to shove herself away and beat in the coward's face who had watched Fred's abuse, year after year, too afraid to say anything to stop it. They'd been nearly the same age, Millie and Pierre. They'd trained together. He'd seen how she'd taken the beatings he'd earned, how her meals would be held back if she didn't meet Fred's expectations. He'd seen everything and done nothing.

Millie wanted to tell Gilbert why Pierre deserved to have his face beaten in, but he was right. She needed to save the anger for later. Pierre would want to find Fred as much as they did, and she could always land a punch on his kidney on the trip to Marigot when he wasn't expecting it. Maybe she could break his nose again.

"Well, isn't that just heartwarming," Nathalie said, voice dripping with sarcasm. "I see the two of you know each other. Mister Goldman, this is Pierre Luc Rousseau, Frederic's solicitor, and younger brother. Pierre, this is Rhiannon's banker, Mister Gilbert Goldman. He's also married to the Butcher, as you can see."

Someone made a choking sound, and Millie reluctantly lifted her face away from Gilbert's coat to see Pierre had gone pale.

"M-married?" Pierre stammered, staring at her like she'd grown a second head. "On purpose?"

"Yeah," Millie snapped, throwing a rude gesture his way. She could feel Gilbert chuckle behind her, easing the pressure of his arm around her waist. "It's not illegal up here, asshole."

"Illegal?" Gilbert asked, but Millie didn't take her eyes off the lesser Rousseau.

"Marigot is more traditional in its view of marriage," Nathalie said, brushing imaginary dirt from her bottle green travelling suit. "Unions between humans and non-humans are not acknowledged unless the non-human blood is one-eighth or less."

"It's bullshit is what it is," Millie said, and spat onto the ground. "They only care if you look human."

Nathalie's expression turned brittle, and she stared down at the offending spot on the ground.

"Charming," she said. "Well, we'd best board our train and get going. Rhiannon arranged for a private express just for the four of us, but the station is already complaining that we're holding up their schedule." She snapped in the air and several valets materialised from the crowd, gathering up their luggage and ushering them toward platform two.

"I hate both of them," Millie muttered to Gilbert as they followed. He had shifted his arm from her waist to her shoulders, even though he didn't need as much help walking that afternoon as he had the evening of the party. This just confirmed Millie's suspicion that the gris-gris in his pocket at the party had been amplifying his hip pain.

"I think they can hear you, darling," Gilbert said, unbothered. He was acting like they were strolling off to have a picnic, not heading to the swamp where people like Fred and Nathalie were the norm. Rich assholes that made survival nearly impossible for anyone else.

"Good."

The private express was the sister locomotive to the one that had exploded out in Scorched Bluffs. It was still painted black, but sporting a new blue smokestack, and the familiarity was welcome in what was otherwise a terrible afternoon. A single passenger car was hooked up behind the coal car, and as they boarded, Millie saw immediately that it was a very fancy passenger car.

"It's what the Colfields use while travelling," Nathalie said, breezing into the small parlour area. She pointed toward one end with a lazy hand. "The bedrooms are down there. The married couple won't have a problem sharing, I presume? And Pierre and I will each take a separate cabin. The water closet is at the far end."

She continued the tour, but Millie grabbed Gilbert and marched down the aisle to the largest of the sleeper cabins. She needed to talk to him, but she needed to get away from the two Marigot assholes before she stabbed anyone Rhiannon cared about.

"Do remember that there are other passengers on this train," Nathalie called out in a saccharine voice. "Tsk, newlyweds."

Only in the safety of the sleeper cabin with the door pulled closed behind her did Millie allow herself to scream into her hands. Gilbert reached over and pulled the nearest pillow off the bed, holding it out to her as a softer option. She took it, thanked him and then screamed again, this time into the bundled down of a bunch of dead geese.

"Better?" Gilbert asked when she came up for air. He wasn't smirking for once. Had she upset him somehow? She was acting like one of their girls, throwing a fit because things were going differently from what she'd wanted.

"No," she said, paused, then gave in: "A little."

Gil sat on the bed, resting his bad leg out in front of him. The cabin was remarkably spacious now that she looked around. Across from the bed was a wardrobe built into the car's wall, and large windows let her see the empty platform roll past as the train pulled out of the station.

"So, would you like to talk about it?" Gilbert asked. "You don't have to, but by the way Frederic talked about his brother, we all thought he was dead."

She sat on the bed next to him, having to hop up onto the mattress. Her moccasins swayed over the floor with the train's slow rock from side to side. Embarrassment crept up on Millie, turning her neck and ears hot. She felt like a child, losing control at just the sight of Pierre, and being the wrong size for everything in the train.

"Fred bought me when I was around eleven," she said, running her hands over the soft fabric of her leggings. "His younger brother, Pierre, was away at boarding school a lot. Their father wanted him to harden up. He didn't have the same killer instinct that Fred and his father did. That I did." Pierre hadn't been around much those early days, only returning home for holidays and the summer until he had finished his schooling.

"He saw everything that was happening. He saw the training that was made for me to fail, and how I'd get beaten after every failure. He saw the other house slaves branded as punishment for small mistakes." She flopped backward onto the soft mattress and stared at the ceiling. It was plated with decorative tin tiles, making every corner of the train car disgustingly fancy.

"He didn't say anything?" Gilbert asked, looking down at her with a frown.

"Of course not," she said, and sighed. "This was Marigot before the war. It was run by masters and cane kings who had the full authority to treat slaves like animals, whether they were orcs, elves, or human."

His eyebrows shot up.

"Yeah," she said with a grim smile. "They never let that secret get out, did they? If you pissed off the wrong person, suddenly papers would be discovered that proved you weren't human enough, and poof, you were property."

Gilbert was quiet for a moment, glancing down at his hands.

"Carpenters don't own slaves," he said. "But I'm afraid to ask if they did in Marigot. Slavery goes against the core tenets of our beliefs. Every person is responsible for and in charge of their own path through life. There's no pre-destined rebirth waiting for men like me, no promise of forgiveness that excused terrible acts. Just a conscience. Yet, I've seen how easy it is for some people to break those tenets." He sighed, looking back down at her.

"Most didn't," she said gently, reaching out to rest a hand on his arm. "But the Wheelers forced them out of most of the city. It's hard to compete with slave labour when you have a heart. Most just couldn't afford to keep running their businesses."

His stormy eyes focused on her, looking for something. Whatever it was, Millie had told the truth. She just hadn't mentioned that many carpenter businesses were scared that they would be the next group deemed inhuman.

"It sounds like a terrible place," he said, laying down next to her. "I can see why you left."

"There are good parts, or there were when I was there. Bakimba square was a weekend market of food, fabrics, and conjure. Even slaves got Sunday off to go to the market to sell goods or to shop. The Bakimbans would play music for everyone to dance, and the Osaugan trading posts would put on a stickball game for everyone to watch and bet on." She smiled, remembering how the gathered crowd of slaves and free people had shouted and cheered for their chosen team. She could almost smell the market now: goat meat stew and fry bread stalls butted up against each other while the spices section smelled like exotic places she used to dream of visiting.

"Did you play stickball?" Gilbert asked. "We had a team at college, but only Osaugan students were good at it."

"Just as a kid," Millie said with a small laugh. "Fred couldn't handle his pet being better at it than he was."

The cabin was silent after that, and Millie listened to the rattle of the car and the steady chug of the locomotive. It was soothing, if she didn't think about where they were headed.

"You're not a pet," Gilbert said, breaking through her thoughts.

"No," she agreed. "But I was supposed to be. A silly, feisty little elf. A novelty for him to show off at parties and duels." She rolled onto her side, looking at his profile.

A strong nose and chin, balanced by his dark brow, that was now pulled into a small frown. She could see why he'd had so much success being smarmy in the past, but liked him much better when he was not. Somehow, the man who she had immediately hated upon his arrival in her town was now her strongest supporter. When she dragged Fred back to Wyndford, Millie would figure things out with Rhiannon. She refused to believe Fred had been right about her.

"He didn't mean for you to be terrifying?" Gil asked, looking over at her.

Grateful for the distraction, Millie smiled and wiggled the ear that wasn't pressed against the mattress.

"No," she said. "I was born that way. After a few years of training, he realised he had bought a real killer, not a girl who had gotten lucky in a brawl against one of his guards. Training got more serious after that. He brought in an older Osaugan warrior to teach me how to track and hunt. Waya Blackwater. He was good to me, he taught me how to use the axes. He didn't treat me like the monster I was becoming. He tried to teach me that being a warrior was more than just being a killer."

Gilbert slipped his arm around her and pulled her close. For once, she didn't argue. Resting her cheek on his chest, she listened to his heartbeat. It was steady, and her own slowed until it beat in time with his. Maybe if she stayed in the cabin as much as possible, this horrible trip would be bearable.

"You aren't a monster," he said, kissing the top of her head.

"I am," she countered. "I killed each person Fred asked me to, and I was happy to do it. Now I have to go back to a city where I was little more than an attack dog." Her ear drooped, and she stared out the train car window, watching the outskirts of Wyndford pass by.

"You're going back as a free woman," Gilbert said. "Hold your head high. That place and Frederic tried to break you, but you won, Mildred. You're so much more than a pet or a monster."

She slipped her arm around him and turned that idea over in her mind. A free woman. Somehow, in all the panic she felt over going back, that had slipped her mind. She'd thought she was going back with less power than she'd had when she left, but that wasn't true at all.

"You're a mother, a deputy, a better friend than certain heiresses deserve right now," he continued. "A wife—"

Reaching up, she caught his face and shut him up with a kiss. Back in Scorched Bluffs, she'd kissed him because she expected to die and wanted to feel alive before Fred and his men attacked her town. Now she kissed him because she wanted to. Because he could have sided with the wealthy women in his parlour the other night, and he hadn't. He had kicked his biggest client out of the house.

"Thank you," she murmured against his lips. "You know, this is the first time we don't have to share a bed with three little girls scared of nightmares..." she whispered. Gilbert pulled back to look her in the eye, his fingertips running along the soft fuzz on her scalp.

"Are you sure?" he asked. "Evil Rhiannon might be listening."

"So what?" She turned, kissing his wrist. "Let her be jealous."

The slow smile that spread across his face was smarmy and cocky and everything that made her hate Gilbert at first. But now it sent a thrill of excitement through her. Millie grinned back.

16

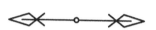

St-Makir's Rest

Nathalie

THE ONE BENEFIT OF travelling with a pair of newlyweds was that it gave Nathie time to speak with Pierre alone about the state of the Rousseau family finances. In short, there were none. Frederic had pissed away any earnings from his biography and any war reparations that had come in. The debt that Harrold Colfield had forgiven was only for the arrears that Fred had incurred in Wyndford. A staggering amount remained in play to some of the oldest, richest families in Marigot. It wore on the younger brother, who had been working as a solicitor to try to pay off what he could.

The downside of travelling with newlyweds was that they were annoyingly immune to sly comments whenever they emerged from their sleeper cabin for food or water. On their last morning on the train, Nathalie even called the elf 'Butcher' to her face and was only rewarded with a mischievous smile instead of a glare. It was terribly annoying.

Their arrival at St-Makir's Rest marked the end of their rail journey and the edge of the sprawling province of Beaulieu. It was as good an excuse as any to force the Goldmans out of their cabin. Knocking sharply on their door, Nathie called out to them in an overly cheery voice that it was time to get ready to disembark.

The cabin door opened, and Nathie looked down to see a cheery elf with her hair braided in the Osaugan style, each side of her head freshly shaved. Full of spite at the lack of any reaction during the trip, Nathie looked the elf over critically and huffed.

"Are you planning to wear your hair like that in Beaulieu?" Nathie asked. "The Osauga are human, you know. You'll embarrass yourself."

The Butcher leaned in, eyes annoyingly bright, and smiled. "I don't give a shit, Wolfe," she said. "It's a common hairstyle. If any Osaugan takes offence, I'll talk to them about it, not to you." The elf reached up and patted Nathie on the shoulder, then unceremoniously pushed her back and out of the doorway. From where he sat, sipping on a cup of tea, Pierre stood up and called out in protest, but didn't hurry over. Instead he stood awkwardly on the balls of his feet, unsure if he should help or not.

"We *are* on the same side, you ungrateful thing," Nathie huffed, straightening the jacket of her walking suit. She brushed off her shoulder where the elf had pushed her.

"We are, so here's the first rule of this engagement," the elf said, pulling on a belt with an engraved tomahawk axe hanging from her hip. "One, don't get in my way, and two, I am holding you personally responsible for that lap dog," Millie pointed at Pierre. "It's on you if he turns on us when the old master families make their presence known."

"That won't be a problem," Nathie said, crossing her arms. "He is not the wilting flower you seem to think he is." Poor Pierre arrived next to her, and Nathie took his arm, resting a hand on his bicep in a show of support. "While you two were occupied with each other, we discussed the state of things in Marigot. Pierre is not the man his brother is. He only wants to salvage the family name."

The Banker sidled up behind his wife, leaning on his cane. He looked from Nathalie to Pierre and back again.

"I'll believe that when I see it," Goldman said. "But I hope so, Pierre. The world doesn't need more Frederic Rousseaus." He rested a hand on the elf's shoulder and smiled brightly at Nathie and Pierre. "Shall we disembark?"

Nathie returned the smile, doing her best to keep the hackles those two had raised from showing through her composure. Somehow, they were perfect for each other, and terrible for everyone else. Surely there had to be a way to get them to argue between themselves instead of with her.

"Yes," she said, "From here we take a riverboat down the Eyatsi to Marigot. The usual route was—"

"Washed out from a storm," the elf interrupted, rolling her eyes. "Not much has changed in ten years, has it?"

Nathie fumed, and it was only the gentle hand of Pierre Rousseau on her arm that kept her from physically lashing out at the short woman. She was saved from further embarrassment by the steward arriving from the rear of the car to announce that they could safely disembark now that the train had stopped at the platform.

"I think you'll find plenty has changed, Miss Argent," Pierre said.

Nathie felt the change in the elf as though it was a change in the air itself. A chill ran through her as she watched the snarky short woman go completely still, and all the light in her eyes died. This was the Butcher, Nathie realised. This dead-eyed thing was the person who had killed her father. Nathie waited for the retaliation, but none came. Instead, the elf yanked open the door to the platform and stormed off the train with the banker in pursuit.

"What did you say?" Nathalie asked Pierre once the other two had gone. "Why did you call her that? 'Argent'?"

Pierre clenched his jaw, eyes fixed on the door that the elf had left through.

"It was her name," he answered with a small shrug. "It was the name Fred gave her."

Nathie felt her body go cold, and suddenly she felt sick. Pulling her arm free of Pierre's, she took a step back and stared at him with wild eyes.

"You used her *slave name*." There were lines, rules of engagement, as the elf had called them. Being rude, sly comments, backhanded compliments were all within those established rules because they were focused on choices and behaviour. Social duels had just as many rules as martial ones, for good reason. The use of a slave name was reprehensible.

"It was *her* name," Pierre said, stepping closer to her. "She just wants to pretend she's not the same person, she wants to play house like—"

"You used her slave name to remind her that to you, she will always be a slave," Nathie said, trembling with disgust. Maybe Mildred had been right. Maybe he was just like Fred, only hiding his true nature behind his softer appearance. "And you said that you were different from your brother." She pulled herself up to her full height, shoulders squared as she stared him down. The previous warmth she'd felt for him curdled at the thought that she might have misjudged him.

"You will apologize to her, or I will use my considerable fortune to make sure that the Rousseau name stays in the mud where it belongs."

In a swirl of skirts, she stormed off, intent on finding the elf to apologise.

St-Makir's Rest was a bustling town, a hub for travellers heading south or north, looking for new opportunities or just looking for a change. Market stalls lined the train station platforms, selling everything from hot pies to good luck mementoes. Tin wheels hung from leather cords next to Bakimban talismans carved into bone and antler. They clattered in the morning breeze as Nathie walked past, searching for the tall banker among the crowd of travellers.

Wyndford had a higher concentration of humans than most towns in Beaulieu. With the abolishment of slavery, newly freed orcs, elves and everyone in-between, had needed to find somewhere to live. Many had moved to towns like St-Makir's Rest, unwilling to bear the shame of taking a job on the same plantations that had once owned them. Several orcs towered over the crowd, a full head taller still than the banker.

"Excuse me, sir," Nathie said, approaching the nearest orc. Tall and broad, his skin was a deep forest green, his dark hair pulled back into a tight braid. Dressed in worn but clean clothes, she figured he would be reasonably familiar with talking with a human lady. Even so, his yellow eyes widened at her greeting, and flicked around them, looking for trouble.

"Yes, ma'am?" he asked, carefully placing his hands at his sides, palms out ever so slightly, to show that he wasn't holding anything dangerous. It was a posture she was familiar with, but it stung more that morning after hearing Pierre call Mildred by her slave name. How many former slaves would have quietly accepted that insult out of fear of retaliation by a wealthy human? There was no more slavery, but social hierarchy was a stubborn thing. Freedom didn't mean equality, not yet.

"I was separated from my travelling companions. I'm looking for a tall human man and a very short pale elf," Nathie said, smiling gently. She hoped to put the poor man at ease, but the orc didn't relax. "Did you happen to see which way they went?"

The man glanced away, toward the river at the other end of town. He pressed his lips together around his tusks and then nodded. He looked worried but kept his voice slow and even for her benefit.

"They headed for the trading post at the river, ma'am." The orc shifted his weight ever so slightly, as though physically weighing the words that came next. "Was that..."

"The Bayou Butcher, yes," Nathalie said. "Thank you so much for your help, sir." She picked up her skirt and was about to head down to the river when the orc chuckled.

"Oh, I don't know about that, ma'am. That's the Ghost of Marigot." He said the title like it was a prayer to one of the messiahs. "My Pawpaw said he saw her fight once, and it was like the bullets went right through her, not leaving a scratch. That she was more spirit than elf."

Nathie's mouth was hanging open ever so slightly as she listened to the man's story. "How do you know the Butcher and the Ghost aren't the same person?" she asked.

She had seen this very elf kill her father during the war. The elf herself had confirmed she was the Butcher, so why had the story changed out in St-Makir's Rest?

"Well, all due respect, ma'am," the man said, dipping his head politely. "The Ghost disappeared at the end of the war. We didn't need her no more. We'd won. But the Butcher came back years ago. Been killing all kinds of non-human folk down in Marigot."

Nathie pressed a knuckle to her lip and let her brows knit together in thought. The orc saw the expression and sketched a quick bow before hurrying off, heading in the opposite direction to the Trading Post. In all her years living in Marigot, Nathie hadn't heard of any more 'Butcher' murders, though the freed people of the Bayou mostly kept to themselves when they could, and they certainly never shared their business with the wealthier class of humans.

"Shit," she said. Nathie knew that the original Butcher had been out west for the last five years, but if there was a copy cat running around using the moniker, that could prove to be extremely dangerous for all of them.

Breaking into a quick march, she crossed the town to the Osaugan Trading Post, where the elf had last been spotted. The trading posts were vital in Beaulieu and beyond, acting as general store, furrier, and post office all at once. The Osaugan network through the swamp and forests let them move goods from one region to another in a fraction of the time it took the Amelian post, even with a fresh fleet of Colfield locomotives.

There was a large shaded porch out front and an older Osaugan man sitting in traditional garb on a cushioned chair, smoking his pipe. He wore his hair in the traditional braid with his scalp plucked bare on either side of it. Black and red paint on his face identified him as a war veteran, though not which side he had fought on. Spotting her, the old man tilted his chin up in greeting, then silently gestured toward the riverboat docked there with an arm that ended below his elbow. Amputees had been common in the regular ranks, but they still shocked Nathie whenever she saw them in person. So much healing magic had been available in the field hospitals, and there still hadn't been enough to save the man's arm.

"Oh, er, thank you," Nathie said, tipping her head and hat in his direction. The man responded with another nod and a long draw on his pipe.

Luckily, she didn't have to look much further. The Goldmans were standing on the dock, speaking to a dark-skinned elf who wore her hair in Bakimban braids, pulled back from her face with a leather tie. Dressed in a long duster coat that smelled like horses, the second elf turned to regard Nathie with suspicious eyes.

"We have a problem," Nathie blurted as she joined the trio.

"That was a *great* apology," Mildred said, deadpan. She turned to the other elf and tilted her head at Nathie. "Annie, this is Ryan's cousin, by the way. A Marigot master through and through."

"Her name was Rhiannon first," Nathie said, trying to make the best of the tense atmosphere. "I apologise for Pierre and have warned him that his actions were unacceptable. If he proves to be as much like his brother as you think he is, then I will have no qualms about buying the remainder of his estate out from under him."

The elves looked at each other, their ears flicking in minute movements that Nathie couldn't decipher. When they looked back at her, the new arrival, Annie, raised an eyebrow.

"That asshole's brother got my mom killed during the war," she said. Next to her, the Butcher winced and looked away. "As much as I'd like to grind both his and Frederic's faces into the dirt, that can wait until we drag them both back to Wyndford for the trial."

"How did you know we'd be here, anyway?" Gilbert asked. The Butcher remained suspiciously quiet, looking out at the river. "It's a long ride from Scorched Bluffs. You must have left a week ago, or more."

Annie crossed her arms and studied the banker for a moment before she bothered to reply.

"Look at you, learning the lay of the land. I'm impressed, Goldman," she said. "I didn't ride, I flew. My auntie sent word two weeks ago that you were coming back and you'd need my help. The Stratton won't be able to make it in time to help, so you get me and auntie instead."

Gilbert nodded, then looked down at Mildred with a small frown. "That makes no sense," he muttered to her. "How could she know any of that?" The pale elf patted him on the arm, but made no effort to explain to him or to Nathie, who desperately wanted to know more. She thought she'd understood all the potential players in this game, but here was a wildcard elf and her mysterious aunt that seemed to be aligned with the Butcher. It seemed not all her friends had died, after all.

"We're glad you're here, Annie." Mildred turned to look at Nathie and took a deep breath. "You didn't know what that name was. You're not the one who should apologise,"

Mildred said. Nathie could see the way the elf grit her teeth, and Nathie suspected that while she had been forgiven, Pierre would have a much harder time. "You said there was a problem?"

"Yes, well," Nathie said, struggling to regain her composure. "I asked a lovely young orc which way you'd gone and he told me something shocking."

"Was it that you're an asshole?" Annie muttered under her breath. Goldman coughed politely into his hand, though it sounded suspiciously like laughter to Nathie. She felt her cheeks get hot, but continued on, knowing that this was a problem for everyone on the dock, Annie included.

"No," Nathie answered primly. "He said you couldn't be the Bayou Butcher, because the Butcher has been killing people in Marigot in the last few years. There is someone out there pretending to be you, or killing under your moniker, for lack of a better name."

Two of the three gathered reacted the way Nathie expected them to. The Goldmans both stared at her, ashen-faced. Annie rounded on Mildred and swatted her on the shoulder. The smaller elf winced and rubbed her arm, but didn't retaliate or complain.

"Mildred, how many people know?" Annie asked, gesturing at Nathie. "Did you go around telling all of Wyndford or something? First Ryan goes and tells the marshal about her past. Now you show up and everyone already seems to know yours." She squinted over Mildred's head at the banker who held his hands up in self-defence.

"Whoever took Fred left a message," Mildred said, shaking out her arm. "It said that the Bayou wants its butcher back. Whoever wrote it is educated. The message was in proper rota grammar, not creole. I thought it was for me, but what if the person who left it wants to draw out the fake Butcher and confused me with the new one?" Mildred frowned, glancing back toward the river.

"The sooner we get to Marigot, the better. Annie, I really need to talk to your aunt about what's been going on. She'll know more about this, I'm sure."

"Who is this auntie?" Nathie asked, unable to help herself. She made a point to know anyone worth knowing in Marigot, and the revelation that there was another Bayou Butcher out in the swamp was bad enough. If the elves had a secret society kept away from humans, Nathie might burst with curiosity.

"Madame Ghat," Millie said for Annie, who suddenly seemed sheepish and scuffed her boot against the dock's wooden planks. "She's a conjure queen."

Nathie felt a chill slip down her spine despite the oppressive heat. Marigot had three queens, but the one who was most respected, the one who others whispered about in the shadows, was Madame Ghat. Not even Nathie, for all her money and good works, had been able to secure a private consultation.

"Oh," she said very politely. "That Madame Ghat."

17

LONG MAN RIVER

MILLIE

MILLIE COULDN'T SLEEP. IT had been easier while they were on the train, hidden away in their cabin and tucked under Gilbert's arm, but every night her nightmares had gotten worse. Now that she was on the river, she was thrust back into the thick of the war whenever she drifted off. Her attempt at a noonday nap had been countered by a dream where she watched her soldiers cut down in front of her over and over until Gilbert had woken her up. Although the others had now retired to their berths, Millie wasn't ready to face more nightmares just yet.

The sloshing of the paddle wheel was as familiar as the way the humidity that clung to her skin even after sundown. The bayou didn't cool off much overnight, unlike Scorched Bluffs. Humidity held the heat in the air, leaving you a sweaty mess no matter what time of day it was. Mosquitoes buzzed by her ears, eager for blood but put off by the oil she'd picked up in St-Makir's Rest.

Magic repellents worked the best for others, but the moment Millie touched any enchanted charms, their spells evaporated, leaving Millie defenceless against the mosquitoes. The oils, an Osaugan recipe of geranium, fir, and vishap glands, were a smellier solution but one that survived skin contact. She'd bought enough to share with Gilbert and Annie, aware that she'd dissolve the enchantment either might try to use by sheer proximity alone.

Alone on deck, Millie rested her arms on the railing and watched firebugs flit through the thick greenery at the edges of the river. The yellow of their abdomens made and remade little constellations as they danced around each other in the darkness. They were one of the few things she'd missed from the swamp.

The glow of light announced Pierre's arrival before Millie heard the creak of his footsteps on deck. She swivelled one ear toward him, but kept her eyes fixed on the night, preferring not to ruin her sight by looking at the bright lantern he held. That was the trade-off, she supposed. Elves could see best in the dark, but their eyes were easily dazzled by bright light once they adjusted to the darkness. Orcs managed the two better, while humans shrugged off the change most easily, but struggled in dim light.

"If you call me that name again, I'm throwing you over the side for the vishaps," Millie warned, still watching the fireflies. Pierre was a good foot taller than she was, but they had been frequent sparring partners in the past. She'd won every round.

"I'm sorry. That was unfair of me," he answered, and the glow of light dimmed. He joined her at the railing, holding the now hooded lantern in one hand. It was still uncomfortably bright to her, but Millie still glanced at him to get a read of his expression. She wasn't the one who had pulled out old scars and torn them open again. Fred had been a difficult man to live with, but at least he'd liked Millie. Pierre hadn't been so lucky.

"It's Mrs. Goldman now, right?" Pierre asked. Millie didn't answer, watching him with eyes that she knew reflected red in the dimmed glow of his lantern. Pierre sighed, and looked out at the water, even though he couldn't see anything other than the firebugs.

"It's been a shock, you know," he said, shoulders drooping. "I'd hoped he went north and would drink himself to death, or finally owe money to the wrong man. That he would just... go away and I would never have to clean up his mess again. Instead, he found *you*. Or you found him, and then he was in custody for a horrible massacre, and that bastard wrote to me, begging me to come and get him out. To clean up the worst of his messes again." He ran his free hand through his hair, grabbing it in a fist and pulling gently at his roots.

It was an old tell, one she'd seen him do countless times as a young man. Knowing it meant Pierre was stressed did nothing for Millie. He had reason to be stressed. Everyone in their travelling party did.

"Yeah, well," Millie muttered, looking back out at the water. "Surprise. Still alive."

Pierre chuckled, but it sounded as hollow as she felt. "I expected you to be the one to kill him, actually. You're his one success, you know. Everything else he ruined–"

"He ruined me too," she snapped. "I survived in spite of Fred, not because of him." She caught herself, taking a deep breath to prevent another outburst like the one she'd had at Wyndford station. Millie squeezed her eyes shut and rubbed her forehead with her thumbs. Being around Pierre made her feel like she was back in the thick of it, her nerves raw and heart so hardened by scars that she could kill a boy holding a rifle and not even blink. She didn't like that part of herself, even if it was what had kept her alive out on the Frontier.

"You're right. I'm sorry," Pierre mumbled. "I panicked when you said I was just like him. Like our father was. I lashed out, just like they would have, proving you right. When he was arrested I thought there would finally be an end to it. I can't believe whoever took him left his hand behind. Why not just torture him after they had him?"

Mildred Argent would have knocked him down and told him that was his problem. Millie Berry-Goldman just groaned. She was tired; she wanted sleep, and most of all, she wanted to find Fred so they could leave Marigot as soon as possible.

"Because whoever it is, they're not after Fred," Millie said. "They're after me, Fred is just the bait."

She heard Pierre gulp next to her.

"Why?" he asked. At least he left the 'Why care about an elf?' part of his question unspoken, but she could hear it hovering between them.

"Fuck if I know," she admitted, resting her chin on her palm. She perked her ears at the muffled sound of a thump somewhere behind them. A door? Or something else? The other passengers had been staying holed up in their cabins since Millie boarded. Even the crew avoided her, some making the sign of the wheel as she passed by.

"I don't have money. The marriage to Gil was supposed to be a last-ditch gamble to keep my girls out of the poor-house, and Rhiannon is the one with all the power in the city. This seems too elaborate for just revenge for something that happened ten years ago." Pierre's question was the exact right one: why her?

Millie scowled down at the water. There were plenty of people who could want her dead after the war, but she wasn't sure why anyone would use Fred to target her when she would have done it the other way around. She pushed herself off the railing with an annoyed grunt and turned to head for the cabins.

"Where are you going?" Pierre asked.

"Wherever the fuck I want," she snapped. If she couldn't sleep, at least Pierre wouldn't bother her in Gilbert's room.

When she reached their cabin, Millie opened the door slowly, peering inside for any surprises. Gil had pulled the straw pallets off the berths and laid them on the floor so that he could fit. He lay diagonally, legs tucked into the recess under the berths where luggage normally was stowed.

He grunted sleepily, and reached out to pull her down next to him.

"Took you long enough," he muttered, "I couldn't sleep without your snoring."

"Again," Waya Blackwater pulled his axe back from Mildred's throat and helped her to her feet. "Remember to listen to your instinct," he said, tapping her breastbone. "Our spirits know the intentions of others, while our minds get caught up on complications. Then your body gets caught by a bullet or blade."

Mildred picked up the hand axes he'd stripped her of mere heartbeats ago. She twirled them one after the other to find the right balance point and adjusted her grip accordingly. Blackwater nodded, his eyes crinkling in approval. Since his arrival at the Rousseau manor, her training had intensified, taking over the language lessons and penmanship that Fred had previously insisted on. For that, Mildred was grateful. The languages weren't so bad, but she didn't see why the perfectly shaped 'q' mattered all that much to a fighter.

She'd asked Fred, once. He'd laughed and hugged her, then asked what she'd rather be doing instead. Blackwater arrived the next week, purchased from the O'Learys. The older Osaugan man had been in poor shape, emaciated and hunched over. The O'Learys had worked him nearly to death in the cane fields, but with proper food and rest, Blackwater had grown strong and quick once more.

Annoyingly quick, as far as Mildred was concerned. She breathed in and launched herself at her mentor. She tried to keep her mind blank, letting her instinct take over as she ducked under a swipe of his axe, and pressed forward, closing the distance between them until she had her heel planted just behind his. It was a stretch, but she was just tall enough now to hook her arm around his throat, feeling his Adam's apple tuck into the crook of her elbow.

She twisted, using her whole body to pull him backward and off balance. He took a half step back with his free foot, but it wasn't enough. She felt him give, toppling down in front of her to avoid a neck injury.

She felt a flush of pride, but it ended the moment he grabbed onto her belt and pulled her down with him. His shin caught her legs and launched her backward, over his head and into the dirt. She landed on her back; the air knocked from her lungs. Millie tucked her legs up, rolling over her shoulder into a crouch, one hand braced on the ground, ready to launch herself back at the older man.

"Hold," he said, getting to one knee. "Better, you went right for my weakness." Grimacing, he pushed himself up to his feet and stretched his back. Even a full six feet away, Mildred heard things pop back into place. She relaxed into a squat and winced at the sound.

"From the fields?" she asked.

"From being old," Waya said with a laugh. He brushed some of the dirt and sunburnt grass from his leggings. "War is a young person's path, Ghostie. Made for hot heads and bodies that do not complain so much as mine does."

Mildred pursed her lips at the nickname. She was probably fifteen years old now, old enough to fight in the Marigot militia. Old enough to have outgrown her nickname. Yet Fred and Blackwater refused to let her fight anyone other than Fred's stupid younger brother, Pierre, or a few of the guards. She won every match against Pierre, who was too afraid to commit to any of his strikes, and by now she won against most of the guards, too.

"We should stop with axes for today," she said. "What doesn't hurt your back to teach?"

Blackwater smiled in earnest now, and he slipped his axes into the belt at his waist. "I think it is an excellent day for a swim, don't you?"

Mildred groaned. A swim meant vishap-infested water and catching fish by hand for supper.

"Tsk, being a warrior isn't just about fighting, you know," Waya said, tucking his axe away. "It's about—"

"—Keeping people safe. That means keeping them fed,"
Millie grumbled. "I know."

Blackwater smiled, cracking his skin along his cheeks as if
his skin were dried mud. Millie watched her mentor's face
crumble away, leaving a muddy, mossy skeleton that started
to rattle and laugh at her.

"You're no warrior, Millie. You're just a rabid dog who
bites the hand who feeds her."

Millie frowned, watching Blackwater's skeleton fall
apart, piece by piece. He was still laughing as his skull fell
to the ground, his jaw open in a permanent grin.

The creak of the cabin door yanked Millie out of the disturbing dream. Her eyes flew open, and before she registered what was happening, she reached up and caught the hand plunging toward her chest. The attacker hesitated, their dark eyes going wide as they found their victim to be awake. Millie used the moment of surprise to wedge her forearm between her and the attacker's hand to keep them from pressing the knife they held further down. As the rest of her woke up, Millie realised she hadn't quite caught the knife in time. The tip had slipped into her chest, not deep enough to kill her, but enough to hurt.

"You killed my family," spat the attacker, leaning hard on the knife. They were part elven, but larger than Millie was, and they had the advantage at the moment. They were an androgynous figure, hair cut too short to pull back, but long enough to get into their eyes. Their expression was wild, their eyes wide and with a panicked hatred, reminding Millie of when a cat got backed into a corner. Desperate people were dangerous.

"I don't even know who your family is," Millie snapped, grabbing onto the attacker's pointed ear and twisting it viciously. The half-elf's head followed, trying to reduce the amount of leverage that Millie had on them, pulling back from the knife. It was enough for her to push their weapon to the side, sinking the knife into the wooden floorboard to her side. Immediately Millie rolled over it, knocking the knife out of the half-elf's hands. They tried to roll with her, scrabbling at the pale ears Millie flattened against her skull.

"That's worse, you monster!" they hissed, shoving an arm under her to try to wrap it around her throat. Millie hunched her shoulders up and tucked her head down like a turtle. Missing their mark, the assassin's arm wrapped around Millie's face, crushing her lips against her teeth. Fine, if people were going to call her a monster, she was done fighting 'fair'. Millie opened her mouth and chomped down on the half-elf's forearm, biting deep into the sweaty flesh. Coppery blood flooded her mouth, overwhelming the salt. The half-elf screamed, but the sound cut off into a pained wheeze. The half-elf let go of her and pulled back, flapping their caught arm in a pitiful attempt to free themselves.

She spat it out and rolled back over, snatching up the knife she'd pinned under her chest only seconds before. Millie punched the knife into the half-elf's chest without a second thought, feeling the blade skip along a rib on its way home. Only then, did she look up to see Gilbert's scowl over the attacker's shoulder, one of his bare arms roped around the half-elf's neck.

"Traitor," the half-elf mouthed, blood staining their lips as their pierced heart pumped their life away. It seeped out onto Millie, hot and sticky.

"Are you okay?" Gilbert asked, looking around in the darkness. He could barely see, and Millie watched his eyes cast about the cabin. The starlight outside was too dim for human eyes, and she realised that darkness had probably saved her life. The half-elf wouldn't have been able to see as well as she could. Their first strike was probably seeking her throat instead of her shoulder.

"I *just* fell asleep," Millie grumbled. Her shoulder throbbed, but it didn't feel like anything important had gotten nicked. Heavy footfalls reverberated through the wood floor, disrupting the steady chug of the steamer's engine.

"Stay back," she warned Gil, and pulled the knife from the half-elf's chest. The sharkskin grip gave her the purchase she needed, despite being coated in the blood of its former wielder. Gilbert pulled the body back with him to the corner of the cabin, making his way by feel.

Freed, Millie got to her feet and crept to the cabin door, peeking out into the promenade that ran the length of the deck. A few cabin doors had opened as curious passengers snooped on the scuffle they'd heard. At the sight of Millie in a nightshirt and leggings both drenched in blood, the doors slammed shut as one. Only Annie remained, bleary-eyed and unsurprised.

"There's a second one," the dark-skinned elf said, rubbing the crust of sleep from her eyes. She pointed with her other hand toward the prow of the boat. "Human."

"You could help," Millie muttered, wiping the worst of the blood from her feet on the deck. She didn't want to risk losing her footing as she set off after the second assassin.

Annie pursed her lips and shook her head.

"Nah, you've got this," she said, and gave Millie a thumbs-up. "I'll check on your banker, though."

Rolling her eyes at her friend, Millie knotted the loose hem of her nightshirt around her waist and crept forward. The ferry's cabins were built on the second level of the boat, clustered in the centre with their doors opening outward onto the promenade that circled around them. It made it impossible for Millie to get a good look at the deck without looping around to the other side where the assassin could be waiting for her.

Wiping the knife blade on her leg, Millie tucked it between her teeth and grabbed onto the column supporting the third deck. Bracing a bare foot against the promenade's railing, she hopped up, grabbing hold of the angled support strut that braced the upper deck against the column like the branch of a tree. Clambering up the outside of the boat, Millie hauled herself up to peer over the top deck for any sign of danger.

An elven crewman was at the wheel, whistling to himself as he gently corrected the boat's course down the Eyatsi, his ears flicking in time to his song. No one else was in sight. The wheelhouse hid the elf from the waist down, but he looked too relaxed to be harbouring the human Millie was after.

She climbed over the top deck's railing, the fancy posts giving her hands and feet purchase. Easing herself over the railing and into a crouch, Millie crept around the back of the wheelhouse toward the boat's opposite side. Sure, she could interrupt the wheelman, but she didn't want to give away her position.

Leaning over the railing on the other side of the boat, Millie spotted a canoe lashed to the main deck, and a human crouched next to it, their back toward her. They had a hood pulled up over their head, which made no sense in the muggy heat but would help keep them from being recognized if anyone spotted them.

The smart thing to do would be to creep down to the main deck and hope the human hadn't gotten away in his canoe before she got there. Millie took a deep breath, took the knife from her mouth and hopped over the upper deck's railing.

The man in the canoe pushed off the moment she was airborne. Millie had misjudged her timing, and now where the figure in the canoe had been was only water. Heart in her throat, she tossed the knife aside and tucked her arms around herself a heartbeat before she hit the water.

It hurt.

The soles of her feet slapped the water, leaving them stinging as she shot deep into the river like a goddamn otter. The water was cool and heavy, the hungry current pulling her forward and down. Kicking out hard, Millie swam for the dark surface. There was no friendly light waiting for her, only the slimy hull of the boat that chugged along as its paddles pushed it forward.

Millie knew her splash would have spooked the local fish and smaller vishaps, but every heartbeat she stayed under was one that would draw the big predators her way. She was pale, like a fish's underbelly, and worse: covered in blood. The perfect bait for a full-grown vishap. The aquatic draconids ruled the bayou and its rivers, chasing the mundane alligators to the smaller waterways. They could see just as well in the murky water as Millie could, and their powerful limbs and tail let them swim faster than anything without fins.

Dragons might breathe fire, but Millie didn't have nightmares about the big blue that had burnt down

Scorched Bluffs, but she did about the vishaps that lurked in the Eyatsi.

By some miracle she surfaced, her hungry gasp for air alerting the remaining assassin to her survival. The ferry had pulled ahead slightly, but the wheel had stopped and a lantern wobbled back and forth on the upper deck as the crew tried to spot who had gone overboard before the river took them.

Deeply embarrassed, Millie ducked back under. Vishaps were drawn to splashing, and Millie didn't feel like providing them with a dinner bell. Kicking for the ferry, she reached the boat's paddle wheel and immediately hauled herself up onto the slimy wooden blades. The water under her erupted as a sub-adult vishap leapt toward her, jaws wide.

With a yelp, Millie jumped to the next wooden blade, tucking her legs up to her chest. The vishap's jaws snapped shut with an audible snap, catching only the droplets of water that fell from Millie's legs.

"What are you *doing*?" Nathalie shouted from the cabin deck. Millie looked up to see her leaning over the railing next to the paddle wheel, dressed in a dark velvet robe. Feeling her ears burn, Millie clambered up to her feet, hopping onto the next paddle blade.

"There's an assassin," she panted, pointing down at where the canoe had been tied and where she had misjudged her jump so badly.

"So you jumped into the river?" Nathalie asked, incredulous.

Heat flushed up Millie's neck and face, and she hated that she was clinging to the paddle wheel like a drenched rat. With an angry huff, she climbed along the edge of the wheel to its spokes. Careful not to get caught in the machinery, Millie edged her way over to where the wheel connected to the boat.

At least, to the elf's relief, Nathalie realised what she was doing and moved to meet her. Wrapping one arm around a support column, Rhiannon's cousin leaned over the railing and stretched her other arm out for her. Millie jumped, grabbing onto the arm and scrabbling a bit as her wet hands slipped on the other woman's skin.

Quick as a snake, Nathalie let go of the column and reached down, grabbing a handful of Millie's soaking nightshirt. The knot she'd made earlier held fast, and Millie felt herself hauled up to the railing. She scrambled over it and the two collapsed in a mess of velvet and soaked elf.

"You are... incredibly stupid," Nathalie huffed, shoving Millie off of her. Happy to oblige, the elf rolled to the side and lay on her back for a moment, catching her breath. It felt like every part of her ached, inside and out. She hadn't had a chance to swim in years, and her lungs felt like they were on fire.

"Yeah," Millie panted, too tired to argue. "Is... the canoe..."

"Yeah, it's gone," Annie said, ambling over with the body of the first assassin draped over one shoulder. "You want this before I toss it over?" Gilbert followed behind, bare chest smeared with blood and leaning heavily on his cane. He held a lit lantern that seared Millie's eyes. She squeezed them shut, rubbing at them until the pain eased.

"Let me check it before you do," Millie said, opening one watering eye. Annie dumped the body next to her on the deck with a loud thump. The half-elf's head lolled toward Millie, and she made a face as it stared lifelessly at her.

Pushing herself into a crouch, Millie reached for the dead half-elf's pockets but hesitated. Her ears flicked back and forth for a moment, and she looked up at Nathalie, Annie, and Gilbert.

"Is something wrong?" Gil asked, brow knit in concern. "Are you hurt?"

"No," she said, flicking water from her ears. "I mean, not badly. I'm just used to Ry telling me that looting bodies is immoral."

Her ears flattened against her head in surprise as Nathalie burst into a peal of laughter next to her. The human woman kept laughing, tears welling up in her eyes from mirth. Reaching up to wipe them away, Nathalie tried to control herself but giggles kept bubbling out of her.

Deeply unsettled, Millie recoiled. She'd been certain the human woman only had two emotions: sulking and snark. Seeing her laugh made the resemblance to Rhiannon even stronger, and Millie hesitated, looking at Gil for help. He was good with people.

"My apologies, but my goodness, the face you made," Wolfe said, fanning her face where she sat. Her normally pale skin had flushed bright pink. "But that is exactly what Rhiannon would say isn't it?" She took a deep breath but dissolved into another bubble of laughter. "Oh dear, I think we've all left our moral compass back in Wyndford, haven't we?"

"Are you going to tell me to be respectful since she's not here?" Millie asked cautiously.

"Good Messiah, no," Nathie said, waving one bloodied hand. "Take whatever you want. I just think we should dispose of the body before someone notices. Go on, Mildred. I have no qualms about robbing the dead."

"It's not robbing," Millie muttered, her ears still folded back. "I'm *investigating*."

Annie smirked down at Millie who glared back up at her. Just because it wasn't true, didn't mean Millie would admit it. She shoved her hands into the body's pockets, patting them down for any other knives that she could use, but Millie only came up with a folded bit of parchment that was now thoroughly stained red with blood. When she opened it, Millie couldn't make out any of what was written there, the blood had so thoroughly stained the paper that the ink was completely blotted out.

Feeling the hair on the back of her neck prickle, Millie was startled to find Nathalie leaning over her shoulder. She smelled expensive, her perfume rich and floral compared to Millie's river water.

"Let me see," she said, glancing at Millie. For the first time since the elf had met her, there was no guile in Nathalie's expression. "I'm something of an alchemist, I should be able to clean that up once we get home and I have access to my full laboratory."

They hadn't been this close since Rhiannon's party, and once again Millie wondered why Ry's cousin was so strange. Feeling her ears get hot, she handed the scrap of paper to Nathalie and scooted further away from her.

"Excuse me, I hate to interrupt but..." a member of the crew hung awkwardly by the corner of the promenade. The lantern in his hand illuminating the dead body in all it's gory glory. "Is that—"

"We were attacked," Millie said, pushing herself to her feet, and pointed at the oozing wound on her shoulder. In the corner of her eye, Millie caught Annie rolling her eyes.

"I'm afraid we've made a bit of a mess in our cabin," Gilbert said, resting a hand on Millie's uninjured shoulder.

The crewmate cleared his throat, his awkward Adam's apple bobbing up and down. He was trying to grow a moustache, but the few strands that he had made his young age painfully obvious.

"I was going to ask if that was everyone who fell overboard," he asked, tilting his head toward Millie. "If so, we can get back underway. Else we need to stay anchored, and the captain has to make a report..." he trailed off and looked meaningfully toward Nathalie.

"Darling, tell the captain that we're all accounted for. In the meantime, we'll sort this little mess out and get the cabin cleaned in time for your next trip," Nathalie said, turning to the crewmate and waving a pale hand toward the dead body.

The crewmate tipped his straw hat in Nathalie's direction and hurried away to signal the all-clear. Millie stared at the human woman in confusion.

"This is Marigot. If there's no body, there's no reason to care, isn't that right?"

"Now," Nathalie said, finally getting to her feet. "Let's get that body overboard and your shoulder stitched up, shall we?"

18

MARIGOT

GILBERT

THE FIRST BLUSH OF sunrise lightened the sky as Gilbert watched Nathalie tie off the last of the neat sutures that closed Millie's wound. As terrible as she was as a person, it turned out that Evil Rhiannon was quite good at stitching up injuries. They'd retreated to the cabin Nathalie had taken, where the human had surprised both Millie and Gilbert with her skill of stitching up the gash on her shoulder. Gilbert perched on the lower berth, his bad leg stretched out in front of him.

Annie had gone back to her cabin to get a bit more sleep, while Rousseau junior had yet to make an appearance. The three of them, banker, butcher, and bitch, were alone.

"How does it feel?" Gilbert asked Millie as Nathalie applied a bandage to keep the mosquitoes away and catch the blood that still seeped from the injury. His wife rolled her shoulder to test her movement, then nodded.

"Like nothing's there," she lied, and Gilbert smiled. He'd seen how her ears twitched as Nathalie had worked and knew it must hurt. But if she was in a good enough mood to lie, then she wasn't in too much pain. "Thank you," she said to Nathalie, ears drooping. Gil rubbed her back, a silent 'good job' for thanking Nathalie when he knew Millie would much rather punch her. The cotton of her shirt was still wet, and both of them would need to change out of their bloodstained clothing before they arrived in the city.

"Hardly a problem," Nathalie said with a small smile that seemed more genuine than any other expression Gilbert had seen her wear. "I worked as a nurse during the war. I've stitched up far messier wounds than yours." Gilbert caught a flicker of sadness that crossed the woman's face.

"Which hospital?" Millie asked, her ears hovering low.

"Messiah Jethram's Grace," Nathalie said, waving one bloodied hand dismissively. "Believe what you want about me, Mildred, but we treated anyone who showed up at our door." She looked around, and Gilbert picked up the bundle of her bunk's sheet, handing it to her to clean her hands. Wolfe hesitated for a moment, then took it with a nod.

"Much appreciated, Mister Gilbert," Nathalie said, rinsing her hands in a basin of water Annie had brought, then scrubbing them clean with the sheet. "This adventure makes me feel young again. I haven't had to stitch anyone up in years. Usually, there's someone on hand who knows a simple healing spell."

"You're still young," Millie grumbled, her ears flicking down and back. "And magic is unreliable." Standing, she rolled her shoulder again and held out her arm to help Gilbert up. He noticed Wolfe's sharp eyes follow the elf's movements closely.

Gil smiled broadly and took his wife's arm. His hip, extra stiff from sleeping on the wooden deck, protested with a flare of pain. He grunted, making a show of his discomfort so Nathalie wouldn't ask *why* magic was unreliable.

"We'd better change into something less bloody," he said to Millie, bracing himself against the top berth. "We're already attracting flies."

THE FERRY ENTERED MARIGOT late that afternoon. The air was soupy with humidity, and even the mosquitoes that buzzed around seemed lazy from the heat. Millie had put on a broad hat to keep the sun off her, but it had the unfortunate effect of making her look a bit like a pale mushroom. Not that Gilbert would dare tell her, she might take it off out of spite and then he'd have to deal with a sunburnt wife. Best to let unaware mushrooms be. Gilbert thought the effect was terribly charming.

She led him to the front deck to point out landmarks. They were just a different kind of landmark than most people might expect to see on a river cruise.

"That's one of the oldest plantations," she said, holding his hand as they slowly chugged past a narrow field of what looked to be enormous grass. "It used to be outside of the city, but Marigot was growing closer every year before the war. We burnt half of it down, but it looks like the owners rebuilt it. It belonged to the Gallois family. They were Ormani royalty that escaped the revolutions by coming here."

"Shame," Gilbert said, giving her hand a small squeeze. "If they'd gotten their heads lopped off back then, they would have saved you a lot of trouble." The boat had passed countless fields of those tall grasses the day before, and it was a sobering realisation that each field belonged to a plantation. "How many slaves did they typically have, do you know?" Gilbert asked. "For one about this size?" The Gallois plantation seemed smaller than some others they had passed by.

"This one? About a hundred," she said, tilting her head back and forth as she thought. "Maybe more. The Gallois family had a basket weaving business too, so they'd have had extra bodies for that."

Extra bodies, a hundred slaves for a small plantation. The numbers were staggering when he scaled up the single plantation to match the many he'd seen on their approach to Marigot. Industrial slavery, Millie had been right when she'd said slaves were valued as little as livestock. Sometimes less.

"Did they get out?" he asked. "The slaves, I mean. You said you burnt half of this one down. Was anyone able to get out before you did?"

Under the brim of her hat, his wife knit her brows together and bit her lip.

"I think so, but... I don't remember," she admitted, glancing up at him. He could see that bothered her, but Gil wasn't sure if what concerned her was that she couldn't remember, or the possibility she had hurt slaves. "We raided up and down the river for years to disrupt their imports and profits. We hit some plantations over and over, sapping their funds and building materials to prevent the timber from going to the secessionist army."

The city of Marigot's levees rose ahead of them, massive bulwarks of dirt that were nearly as tall as the paddle steamer's funnels. A few children were perched on the top of the levee to the right, watching the steamer come into town under the hot afternoon sun. One stood and let out a whoop before they ran along the levee, disappearing down the far side of it.

"Can I ask you something?" Gilbert said, glancing back at Millie. "Why do you call them secessionists instead of the Marigot Rebels? That was their official name, wasn't it?"

Her face twisted, but by now Gil knew when her disgust was directed at him, and this wasn't it. Millie watched the levees drift past for a moment before looking back up at him to answer.

"What were they rebelling against?" she asked, summing up her answer with a single question. "The people who started the war were practically kings on their own plantations. Amclian laws stopped where the land deeds started for these families. What masters did on their land to their 'property' was their right, even if it was horrific." She looked away again, focusing on a cluster of huts built on the river side of the levee, standing on stilts in the water itself, with a ladder down to a lashed canoe that floated lazily in the muddy water.

"They weren't rebelling against injustice, or any of the other bullshit they made up to validate themselves," she said. "They called themselves rebels to feel good about what they were doing, and to pretend they were just to resist the new abolishment laws. All they were doing was protecting their wealth." She shook her head.

"When the slaves revolted, or tried to, they called us traitors to avoid losing that precious illusion," Annie said, walking up to join them at the railing. "Ma bought my freedom before the masters stopped honouring that law, and sent me out to live with Auntie Ghat in LaFlotte, a freed folk village hidden in the swamp." Annie sniffed, looking out at the huts in the water.

"Millie won't tell you, but she helped," Annie added. Gilbert glanced over at his wife to see her face had gone pink. "Talked the Rousseaus into it when they didn't want to let me go. Ma was strong, a powerful worker. They wanted as many of her babies as they could get. She made sure they didn't get any, though."

Somehow, that concept had eluded Gilbert until now. Of course, farmers bred livestock, masters who saw people as livestock would do the same. Millie's earlier comment now made horrifying sense. The thought made him sick, and he had to take a deep breath of the muggy air to settle his thoughts. The air had changed since the boat pulled into the city. Before it smelled mostly of bugs and leaf decay, now it smelled like sewage and people.

"I didn't do that much," Millie muttered, reaching up to rub her shoulder. Gilbert gently swatted her hand away before she could pull her fresh stitches. He was rewarded with a mild glare, but Millie lowered her hand. "I just pointed out that there'd be more children if they didn't make Clem hate them for keeping you around."

"Were there more?" Gilbert asked, wrinkling his nose. "Babies?"

"Nah, Ma got a tea from Auntie to stop that from happening," Annie said with a smirk. "The spirits like us folk more than the masters. We were the ones working the land

and making offerings to the fields, after all. Gold doesn't mean much to fertility spirits, but working the soil sure does."

They were quiet until the paddle steamer reached the dock. A wooden platform was built, with steps leading up to the top of the levee, while the dock itself was lashed to one side of the stairs and to two tall anchoring poles on the other side. Rings in the wood suggested that the dock could be adjusted with rising and falling water levels, a brilliant solution, in Gilbert's opinion.

The stairs were full of people, with each platform between flights crowded with onlookers that were watching the boat paddle up to the dock. The people were all shapes and colours, from dark-skinned humans that made Hal look pale in comparison, to burly orcs with their hair in topknots and braids, to a handful of arroyans with visible horns, their unnatural skin tones gleaming like gems in the afternoon sun.

"Millic, darling," Gilbert said, feeling something strangely like stage fright. "Is there usually such a large crowd when boats arrive in town?"

"Nah," Annie said, chuckling. "They're here to see the Butcher herself. It ain't every day that you see a living legend." She pushed herself off the railing and backed away from Gilbert. "I'll meet you at Auntie's shop. Try not to kill anyone before that, okay?"

Annie hopped over the side of the railing and burst into a flutter of feathers that Gilbert recognized as some kind of hawk. With a few powerful flaps, Annie was gone, soaring over the city and leaving them both to face the gathering crowd. As the paddleboat approached, a series of jeers rose from the dock.

Next to him, Millie sighed heavily. Gil draped his arm around her shoulders, giving her a gentle squeeze of support.

"How worried about the crowd should we be?" he asked, squinting up at them. There weren't any torches or pitchforks out yet.

"They're here to enjoy the show," she said, leaning into him. "But we'll need to be careful after dark. Marigot loves a good riot, and they haven't had one in years, according to Annie."

Looking around the boat deck, Gilbert spotted Nathalie and Rousseau Younger making their way through the crowded deck toward them. To his surprise, Wolfe was dressed in a pair of leggings and a loose linen shirt under a linen vest and suit jacket. He didn't think she could exist unless she was wrapped in silk or the finest wool on the market. She was also walking with a swagger that she hadn't had before. She had more in common with Rhiannon than they'd first thought, Gil realised, watching Pierre trail behind her like a puppy.

"Splendid," Nathalie said, spotting Millie's hat. "I was going to offer one of my own for your use, but I fear it wouldn't have fit your petite head. Pierre and I have been discussing things, and I think the best place to stay while we investigate is Pierre's home."

"No," Millie said immediately, having to raise her voice over the crowd. "Absolutely not. I'd rather sleep outside. In the rain."

"Mildred," Nathalie said, remarkably patient. "Can you name a location in town we would have access to that is better built or fortified against attack?"

Gil watched his wife open her mouth, then snap it shut. Her ears were hidden by the brim of the hat, but he'd bet his bank they had just flattened against her skull.

"How about," Gil suggested, "We go to the door? I can learn where it is and pick up some of the family ledgers. Millie can decide if she'll feel comfortable staying there, and if she isn't, we'll find another solution." He smiled at Nathalie and Pierre, and felt a strange little bubble of pleasure in his chest as Millie squeezed his hand in a silent thank you.

"Fine," Nathalie said, trying to maintain her earlier patience, but Gilbert noticed one of her eyebrows twitched up at the arch. Aha, one of her tells. The woman was remarkably good at masking her emotions when she wanted to.

"Pierre, shall we?"

The younger Rousseau had been staring at the gathered crowd, looking a little ill. At Nathalie's question, he snapped back to attention and smiled shyly at them. He lifted his arm for Nathalie to take, dropping it as she waved him away. His ears turned bright pink and Pierre smoothed his vest in a thinly veiled attempt to pretend nothing had happened.

"Ah, yes. Erm. Shall we ask the dockhands to clear a path, then?"

19

THE VIPER'S NEST

NATHALIE

THE ROUSSEAU TOWNHOME WAS impressive, even in disrepair. It had been built a hundred years ago out of imported stone, allowing it to survive generations of fires that swept through the city. With a bit of work and enough financial investment for repairs, it could be beautiful again, of that Nathie was certain.

"Here we are," she said, opening the door of the carriage and climbing down without help from the driver. Messiah, it felt good to be wearing comfortable clothing once again. She loved the drama that a good silk skirt swish could add to a moment, but if assassins were after them, mobility was best. Nathie placed her hands on her hips and looked up at the home, already planning out what would need to be done. The grout between bricks would need to be repaired and the wooden porch that circled the home looked like it was one season away from rotting off the building completely.

"It looks..." the elf spoke, and Nathie turned to watch her with what was certainly too hawkish of an expression.

The elf's face screwed up as though the home smelled of shit. "It looks awful. And you live here?" she asked, looking at Pierre.

Ears turning red, Pierre pulled out a ring of keys. He mumbled something about modest living and sorted through the keys until he found the one he was looking for. Walking up to the front door, he brushed some curtain moss aside and unlocked it. However, instead of stepping back and holding the door open for the gathered party, Pierre stood in the doorway and dropped his head.

"I need to apologise again, I'm afraid," he said, turning to the elf and her husband. "My brother did terrible things to both of you. I read about what happened in Scorched Bluffs and Wyndford. I had hoped for years he would get better, but he grew worse." Nathie cocked her head as she watched Pierre pluck nervously at the keys on the ring, as though they were worries that could be pulled off with enough effort, like flower petals left to drift on the river out to the sea to be forgotten. Pierre was not a brave man, so it made Nathie proud to see him admit his wrongs to the elf whose legacy he struggled with.

"But most of all, Mildred, I *am* sorry for everything. For every year I didn't tell him to stop, every sparring bout where he told me not to hold back, even though you weren't supposed to hit me—"

"Yeah, but I won those bouts," Millie said, watching Pierre in cautious confusion. "And I definitely hit you. I hit you a lot."

Pierre smiled and cleared his throat, reaching up to rub his nose self-consciously.

"That you did, even when you were half my weight. But, I hold true to what I said. He got away with so much because I never spoke up. I've regretted it since the end of the war when you disappeared. I figured he had finally killed you."

"This is all very lovely," Nathie said, "But perhaps it is also a conversation best held inside? Marigot is full of little birdies who love to eavesdrop."

The elf went ashen, all warmth draining from her face to leave her skin a dead white. Oh, did something finally scare her? How curious.

"I can't," Mildred admitted, eyes fixed on the door. "I can't go in there again. Gil, I'll wait outside. If either of those two tries to hurt you, shout." The elf visibly shuddered just from glancing over at the window. Nathie followed her gaze, but couldn't see anything other than a stained lace curtain through the dirty glass.

"Oh, come off it, Mildred," Nathie said, losing patience. "It's just a house. I can search it first if you're afraid of ghosts." She reached past Pierre and opened the door. It always stuck a little, and Nathie lifted it by the handle and leaned her shoulder into the door to get loose from the frame. The house looked better on the inside, but the smell of damp wood lingered in the doorframe.

Pierre followed her inside, but the elf stayed stubbornly outside. When Nathie turned to see what was keeping her, she was met with a wide-eyed lilac stare. Glancing up at the husband, Nathie saw a deep frown on his face.

"What?" she asked, a sinking feeling in her belly.

"You knew how to open the door," Millie said. "You didn't push until you lifted it by the handle to get it over the warped part of the frame."

Nathie huffed, feeling her cheeks flush hot. Dammit, she should have just waited for Pierre to open the damn door. "I'm certain that this is not the only house with a warped door frame, Mildred. It's been a wetter summer than usual. Most buildings are warped."

The elf's eyes snapped into narrow slits, and she stalked up to Nathie, watching her like she had the night of Rhiannon's soirée: like Nathie was a snake, ready to strike. Nathie's instincts told her to shove the small woman back, but she knew that instinct was a poor master when faced with hot tempers. Better to remain outwardly calm and appraise the situation. Cooler heads prevailed in difficult situations.

"How long have you and Pierre known each other?" Mildred asked, prowling back and forth like the little beast she was.

"Wh-" Pierre answered, but Nathalie held up a hand to forestall him.

"Two years," Nathie said, chin high. "He was the executor of my latest late husband's estate. And I can assure you very much that he is nothing like his brother."

"How do you know?" Mildred asked, still prowling. "Have you ever met Fred? Has Pierre shown you the cellar?"

Nathie's composure was wearing thin, and she rolled her eyes at the elf's dramatics. After the attack on the boat, she'd let herself relax a little, which had been a mistake. The elf was unstable, and giving her a reason to distrust Nathie would be a dangerous mistake. To keep a level head, Nathie took a deep breath and held it for a moment.

"No," she admitted. "I have not met 'Fred', much to my relief. Though I have bought up some of his debt as a favour to Pierre. We consider it an investment in rebuilding the Rousseau name into something better."

The elf spat onto the cobbles in front of the door. Disgusting.

"Some things should die, the Rousseau name included." She glared at Pierre and jabbed her finger in Nathie's direction.

"Show her the cellar before she spends any more of her money on you. Show her, or I'll know you're just a lesser version of Fred." Spinning on her heel, Mildred started marching down the tree-lined walkway out to the street.

"Pierre, why don't you fetch me those ledgers ready?" Gilbert said, putting on a smile that Nathie wanted to slap off his face. "I'll be by tomorrow with Miss Annie to take a look. In the meantime, I'd suggest thinking about how many husbands the lovely Nathalie has had, and asking yourself why so many have died."

Bastard.

"Are you going to claim I poisoned the one who died in the war too?" she shouted after him. "I would have never hurt Teddy!" The banker just smiled and waved at them before he turned and limped after his wife.

"Those two are made for each other," Nathie spat, struggling to control the sudden roil of emotions that the banker had just set off within her. She was supposed to be the one in control, with multiple strings to pluck from the shadows, while they were supposed to be focused on finding Frederic. A hiccup caught in her chest, and Pierre's warm hand rested on the small of her back, gently pulling her into his arms.

They'd played at being strangers since Nathie's arrival in Wyndford, but now the cost of depriving each other of support was for nothing.

"I know," Pierre said, gently guiding her inside. "Ted was a good man. Goldman was just looking for a way to hurt you." Nathie sniffled and pressed her cheek against Pierre's shoulder. He wasn't like his brother. He couldn't be. Pierre was like Ted, a good man, struck by some horrible circumstance in life. Ted was killed too young, while Pierre had the misfortune to be a Rousseau.

"What did she mean about the cellars?" Nathie asked. "You said they'd flooded."

"They had, but I can show you regardless if it will help ease your mind about me," he said. Gentle fingers wiped away a few stray tears, and he pressed a light kiss onto her brow. "But, darling," he hesitated. "I worry that after you see what my family has done, you might agree with what Mildred said about the family name."

Nathie sniffed, pulling back from him just enough to look him in the eye. Those soft, thoughtful blue eyes that always gave his mood away, no matter how hard he tried to hide it from her. No, this man couldn't be as bad as his brother. Nathie had been married to men like Frederic before. She would have noticed that taint in Pierre, wouldn't she?

"Show me," she said.

THE CELLAR SMELLED OF brackish mud, and flies buzzed about in the darkness as Pierre led Nathie down the creaky wooden steps to one of Marigot's rare cellars. The city was built on the Eyatsi river's delta, shifting mud and silt that regularly spat out anything you tried to bury in it. Cellars flooded and collapsed, graves spat out coffins and bones. Locals said the city wouldn't let you forget your sins, but Nathalie used to think that was just an attempt to explain the strange behaviour of the soft ground. Since meeting the Butcher, Nathie was no longer sure it was just a story.

Along the brick walls of the cellar, runes were drawn in chalk to hold the water out. More permanent spells would have to be applied later, using paint or ink to re-inscribe the walls with the water-repellant spell, or the Eyatsi would seep back in. Drifts of silt covered the flagstone floor from the last flood, still damp enough to show a single set of footprints that led from one chalked rune to another. The only person who had been down here was the mage Pierre had hired to shore up the foundations.

"I don't see what's so shocking about this," Nathie said, uncomfortably aware of how the damp bricks muffled her voice. Odd, didn't brick echo?

"You will," Pierre said, shoulders sagging. He crossed the room to where the silt was thickest on the floor. He held his lantern high to give Nathalie enough light. "Here," he groaned, pointing at the wall opposite the stairs.

Nathie spotted a lump in the silt. Crouching, she brushed off the top layer of mud to reveal a loop of rusted metal. A chill ran through her, but she had to know. Hooking a finger through the metal, and pulled. Many links were rusted together, lifting in stiff spans crusted with mud that only broke loose when the weight of the chain pulled the links apart.

At one end, the chain ended in an iron cuff, sized for a child. Or, as Nathie realised with a sinking horror, one tiny elven woman. She pulled on the chain, and it clanked as it pulled taut against the ring that had been set into the stone floor many years ago.

"He kept her in here?" she asked, looking up at Pierre. He looked sick, his face pale and sweaty as he slowly crouched next to her.

"Her, and others," he said, reaching out with his free hand to dig through more of the silt. This chain ended in a much larger cuff, one that could have closed around Nathie's calf with an inch to spare. Pierre dropped it back into the silt with a clank.

"Why?"

Pierre pressed his lips together, his beautiful blue eyes fixed on the shackles in front of him.

"Because it made him feel powerful. But after the war, it was just her down here until he moved to Wyndford. I thought he'd killed her up there, finally put her out of her misery after what he did to your cousin's family. But he didn't. She got out, somehow."

"But..." Nathalie stammered. "But the Colfields were killed several years after the war. He kept her down here all that time?"

Now he looked at her, pained.

"And you knew," she breathed. Finally, the elf's actions made sense. They were unhinged, but would Nathie have done anything differently if faced with a man who'd let her rot in a flooding cellar for over three years?

"I knew, and I was too afraid to stand up to my brother," Pierre said. "He was a war hero, and I had been overseeing training up north, near New Haven. I was well clear of the fighting for the duration. By the time I returned to Marigot, he had already been awarded the Hero of Amelior title, and she was already locked up down here. I told myself I wouldn't be able to do anything, that if I argued with him, Fred would have killed me."

The cellar was closing in on her, the stink of river mud clogging her throat. Nathie scrambled to her feet and raced up the cellar's steps and out of the home into the relatively fresh air of Marigot. She gagged, thinking about how trapped she had felt in some of her marriages. When Teddy had died, Nathie had lost herself for a while. She'd been put in an asylum for a few months until she had regained her sanity. The rooms had been small, spartan, dark. They'd been cages at best, oubliettes at worst. Nathie could still hear the wails of the forgotten on her bad nights.

The humid air of Marigot was as thick as ever, but after the claustrophobic cellar, it tasted like manna from the Messiah. Hands trembling, Nathie hugged herself and tried to hold the contents of her stomach in place.

Three years. Three years of solitude and darkness at the mercy of Frederic Rousseau. It was enough to drive anyone insane. Nathie had barely survived her few months at the asylum, and only escaped when she pretended to be well and docile, agreeing to marry her second husband, who vouched for her sanity.

When Mildred had been let out, she'd been told to kill Rhiannon. Yet, instead of acting like the broken attack dog Frederic had meant for her to be, she'd saved Nathie's precious cousin. She'd hidden Rhiannon for years on the frontier, and even now she'd avoided killing Nathie, who had been nothing but terrible to her since they met.

"Nathie?" Pierre had hurried after her, but now she heard his steps slow as he approached. He'd always given her enough space, but now she wasn't sure if that was because he was thoughtful or because he was a coward.

She wiped the water from her eyes with her sleeve and looked at him with as clear a mind as she could manage. He looked ashamed, sad, afraid. Everything he should be. All Nathie wanted to do was run back into his arms and tell him she forgave him, an urge that frightened her. How many times had Mildred reassured Frederic, only for him to turn around and imprison her for so long?

"She was right," Nathie said, sucking down ragged breaths. "You're no better than he was. Is."

"I'm sorry," he whispered. "I would do anything to go back and change things. We're going to find him, and once he testifies for your cousin, I'm going to let Mildred do whatever she wants to him. I'll hide the body. I'll fabricate a story where she was elsewhere, whatever she needs. Because as much as he's hurt your cousin, as much as he's hurt me... no one else has suffered at his hands as she has." He reached for her, and Nathie reacted without thinking. She pulled her knife from her belt and held it to his neck, only realising what she'd done as she saw the glimmer of fear in her beloved's eyes.

"Don't touch me," she hissed, backing away from him. She had trained for years to be fit enough to kill any man or elf, but she'd never wanted to hurt Pierre. She'd let him in, let him meet Owen, told him about her time at the asylum and what she'd done to get out. His betrayal cut deep, and Nathie wasn't sure if she could hold off her rising panic for much longer. Her gentle Pierre had helped his brother torture Mildred for years, and the night she'd told him how awful it was to be locked away in the darkness, he had said nothing. He had done nothing.

"You say you're better than Frederic? Prove it," Nathie said, feeling her heart break. Words were so easy to speak, but it would only be action that proved to her that Pierre was more than a Rousseau.

Mildred had been right. Some names were not worth saving.

20

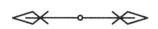

WHERE THE HEART IS

THE RED HAND

MARIGOT HAD A VIBRANCY to it that no other city did. The Red Hand had travelled widely in their years, seeing everything from the granite and gold capitals of the Rodinyan Empire to the clay-baked Omphalopolis in the Northern Caliphates. Each had its charm, but no city breathed as Marigot did, and none bled like it either.

Every street was a wonderful cacophony of life: Bakimban fishmongers by the pier offered fresh morsels to tempt chefs and housewives alike into buying the day's catch. Osaugan children occupying any cleared space for impromptu stickball games, their bets reverently placed to one side so the food wouldn't get trampled. The winners would share their meal with the losing team, a show of sportsmanship that the Red Hand had yet to find in any other sport. Two blocks downriver, and there would be the loser of a different game, bleeding out in an alleyway after losing a duel to some slighted dandy. The washerwoman who found him just stepped over the dying man, carrying her laundry to hang out in the late afternoon sun.

Marigot was a holy city, a city of life and death and the ever-present Messianic cycle playing out and feeding the spirits that called the city home. It rejuvenated the Hand after their long journey from Wyndford. The aches of the ferry's narrow berths eased with every stride, and the Hand found themself wanting to continue their walk rather than return to the safe house where a very drunk Frederic Rousseau waited.

The Red Hand shortened the leash of the dog that trotted next to them and the scarred and heavily muscled bull terrier fell to heel with perfect obedience. The dog had given them some trouble when the Hand had first returned, but a few disciplinary measures and a gris-gris sewn onto its collar had rectified the poor behaviour. Disobedience was not tolerated from any of the Hand's underlings, especially not from a dog.

Ahead, a familiar pale figure stood on the corner, back towards the Hand. The elf stepped out into the street to flag down a cab, putting herself at risk of being trampled without a second thought.

The Hand's heart skipped a beat. It was one thing to find her lurking in the fog of Wyndford, but it was wholly different to see her in her natural habitat. The Butcher was back in the Bayou, and soon she would be made to face the consequences of her actions. Marigot had lost its former glory, and many good families had lost their fortunes and names because of the Butcher's war. The Hand's lovely city was still a shadow of itself, but with the blood of the Butcher, it could be restored to its former self.

The Hand smiled, watching as the elf and her husband climbed into the cab. The Hand didn't need to hear where the elf was going. They already knew.

Soon it would not be the dog falling to heel when the Hand took their regular walks through the city. It would be the most dangerous elf Marigot had ever seen.

21

HOMEFRONT

RHIANNON

RHIANNON SAT OUT ON the garden's terrace, watching four children chase three dogs of vastly different sizes across the lawn. Hands curled around a cup of tea, she let herself smile as the puffball puppy named Freckle zoomed between the legs of Fyodor, much to the mastiff's consternation. Owen had been reluctant to play with 'babies' as he'd called the trio of little girls, but had quickly given in to join them on the grass.

"Thank you for inviting them over," Gilbert's dad said, rubbing his forehead. "God only knows if this will be enough to wear them out by evening." Avrom Goldman had a fierce expression most of the time thanks to his intimidating eyebrows, but this afternoon, he simply looked exhausted. "I checked their milk at night to make sure their mother hadn't given them coffee by accident."

"I thought Owen could use some friends," Rhiannon said, watching her nephew chase Rasha to the tiny elf's delight. "He just got to Wyndford for the first time, and now his mother had to go back to Marigot before he's had a chance to get settled."

Avrom harrumphed and reached for his own mug of tea.

"Bad business, all of this," he muttered into the cup. "It's never a good sign when people start painting messages on walls. That Rousseau's been more trouble than he's ever been worth. First trying to kill Gilbert, now disappearing and leaving his hand behind. What a schmultz."

Rhiannon wasn't sure what 'schmultz' meant, but she agreed that what had happened was worrying. Rousseau had been the key to Uncle Harrold's trial and if they couldn't find him in time, the case might get dismissed. While her father's will was abundantly clear that the personal finances were to go to his surviving child, the company was split between her father and his murderous brother.

She couldn't let Harrold take the company from her, not after he'd taken everything else.

Stepping out onto the terrace, her butler, Murphy cleared his throat to catch her attention.

"Miss Rhiannon, Detective Stratton and Sergeant Duncan are here. Shall I show them out here? Or to the study?"

Rhiannon pursed her lips, but Avrom beat her to the decision. Waving a gnarled hand, he motioned for her to go inside.

"I'll watch the gremlins out here," Avrom said, his tone affectionate, even if his words were not. "It's better not to talk about such serious things around them." He added, more solemnly. "Those little ears are far sharper than any of us would like."

Rhiannon smiled. That much she knew. How often had she said something to Millie only for a pair of wiggly little ears to overhear? The smile faded almost immediately as Rhiannon thought about the expression on Millie's face when they'd last spoken. A careless word and she'd cut her friend to the heart. Millie's impassive mask was familiar, but until that night, Rhiannon had only seen it used on others. The thought that her friend didn't trust her enough to show her true self hurt, but that didn't change Rhiannon's duty to the company.

Excusing herself, she headed into the house. She took a few steadying breaths before heading to her study. Allan and Hal stood inside, looking around the room.

Dark-skinned and observant, Hal was Gilbert's friend and a Stratton Detective. The agency had a sterling reputation for solving mysteries, and while that had been dangerous when she was living as Ryan Collins, his skills were needed now. Hal had a way with people that Rhiannon didn't. He was charming, with warm dark eyes and a friendly smile that had a way of making you feel at ease until you confessed your darkest secrets to him.

Allan was looking at the painting of her father, hands tucked into the pockets of his uniform, the brass buttons on his broad chest gleaming in the morning light that streamed in through the study's windows. It was still strange seeing him like this, but neither of them was covered in prairie dust these days. His coppery hair seemed even redder without the dust, though Rhiannon wasn't sure why she kept noticing.

"Detective, Sergeant," she greeted them both. Once she had, she dropped the titles. They would just make Allan uncomfortable and remind Rhiannon that she was no longer a Sheriff, but simply a 'Miss'. "Thank you for coming. Hal, has Allan filled you in?"

"Miss Rhiannon," Hal said, reminding her nonethe-less as he lifted his hat in her direction. He smiled his trademark smile and Rhiannon found herself glad that he hadn't been available to leave when Gilbert and Millie had. She needed him here. "He started to, though I'm afraid there's some context I'm missing. Perhaps after we talk here, we could visit the jail so I can get a better look at the scene?"

"The warden might complain, but I'm sure he'll let us," Allan said, holding his hat in front of him and fiddling with the brass badge sewn onto it. "All he's done since it happened is complain and try to convince me he had nothing to do with it."

"Which sounds like he definitely had something to do with it," Hal said.

"Maybe," Rhiannon said, gesturing for the men to take a seat. They waited until she did, like the gentlemen they were. "Millie, Gilbert, and my cousin have gone to Marigot to get Rousseau, but I don't plan to sit on my hands while they're gone. I want to find out how someone got into the jail unnoticed, and then back out again, this time with a man who'd just lost his hand."

She frowned, resting a knuckle against her lips.

"There should have at least been a blood trail from Fred," she muttered.

"Maybe they had a healer with them?" Hal suggest-ed. "Or a way of stopping the bleeding and controlling Rousseau long enough to get him outside."

Allan cleared his throat lightly.

"He was also injured. Depu- er, Ms. Berry, shot him in the leg back when she rescued the Goldmans. It hasn't healed right and I don't think a man as big as Rousseau could just be given a piggyback out the door." Allan frowned, scratching his chin. "Well, maybe, if you found someone who's just as big."

Hal spun his bowler hat between his hands, deep in thought.

"Let's start off with everything we know," he said, hanging his hat onto the arm of his chair so he could count off the items on his fingers. "One: Rousseau was injured twice over, and wouldn't have been able to walk out under his own power. Two: whoever took him has a reason to stop the trial or prevent Rousseau from sharing other secrets that haven't come to light. Three: they know enough about conjure magic to set up that display for the guards to find."

"Four: they either bribed or threatened whoever saw them leaving," Allan added. He frowned, looking down at the hat Hal had been spinning. Then at his own hat, turning the badge sewn onto it this way and that.

"Well shit," Allan muttered. "It was an inside job, wasn't it? Just like how you and Berry were law, but used it as a cover to steal all that stuff. No one asks what a guard is doing with a shackled prisoner."

Rhiannon felt her cheeks get hot. She'd never liked that part of living out in Scorched Bluffs. They'd tried to do things legally, but sooner or later, survival became more important than morals. It was why they'd only stolen from her family's company.

"Sounds like we need to see if anyone's not shown up for their shift," Hal said, putting his hat back on.

THE JAIL WAS IN an uproar. Even from the warden's office, Rhiannon could hear prisoners shouting and banging against their cell doors. Guards kept hurrying past the open office door, heading for the cell blocks with batons in hand.

"Is this a riot?" She asked Allan, raising her voice to be heard over the cacophony. Rhiannon supposed she should be nervous, but after a dragon attacked her town, a riot seemed like a pleasant afternoon in comparison.

"Uh," Allan said, sidling over to the door to peek out down the hall. "I don't know. I always thought riots had fires and stuff."

"I'd say it's almost a riot," Hal said, standing by the warden's desk with his hands behind his back. The desk had papers strewn across it, and a nearly finished whiskey bottle sitting in one corner that Hal had immediately re-stoppered. The room was still thick with heady fumes.

The warden himself was 'on his way', though Rhiannon suspected that might take a while given the state of the jail. Crossing over to join Hal at the desk, she looked over the papers left out in the open. A few telegrams from the governor demanding information, and a half-written report was set next to a full report about Rousseau's 'escape'.

"He was rewriting it," Hal said, pointing to the description of events. "No mention of Rousseau's hand, and blames him for the whole thing. Said he killed two guards and his own steward, Lionel."

At the door, Allan frowned.

"Look, I don't like the guy, and I'm sure Rousseau killed a lot of people, but I don't think he cut his own hand off." He peeked down the hall again and slowly closed the office door. Once it was closed, he joined Rhiannon at the desk, pulling over the original report. He squinted at it, mouthing some words as he read.

"I think he was trying to cover his a—" Hal hesitated, looking at Rhiannon. "This is weird," he said. "Do I swear in front of you because you used to be a sheriff and have heard worse? Or do I not because you're a lady of society?"

"He's covering his ass, yes," Rhiannon said, her lips twitching up into a small smile despite the situation. "I might not be a sheriff anymore, but I'm not about to faint if I hear a curse word."

Hal held his hands up in defence.

"Just checking."

Rhiannon folded the pair of reports and slipped them into her pocket. If she didn't take them now, the 'not riot' in the cellblocks was the perfect excuse for the warden to have the original go missing. She refused to let that happen.

"Ry, you aren't... stealing the reports, are you?" Allan asked.

"No, I'm protecting them," she said without looking up. The rest of the letters and papers on the desk were safe to ignore, so she checked the drawers one by one until she found a scrap of paper crumpled up into a ball and tucked into the back corner of a messy drawer. Unlike all the rest, faint lines were printed onto the paper, suggesting it was from a ledger of some sort.

Pulling it out, Rhiannon smoothed out the wrinkles as best she could.

"That's a page from the shift book," Allan said, pointing at the column of names and then to the columns with various malformed X's in them. "We have one just like it down at the station. Here, this one logged in for the night, but there's no matching mark for signing out."

"What if that guard was one of the two dead ones?" Hal asked.

Allan shook his head.

"If someone gets hurt or killed, you're supposed to mark what happened in the column where they should have signed out." He flipped the page over and tapped where two rows had numbers hastily written in the columns, which had been crossed out. Rhiannon didn't need to check the reports in her pocket to see if the number matched. There was no other reason to mark it out and hide the shift log.

Turning it back over, Rhiannon read the name of the man missing a log-out mark.

D. Gallois.

A wail rose from deep within the prison, followed by another and another as guards sounded the alert.

"Well, there's our cue to leave," Hal said, handing the log page to Rhiannon. "Sounds like it's officially become a riot."

"That's the alarm for fire, then?" Rhiannon asked, safely tucking her rescued pages away.

"A small one," Allan said with a nod. "If it was a big one, you'd just hear the guards running." He ushered Rhiannon toward the office door, his hand on the small of her back. "I've learned a lot of these guards aren't terribly interested in prisoner safety."

Rhiannon frowned. She opened the office door and immediately checked down the hall to see if there was any sign of fire.

"Other way," Allan said, taking her by the shoulders and steering her toward the exit. "You're in skirts with critical evidence in those pockets. Fire bad, Ry. Fire *bad*."

Hal trotted past, opening the door of the jail so the trio wouldn't get slowed down. Rhiannon was torn. Allan had made good points, but it felt wrong to escape a building that was facing fire. Wyndford was built out of the local granite, but so much of the city was still just wood. She'd learned in Scorched Bluffs how fast and how deadly fire could be.

"What about the prisoners?" she asked, as Allan continued to steer her away from the jail. A glance over her shoulder told her that while there was a plume of smoke, it wasn't very large. Yet.

"The fire brigade's just arrived," Hal said, pointing at a cart full of mages that drove past. Several firefighters were already forming sigils with their hands, preparing the rain spells that would keep the fire contained.

"This isn't Scorched Bluffs, Miss Rhiannon," Hal said. "They'll manage alright without our help."

Rhiannon wasn't fooled. What Hal was really saying was that the prison would manage without *her* help. A lady of society, the last Colfield, the darling of the city and a precious thing to be protected as though she were made from porcelain.

She scowled the entire ride back to the manor, alone in her carriage. Allan and Hal stayed to help fight the fire, naturally.

The manor was quiet when she returned. Murphy greeted her at the door with a blessedly hot cup of coffee.

"Master Owen is enduring his lessons," Murphy said with a twinkle in his eye. "I'm sure he wouldn't mind if you interrupt him."

"In a while," Rhiannon said, savouring the smell of coffee. "Could you have a bath drawn for me? I'll be in the study until it's ready."

"Of course, Miss."

The study was the safest place for the papers she'd taken, and it was also rapidly becoming a sanctuary among a house full of ghosts. Pulling open a drawer, Rhiannon paused at the sight of the two sealed letters Millie had left behind. Sliding the pilfered evidence under the stack of letters from suitors, she glanced back at the note Millie had written.

'For when you feel alone.'

Rhiannon sighed. On one hand, she was still a little annoyed at her friend for refusing to understand why she couldn't go to Marigot. On the other, Millie rarely offered unsolicited advice. If she did, especially while upset at Rhiannon, the letter was definitely something she should read.

Picking up the envelope, she flipped it over and pulled out the letter. It was a single page, written in Millie's plain handwriting.

I don't know if I'll be able to survive this trip. I never lied to you, but I hid how bad things were in Marigot and I shouldn't have. I'm sorry.

I can't be there for you right now, but there is someone who will protect you with his life, and always act in your best interest, even if you don't want him to. You need to trust him now. Allan might be a bit weird, but he's a good shot and smarter than he lets on. Trust his instinct, and trust that he is interested in you *and not your money.*

Remember: you don't owe the fancy people shit. Be happy instead of whatever they want you to be.

- M

Rhiannon blinked, then felt her face grow hot. She put the letter face down, as though that might stop the blush that consumed her face. Millie must be wrong, but she hadn't been teasing in the letter. No jokes about Allan's hair or intelligence.

Burying her face in her hands, Rhiannon thought about how Allan had placed his hand on the small of her back to get her out of the prison. How bright his smile had been when he'd spotted her the night of the soirée and how she had felt secure around him despite the dangers they were facing. How her stomach had fluttered when she saw he was in Wyndford.

Now what was she supposed to do?

22

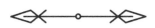

THE ONLY JUST WAR

MILLIE

MILLIE HAD FLAGGED DOWN a cabbie who had tried to ignore her at first. When she stepped into the street to block the horse, the driver relented with a nervous smile. The elven orc seemed relieved when Gilbert climbed into the buggy, as though his presence could temper Millie's terrible mood. Well, he did, but Millie sure as hell wasn't going to admit that out loud. She climbed up after him and gave the driver directions for Madame Lavoie's shop.

Annie had mentioned it was at the edge of the Bakimban quarter and the Osaugan summer village. While not technically a seasonal village anymore, the Osaugan quarter's wattle and daub homes were built in a different configuration that refused to align with the half-planned streets of the rest of the city. Homes ringed the central hut in a horseshoe shape that aligned with the east rather than Marigot's roads, which angled southeast to match the river's course. 'Village' was still the best way to describe it.

"Was that the house with 'the cellar'?" Gilbert asked, draping his arm around her shoulders once she was settled.

"It was," she said, focusing on the buildings that rolled past. The neighbourhood they were in, Sainte-Heverèle, had been part of the old city ringed by a defensive wall the last time she had seen it. It looked the same at a glance, but individual homes had changed. The orange trees in front of O'Leary House had gone, replaced by saplings that would take years to grow as tall and fruitful as the ones she had burnt down.

A curtain twitched in a window, and for a moment, Millie grabbed Gilbert's shirt, ready to throw them both to the floor of the cab. But there was no report of a rifle. Just someone looking out the window. It didn't help her growing paranoia to know that people really were watching her every move.

"That bad, is it?" Gilbert rested his other hand over hers and gently helped her let go of the shirt. She had mussed it, leaving sharp creases where she'd grabbed a handful. "We'll find him as soon as we can, then you can leave this place and never need to come back."

"I used to love this place," she admitted, feeling torn. "I loved how clean the streets were compared to where I lived before Fred bought me. How shiny everything was kept, from the saddles of horses to the glass windows. Like people actually cared about the place they lived." Now it just made her feel sick.

The smoke made it hard to breathe. Someone had thrown burning oil onto O'Leary's orange trees, and now the fire had spread to the houses that flanked them. The Rousseau house would be in danger of catching, but it was built with stone for a reason, and had survived every fire the city had thrown at it. It could survive one more.

Crouched behind an overturned carriage piled with loose cobbles and expensive furniture, Millie turned to count how many of the Irregulars were still with her. They'd lost Delilah at the gate to the Old City, holding it open and providing cover by sending volleys of fire over the makeshift barricades the secessionists had constructed.

Akhun had died the week previous, catching a cannon-ball before it slammed into Millie and the others. It had killed him, but he'd saved the rest of their squad. Now the shark-toothed Remi and a handful of others crowded along the cover, their heads low to avoid potshots.

A hawk swooped down, flapping awkwardly as Millie reached out and caught it before it hit the cobblestones. Her chest wrung her heart tight as she spotted the blood. In a shower of feathers, Clem lay in Millie's arms. A mockery of how Clem used to hold Millie those first few nights at the Rousseau house, promising a little girl that she would do everything to keep her safe.

"Clem," Millie whispered. "How bad is it?"

"Report first, Sergeant," Clem said with a bloodstained smile. "O'Leary and his men are in the courthouse, ready for a last stand." She lifted her hand to Millie's cheek and placed a bloody handprint there, careful not to smear it.

"No masters," Clem whispered.

"No kings," Millie finished for her. She did what she could for her friend, making sure she had a revolver and bullets. But they both knew that by the time anyone found her, they would only find her body. It tore something inside as Millie turned to the rest of the squad and issued their orders of attack.

Something soft was placed in her hand, and Millie flinched back to the present. Blinking, she found her cheeks wet, and Gilbert's handkerchief in her hand.

"Do you want to tell me?" he asked.

"That's the building where we found O'Leary," she whispered, unable to look at the High Court of Marigot as they passed it by. "I just, I keep going back there," she admitted. She squeezed her eyes shut and shook her head. 'There' wasn't right. "I mean, back then."

Gilbert gently pulled her into a hug, and she felt him press his lips to her hair, feeling his exhaled breaths tickle her ears.

"Carpenters are supposed to be peaceful people," he said, his voice a rumble in his chest. "We're not supposed to fight wars. We're supposed to respect the choices of others so long as they don't hurt or kill someone else. But, the more I see here..." he trailed off, and sighed into her hair. "The more you tell me, the more I think that there isn't always a choice, is there?"

She shook her head, suddenly tired.

"Delilah, Madame Ghat's older sister, she fought with us. She was terrifying, as good with a weapon as she was with magic, but I remember her telling me that the only just war was one for survival. There was talk of abolition for years before the revolt kicked everything off. Years of negotiation, years of attempting to compromise, reinstating the old laws of being able to buy our freedom with our earnings, so that the Masters wouldn't lose money on their 'investment'. The Union even declared war but held off on the actual fighting, waiting for Marigot to agree to abolition."

She took a shaky breath and lifted her head to look out at the city once more.

"It didn't work," Gilbert said, gently.

"No," she agreed. "It didn't. Fred told me we'd get married once it was legal, that we had to fight to change our lives, to get a chance at being happy. I think he meant it at the time, but the things we saw and the things we did during the war... they changed all of us. He wasn't a good man before the war, but he was a monster after it."

She'd become a monster, too.

"But you won," Gilbert said, nudging her and pointing out at the city. "You survived. You made sure that everyone else who couldn't fight had a chance to survive, too. I highly doubt the Rousseaus were the only ones with such a cellar."

"They weren't," Millie confirmed. Out on the plantations, masters didn't bother with a cellar, but in the city no one wanted their slaves keeping the neighbours up at night. She never wanted her daughters to listen to the way someone's screams grew more shrill as panic and pain set in. She would die keeping them away from Marigot and its awful past. All the beautiful clean streets in the world weren't enough to scrub the memory of those screams from her mind.

The Bakimban quarter's lively sights and delicious smells replaced the wealth and cleanliness of Sainte-Heverèle. Millie took a deep breath, savouring the heavenly smell of heavily spiced fish stew which the quarter was known for. It used to be her favourite meal to sneak whenever she was free to find her own meals. Bands were setting up on street corners, their shiny bugles and tin guitars gleaming in the evening sun.

While it was called the Bakimban quarter, the residents were from all over. Yes, some traditional families still lived there, fourth-generation free settlers that had moved to Marigot when they heard the city needed skilled fisherfolk. Human, elf, orc, and everything in between, Bakimban kingdoms had intermarried centuries ago when the slave trade first threatened their borders. Now, they were the example that Millie had held up to Fred when he'd argued that equal existence would be impossible. Their skin was dark, hair tied into braids that were often dyed red with special dust that kept the mosquitoes at bay.

Annie had lived there with Ghat after the war until she was old enough to decide she wanted to head out west and learn how to work a ranch. Millie had wondered if she missed the smells and sounds, but returning to Marigot was much easier when you could fly.

"I rather like this part of town," Gilbert admitted.

"You haven't even tried the food here yet," Millie said with a small smile. Her chest still ached, but the friendly chatter of neighbours around them helped soothe her old wounds. "This is the part of Marigot I've missed. The part of the city that comes alive," she said. "After we speak with Ghat and Annie, you need to try the fish stew. Oh, and the bayonet beignets," she added. "They stick the beignets on a skewer. It's not a real bayonet, but..." she trailed off, a little embarrassed.

"That sounds like a marvellous idea," Gilbert said, a calm smile spreading across his face. He didn't tease her about being excited about food, though she knew it was only because he felt bad for her. Millie suspected that the moment she was feeling less rattled, she wouldn't hear the end of the beignets.

The cab clattered to a stop in front of a tidy-looking conjure shop. The painted sign was simple, 'Mme Lavoie's Conjure Cures' lettered in a sunshine yellow paint on black. A single yellow snake decorated the sign, Ghat's personal emblem.

"You're okay with snakes, right?" Millie asked Gilbert, giving his hand a pat before letting go and climbing down from the cab.

"In theory," he said carefully. "I don't know much about them other than what you told me on the train: the ones with white mouths are venomous and to leave them alone." He accepted her help as he climbed down after her, his bad hip giving him some trouble.

"Well, Annie tells me the one in here will be fine," she said, opening the door for him. The conjure shop smelled mostly like spices and dried herbs, and frankincense nuggets were burning on a small coal brazier that stood on the shop's counter, with a large gold and white python curled around the brazier's base, soaking up the heat that radiated from it. It didn't move as they stepped inside, other than to flick its tongue into the air and taste who the new arrivals were.

The rest of the shop was a tidy clutter. Carved idols and amulets stood on one shelf while prayer candles made of snake fat and tallow were on another. Drying herbs hung from the beams overhead and a table in the centre displayed embroidered altar cloths in vibrant colours. Behind the counter was a curtain pulled across a doorway with a neatly lettered sign 'Do Not Enter'.

"That is a very large snake," Gilbert said, freezing in place the moment he realised it wasn't a statue.

"That, I believe, is Mulatiwa." Millie stepped around him, walking up to a respectful distance from the snake. It raised its head to get a better look at her, then flicked its tongue again, and stretched out, bringing its snout closer to her face. "I think. Annie mentioned him once."

"Hello," Millie said cautiously. She knew how to deal with snakes that were just snakes. She didn't know how to deal with snakes that were also part spirit. The snake turned and slithered onto her shoulder, climbing up to drape itself around her like a slithery, heavy scarf.

"Should I help?" Gilbert asked in a whisper, then frowned and looked at the snake. "How could I help?" he asked himself.

"I don't know," Millie whispered back. She'd been concerned when a coil wrapped around one arm, but at the moment the snake seemed to be content to drape across her shoulders. "Uh, good... boy?" she said awkwardly. Gilbert's eyes were wide, and he was staring at the snake with a mixture of awe and fear. As was probably appropriate.

The snake looked over toward the curtain a moment before it swished to one side. For a moment, Millie was certain it was Delilah who stepped out of the back, her dark skin mossy green and her ears long and pointed. They had the same nose, the same sharp eyes that were too dark to tell if they were brown or green unless the light caught them just right. The masters called elven orcs 'goblins', but Millie thought they looked the way the ancestral elves must have before they lost their green skin as they became more nocturnal.

Despite the family resemblance to Delilah, the way Ghat moved was completely different. Dressed in a white blouse and skirt, she wore her hair up in a white duku, a headscarf that wrapped up hair that Millie knew was dark and curly, into a tight pile on top of her head. Ghat was regal, unbroken from the years of backbreaking work that her elder sister had suffered.

"Well, well," the conjure queen said, placing her hands on her hips. "Mulatiwa caught us a little white mouse for dinner." Ghat clucked her tongue and walked around the counter, circling Millie with a critical eye. One she then turned onto Gilbert, who smiled his charming smile and immediately drew a frown from the priestess.

"And a *husband*? Ghost, what kind of trouble have you gone and got yourself into?"

Millie reached into her pocket and pulled out the pair of gris-gris she'd collected from Rhiannon's party. Holding them out, she watched both Mulatiwa and Ghat snap their attention to the little pouches. The snake stretched out, flicking his tongue out repeatedly at them, trying to taste what was inside.

"Someone planted these on me and Gilbert at a party up in Wyndford. I need to know who made them."

Ghat plucked one bag from Millie's hand and examined the fabric and stitching through narrowed eyes. The snake slithered from Millie's shoulders to Ghat's. He had more room there anyways.

"You are lucky you are what you are," Ghat said, looking from Millie to Gilbert. "These are dark spells. I can tell you what their intent was, but it will take time to get the spirits to tell me who made them." She picked up the second gris-gris and walked back behind her counter, pulling a small pair of snips and tweezers from a hidden shelf underneath it.

"Tell me, Gilly Boy, has Mildred told you what she is?" Ghat asked, carefully snipping the red threads that held each gris-gris closed.

"I figured it out on my own," Gilbert said, moving closer now that the snake's interest was focused on the little pouches. "Watching her fight a dragon with only a knife tipped me off that she wasn't a normal deputy."

"I don't think she means finding out that I was the Butcher," Millie said, her hand catching his before she realised what it was doing.

"Correct," Ghat said, "But that can wait just a moment longer." She pulled the red thread free from the first pouch and unwrapped it, revealing the collection of components inside. A bullet, a dried hot pepper, a scratched-up penny and a bit of white cloth stained with a few drops of blood long dried.

"This was designed to hurt, to reopen a healed wound," Ghat said. She looked up at Gilbert. "Yours. Whoever made this knew you had been hurt badly and wanted you distracted by that old pain."

"Lovely," Gilbert said, dry as a bone. "What about the one that Millie found on her dress?"

Ghat snorted and looked up at them, slips twitching into a smile. "You got her to wear a dress? Impressive." Before Millie could argue, Ghat unwrapped the second pouch, and all humour dropped from her face.

"This was to control you, Ghost," she said, picking up the spell components and setting them out one by one. "A chain to keep you bound," she pulled a bracelet of fine iron chain from the gris-gris. "A snake fang to make the spell stick, a piece of brick from the high court building, and this..." Ghat unfolded a slip of crumpled paper to reveal that it was the receipt Fred had written for Millie's purchase, twenty years ago.

"Someone out there wants you under their spell, Mildred," Ghat said. "You're damn lucky they didn't know you drain magic."

Her body had gone cold the moment Ghat unfolded the purchase slip, and Millie struggled to hear what else the other woman was saying.

"Who would have access to that receipt?" Gilbert asked. But there was only one answer.

"The Rousseaus."

23

THE TRUTH

NATHALIE

NATHIE'S FIRST INSTINCT WAS to return to her house and hide from the world at the bottom of a very expensive wine bottle. Her townhome had been closed for the season, but she wouldn't need much. Her bedroom, the kitchen, her laboratory. She'd started walking at a clipped pace, leaving Pierre behind to sort out what he planned to do, and let her feet choose her path for her.

They did not take her home, but carried her through the Bakimban quarter, dodging street food vendors and musicians alike. Even the thought of food turned her stomach, and she clenched her teeth to keep from gagging. The food was delicious when she was in less of a state, but as it was, all Nathie could do to keep from breaking into a run to get past the smells.

Mme. Lavoie's shop was a welcome relief, and Nathie slipped inside without knocking. Four heads swivelled to stare at her, one reptilian. Nathalie took a deep breath and marched over to the elf, preparing the speech she had been rehearsing the whole way over.

"He showed you the cellar," Mildred said, catching her out with a single glance.

"He did," Nathie said. Her usual eloquence had evaporated down in that hellish hole in the ground. "I must apologise. I didn't know how bad things had been and I didn't want to know. Since we met, I have been nothing but rude to you and kept secrets."

Mildred raised her eyebrows, but Nathie wasn't done. She held up a hand, stalling the elf's questions.

"I've spent half my life hating you," she continued. "But then you saved Rhiannon. I met you, and while you're a horrible feral gremlin with little regard for manners, you are not the monster I had been led to believe that you were. It's time I tell you the truth, Mildred."

"Enough, I'll have Annie put on some tea and we can discuss this upstairs," Ghat said. "Some things are best said in private, are they not Ms. Wolfe?"

Nathie nodded, her cheeks getting hot. She felt very much like she had as a little girl when her tutors would chastise her for making up stories instead of repeating history as it was taught. But historical events were never truly the way they were taught, were they? A violent butcher kept trapped for years underground, and when she escaped, instead of carving a righteous swath through anyone that had wronged her, the Butcher had saved a wealthy young woman from death and taught her how to survive on the Frontier, keeping her safe and hidden for years.

That didn't match the stories of the Butcher at all.

"Come," Ghat said, scooping up the remains of something from the countertop in front of her, and walking out to a narrow wooden stairway that had a thick hemp rope drawn across it. The snake draped around her neck reached down and used its head to unhook the rope for her, letting the rope fall to the side with a thump as it struck the wood of the shop's wall.

Mildred gestured for her to go first, and Nathie supposed she deserved that. Creeping paranoia whispered that the elf would split Nathie's head open with a single swing of her axe, but she'd had plenty of opportunities to do so on the train and boat ride into Marigot. No, the one thing that they had in common was a love for Rhiannon that would hopefully stay any murderous impulses. As difficult as it was to admit, the elf had been doing a far better job at playing nice than Nathie had.

The upstairs was split into a kitchen and sitting room, with a bedroom beyond, separated by a curtain of colourful cloth, woven in a geometric pattern common to Bakimban cotton. Annie looked up from where she lay on the bed, and with a gesture, made the curtain pull itself across to hide the bedroom completely. After a small shuffle, the dark-skinned elf emerged from behind the curtain in a simple pair of slacks and camisole.

Her skin was smooth, free of the old brands that marked the shoulders of so many of Marigot's adult residents. Catching Nathie looking, Annie winked and flexed her arms to reveal a ripple of defined muscle. Nathie felt her cheeks warm again and quietly took a seat at the simple wooden table that sat in the middle of the room. The chairs were mismatched but sturdy, each with a knitted cushion to sit on for comfort.

Mildred took a seat opposite, with Gilbert sitting between them with a warning glance at Nathalie. Clearly, he intended to be a buffer between them, and Nathie was grateful for it. What she was about to say would surely drive Mildred into a rage.

"Now, go on, Ms. Wolfe," Ghat said, sitting on the other side of the table, the snake coiling to rest its head on one of its loops, unblinking eyes staring at her. Nathalie had to resist shuddering. The python's eyes glinted with intelligence that went beyond what any mundane reptile had.

"You were saying you've spent half your life hating me," Mildred prompted, without the grace to look like the topic interested her. Well, it would. The elf wasn't that good an actress to hide her reaction to what was to come. Nathie picked at the hardened skin on her thumb, a nervous habit she normally stifled around the elf.

"I did, and I meant to spend the remainder of it hating you," Nathie agreed. "In fact, I hated you so much that when I heard you were alive, I reached out to Pierre to make a plan. He wanted Frederic to hang. I wanted you to hang with him."

"Lovely," Mildred muttered, rolling her eyes. "What did I do to earn such devotion from a lady like yourself?"

"You killed my father," Nathie said simply, folding her hands into her lap to keep from drawing blood on her thumb. "I saw you do it during the war."

A sick satisfaction filled Nathie as Annie dropped a mug over by the stove, clattering loudly as the tin vessel dented and rolled away. Mildred and Gilbert's mouths had gone slack, and only Madame Ghat and her snake seemed unsurprised.

"You told Rhiannon, didn't you?" Mildred asked. "That's why she'd been acting strange."

Behind her, Annie scooped up the tin mug and, using her thumbs, popped the dent out with a little 'tink'. The water was nearly at a boil, and Nathie sincerely hoped whatever tea was being made had a sedative quality. Her nerves were all in knots, and she was desperately tired after learning about Pierre's complicity.

"I did," Nathie said. Under the cover of the table, she gave in and worried at the hardened skin next to her thumbnail, picking at it mindlessly. "I fully intended to drive a wedge between the two of you so that when you hung, she would be less upset. But I didn't make up any stories about you. I only told her what I saw and what happened to me after you killed him."

Annie poured water from the kettle into the iron teapot, but Nathie noticed how she had her ears perked and pointed toward the table where the rest of them sat.

"Oh," Mildred said. "I'm sorry I killed your father."

Nathie waited, but frowned when she realised that was the entirety of the elf's apology.

"That's it?" she hissed, standing up and planting her hands on the table. "You killed my father and destroyed my life! My great-uncle sold me off to get married, twice! He would have a third time if his greed hadn't taken care of him for me. I was no more than a piece of meat to sell to the highest bidder." She angrily pushed some loose strands of hair from her face and jabbed a finger in Mildred's direction.

"You caused all of that, and the best you can say is 'I'm sorry'?"

Mildred shrugged, ears low.

"I *am* sorry," she said. "But I can't go back and change what happened, no matter how much I might want to." Nathie hated the way Mildred was looking at her. It wasn't quite pity, but it was close.

"Do you even remember doing it?" Nathie asked, voice dripping with venom. "Or was my father just another face-less target?"

"I don't remember him," Mildred said, looking down at the table. "I'm sorry. I don't remember a lot of the people I've killed, the war blurred into a tangle and I haven't been brave enough to pull those memories apart."

Nathie wanted to be furious, but the elf's answer knocked the wind from her. Suddenly, she was exhausted and wanted nothing but to climb into her own bed and sleep. She straightened, smoothing back her hair and tuck-ing it into the pile atop her head.

"I haven't decided if I still want you to hang, but I want you to know that even though you killed my father, I would never want you to go through what you did at the hands of the Rousseau brothers." She sniffed, chin high. Her mask was cracking, but she could hold on until she was safely home.

"When you're ready, I'll have a room prepared for you at my townhome. Just ask a cab to direct you to Wolfe House. I should have the note from the assassin cleaned up for you by the time you arrive."

"You aren't going to poison me or anything?" Mildred asked, lifting an eyebrow. "I probably deserve it."

Annie snickered, and Ghat gracefully elbowed her niece in the side without so much as a glance in Annie's direc-tion.

"You do, but that doesn't help us catch Frederic, does it?" Nathie asked. "I need you as much as you need me. There are survivors of the war who would pay anything to have your head on a platter, but you don't know who they are. I do." Wrestling her emotions back into the depths of her heart, Nathie brushed some dried silt from her hands. A small smear of blood told her she had picked at her thumb too much. She wiped it and the silt off onto her legging.

"Just know that after we have him, I will demand the satisfaction of a duel. I figure it is the only fair way to resolve this issue." She pulled a glove from her belt and tossed it onto the table. It got halfway before the snake darted forward and snapped it from mid-air. With her kid glove hanging from his mouth, the snake slowly pulled back to coil around Madame Ghat's shoulders. It looked very pleased with itself and made no move to swallow or drop the glove it had snatched.

"Alright," Mildred said, turning from the snake back to Nathie. "I agree. Once this is over. You might not get that glove back, though." The elf's husband looked at her with a frown, but remained quiet.

"I have other gloves. I'll go prepare the house." Nathie looked at the glove and let the snake have it. Nodding to Madame Ghat, she excused herself and hurried down the stairs and out of the shop. She held the tears back until she reached the street. Hailing a cab, she breathlessly directed it toward her home. She didn't see the gathering clusters of humans near the shop through her watery vision.

24

Discipline

The Red Hand

Madame Lavoie's shop was a pillar of the Bakimban quarter, as was the woman herself. Notoriously picky with her clients, the conjure queen herself had become well respected and even feared in Marigot for how effective her gris-gris were, and the powerful network of information that she seemed to have at her fingertips.

What a shame it was that she helped an old friend. The Red Hand had quietly let the old families know who Ghat Lavoie was harbouring among her conjure curios. There was not a family untouched by the Butcher's actions among Marigot's elite. Everyone had a brother, a father, an uncle who had died because of her. Directly or indirectly, her hands were stained red with Marigot's sons.

The aggrieved families sent who they could. Gallois, the hulking muscle that had carried Frederic from Wyndford Jail, stood next to the Hand, tucked into an alleyway across the street from Lavoie's shop. The dog whined softly at their heel, eager to get started on the hunt for the elf. They would need to find her before anyone else could kill her.

It was crucial for the Hand's plan that she was taken alive, preferably in one piece.

"Go on," the Hand said, handing Denis Gallois a bottle of high-proof rum. A rag had been soaked in it and shoved into the neck, a wick ready to be lit. The makeshift fire bomb had been made popular during the war by the Butcher's soldiers and had been regretfully called a 'Marigot cocktail' since.

"At my signal," the Hand said. "Not a moment before."

Gallois tilted the bottle in a mock cheer.

"Happy hunting, boss."

The dog quit its whining as the Hand headed deeper into the alley. They'd loop around to the rear of Lavoie's shop to cut off the most likely escape route that the elf would take. The dog would chase her, catch her, and then the Hand would take over to incapacitate her. Gallois wouldn't be needed for the Butcher's slight frame. Instead, he would block any attempts by the others in the shop to follow her.

The Hand loved when a plan came together. By the end of the night, they would have the Butcher in hand, and the city would be reminded of who truly owned its streets. Any opposition would be crushed, the way it should have been during the opening days of the war.

25

A Soul's Cycle

Gilbert

The sitting room was quiet in the wake of Nathalie's departure, with both Millie's and Annie's ears perked to listen to the human woman's footsteps. Only when the front door creaked did their ears return to their normal posture. Millie's were low, Annie's neutral.

The snake hissed gently around its stolen glove.

"So, she has a death wish, then?" Gilbert asked, picking up his tin cup and blowing the steam from it before he took a small sip. The tea was herbal, a soothing relief from the flood of emotions that had been running rampant all day.

"Why else would she ask for a duel?" Annie said, taking the chair that Nathalie had left empty. Reaching over, she stroked the snake's head. Gilbert watched, fascinated, as Mulatiwa leaned into the touch. Gilbert might be a city boy, but he was certain regular snakes were not this friendly, and he had no inclination to go find out if he was correct.

"I'm not going to kill her," Millie said, frowning down at her mug. "It's bad enough I can't remember killing her father *in front of her*. I feel like that would be something that stuck out, but..." she trailed off and rubbed her face with a low groan.

"The fog of war affects more than just the moments of battle," Ghat said, sipping her tea delicately. "It clouds our memories long after. Do not hate yourself for this, Mildred." Her dark eyes fixed on his wife, and Gilbert reached under the table to take Millie's hand.

"How can I not blame myself?" Millie asked, but she squeezed Gilbert's hand. "I was the only one left, and I was the worst of all of us."

"You were not worse than that rat-man," Ghat said, bluntly. "What was his name, Remi? Annie told me you killed him out west. As you should have done, that man was no better than a rabid animal. As for Delilah and Clem, they made their choice. They fought, knowing that they might die. You were not responsible for losing them, Millie. No matter what that bastard Rousseau told you."

Millie paled, her ears drooping lower. She hadn't mentioned that Frederic had told her that, but it fit with what Gil knew him to be like. Cruel, always looking for a way to twist the knife after an insult. Of course, he would have told Millie that the death of her friends was her fault. How better to hurt her?

"May I ask a question?" Gilbert asked. He didn't want to let Millie think too long on what else Frederic had told her, especially after having to face the house where she'd once been kept a prisoner. "Downstairs, you mentioned Millie was lucky to be what she was, and you didn't mean that she was the butcher. Could you explain what you meant?"

Ghat and Annie looked at each other, then back at Gilbert.

"Magic is part of our lives," Ghat said. "More than most truly understand. The great wheel of life does truly exist, but we are not endlessly reborn as the self we are now. When we die, when anything dies, we become spirits. Ancestors. As living beings, we breathe air; but as spirits, we breathe magic. We live in magic until that magic solidifies around us once again and we are born into the world, ready to experience life from a new perspective."

Ghat motioned to the cabinet and Annie got up and went to it, bringing back a jar of salt. When she got back to the table, she opened the jar for Ghat and set it by her aunt's hand. Picking up her tea, Annie took a seat again and took a sip.

"This is the true cycle of life, the wheel of existence, whatever you prefer to call it," Ghat said, picking up a handful of salt and carefully pouring it from her hand to form two arcs that made a circle, with only a finger's width of bare table between the arcs, breaking the circle. "We live, we die, we live as a spirit, we are born again into flesh. It's not just people, but all animals and plants are just as important to this cycle as we are.

"What makes mages special is that they can manipulate this spiritual world and use that magic to manifest changes in the physical world."

"Like Sweetpea's storms," Annie said. "Or how I change into a hawk. It takes focus and practice, because if we aren't able to keep the magic contained within our spell, it dissipates. Or we experience what's called a blowback and our spirit can get knocked loose as the magic forcibly returns to the spirit realm."

Gilbert made a face. That sounded like it hurt.

"Every so often, a very special person is born," Ghat said, and reached over to rest her empty hand on Millie's shoulder. "Her Ghost Eye ancestors were not entirely wrong with their belief that Millie is half-spirit. But they expected her to be on one side of this cycle, when she is on the other." Giving Millie's shoulder a gentle squeeze, Ghat let her go and tapped one gap in the salt circle.

"The people born that bridge the gate of death to spirit are considered founts of magic. Every breath they breathe fills the world with energy that mages can use. In all societies, these people are prized, because their presence makes spells more powerful, and they themselves can be extremely powerful magic users."

"And then there's Mildred," Annie said, a small smile on her face. "Our pale friend is at the other gate. She's what we call a life-bringer. She absorbs magic and funnels it into our physical world."

Millie sighed and finally took a drink of her tea. Gilbert supposed it must have cooled, since she didn't wince.

"So that's why the spells don't work around you," he said, watching her squint into the bottom of the tin mug. "But Sweetpea—"

"Sweetpea cheats," Annie said with a laugh. "Arroyans learned how to skip back and forth between the two worlds using shortcuts. Whenever you see Sweetpea cast a spell around Millie, she floods the space with magic to act like a clogged funnel, so her spell will still work despite Millie soaking up magic."

"So basically, I'm a sponge, but I haven't figured out how to take the magic I soak up and make anything with it. It just happens whether I want it to or not. Sometimes, like with the gris-gris, soaking up magic isn't so bad. Other times like when I get stabbed and can't be healed, soaking up magic is bullshit."

"Grannie Whitewing brews a tea that kicks Millie further into the spirit world so she can get healed," Annie said. "She refuses to let anyone else from outside their clan try it, something about it being too dangerous." Annie sighed, sulking at the thought.

"That was a lot of information," Gilbert said, trying to digest it all. "So some people are water fountains, and Millie is a sinkhole."

Under the table, his wife, the sinkhole, let go of his hand and punched him lightly in the thigh. Glancing at her, Gilbert saw she wore the faintest smile on her lips. He smiled back, broadly.

"You two are worse than love-struck puppies," Annie muttered.

"So," Gil said, catching his wife's hand again. "Now we know something about who made the gris-gris. Whoever it was, it couldn't be Pierre Rousseau. If he grew up with her, he would have known not to bother with a gris-gris, correct?" He looked at Millie for confirmation.

Frowning, she reluctantly nodded.

"Fred didn't tell many people, but Pierre would have known magic doesn't work around me. Unless he forgot in the last five years, he wouldn't have bothered getting a gris-gris made." Millie finished her tea and sat back in her chair, thinking.

"So, if it wasn't Pierre, who was it?" Gilbert asked. "And how did they get a hold of the receipt from the Rousseau home?"

Millie groaned, tipping her head back. "We're going to need to ask him who might have got a hold of it."

"I'll ask," Gilbert said. "Tomorrow, I'll go to Rousseau's house and look through those ledgers and see what I can find out. You should go with Annie or Nathalie to find out what you can about the surviving assholes from the war."

"Hell no, I ain't going near those secessionist assholes," Annie said from her seat.

"You and Nathalie should go find out what you can about those surviving secessionist assholes," Gilbert corrected himself, not missing a beat. "I wish we could wait for Hal to get here, but I don't think the people that have Frederic will wait for our favourite Stratton to arrive."

Millie straightened in her seat and opened her mouth to argue. Before she could, Gil brought her hand up and kissed it.

"I know they're not after Fred, they're after you," he said, watching her turn pink from ear tip to ear tip. "But Pierre might know something, and I'll pry it out of him by giving him something he's probably never had."

"What's that?" Annie asked, making a face. "Balls? A spine?"

"A friend, Annie," Ghat said, swatting her niece's shoulder. "Tsk, you went and picked up all your sass from Mildred because it certainly didn't come from me." Ghat smiled, revealing slightly larger canines than a regular elf's. "Now, Gilbert. Let me make you a cream for that hip of yours. It won't be as effective as a gris-gris, but if you're going to be married to Mildred, regular herbs will be more effective."

WITH A SALVE FOR his hip and a tea for his wife to sleep, Ghat told Gilbert and Millie that they could leave. The stairs gave Gil less trouble going down than they had going up, but Millie took them slowly, ready if he needed help. He smiled, about to thank her, when he noticed her ears twitch.

Fire exploded from the shop window. The small, distorted panes of glass shattered inward, tearing apart a display table of sewn poppets and lighting them on fire. His heart leapt into this throat, and Gil grabbed Millie, diving for cover behind Ghat's counter. He tried to take the brunt of the impact, grunting in pain as he landed on a pile of sticks that snapped under his weight. As he pushed himself to his feet, Gilbert saw he hadn't landed in a pile of sticks at all. He'd landed on a pile of bones. Some were small, but others weren't. Gil wasn't familiar enough with the inside of people's bodies to know if they were humanoid or not.

"Get down!" Millie shouted over the crackle of hungry flames.

For a moment, Gil thought she was talking to him. He blinked, spotting Ghat descending the stairs with wide eyes. The world around him slowed down as his heartbeat raced. Gil watched the conjure queen walk toward the fire, confusion plain on her face. The world snapped back to its normal speed as another bottle smashed into the shop.

Ghat spun on her heel and pointed behind Gilbert toward the back of the shop.

"Get out!" she hissed, lifting a hand toward the flames. They'd spread rapidly over the dry goods, smoking fiercely as the fire consumed the wall of herbs hung up to dry.

Gilbert shoved the tin of cream into his pocket as he and Millie scrambled to their feet. She grabbed his hand tight, leading him beyond the curtain to the rear of the shop. Gilbert blinked as they passed some altars with bones and bread laid out in front of them, others with thick tallow candles that would only add further fuel to the flames. Another smash and whoosh from the front of the shop suggested that the sooner they all got out of the burning building, the better.

Reaching the back door, Millie unlatched it and kicked it open.

"Oh, thank God," Gilbert muttered as they emerged into Ghat's back garden. All kinds of herbs and flowers were growing, most of which were completely new to him. For example, the strange ghostly flowers that seemed to rustle and dance of their own accord not more than a foot away from him.

"Wait," Millie gasped, throwing her arm in front of him.

"Snakes," Gilbert said, shuddering as the garden came alive with scaly bodies slithering away from the fire, heading for the narrow alley between Ghat's garden and the one of the building opposite. Some were thin grass snakes, too small to be of any concern, but others were thick muscular things, as thick as Gilbert's forearm with a pale line across their mouths.

"Which ones are dangerous?" he asked, eyes flicking from snake to snake. None of these looked friendly, like Mulatiwa had been.

Screams rose from the mouth of the alley as the snakes fled.

"All of them," Millie said, picking her way forward as the last stragglers slithered past them. "I think they just cleared out an ambush for us. Don't block their way and we should be fine."

"Wonderful," Gilbert said, careful not to lose his balance and fall onto any of the unhappy vipers. "I hope whoever was there got bit on the ass."

His wife laughed, and Gilbert felt giddy enough to join in. Their first day in Marigot and already Rhiannon's cousin admitted to wanting to kill Millie, Pierre revealed himself as a cad, and now Madame Lavoie's shop was burning down while a flood of snakes cleared the way for escape. Reaching the back alley, Millie looked up the block and Gil glanced down it, spotting a confused-looking washer woman holding her basket of laundry over her head and a familiar hawk wheeling in the darkening sky. It seemed Annie had already made her escape.

The thud of paws on dirt and a low snarl were the only warnings Gilbert had before a muscular dog sprinted out of one of the other gardens and leapt for Millie's throat. She reacted quickly, snapping her arm up to catch its jaws just as it reached her. The dog slammed into her, knocking the elf flat.

He hadn't been fast enough to block it, but Gil reached down and grabbed it by the collar, hauling the dog off her before it could get to her throat. The dog didn't fight it, and as he pulled it away, it licked at its bloodied nose. It seemed to be as confused about what was going on as Gilbert was, even turning to lick at his hand with big brown eyes.

"Ow." Millie said, pressing a hand to her chest where two dusty paw prints showed the point of contact. A dark stain was spreading where Nathalie had stitched up her shoulder only hours before. The dog whined, hanging its head and looking over at Millie.

"Are you alright?" Gil asked, turning to keep his body between the dog and his wife. "Your stitches..." He held out his hand to her to help her get up. She took it, wheezing, as he pulled her to her feet. She shook her head, looking at the dog. He was heavily scarred, with both his ears and tail docked in cruel fashion. He also seemed completely uninterested in launching another attack.

"Later," Millie wheezed. She staggered to her feet; one hand pressed to her shoulder.

"Careful," Gil warned as Millie reached a hand out for the dog to sniff. She was greeted with enthusiastic licks on her hand, and the wagging of the dog's whole rear end.

"On his collar," she said, reaching under the dog's chin. With a quick yank, she pulled a small packet of dark wool free. A gris-gris, the same as the ones that had been planted on both of them at Rhiannon's party. "This must have made him aggressive," she said, turning the little bundle over in her fingers.

Behind them, the door slammed open, and Millie and Gil turned to see a sooty Ghat emerge from her shop, Mulatiwa draped around her shoulders. The elven orc was furious, her teeth bared as she stomped through her garden, unbothered by the risk of venomous snakes.

"You killed all the warding spells," Ghat said, jabbing a finger at Millie. "Now look at what they've done." Her voice cracked on the last word, and tears welled up in the other woman's eyes. "Look!"

"I'm sorry—" Millie said, but the conjure queen cut her off with a brusque wave of her hand.

"You didn't set it on fire," Ghat said, her voice harsh from inhaling smoke. "Ten years I served these people. Ten years, and so little has changed. Still nothing but frightened dogs who put their tails between their legs when the masters arrive." She spat onto the ground and made a gesture that looked suspiciously like a curse. Gil let go of the dog's collar, to scoop up the cane he'd dropped in the scuffle.

"Time to go," Millie said, pointing down the alley to where the screams had come from moments earlier. A cluster of masked men and women had reached the back alley. One hopped forward and launched another flaming bottle their way. Quick as lightning, Millie darted forward, catching the bottle in both hands before it could smash into the ground and spray fuel over them. Gilbert grimaced, expecting the bottle to erupt into flames.

The masked group paused, unsure of what to do. It gave the elf the opening she needed. Launching the bottle directly at the ground in front of the men, she pulled her axe from her belt and readied it.

"Gil, Ghat, get to Wolfe's house," she said, breathing through her teeth. The conjure queen didn't need to be told twice. She spun on her heel and sprinted away, launching herself up into the air as a hawk the moment she could. Gil, however, swaggered up next to his wife, cane at the ready. God give him strength, because he was about to do something stupid.

"Unlike our magic friends, I can't fly," he said, shrugging off Millie's glare. "But this cane is solid ironwood, and I was a champion fencer, you know." He smiled at her and scythed the cane down onto the outstretched arm of a man who ran toward them. The cane connected with a sharp crack, and the man staggered back with a scream, clutching his arm to his chest. A knife tumbled out of his hand, and Gilbert kicked it away, sending it into the thick garden across from Ghat's.

The injured man let out a bellow and bull-rushed Gilbert, shoulder low. Gil pivoted on his good leg, swatting down hard with his cane to connect with the back of the man's head as he passed. The man crumpled, crashing into the short wooden fence that separated Ghat's garden from her neighbour's.

The stray dog rushed ahead, launching itself at one of the three attackers that had avoided the fire. Just like it had with Millie, the dog knocked the woman over. This time, however, the woman wasn't met with kisses. Muscular jaws closed around the woman's arm and the dog immediately started throwing its muscular body side to side, causing chaos as one of the other thugs grabbed onto it to pull it off the woman.

Two men were on fire, screaming as they rolled around in the dirt. One was busy with the dog, and the remaining man sprouted Millie's axe from his forehead. He wavered on his feet, then crumpled into a heap in the dirt, staring at the sky.

The man wrestling with the dog glanced over his shoulder and realised he was the only fighter left. He reached for the holster at his hip, but it was clear to Gil that this man was no gunslinger. After spending time on the frontier with his wife and her terrifying friends, Gil had seen them draw their weapons so quickly that their bullet hit its target before he could blink.

This man was fumbling with the hammer when Millie rushed him. She wrested the revolver away from the remaining man, flipped it around on a finger, and pressed the barrel to the man's forehead. The man blinked, looking from Millie to Gil, as though the banker might help. Gilbert brushed a bit of ash from his shoulder and placed both hands on the head of his cane with a smile. His hands trembled from adrenaline, and he tightened his grip on the cane to keep them steady.

"Are you going to tell me who sent you? Or should I just kill you now?" Millie shouted over the sound of the fire, cocking the revolver's hammer.

The man held up his hands, and Gilbert noticed one twitch forward. So did Millie.

The gunshot cracked through the roar of flames from Ghat's shop, and the man fell.

"I don't think he was going to tell you," Gilbert said, walking over to pull the dog off the lone woman. She'd turned pale and was trembling, her eyes unfocused. The dog wiggled his butt, pleased he'd done a good job. He smiled up at Gil, his bloody tongue hanging out the side of his mouth.

"Good boy," Millie said, patting the dog on the head as she bent to retrieve her axe from where it was lodged in a man's forehead. Bracing her foot on the man's shoulder, she pulled the axe free with a squelch, and wiped it clean on the downed man's clothes.

"How worried should we be about the police?" Gilbert asked, realising that while he'd heard shouting earlier, no one seemed to have arrived to investigate the fire, or the sounds of fighting.

"They won't be coming until the fire's out," Millie said, crouching by the man she'd shot. She checked his pockets, pocketing any spare bullets she found. At one pocket, she paused, and pulled out a money clip with a stack of banknotes and a small gris-gris. Gilbert leaned over her shoulder, counting the thickness of the clip and doing some quick math.

"If that's how much leg breakers make down here, I'm even more impressed Rousseau found himself in debt," he muttered, coughing into his sleeve. The smoke from the store stung his eyes and nose. Whatever herbs Ghat had kept in there were also making him feel just a little giddy. Millie handed Gil the money, and he looked down at it in surprise.

"What?" she asked as he looked at her in confusion. "You're a banker. Money is your thing." It was hard to argue with logic like that. Gil tucked the money away, making a note to open an account for Millie when they got home. She might not want this man's money now, but it could help pay for a new shop for Ghat when everything was over.

With no more reason to stay, and acrid smoke chasing them out of the back alley, Millie, Gil and the dog hurried out onto a side street. The elf led the way, splattered with blood and with a nasty-looking burn on her wrist. Gil gently caught her hand once they were a few blocks away, pulling her to a stop out of the way of the street they were on.

"Is this from the bottle?" He asked, pulling his handkerchief from his pocket. It was clean and would help dirt from getting into the burn until they got back to Wolfe's home, wherever that was.

"Yeah," Millie said, reaching down to stroke the dog's head with her other hand while Gilbert inspected the burn. "The wick got me when I caught it." Carefully, he wrapped it in the clean handkerchief, realising with a laugh that it was the cleanest thing on either of them. Both were covered with ash and soot, making Millie look even more like a ghost than usual. He leaned down and kissed her forehead, then made a face and spit the ash out that he'd accidentally picked up.

"That was a mistake," he muttered, wiping his mouth on his sleeve.

"Do you regret marrying me?" Millie asked, looking up at him. Gilbert shook his head, spitting again to clear his mouth.

"Not at all. The mistake was kissing your face before you've had a wash," he said. He didn't need to think about his answer. It was the truth. "Back in Scorched Bluffs, marriage was the simplest way to ensure all our daughters would be safe. Even though we both survived the attack on Scorched Bluffs, the only questions I had was if I was holding you back from being happy, and if you knew how cute your snores are."

Millie rolled her eyes, but her ears flicked a bit, rising from a mopey droop to a more relaxed posture.

"No," he repeated, serious now. He reached out, brushing his thumb over her cheek, leaving a streak of clean skin, shocking in how pale it was against the soot. "I knew you had done bad things during the war, though now I'm certain half of those are just stories. I saw how devoted you were to your daughters and your town, and I saw it again when you agreed to come to this god-awful city for

Rhiannon. I don't think she meant to be so cold to you, back in Wyndford. She just needs time to think."

"Ghat's sister and Annie's mom both died on my watch," Millie said, her voice growing rough. She blinked rapidly, but he could see the tears forming on her eyelashes. The dog whined and placed his heavy head on her arm. "Delilah and Clem were the women that I saw as a little girl and thought, this is how people should be. They took care of me when I needed it, and they supported me when Fred named me sergeant over everyone else. They showed me how to be the deputy you met at Scorched Bluffs. Clem and Delilah were more family than my mother ever was." She took a shaky breath, looking up at him. "And I couldn't save them. I had nothing worth living for, but here I am still breathing while they—"

Gilbert pulled her into a gentle hug and rested his chin on her braid. The dog pressed his face into her with a soft whine, wanting to help.

"I don't think Madame Ghat or Annie blame you for what happened," Gilbert said, stroking her back. "War is a terrible thing, but like you said: there is only one just war, and that was the war you were fighting. The war you're still fighting."

She nodded and heaved a sigh that seemed to drain her petite frame of tension. She held onto him for a while, and he didn't press her any further.

"I think you just stole another dog, though," Gilbert teased. "First Freckle, now this old boy."

"This one stole himself," Millie huffed against his chest, her voice muffled. Gently, cautiously, Gil felt her wrap her arms around him.

"My wife, the dog thief," Gilbert said, rubbing her back. He knew he wasn't the one who could reassure Millie that Annie and Ghat didn't hate her. If he could lighten her mood just a little, Gil hoped she'd be able to believe the two other women when they were ready to have that conversation.

26

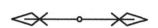

In Strange Company

Millie

Millie turned the revolver over in her hands as she and Gilbert rode to Nathalie's home in yet another cab. The absolutely not-stolen dog lay at their feet, his head resting on Millie's boot. The gun was well made, not one of the clunky early models that had been issued to the Marigot army during the war. The maker's mark stamped into the polished frame of the gun was from a company she didn't recognise, but she knew she could find out more about it at the local trading post. If the gun was as good quality as it looked, it and the money she'd found meant the 'leg-breaker' she'd shot was actually a member of one of the old families.

"You're keeping it, aren't you?" Gilbert asked, and Millie started, realising he'd been watching her fiddle with the gun the whole ride.

"Of course I am," she said. Then quickly added, "To help the investigation, obviously." He smirked, but for once he didn't call her out on the half-truth. The gun would help narrow down who was sending people after them, but it would also help by shooting people coming after them.

The cab rolled to a stop, and the dog whined at the door until Millie opened it for him. The scarred terrier hopped down from the cab like he was used to it, just making everything more confusing. Tucking the gun into her axe belt, Millie helped Gilbert down from the cab and turned to look at the Wolfe house while he paid their fare.

The house's second-storey porch had flowering plants and curtain moss lining it, but all the blooms were shades of blood red while the surrounding homes had riots of colour. Ominous black wrought-iron gates topped with sharp points stood ajar, imposing enough to make any un-wanted visitor think twice before calling. The dog didn't think twice about trotting up and sniffing the gate, leaving his mark on one of the wrought iron posts.

"Of course, that's her house," Gilbert said once he got a good look at it. "A friend told me she's called the black widow of Marigot." He frowned lightly, and looked down at Millie. "Why does Marigot give everyone weird titles like that? Black Widow, Ghost, Butcher?"

"It sounds better in songs?" Millie guessed. "Marig-ot does a lot of things differently than other cities." She slipped through the gate first and tested it by nudging the gate door further. It swung soundlessly, the hinges well-oiled and in good repair. It would make it hard to hear anyone sneaking in, but houses like these usually had wards for people that were not magic sponges.

"Like not calling the police when four people die in the street," Gilbert agreed.

Millie looked over her shoulder and shrugged at him. The men had attacked them in front of Ghat's shop. That was basically asking to get killed if you knew anything about Marigot. You attack someone, you'd better hope you kill them first, or they'd have free rein to hunt you down and finish what you'd started. The city guard would show up when they realised the dead men and women in the alley were masters.

The front door of the house opened and revealed a curvy elf with deeply bronzed skin in a servant's dress, her dark curls pulled up into a bun on the top of her head. The woman took one look at Millie and her eyes flew open. Even though the other elf was a good six inches taller than Millie, she practically fell over herself to get out of the way and let them in.

"Mrs. Butcher, I mean Mr. and Mrs. Goldman, Lady Wolfe is resting, but I have food and your room prepared. I'm still preparing the rooms for Madame Lavoie and her niece, but please, follow me."

The dog trotted in like he owned the house, and Millie winced, hoping he was house-trained.

Ghat and Annie were waiting in the dining room, with Mulatiwa draped around the conjure queen's shoulders. Even the snake looked sad as Millie walked into the room, Gilbert on one side and the dog on the other.

"Mildred," Annie said, eying the dog. "Did you steal—"

"No," Millie grumbled, taking a seat at the massive mahogany table. To her relief, the dog lay down at her feet with a heavy sigh and closed his eyes. Someone had trained him not to jump on tables, then. That was a relief. Millie didn't need more reasons for Nathalie to hate her. Killing the woman's father was enough.

"I can't believe it," Ghat said, spinning a spoon on the tablecloth, one half-turn at a time. "The shop, gone. And not one of my neighbours tried to help." Her long green ears swooped down. "I helped them with everything. Fertility gris-gris, purging tea, sorting out grumpy ancestors, and when I needed them, they hid in their shops. Too afraid of some humans with fire to help."

They sat in silence for a moment, all of them looking down at the pristine white tablecloth.

"Millie killed a bunch of them," Gilbert said, reaching for a glass of water. "If that makes you feel better. I'm afraid I'm not sure how moral you are yet, Madame Lavoie."

Annie coughed and took a sip of water to hide the smirk on her face.

"A little," Ghat said with a sigh. "But without my shop and my altars, most of the spirits have fled. It will take time to coax them back, and I worry we don't have such a luxury. If these people are bold enough to burn down my shop, they believe themselves untouchable. I fear we will need to call on the ancestors for guidance. Grandmaman will find out whose blood was on that note. Bring that hand of Rousseau's too."

Gilbert looked at Millie, raising his eyebrows.

"It's just the ring," she explained, ears getting hot. "I took it when no one was looking back at the jail. I figured Ghat could use it to track down where Fred was."

"Oh, well, that's fine," he said, leaning back in the chair. "I was worried it might be his entire hand rotting away in our luggage."

Millie took a long drink of water, glad she had not gone with her initial plan, which had been exactly that. Wrap the hand in cloth, bring it to Marigot, find its owner. She'd settled on the ring since it didn't smell, and it was much easier to hide than a whole man's hand.

"Who is Grandmaman?" Gilbert asked Ghat. Annie winced, and her aunt's ears drooped even lower.

"My grandmother," Ghat said. "She is the Granddame of conjure in Marigot. The highest high priestess, if you prefer. She only speaks with supplicants who are endorsed by one of the three conjure queens of Marigot. It is the queen's responsibility to ensure the supplicant makes a proper pilgrimage to her." Ghat looked down at the spoon in her fingers, the silver reflecting the candelabra's light from the table.

"She is very... demanding," Ghat admitted.

"She's also been dead for years," Annie said, wrinkling her nose. "She's going to smell terrible."

Ghat reached out and flicked her niece's ear. Annie ducked her head and winced, rubbing the offended ear tip. Millie pressed her lips together to keep a straight face. She had been on the receiving end of those ear flicks many times from Delilah. The amusement curdled on Millie's tongue, replaced by grief.

"I just mean that undead really smell after a while," Annie muttered. "Especially in the swamp."

"The local priests don't have a problem with her being... like that?" Millie asked, arching an eyebrow. Privately, she agreed with Annie, any undead out in the swamp would smell awful after a day. She couldn't imagine how one had lasted years without falling apart. "I thought the undead were still illegal."

Ghat bared her teeth, showing off her sharp canines. If there'd been any warmth in the expression, it might have been called a smile. Instead, it looked more like a grimace than anything else.

"The church only cares about the soul. Our body is just an empty vessel after we die. Grandmaman skipped waiting to be reborn in a new body: she returned to her old one before it was cold."

Annie rolled her eyes.

"They're scared of her," the other elf translated for Millie. "As long as she stays out in the swamp, the church is happy to pretend she's nothing more than a bogeyman in children's stories. Like with you being the Butcher."

Millie frowned down at her water glass. What would the singers of bogeyman stories think of the Bayou Butcher going to meet the undead conjure grand dame in the depths of the swamp? It would be the kind of story little girls begged to hear every night, even though it would scare them silly every time.

For the first time since arriving in the city, Millie had a moment to think about her girls back in Wyndford. She trusted Avrom and Arnaud to look after them, but her girls were a handful, always getting into things they shouldn't. Hopefully Sarah would be alright. All three of the girls had been having nightmares since the encounters with Fred, but Sarah was so sensitive compared to the other two. She'd had to face Fred's horrific treatment, and more than Fenna and Rasha, she struggled with sleep.

"Sorry to interrupt," the maid said, carrying in plates of food. "All the rooms are now ready, and I can show you to them after you eat. Ms. Wolfe sends her regrets, but she is not feeling well enough to join you this evening."

It was a distraction from the pang of homesickness that cut deep into Millie's heart. The dinner was a simple but filling meal of fish and vegetables. The fish was fresh, blackened in a skillet with herbs and lemon. After a week of travelling and eating fried or cold food, Millie was almost ready to give Nathalie a hug for serving them something normal. Almost. The dog was served a plate of plain fish, which he noisily devoured at Millie's feet before licking the plate clean.

The maid, Ruth, showed them to their room, and left them staring at the sheer density of the decor inside. Millie wasn't about to claim she had any taste when it came to fancy people decorating, but there were gilt vases, framed paintings of tall ships on the ocean, a velvet fainting couch with a pair of folded towels perched upon it that had embroidered edges, and the four-poster bed looked like it belonged in a cathedral instead of a bedroom.

"Are all Marigot homes—" Gilbert started.

"No," Millie said, edging toward the bed, careful she might somehow damage it. "The Rousseaus loved bright yellows and white. They showed their money by how hard it is to keep those two colours clean. This is..." she trailed off, at a loss for words, and poked the bed. It felt soft, and she guiltily wondered how nice it would feel to curl up on it.

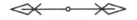

"I DEMAND SATISFACTION!" PAUL O'Leary threw his glove down onto the table, upsetting the piles of coins and cards that were the source of the disagreement. "You never win this much, Fred. You must be cheating."

O'Leary's dog stepped up behind his master, a broad half-orc who had one tusk missing and a nasty-looking scar down the side of his face. Trouble had been brewing for the last year, as the threat of war with the rest of the Union became increasingly likely. Beaulieu was the largest province, and by far the wealthiest, but it was weak to attack with a soft border and a lack of powerful cities to protect the wide expanse of vulnerable farmland.

Fred had told Mildred that he was certain things would come to a head before the next storm season, and a single glance at O'Leary's face told her that Fred was right. Paul had expected Fred's support in preparing an army against the Union, but privately, Fred was for abolition. He had experience the others needed, having served down on border skirmishes with the Nahuatl last year. Millie had been left behind with a critical task: to plan a revolt with the slaves of Marigot. O'Leary might have heard whispers, given how furious he'd been all evening.

"Fine," Fred said, placing his cards down. "I accept your challenge. I name Mildred Argent as my champion, and the street outside tonight as the time and place."

Masters rarely fought in duels. Instead, they nominated a trained slave to risk death for them. Losing a years-long investment still hurt, but not as much as catching a sword in the gut. Millie stood, her dress rustling. The men at the table and their retainers burst out laughing. O'Leary just looked even angrier. He'd been expecting Blackwater, or one of the other fighters the Rousseaus kept for just such a purpose. Now, he stared at her with hatred in his eyes, and Millie understood why.

This seemed like a joke, an insult to his champion's abilities. It wasn't.

"Fine, I'll fight her myself. It's time to teach your pet a lesson."

They met outside, Mildred having changed out of the dress and frills into a pair of leggings and the plain camisole under her whalebone corset. She knew how small she looked, and she knew O'Leary would think she was an underfed plaything. He hadn't seen the years of honing Fred put her through, the nights of sparring after her daily tasks, the way Fred had insisted she learn how to eat the pain and let it fuel her.

"To the death," O'Leary shouted, "With swords." Someone provided lightweight sabres, the kind the Union army issued to officers. Millie took one and tested its balance. It was very similar to Fred's, and she felt a rush of gratitude for the painful lessons he had been putting her through since his return from the Nahuatl border. She preferred her axes, but she could make anything with an edge dance in her hands.

"You heard him, Mil," Fred drawled. The others laughed, expecting a disaster. "Go get him."

Slaves could not harm masters. It was an ironclad rule in the Marigot culture. There was only one exception: a slave could kill to defend their own master from harm, such as a duel. Most slaves were beaten down until they couldn't think of raising a hand against any master, but Millie had never been good at submission.

O'Leary saluted with his sword, drunk on anger and wine. Millie returned it, sober in every sense of the word. He lunged, a simple thrust that wobbled. Millie swatted the thrust aside, hard. O'Leary had time to look shocked before she darted past his guard and slashed. His face was still shocked as his head toppled to one side, spraying Mildred in hot blood.

"No more masters," Mildred said, baring her teeth in a predator's smile. She reached out casually and pushed the headless body so it topped over. "No more kings."

Of the gathered men and their attendants, only Fred was smiling. The rest had their mouths open in abject horror at how quickly the duel ended. Mildred watched the masters realise that not only was abolition coming, but it was coming for their heads.

One by one, the masters bled as slashes appeared on their bodies. Millie frowned, taking a half step back. This wasn't right at all. She'd only killed O'Leary the night of the duel. She and Fred had mobilised their militia that night, re-treating into the swamp to link up with the Union.

Fred staggered, his hand gone. He clutched his stump to his chest and stared at her in horror. Gallois sprouted her axe in his chest and looked down at it in surprise. Something was wrong.

Behind her, the sweet voice of Clem warbled a lullaby that she used to sing to Annie and Millie at night to soothe them after a hard day's work.

"You killed us," Clem sang. "You led us to war, and you killed us dead. A bloody crown for our butcher's head."

Millie woke with the memory of blood on her lips and a sword in her hand. She lay still, ears perked for the last strains of Clem's song as her heartbeat slowed. Gilbert mumbled something about tax rates under his breath and rolled over with a groan. Relieved she hadn't woken him, Millie slipped from the bed to get some fresh air. The dog had fallen asleep by the door, and he huffed in his sleep, back paws twitching from a doggy dream.

Stepping out onto the porch, Millie closed her eyes and took a deep breath of the night air. It was still hot and muggy, too humid to cool off much overnight. She smelled a storm on the horizon, the subtle shift of air to ozone, with the heavy earthy scent of rain. It was storm season, but she'd hoped that they would be lucky to get Fred and get out of Marigot before anything nasty blew in.

She was not alone on the porch.

Ghat sat on the wooden planks, knees tucked up to her chest and her back to the home's plaster wall. Wordlessly, Millie walked over to join her. It was easy to forget how young Ghat really was. She held herself with a regal poise that commanded respect, but she was still young.

"I'm sorry," Millie whispered, sitting down next to her. "I should have known whoever this is would punish anyone caught helping me. I shouldn't have put you in that position."

Ghat pursed her lips and shook her head slowly.

"You were not the one who disappointed me, Millie," she said, her voice raw. "I forgot what people are really like. Things after the war, they're not great. But they are getting better. It was easy to look at my shop and think that I meant enough to the city to be safe."

Millie slipped her arm around the taller woman and pulled her down into a hug.

"Not all people," she whispered, thinking of how carefully Gilbert had wrapped up her wrist after they'd escaped. "But too many."

Ghat sighed and lowered herself to lay her head in Millie's lap like she used to, before the war.

"I'm sorry I never came back." The words were bubbling up in Millie's throat, and she felt like if she tried to stop them, she'd choke. "I should have visited you as soon as I could."

"You still sent word," Ghat murmured, watching the wind ruffle the petals on Nathalie's dark flowers. "I should have gone with Annie when she left, but I thought I had a community here."

They sat there in silence for a while, neither willing to talk about who was missing. Millie closed her eyes and pictured Delilah like she'd been back when they'd met. Quick to smile, Dee was always humming a song under her breath while she worked. It didn't matter if it was while she was braiding Ghat's hair, cleaning out Millie's latest scrapes, or helping teach baby Annie how to talk. She and Clem had taken in the strange albino elf that Fred dropped off at the dormitory and showed Millie how to get by in the Rousseau household.

She tried to picture Delilah's smile with its sharp canines, or how Clem got shy when Delilah would kiss her on the cheek in front of others. But every time she nearly got them right, the rot of her dreams would set in.

"I was scared," Millie said, finally opening her eyes. She swallowed the hot lump in her throat. "Not of facing the masters, but I was scared you and Annie would hate me for what happened. I hated myself so much." She lifted a hand to wipe away the tears building on her lashes. "I promised you I'd keep her safe, and I couldn't."

Millie looked out at the city, rebuilt so thoroughly that it seemed like the war had only been a bad dream. She'd lived it and kept reliving it, but being back with no sign of the fighting made Millie feel like she had dreamed all of it. That maybe Clem would step out to join them, a hint of grey creeping into her curls. Delilah would have laugh lines from the dumb jokes Clem and Millie would make, and Millie's little girls would have had two more aunties to watch over them and teach them bad words.

"It wasn't your fault," Ghat whispered. "It was war." She let out a shaky sigh, and reached up to wipe the back of her hand over her own eyes. "She visited me, you know. After the war was over. You were missing, and there was that ridiculous rumour about you performing sacrificial magic. I knew it was bullshit, but it wasn't safe to tell anyone. I kept waiting for her and Clem to come home." She pushed herself up, out of Millie's lap.

"They told me they wouldn't be coming back, but to wait for you. That you had made it, somehow." Ghat pressed her hand over her mouth, and Millie watched how it trembled with the effort of keeping the grief at bay.

"I'm so sorry, Ghat," Millie whispered. The tears were falling freely now, salty on her lips.

"They were always our big sisters," Ghat said, a fragile smile on her face. "They wanted me to know, so that I wouldn't worry. They wanted us, all of us, to be able to live the lives they'd fought for." The smile dissolved. "And tonight all I can think of, is that everything I'd built in my life is gone."

Millie rose up onto her knees and pulled Ghat into a tight hug, her own shoulders shaking.

"Not everything," Millie whispered, slowly rocking the other woman. "It's my turn to look after you. Once we find out who did this, I'll make sure they never can do anything to you again. We can get you another shop, or a place to stay until you're sure of what you want to do. Anything you want, Ghat." Millie pressed her nose into Ghat's braids and held her tight.

"I've missed you," Ghat whispered.

27

HANDPRINTS

THE RED HAND

THE AMBUSH HAD BEEN a disaster. The Red Hand stood in the back alley behind the smouldering remains of Madame Lavoie's conjure shop, staring down at the bodies the Butcher had left behind. Two loyalists were dead from fire, one from a broken skull, one from the Butcher's axe, one shot and one left alive but in shock with a savaged arm.

That wasn't even counting those who had been bitten by palemouths the Butcher had sent after them.

"She took my dog," the Hand said to Gallois. The large man crossed his arms and looked over the carnage. Like the Hand, Gallois was impressed. One little elf had filled the alleys with snakes, set two of his men on fire, and converted the dog to her side. They had heard no stories of her using magic, but how else had she been able to take control of animals?

"She's stronger than we thought," Gallois said. "I didn't doubt you at the beginning, but..." he trailed off, eyes returning to the burned bodies. "You're right. She's perfect."

The Hand smiled, clapping a hand on the man's meaty shoulder.

"I had my doubts when we first found her, too. There's no shame in that, my friend," they said. "But I think it's clear we underestimated her. That was my mistake, and one we will rectify tonight. The guard will deal with the bodies, I need you with me for this."

The conjure shop wasn't far from the river, and it was a short walk to reach the inhuman quarter of Marigot, where freed inhumans had settled after abolition was finally enforced. The streets were quiet. None of the residents wanted to be the next business to receive a delivery of firebombs. Most would need to report to their work at sunup, which meant this was the quietest neighbourhood in all of Marigot once the sun went down.

The Hand pulled a small gris-gris from their pocket and whispered the dedication to draw in spirits of stealth and darkness. Gallois would solve any issue with witnesses, but it was easier to have none at all.

In the corner of their eye, the Hand spotted a ghostly figure flit from shadow to shadow. They smiled, grateful their request had been granted. The spirits were hungry, and the Hand made sure to always feed those in need.

"The bakery," the Hand murmured to their companion. Gallois nodded and pulled an axe that resembled that of the Butcher's from his belt. It glinted in the night with unnatural light, and for a moment, the Hand saw their favourite spirit reflected in the blade. Glowing eyes, their face more shape than features.

The Hand smiled and opened the bakery door, motioning for Gallois to take the lead.

28

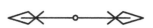

FAMILY REUNION

RHIANNON

RHIANNON SPENT ANOTHER RESTLESS night in bed before she finally gave up on sleep as the first blush of dawn touched the sky. Fyodor had taken to sleeping at her feet. His deep breaths were calming throughout the night, but it made getting up unnoticed a thing of the past.

Sliding her feet out from under the sheet, Rhiannon murmured reassuring words to the dog as he lifted his head and looked up at her with bleary eyes.

"You can stay here," Rhiannon reminded him, but the dog groaned and heaved himself up to his feet and jumped down from the bed with a loud thud. She winced, waiting to see if she heard anyone else stirring. A few of the staff would already be up, but that didn't mean Fyo had to wake up the entire household.

"Gentle feet," she whispered to him, climbing the rest of the way out of bed. On these floors, she didn't make a sound, but Fyodor had spent the last five years living on dirt. He'd completely forgotten his puppy training on how to land and walk quietly in a house with other people. At the command, he lifted one paw, tilting his head uncertainly.

"That is a very good paw," she agreed, taking it and shaking it. She'd have to spend some time training him soon, after this mess with Rousseau was cleared up.

A gentle knock at the door announced that her getting out of bed had not gone unnoticed. Rhiannon pulled on her robe and crossed her room to the door. On the other side, she heard whispering and a faint whine. Ah, Owen must be awake.

"Good morning," she said with a smile, opening the door to two expectant faces. Owen smiled, revealing a missing front tooth, and Agnar hopped from one front paw to the other in excitement.

"Can Fyodor come out to play?" Owen asked. "We'll be quiet, out in the garden."

Rhiannon doubted that any of the three would stay quiet, but the garden was a much better place for them than inside.

"Let me get dressed and we'll both come out. How does that sound?" She said, crouching down in front of him with a smile. Some time with her nephew sounded like a wonderful break from going over the same worries about her uncle's trial for the umpteenth time. "Will you wait for just a few minutes in your room? I'll meet you there."

Owen nodded vigorously.

Rhiannon was about to stand when she thought of something. One name on the jail guard log was 'Gallois'. It was a long shot, but it sounded Ormani. Owen was still young, but he was a sharp boy, and his mother would be sure to tell him about which families were friendly to theirs and which were not.

"Owen," she said, brushing some of his wild hair from his face. "Do you know a family called 'Gallois'?"

The boy giggled.

"You say it funny," he said. "There's no 'ess' at the end. It's 'Gal-wah'. A boy at school, Georgie, he's a Gallois. He's nice, but his big brothers are real mean. I beat one up because he was mean to Georgie." He puffed out his chest. "I'm real good at fighting."

Rhiannon's smile grew wider. Of course he was. He was Nathie's son.

"I bet you are. I'm not bad myself, you know," she said with a wink. "Okay, I'm going to get changed and I'll meet you two in your room." Owen nodded and took off at a sprint, heading to the room he shared with his nanny. Rhiannon squeezed her eyes shut, saying a silent prayer to her staff, asking them for forgiveness.

She stood and closed the door. So Gallois *was* a name from Marigot, though that meant nothing on its own. But it was a start. Rhiannon knew where she could get more information, but she'd been avoiding the thought since she found out Rousseau had been taken. It made her sick, but if anyone in Wyndford knew who might want Rousseau gone, it would be Uncle Harrold. The man who had paid him to kill Rhiannon and her family.

"Absolutely not," Hal said, having just spat out some of his coffee. He and Allan had been sent for once the day reached a reasonable hour, and the two men had arrived promptly, giving a breathless and windblown Rhiannon an excuse to sit after playing with Owen and the dogs. Now they were seated with breakfast and coffee, for which Rhiannon was especially grateful.

"What he said," Allan said around a mouthful of toast. "Even if your evil uncle didn't kill you on sight, it would be bad for the trial. He could say you intimidated him or something."

"I plan on intimidating him," Rhiannon said, sipping her coffee. She reached for some of the sliced apples on the fruit tray. She had expected the men to be concerned and had prepared her arguments before they'd arrived. "Uncle Harrold wouldn't tell us anything without having a reason to do so. I plan to offer a stick and a carrot to help give him that reason." She bit into the fruit and sighed in pleasure. Fresh fruit had been a rarity out in the Bluffs. Now it was something she indulged in almost every morning. It wouldn't be long before they were out of season, and Rhiannon planned to have her fill until then.

"Okay, so what's the carrot?" Hal asked, dabbing some stray coffee drops from his vest with a napkin. "Assuming the stick is that you make him go missing."

"Speaking on his behalf at sentencing," Rhiannon said. "He's going to hang. We all know that. He knows that. I would request the judge to change the sentence to life imprisonment."

The table was quiet, and Rhiannon looked from Hal to Allan. They looked at each other, but it was Allan who turned back to her and nodded. Hal pressed his knuckles to his lips and frowned at the fruit.

"And you're sure you're willing to make that concession?" the detective asked, looking up at her. "I don't mean to doubt you, I just want you to be absolutely certain. This man did something terrible to your family. Most people would want to see him hang, no matter the cost."

"I'm certain," Rhiannon said with a confidence she didn't feel. She squared her shoulders and placed her hands in her lap. She couldn't sleep at night, kept up by the ghosts of her family memories. Rhiannon had always prided herself on her family's values of temperance and fairness. The death of Harrold wouldn't bring the missing Colfields back, no matter how much she wished it could.

"I've thought about this for a while," she said, smiling slightly at both men. "If Rousseau cannot be found, I would rather Harrold face justice and live, rather than walk free because I wanted his death."

"Alright, I'm going with you though," Allan said, his brown eyes clouded with worry. "Both as a police officer to monitor the situation, and because I don't trust that bastard a single inch."

Rhiannon felt her smile warm, and she watched the tanned skin of his ears grow bright. Millie's letter stuck in her mind, and suddenly shy, she looked back at her apple.

To her left, Hal groaned under his breath.

"Not this again," he muttered. Rhiannon pointedly ignored him, feeling her own cheeks grow warm.

"Harrold might not agree to see you," the Stratton said at normal volume. "But if you're willing to put that offer forward, I think it's worth a try." Hal sighed and poured himself some more coffee. "Too bad Berry isn't here. She'd be a great ace up our sleeve if we needed to use the stick method."

"She would," Rhiannon agreed, feeling her gut twist up into a knot. She shouldn't have let her friend leave without apologising. But what was done was done. Rhiannon would just have to wait for Millie to get back to talk about what happened. "But we're going to have to work with who we have."

Hal paused, coffee halfway up to his lips. He slowly set it down.

"You know," he said thoughtfully. "I think I know someone who would make a suitable replacement."

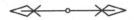

RHIANNON AND ALLAN WAITED in front of the house where Harrold was being kept under arrest. It was similar in size to the Goldmans' home, one of the tall greystone townhomes that sprung up in Wyndford for the upper middle class. While it grated on her that Harrold could live in moderate comfort, Rhiannon knew her uncle would see this home as much of a punishment as an actual cell would be. Given how easily Rousseau had been removed from the jail, the townhouse turned out to be the more secure option as well.

One of the police officers assigned to guarding Harrold stepped outside and greeted them all with a respectful nod. Stocky and short, the officer was almost certainly part dwarven, though it would be improper to ask. The dwarves largely kept to themselves in the steelworks quarter, but it was not unheard of for one of them to have a relationship with a human. Never with an elf or orc, though. At least not as far as Rhiannon knew.

"Sergeant, Miss. Colfield," the officer tilted their head back toward the home. "Corporal Plackitt at your service. The grumpy old bastard agreed to meet with you. For your safety, he'll be restrained to the chair by a shackle. If you feel uncomfortable or unsafe—"

Rhiannon smiled. Plackitt. Colfield Rail worked with the Plackitt refinery to buy iron for rivets. Definitely dwarven, in that case.

"I'll be fine, Corporal," she said. "We're just waiting for Detective Hal Stratton to join us." She looked up the street and saw a cab round the corner. As the horse trotted closer, Rhiannon spotted a familiar bowler hat. "I believe that's him."

Hal apologised before the cab even pulled to a stop. The severe-looking woman sitting next to him had her arms crossed over her chest and watched Rhiannon through narrowed eyes. Ah, so this was Millie's stand-in. Rhiannon had to admit the woman had quite a presence.

"This is Tabea. She works with Gilbert. Tabea, this is—"

"I know who you are," the woman said, her canines too long to be elven. Her ears were pointed, but immobile, and Rhiannon would have bet a dollar that under her hair hid two nubs of horn that hadn't grown in.

"Well, thank you for joining us," Rhiannon said, holding out her hand to shake.

The lower arroyan woman looked at it with a scowl, then marched past them all to the door.

"I am between meetings and since Mister Goldman is off on some *adventure* for your sake, I need this to be over quickly so I can get back and make sure we keep making you more money," Tabea said, opening the door. Hal shot Rhiannon an apologetic look and hurried after her.

Rhiannon blinked, and Allan sidled up to her.

"How are there two of them?" He muttered under his breath. "No wonder Goldman liked Berry so much."

Rhiannon bit back a laugh and covered her hand with her mouth to keep it from escaping. Tabea's demeanour explained why Gilbert had taken an immediate interest in Millie back in the Bluffs. She took a deep breath to regain her composure and followed Hal inside.

The home was furnished, but not lavish. There were no heavy vases that could be used as weapons, and all doors had been removed from their hinges, leaving Harrold no privacy to hurt himself or try to escape. Rhiannon paused at the parlour doorway, looking over at her uncle.

He was older than she remembered at his arrest. Always a slender man, Harrold was now almost gaunt, the dark circles under his eyes cast his sharp cheekbones into high relief. His silver hair was well kept, but she saw the way his hands trembled where they held onto the arms of the chair he was shackled to. Confinement did not agree with Harrold Colfield, and the knowledge he would find a lifetime in it to be punishing was enough to assuage any last-minute doubts Rhiannon might have had.

"Well," Harrold said, taking the moment to study her. "It looks as though the city isn't agreeing with you as much as you hoped it would. No pet elf to threaten me? Tsk." He clucked his tongue and shook his head. "Has she abandoned you so soon?"

A gentle hand rested on her back, and Rhiannon glanced up to see Allan standing next to her.

"Don't let him get to you," he whispered.

"She's away on other business," Rhiannon said, reining in the flush of anger at hearing Millie called a pet. Allan was right. Harrold was trying to get her angry so she would jeopardise the upcoming trial. She wouldn't let him have that satisfaction.

"Do you know why I'm here?" she asked, taking a seat on the sofa across from him. Tabea sat next to her, arms still crossed and looking as sharp as Millie ever had.

"To get something, I presume," Harrold said, leaning back in his chair. He folded his hands together in his lap, though it did little to hide the tremors. "Why else would you offer me a chance at survival? You're still a Colfield, after all. You know better than to make a bad deal."

Hearing Harrold call her a Colfield caught in Rhiannon's chest, tugging sharply at her heart. She didn't realise until that moment how badly she'd wanted to hear that, to be recognised as a member of the family... but not from Harrold. The man she wanted to hear acknowledge her as an adult of the family was dead at the whim of his brother.

"I am," she said, keeping her voice even. "Someone broke Frederic Rousseau out of Wyndford Jail. I'd like to know what you know."

Harrold blinked.

"You think I arranged this?" He asked, lifting his sparse eyebrows. "Oh little Rhiannon, I would rather he died in that cell. As you can see, my movements are monitored from the moment I wake up to the moment I go back to sleep. I had no way of arranging for such an escape."

"Well, that's the interesting part," Rhiannon said, keeping her expression cool and detached. It helped cool her temper, and she needed to be calm to deal with Harrold. "Whoever took Rousseau only took most of him. They left his hand and a message. We know you weren't involved, but whoever took him could just as easily use what he knows against you."

It was just a flicker of worry that creased Harrold's brow, but Rhiannon spotted it. Next to her, Tabea leaned forward, eyes suddenly fixed directly on Rhiannon's uncle with shark-like intensity.

"Why would anyone listen to some drunk?" Harrold asked. "If he's gone, that serves me just fine. You plan for me to hang, so anything Rousseau says would be useless against me."

"There are worse ways of dying," Tabea said, playing her part beautifully. "Maybe the rope is the wrong length. Maybe you don't die at the drop. There are plenty of ways someone could still hurt you, old man."

Harrold glanced at the arroyan woman, then back to Rhiannon. The crease on his brow had returned, giving away just how much Tabea had unnerved him. Rhi made a mental note to tell Gilbert to give his secretary a bonus after this.

"You offered to pay Rousseau's debts. Who did he owe money to?" Hal asked.

"That's what you want?" Harrold asked, the worry deepening into a frown. "Little girl, if I told you, your clemency would be undone by the retaliation I'd face for opening my mouth. Some debts can only be paid in blood. Those are ones I couldn't pay off for Rousseau, even if I was so inclined."

He coughed, holding a handkerchief to his lips.

"No, no," he said, shaking his head. "I choose the noose."

29

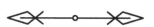

BLOOD ALCHEMY

NATHALIE

NATHALIE'S LABORATORY HAD REPLACED her most recent husband's study. The daylight streaming in through north-facing windows provided good light that wasn't direct enough to damage her ingredients, and she could open the windows to allow fresh air to circulate while mixing pungent concoctions.

Removing blood was a relatively simple process. She had removed countless blood stains from silk, satin, cotton, and more. Having an active and extremely curious eight-year-old boy meant there were scrapes and cuts aplenty in her household. Rather than replace rugs, sofas, and clothing every other day, Nathalie had learned how to remove the stains instead. Paper was like fabric, just a little more delicate. So long as she wasn't distracted, Nathalie was confident she could get the blood off the assassin's note.

Plucking a small vial from her shelf, she double-checked the label even though she knew exactly what each vial contained. Vishap acid, carefully harvested and kept in dark glass to keep the sun from breaking the precious substance into useless saltwater. Putting on a pair of thick vishap-skin gloves, Nathie measured out two drops into a flask of water. Next came a pinch of dried ghost flower root to transform the acid into a solution that would eat the blood, without destroying the paper it had soaked.

Stirring the concoction, Nathie ignited the heating element the flask sat on. The round iron disc flickered and sputtered out, refusing to warm. With a frown, she checked that the disk was properly seated in its cradle of clay. It was. Nothing had marred the runes stamped into the iron either, so why wasn't it working?

Nathie's frown turned to a scowl. She straightened, turning around to look at the room. Mildred was standing with her back toward Nathalie, looking over the books on her shelves. She hadn't even heard the other woman come in. That was disturbing. Nathie prided herself on being aware of her surroundings. Mildred might not be an immediate threat, but no one should be able to move that quietly. It defied nature.

"You are interrupting my work, you know," Nathie said, throwing her gloves onto her desk with an audible 'thump'. The elf's ears perked at the sound, and she turned around to smile a bit sheepishly.

"Sorry. I was curious, but I didn't want to make you jump while you were working on anything dangerous." Hands tucked behind her back, Mildred walked over to peer at the flask that sat on the still-dark heating element. "Is it broken? What's it supposed to be doing?" she asked, reaching a finger out to touch the metal. Nathalie slapped it away before Mildred could destroy the magic in the runes for good.

"That is supposed to warm up, but *strangely,* it is not working," Nathie said coolly. "Do you have anything to say for yourself?"

Mildred straightened, rubbing the back of her hand with no sign of remorse. She looked at Nathie with those lilac eyes that had once haunted Nathalie's dreams, but now just haunted her days. It would have helped if Mildred were uglier, Nathie thought. As horrid as that was, she could hold fast against eyes like that if they weren't part of a woman who was so... so... infuriating.

"Oh, right," Mildred said. "You weren't at the shop when Ghat explained. You know how water has springs, where the water comes out of the ground?"

Nathie arched an eyebrow. Where the hell was this going?

"I'm the opposite. A sink hole for magic," the elf said, still watching her intently.

"I've never heard of that before, but of course you are," Nathie said, rolling her eyes. "You couldn't just be a normal elf. You had to be a weird one. Now, will you step out into the hall for a minute so I can heat the solution?"

The elf relaxed, breaking the intense stare, and smiled. Nathie felt like she'd passed a test, but wasn't sure what the test had been for.

"Sure," Mildred said, looking over the vials of ingredients Nathie had on her shelves. She reached up and picked up one jar with thin tubers that had grown in tendrils, suspended in a saltwater solution to keep them fresh. "Oh, you have wytchroot? Can I have some?"

"Out," Nathalie said. "Why would you even want wytchroot? It's used for toothaches and warts." She took the jar from Mildred's hand and placed it back on the shelf.

Then she gave the elf a little (but not gentle) shove toward the door.

"I'll let you know when I'm done," Nathalie grumbled. "Shouldn't you be bothering your husband anyways?"

"He's gone to see Pierre already," Mildred said, hesitating at the door. Nathalie scowled at her, but the elf seemed unphased. Turning back to face her, Mildred took a deep breath like she was about to vomit.

"I'm sorry, you know," she said, watching Nathalie with those disconcerting eyes. "About Pierre."

Nathalie felt her mental walls snap up to guard herself against whatever the elf was about to say. She didn't want to hear it. Pity from the Bayou Butcher would be a blow to Nathie's ego that she wasn't sure she could ever recover from.

"Pierre made his own choices," she said. "I'd rather not talk to you about it."

"Because I know how much it hurts," the elf said, looking away. "Because I'm the only one who can understand the pain that comes with loving a Rousseau." She smiled to herself, and Nathie wanted to shout at her to leave, but her voice seemed to get stuck in her throat. Unfortunately, Mildred took her silence as a sign to continue talking.

"It's funny. I used to say the same thing you did. That Fred wasn't a brute like his father was. That his offer to fight in exchange for our freedom was a sign he was different. That he was better."

"I know what men like Frederic are like," Nathalie said. Her voice sounded distressingly weak, wavering even to her own ears. "I was certain that I'd know the signs if I saw them in Pierre." But she had missed them, hadn't she? "I should have listened, back on the train. When he used your old name."

Mildred smiled, but there was only sadness in her eyes.

"Maybe. Maybe I'm wrong, and maybe Pierre can change," the elf said gently. "I have. And if I could change, there's hope for him."

Nathie wasn't sure how she could answer that. It was clear from their interactions that Mildred had indeed changed from the blood-thirsty sergeant that led the sacking of Marigot. Nathie had seen her with her daughters, doting and motherly while one was yelling about strangers. How many times had Nathie sent barbed comments the elf's way, only for Mildred to keep her temper in check? And most importantly, Rhiannon loved her. That should have been enough for Nathalie to realise the elf had changed.

"I will keep that in mind," Nathie said, surprising herself as she realised she meant what she said. "However, I really must ask you to step outside or this process won't work."

With a small nod, Mildred finally opened the door and stepped into the hallway. Nathalie shut it behind her and locked it to keep the elf out until she was done. Returning to her desk, Nathie braced her hands on her worktable and closed her eyes. She took a few deep breaths to calm her nerves. There were times when she could allow herself to feel her full emotions, but it was not when she was handling strong acid and a delicate note.

Feeling her heart calm, she opened her eyes and set to work. Nathie ignited the heating plate again and was pleased to see the runes flare to life. She didn't need to boil the solution, only warm it enough so that the ghost flower root and the acid reacted, turning the solution a faint blue.

The moment the solution darkened, Nathalie took the flask off the heat and poured it over the stained note in a low glass tray. The blood fizzed on contact, building up a pink foam as the solution ate away the stain, leaving the paper behind. With a small pair of tongs, Nathalie agitated the paper slightly. She could see the ink appear as the blood faded. It was a brief note, but there was a splotch, an emblem of something in the lower right corner that was still too stained to make out.

Setting the tongs down, Nathalie started toward the door, only to see it crack open just wide enough for Mildred to stick her head inside.

"Is it ready?" she asked. Looking from Nathie to the desk, where steam rose from the tray.

Nathalie frowned. "I locked that."

"I know," Mildred said, slipping inside. "It's a pretty good lock, too. Good choice." Walking up to the desk, the elf completely ignored Nathalie's glare and frowned down at the paper. "It's eating the mark," she said. "Is it supposed to do that?"

"What?" Nathalie turned and lifted the paper out of the solution with her tongs. Immediately, she dipped it into a jar of water and swirled it around to stop the reaction. But the damage was done. Whatever sigil or mark had been at the bottom of the note had been eaten away in blotches, leaving it indecipherable.

Heart sinking, Nathalie pulled the paper from the water and smoothed it out onto a cotton pad that would absorb the water, leaving the note to dry flat.

"I don't understand," she said, squinting at what was left of the mark. "The solution only eats blood. It shouldn't have eaten any of the ink. The ghost flower should have stopped that."

"Well, it didn't," Mildred said unhelpfully, pointing to the remainder of the note. The black ink used there was perfectly legible, written in an elegant hand that made Nathalie think of Pierre's handwriting. There were differences, to be certain, but perhaps the author had attended the same school Pierre had? It was worth asking.

"The woman who killed your parents will be on the next ferry. Take her, and the chattel debt is gone," Mildred read. "Signed, blotch."

"What's a chattel debt?" Nathalie asked. "Is that over livestock?"

The elf's ears drooped, and Mildred looked up at Nathalie. She wasn't sure if it was pain or grief that clouded the elf's expression, but the two were so often bedfellows that it didn't matter.

"Not livestock," Nathalie said, feeling ill again. "People."

"People *were* the livestock." Mildred sighed, looking back at the blotch. "It could be anything, but it's not your fault. I think whoever sent this signed it in blood. My guess is a master who survived the war."

The elf frowned. "You know, the message on the wall in Wyndford Jail was written in fancy people's grammar. Not informal Orman."

"Fancy? Do you mean it was written in proper grammar?" Nathalie asked, wondering if she should go back to hating the elf. She seemed to be more annoying as an ally than she had been as an enemy.

"Same thing," Mildred said with a shrug. She looked up at Nathalie's cabinet of ingredients and picked up a small jar of powdered striped frog. "Whoever we're looking for is one of the old families. How many are left? O'Leary had a whole squadron of children, but all his sons fought and I killed one leading up to the war."

"Don't touch that. It will knock you right out if you breathe it," Nathalie said, taking the jar from Mildred's hand and putting it back onto the shelf where it belonged. "Aside from O'Leary, there are the Wolfes, which are myself and my eight-year-old son. There are the Pacquets, although they hit hard times after the war. I don't know if they could hire anyone these days. But they still exist. Pierre is all that's left in Marigot of the Rousseaus, and the Gallois' have one surviving son from the war, but plenty of grandchildren." Nathalie pursed her lips as she thought.

Many of the truly wealthy families survived, but had reduced how prominent they were in Marigot, preferring to lie low and continue life as best they could without drawing more shame from business partners in the Union over losing the war.

"I have to visit someone that might help," Mildred said. "At Rhiannon's party, someone planted a gris-gris on me."

Nathalie straightened in surprise, looking at Mildred with wide eyes. Conjure hadn't found purchase up north like it had in Beaulieu. Partially because there had been fewer Bakimban settlers where it snowed, but also because there hadn't been nearly as many slaves who needed to keep their magic subtle to avoid angering their masters. After all, why would a mage ask for something to happen when they could make it happen on their own?

"Who?" she asked, bristling. How dare someone (other than herself) harm one of Rhiannon's guests?

Mildred made a face and lifted her hands. "I don't know. It was a big party, and I was trying not to make a mess of it by punching some rich asshole in the face. At first I thought it might have been you. I didn't think it was related to Fred or anything, just a way of getting me out of Rhiannon's life. Not that it would have worked. Rhiannon's like a sister to me. I'd do anything for her."

Nathalie felt a pang of regret that she hadn't thought of that earlier, though she supposed it wouldn't work any better in the elf's presence than the heating element had.

"Besides, I don't see any evidence of you making them here," Mildred said, looking around at the laboratory. "And the spell is one I don't think you would cast on anyone. It was specifically to call a slave to heel."

She had no words for that. Nathalie would have considered a gris-gris to make Mildred less in control of her emotions, one to make her go away, to have discord in her personal connections, but no, she would have never thought to bring the woman to heel.

"That's why you were visiting Madame Lavoie?" Nathalie asked. "Is she the one who will be able to tell who made them?"

Mildred shook her head.

"No, I have to visit someone else. I might be gone for a while, and I have to go with Ghat alone. Her rules, not mine," Mildred said, holding up a hand before Nathie could complain. "Please, stay safe while I'm gone. The closer we get to finding out who is responsible, the more vicious they'll get."

There wasn't a single thing the elf could have said that would have been more shocking to Nathalie. She blinked, dumbfounded, as the pale elf patted Nathalie's shoulder and slipped out of the room. Nothing that woman did made any sense to Nathalie, especially lately. If she was a killer, why did she care so much about people who didn't like her?

But Mildred had just told her.

'Rhiannon is like a sister to me.'

What a shame that Frederic Rousseau had wasted that loyalty for so long. Nathalie closed up her cabinets, too distracted by thoughts of the elf to notice her jar of powdered frog was missing.

30

ROUSSEAU HOUSE

GILBERT

GILBERT ALLOWED HIMSELF TO sulk on the short walk from Nathalie's house to Pierre's. Millie had woken him up early with the news she might not be back that night, and then practically shoved him out the door for him to get started with Pierre.

She'd also given him the gun she'd taken off their attackers, and told Gilbert not to hesitate if he needed to kill anyone. He supposed that was Millie's way of telling him she cared. That and the way she'd drilled him that morning on how to load and fire the revolver until she was satisfied. The thought brought a small smile to his face. You could take the elf out of the army, but you couldn't take the sergeant out of the elf.

The air had changed that morning, a cooler breeze sweeping in from the ocean and dark clouds roiled overhead. It would rain before the day was out. Gilbert just hoped the weather held until he arrived at the sad excuse for a home called Rousseau House. As he approached the gate, Gilbert felt a prickle run up the back of his neck.

He glanced around, but this early, the only people on the street were servants tidying up the lavish homes of their, well, not owners. Not anymore. But how different was life for the non-human servants, really? He supposed they didn't get branded anymore, but that should have been a baseline humanoid right.

Something moved across the street: a curtain in a window of the house with young orange trees rippled gently. Whoever had been peering past it was gone. Gilbert studied the house, noting the expensive upkeep on wrought-iron gates similar to Nathalie's. Only these were whitewashed to look bright and inviting while each post ended in a spike. The cherry trees would eventually grow tall enough to offer shade and privacy, but the saplings were still too short to hide any snooping neighbours from view.

Making a note to ask Pierre who lived there, Gilbert continued on.

The front door was in no better repair than it had been the day Millie had caught out Nathalie and Pierre's relationship. Gilbert stepped up and rapped sharply on the wood, finding it slimy to the touch. He wasn't sure how Millie had survived this city for so long. Everything was damp all the time, mould grew everywhere, and the bugs were atrocious.

The door clunked and lifted before swinging inward. Pierre peered out at Gilbert with bleary eyes. He blinked twice and straightened, running a hand through his messy hair. It looked like the man had had a rough night, dark circles already staining the hollows under those blue Rousseau eyes. Gilbert felt an urge to punch the man and shook it off. Pierre was clearly a coward in the face of his terrible older brother, but Gil had put up with Frederic long enough to know how easy it was to just ignore the man's behaviour to avoid an outburst.

"Did I wake you?" Gilbert asked, arching an eyebrow.

"No, no," Pierre mumbled, stepping aside to let Gilbert inside. An orcish woman, stooped with age, was sweeping the front hall fruitlessly. "Just a little," Pierre confessed as Gilbert stepped into the home. The smell of damp and mildew was present, but less than Gilbert had expected, given the state of the home's exterior. "I had to get up anyways."

Good God, the man had no spine at all, did he? He couldn't even admit Gilbert had inconvenienced him.

"Well, if you show me to the ledgers, I can start reviewing them while you get yourself sorted," Gilbert said with a nod. "Looks like you didn't sleep very well."

Pierre smiled at Gilbert and it was about the saddest thing he'd ever seen in his life.

"I showed her the cellar," Pierre said. "Nathalie, I mean."

"I know who you meant," Gilbert said with a small sigh. "Millie told me about the cellar. Nathalie told us she'd seen it. She also told us what you two had planned for the trial, so all the secrets are out in the open now and I'd appreciate it if you go wash up and pull yourself together."

Pierre had the decency to look embarrassed and nodded.

"Marga," he called out to the orc woman, but she kept sweeping, her head down. He cleared his throat and shot Gilbert an apologetic look before walking over to her and tapping her elbow. Looking up at him, then at Gilbert, Marga huffed.

"Pierre, you should have told me your guest had arrived," she said, straightening her apron. She bobbed her head at Gilbert before tottering off, leaning on the broom like it was a walking stick. "Goodness, I'll go put the water on for some coffee."

"I'll show you to the study where you can get started," Pierre said, waving Gilbert to follow him. The townhouse had opulent bones, with high ceilings to help with the heat and crown moulding ringed every room. They headed up the wide staircase, its mahogany steps still firm in the pervasive humidity of the swamp. They barely creaked under the two men as they reached the second floor, where Pierre led Gilbert to a room off to the right.

"This is where I spend most of my time, admittedly," Pierre said, opening the door and stepping aside for Gilbert. "Unlike many of my peers, I actually have to work for a living."

The study was tidy, with shelf after shelf of leather-backed books on law and agricultural regulations dating back to pre-war times. The wooden desk inside was much more modest than the beast that had been at Frederic's house before Millie blew it up. Pierre's desk was simple in comparison, and stacked with ledgers, familiar in how wide and squat they were in comparison with the law books that dominated the space.

"Marga will bring up refreshments shortly, and I'll be back as soon as I—" he paused and looked down at himself. Pierre frowned. "Resolve this. Apologies again."

"See you soon," Gil said with a nod. Without waiting for Pierre to leave, Gil made his way over to the desk and sat, stretching his bad leg out in front of him with a small groan. The salve Madame Ghat had provided helped in the morning, but the incoming weather made the newly healed joint ache. Suddenly, Gil regretted every time he'd teased his father about his bad knees. It was far less funny to learn that joints really could hurt before a storm.

Pulling the stack of ledgers toward him, Gil saw Pierre had thoughtfully organised them in chronological order, starting with the most recent book on top. Gilbert set it aside and pulled out the ledger of the year the war began. Opening it, he flipped through until he spotted a name he recognised.

MILDRED ARGENT (S) — PURCHASE OF ONE WRIT OF FREEDOM FOR W. BLACKWATER, $600.

Gilbert ran a hand over his face, holding his chin as he read that entry over again. How a slave was expected to save up that much money at all was shocking, but to save up that much and then spend it on someone else's freedom? It felt like a long time ago now, but back in Scorched Bluffs, Millie had told him she was a bad person. Gilbert knew bad people. He'd handled their money for his entire career, and it was only when Rhiannon moved her funds to his bank that Gilbert had an ethical patron.

Millie had bought her mentor his freedom, and still thought she was a villain who deserved the hatred she faced on the street. Pulling a scrap of notepaper over, Gilbert copied the line down, and flipped through, searching for a different name. It was on the same page; the purchase listed as occurring the day after Millie's.

CLEMENTINE LA PAZ (S) — PURCHASE OF ONE WRIT OF FREEDOM FOR A. LA PAZ, $200.

A few lines below, a third familiar name.

DELILAH LAVOIE (S) — PURCHASE OF ONE WRIT OF FREEDOM FOR G. LAVOIE, $400

They knew the war was coming, Gilbert realised. And they'd bought freedom for the people that couldn't fight.

Annie would have been a young girl back then, Blackwater might have been getting old... He wasn't sure of Ghat's age and instinct told Gilbert that it was best not to ask, but she must have been the younger sister or the daughter of this 'Delilah'.

The door opened, and Marga entered, tottering in with a tray of coffee and freshly buttered toast. Her rheumy eyes twinkled and her silver hair was pulled back into a bun from which wild strands had made their escape some time ago.

"Coffee, sir," she chirped, making her careful way to the desk where Gilbert sat. He rose, intending to help her, but she clucked her tongue at him the moment he did.

"No, no, I saw you with your cane," she said, staring him down. "You need to sit, poor thing. Did you get injured in the war?"

Gilbert blinked. He rather thought he looked a touch too young to have fought, but there had been rumours of the Marigot Rebels enlisting boys to fight, as the secessionists grew desperate.

"Ah, no, this is rather recent, I'm afraid," Gilbert said. "Marga, right? How long have you worked for Pierre?"

Settling the tray on the desk next to Gilbert, Marga lifted the coffeepot with trembling hands and poured Gilbert a cup, the hot liquid nearly escaping once or twice. Gilbert eased his outstretched leg further away from the woman.

"Oh my, I've worked here since I was born, Sir," she said with a smile that turned her face into a lovely mess of wrinkles. "I watched Pierre grow up into the lovely boy he is, always so kind and thoughtful. He is."

Gilbert smiled back, though his opinion differed from Marga's about the youngest Rousseau.

"Did you happen to know an elf that worked for—"

All warmth dropped from Marga's face, and she looked at Gilbert like he'd brought up the dead. Leaning over the tray, Marga stared into his face with her bloodshot grey eyes.

"Do not mention her," Marga said, waving a gnarled finger under Gil's nose. "To mention her is to summon her, and my good boy Pierre doesn't need her to ruin him like she ruined Freddie. Pierre is a *good boy*, sir. Let him stay that way."

Gilbert debated mentioning that he was actually married to the 'her' in question, and that she was off slogging through a swamp on some godforsaken pilgrimage, so she wouldn't show up anytime soon. Instead, he put on his best schoolboy apologetic look and pressed a hand to his chest.

"My apologies, Marga. What did she do to Freddie?" He could barely say the name without laughing. Frederic, the illegitimate war hero of Amelior, violent drunk, and torturer of elves, was called 'Freddie' by the staff.

Marga shook her head and backed away.

"No, no," she muttered. "No, I can't. I won't. I won't. She's gone. She's *dead*." The orc tottered from the study, muttering under her breath about ghosts. She nearly bowled over Pierre, who had just reached the doorway in fresh clothing. Pierre let Marga by, brow knitting in concern.

"You asked her about Mildred," he said, walking over to join Gilbert at the desk. "You shouldn't have done that. Marga's a sweet lady."

Gilbert lifted his cup of coffee and blew the steam from it. It smelled earthy and dark, far fresher than the stuff he could get up in Wyndford. One benefit of living so close to the Nahuatl border, he supposed. He took a small sip and set the cup down to cool for a little longer.

"What happened?" he asked, tilting his head toward the hallway. "Why does she think talking about Millie will 'summon' her?"

Pierre sighed and ran a hand through his hair. It was brushed now, and the man had washed, making him much better company.

"There's been rumours among the non-humans and Bakimbans that the Butcher never left," Pierre said. "But I knew where Mildred was for three years and after that, I figured she was dead. I knew it couldn't be her committing any murders, but the rumours were all the same. A family or couple would be killed with an axe, no witnesses, no survivors. Marga believes the recent killings are Mildred, or Mildred's ghost."

He shrugged and poured himself a cup of coffee, adding two spoonfuls of sugar to it with a silver teaspoon. Gilbert watched, unable to stop from trying to figure out how much sugarcane had gone into making those two spoonfuls, and how many workers were needed to grow and harvest it.

"So there are two Butchers," Gilbert said, waving away Pierre's offer of sugar. "Millie wouldn't target non-humans, though." He frowned, trying to make sense of it. Gilbert wished Hal was here. He'd know the right question to ask to unlock more information. The best Gilbert could do was try to imagine what his friend would say. "Not without a reason," he murmured. "No one kills without a reason, so what do the victims all have in common?"

Pierre raised his eyebrows.

"Well, they're all freed slaves, or families of freed slaves, but so are most residents of Marigot at this point. They outnumbered freeborn humans four to one before a bunch of orcish folk left to set up their own town in the bayou."

Four to one. That number was staggering. Four slaves to every Pierre, Fred, and Nathalie. Working to make their lives as smooth as possible by providing food, shelter, entertainment for fractions of pennies.

"Well, I suppose the question is, who stood to lose the most from the war?" Gilbert murmured, tapping his knuckle against his lips.

Pierre's expression turned grim, and he set his cup down.

"Every single master family," he said. "We, and one other house, joined the Union. A few stayed officially neutral, like Nathalie's. Her father didn't want to risk retaliation from either side, but ended up dead by Mildred's hand anyways." Pierre rubbed the back of his neck and sighed.

"I don't blame Mildred, you know," Pierre said, looking away. "It's hard to understand if you've never been in battle, but I saw the soldiers coming back from the front. They were so thin and they were haunted by what they'd seen." Gilbert watched Pierre's face grow tight and noticed the creeping colour on his ears. Was Pierre ashamed he'd never fought?

"For all his failings, of which there are many," Pierre continued. "Mildred and my brother stayed behind enemy lines to harass and sabotage the Marigot army. After the first year, we couldn't get supplies through to them, not by river or rail. They had to survive on their own for the rest of the war. When Nathalie told me her father was killed, I could only assume it was because they needed something he had, and couldn't risk a master telling the Marigot army where they were."

Yes, Gilbert thought, watching the flush spread to Pierre's cheeks and neck. He was ashamed he'd never seen combat while his older brother was being a war hero. The lesser Rousseau, indeed.

Gilbert lifted his coffee and took another tentative sip. It had cooled enough in the thin china cup that it would no longer scald his mouth.

"Have you told Nathalie that?" Gil asked. "That you don't blame Mildred for this?"

Pierre shook his head. "How could I? This was her father. She watched it happen. She told me she had nightmares about ghost elves for years." He looked up from the floor and met Gilbert's eyes.

"Do you tell Mildred when you don't approve?"

Gilbert snorted.

"Frequently and loudly, but she doesn't listen," he said. "But I still tell her, because whatever this marriage of ours is, it's honest. I married her knowing she was the Butcher, and she married me, knowing I was a financier." He hadn't realised it until he said the words, but it was true. There were no secrets between him and Millie since Scorched Bluffs. A few misunderstandings, but she hadn't hidden how frightening the Rousseau house had been for her, or the concern that she might slip into old habits while in Marigot.

"I don't think it's the right time," Pierre muttered. "She just found out about the cellar."

"I think it's exactly the right time," Gilbert said. "She found out the worst thing about you, but you made her find out from someone who has hurt her badly. Just tell her the rest, and see if you can pry out whatever secrets she's keeping in that iron thing she calls a heart."

Pierre shot Gilbert a glare.

"It was a joke," Gilbert said, rolling his eyes. "Go on, I'll be fine reading these. I promise I won't antagonise Marga any further."

With a deep breath, Pierre stood and smoothed out his vest. Nodding to himself, he left Gilbert in the study and called for Marga to let her know he was stepping out.

Gilbert waited, ears straining to hear Pierre descend the stairs, and only when he heard the thud of the door close did he stand and limp over to the bookshelves of pre-war legislature. The ledgers out on the table were incomplete. He could see as much while he'd skimmed for information on Millie and her friends. Fred might not have been good at keeping his books in order, but this was Marigot. No doubt he'd had a slave to handle them until war broke out, and a slave wouldn't risk leaving anything undocumented in case his master asked where the last ten dollars had gone. Not when a master could kill you on a whim.

So where were the secret ledgers hidden?

31

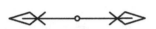

FERRYMAN'S PILGRIMAGE

MILLIE

GHAT AND MILLIE PADDLED upriver, with Mulatiwa draped along the canoe's yoke. They'd left right after Nathalie had finished cleaning the assassin's note, with Millie leaving the dog in Annie's care for the time being. The women made up the lost time on the water, digging in against the Eyatsi's current until they turned up one of the river's tributaries and into the swamp proper.

Despite the canoe's narrow profile, fighting the current left Millie's shoulders aching by the time they reached the flat, brackish water. For a moment, she closed her eyes and breathed in the earthy smell of rotting leaf matter as if it was perfume.

As a girl, Millie's father brought her out to the swamp to learn how to fish and catch frogs. After his death, she hadn't returned until it was with Blackwater, who taught her how to survive in the wild: which snakes were venomous and which frogs oozed poison. He'd taught her that vishap eyes shone red in low light, just like hers did. He'd also taught her how to navigate the endless labyrinth of flooded trails, reedy clumps, and sunken logs. Despite the unpleasant smell, the swamp had been the home of so many good memories that it always felt like a homecoming.

"You are so weird," Ghat muttered from the rear of the canoe.

Millie smiled over her shoulder and made a show of sniffing the air.

"Do you think your grandmother will accept me into the family if I ask?" Millie teased. Ghat snorted and shook her head, but the elf spotted the way Ghat's lips twitched upward in an almost smile.

"If you ask, she might turn you into a pasty white toad," Ghat said, shaking her head. "I'm still surprised she ever let you into LaFlotte."

A small community of escaped slaves, LaFlotte was named after the rafts the town was built on. While the floating foundations put the residents at risk of vishap attacks, it had made hiding the community from bounty hunters much easier. The town floated around the swamp, and could scatter if the need arose. It made finding the place difficult, but Millie had smuggled in food and goods from Marigot both before the war and during it. Hell, she'd even helped slaves escape as part of the Ferryman network, guiding them through the swamp to the relative safety of LaFlotte.

Millie had never met Granddame Lavoie, though she had heard about her from Delilah and Clem. During the war, Ghat's grandmother had still been alive and oversaw the protection of LaFlotte. She decided who was allowed to find the hidden town and who was not. Millie had only been allowed to its very edge to trade, while Annie and Ghat had lived there for the duration of the war.

Granddame Lavoie was also a name that was never to be mentioned in front of a master, no matter how kind they might seem. To do so would bring poor luck down on whoever let the secret slip until such a time as the person could convince the master the woman was merely a folktale. The Granddame had become as much a legend as the Bayou Butcher, said to be born in the swamp itself and taught conjure by the spirits that called it home.

"Here we are," Ghat said, dipping her paddle down and resting it against the muddy bottom to keep the canoe from drifting. Mulatiwa slithered over from his perch and coiled himself around the paddle and thwart, one of the cross beams holding the canoe's shape. With the snake acting as their anchor, Ghat let go of the paddle and opened her pack, digging into it.

"I can't believe you're making me walk the rest of the way," Millie muttered, turning around in her seat and pulling off her boots. They'd get stuck in the mud if she tried to wear them, so she was leaving them and most of her kit in the canoe where it could stay dry. As dry as anything got in the bayou's humidity, anyways.

"If you want to speak with the Granddame, you must make a proper pilgrimage," Ghat said, and tossed her the flask. "Don't fuck it up." Millie caught the flask and uncorked it, sniffing what was inside out of habit.

"It's tea, Mildred. You need to see the spirits if you want to find her home."

"Do I drink all of it?" Millie asked, hefting the flask. It wasn't large, at least. She made a small face at the prospect of seeing spirits. The spirits around the Ghost Eye camp were one thing, since they were kept fed and happy by Grannie Whitewing; but according to Ghat and Annie, the spirits of the swamp were feral, hungry things.

"All of it."

"Great," Millie said dryly. She took a sip, and once she was certain the tea was only lukewarm and not hot, downed the flask in a few gulps. It was bitter and floral, surprising Millie with how pleasant it tasted. Usually, medicine and spells tasted awful. She recorked the empty flask and tossed it back to Ghat.

Millie carefully climbed out of the canoe, balancing her weight with one hand on either gunwale as she stepped into the murky water. It was refreshing as long as she didn't think about how many snakes and vishaps were in it. Hopefully, Ghat's tea would leave her clear-headed enough to avoid them, or she might end up returning with half as many arms as she started with.

"Here." Ghat lit a lantern and held it out for Millie. "This will tell the spirits you are coming to seek knowledge, so long as it is lit, it will grant you safe passage."

Millie picked up the lantern and frowned as it immediately flickered. It felt full of oil, so that wasn't the problem. The wind had picked up, promising the storm's arrival was imminent, but the lantern was shielded by glass.

"Ghat," she asked, wary. "Is this lantern magic?"

"Have a good walk, Mildred."

Grumbling about weird-ass rituals and weird-ass magic, Millie headed deeper into the swamp. She felt forward with her foot on every step to avoid tripping over a sunken branch or log, feet sinking into rotting leaves and mud.

"Oh, fine," Ghat said, "Go on then." Millie turned and watched as Mulatiwa slipped into the water, his golden and white scales glowing in the murky water. He swam over to Millie, his snout poking up above the water, and Millie could have sworn the snake smiled.

"Oh, thanks, buddy," Millie said, running a cautious hand over his head. He was bigger than he'd been in the canoe, she was certain of it. Maybe it was the tea taking effect, or maybe the snake just liked to be big. Millie, all five-foot-nothing of her, wouldn't mind feeling tall once in a while. Wiping her hand on her shirt, she pulled out her axe and started forward.

It was slow going. Every step Millie took had to be tested first, and she couldn't risk standing in one spot for more than a second or two. Out here, the silt was so deep that if she didn't keep moving, she would sink down until she got stuck. Then it wouldn't matter if she had a lantern or not. The vishaps would finish her off.

Fireflies danced between the curtains of moss that hung from scraggly trees, and from the corner of her eye, Millie spotted a blue light deep in the swamp, beckoning her toward it. She ignored the will-o'-the-wisp, well aware that the light was the glowing tail of a particularly nasty species of basilisk. Their tails glowed blue, and the animal would use it to lure unsuspecting prey toward where they waited, hidden underwater.

The mud was too fine and too deep to risk venturing out onto the battlefield to collect the bodies.

Millie stood watch while the others rested, her back to the camp and the orange glow of the campfire's coals. It provided the few humans of the company with enough light to avoid tripping over the tent ropes, but it was bright enough to ruin her night vision if she spent too long looking in that direction. Instead, she watched the dark field ahead.

What had once been left fallow was now churned to a quagmire by Unionist and secessionist alike. vishaps, able to crawl through the mud with ease, paid no mind to what colour the corpse wore. Covered in mud, the bodies all looked the same.

"It reminds me to be humble," rumbled Akhun. As usual, he had crept up on her, stepping so quietly that not even elven ears could hear him coming. Millie looked over at her friend as he crouched, sitting on his heels. He was still almost as tall as she was, even then. Backlit by the fire's embers, every scar and craggy wrinkle carved deep into his green skin as though it were stone. He squinted out into the night, his already narrow eyes turned to slits as he watched the battlefield.

"Because we can be eaten?" Mildred asked, looking back out at the dreadful feast. Eyes shining red in the campfire's light, one vishap wandered close enough for Millie to get a good look. His crest was flushed red, protecting his supple neck from the bites of predators. The rest of his long body was plated with bone, mottled blue and yellow. Powerful limbs pulled him through the mud, his rudder-like tail dragging behind him. Lifting its head, the vishap sniffed at the air in the camp's direction. Millie raised her rifle and sighted down it.

"One shot won't kill it," Akhun warned.

"I don't need to kill it," Millie said, waiting to see what the animal would do. "I just need to make it bleed."

Akhun rumbled in agreement. The vishaps of the swamp were cannibalistic. Any injured animal was irresistible to them. Even a bull male of their own kind.

The vishap swung its head away and sniffed the air again. Catching the scent of something far tastier, it swung around and headed deeper into the battlefield.

"Not because we can be eaten," Akhun said to her earlier question, resting his elbows on his knees. "Because this was the only way to be free, Mildred." She looked down at him with a frown. He turned to look up at her, his scarred and craggy face splitting into a smile. The hole in his chest bled red embers that drifted off into the night air, consuming him from the inside out.

Millie rubbed her eyes with the back of her hand, trying to scrub away the memory. Akhun hadn't stood with her that night. He'd been one of the corpses on the battlefield. In the morning, Clem had sailed overhead, searching for his body, but the vishaps had taken it in the night.

Back in the swamp, Mulatiwa bumped his head into her thigh, bringing her back to the present. He was as thick around as she was now, his head the size of a tombstone. Millie flicked her ears, trying to stay focused. While distracted by the memory, Millie had stopped moving and her feet had sunk into the fine mud. She wrenched one foot free and stepped forward. Slamming the spike of her axe into a nearby tree trunk, Millie hauled herself forward, freeing her other foot.

Yanking her axe free, Millie continued and tried to ignore the shadow that walked beside her. It was the tea; she reminded herself. It was making her slip between the physical and spirit worlds. Of course, she was seeing ghosts, even if they were only ghosts that haunted her memories.

"I can't wait for this to be over," she told Mulatiwa. The snake chuckled, a deep rumbling laughter that Millie felt in her chest.

You will sssssssee. Sssssssoon.

The snake lifted its head out of the water and looked back at her, waiting. The snake was talking. Unconvinced that Ghat's tea was helpful and not just causing her to hallucinate, Millie shrugged. The snake was talking. There were worse things the snake could do than talk. At least it wasn't a fucking Vishap singing Wheeler hymns.

"Okay," Millie said to Mulatiwa, stepping over a sunken log and following him. The lantern, which had been sputtering, now burned steadily, its golden light almost comforting. But it was the lantern's light that cast the shadows which seemed to follow her, whispering about the Bayou Butcher, whispering about the Ghost of Marigot. Whispering about Mildred Berry.

"Go!" Delilah shouted, shouldering the old city gate open and planting her feet so that the human soldiers on the other side couldn't push her back. Bullets peppered her, each sending up scarlet embers that drifted through the smoke overhead.

"Tell Ghat," she said, throwing a flaming Marigot cocktail over the nearest barricade. The men behind it screamed as the bottle burst and fled like rats, unable to put themselves out. "Tell her I don't regret it. I don't regret it for one moment." The last bullet shattered Delilah into a thousand embers, caught by an updraft, and spun up into the sky.

Millie stood on the bloody cobblestones just outside the old city centre, and stared at the place her friend had once stood.

"Don't," Millie warned, gritting her teeth. Her throat was hot, and she forced herself to keep moving, mostly by feel. Her eyes brimmed with tears and she could swear she heard Delilah's voice among the whispers from the trees.

"Don't show me more," she whispered to the swamp. Millie wasn't sure if she was threatening the spirits or begging them to stop. She closed her eyes. "I never forgot, I don't need to see—"

Further into the city, Millie crouched behind an overturned cab and watched the dark, smoky sky. Clem spiralled down, trailing embers from where a bullet had pierced her chest. She dissolved into her human shape as she fell into Millie's arms. This time, Millie didn't ask for a report or issue any orders. She curled around her first and closest friend and wept, begging Clem to forgive her.

"Forgive you? For what?" Clem smiled, already falling apart in Millie's arms. "We saved Annie and gave her a world where she can be as free as she'd like. Isn't it funny? You held me that night the same way I held you when we met." A callused hand caressed Millie's cheek, wiping away the tears there. "I love you, kid."

Millie doubled over and sobbed. Clem's warmth was gone, and Millie's arms held only air. She remembered that, holding Clem against her chest as she'd bled out. Just like how Clem had gathered up a scared little girl on her first night as a slave and held her right alongside her newborn.

"It isn't fair," Millie shouted at the gathered spirits. But she knew that of anyone in the world, these souls would understand that war was never fair. It took good people too early and spat out broken ones by the end.

Akhun, Delilah, and Clem had better reasons to live. They'd had family to love and lives to live... but it was Millie who had survived the war. A cruel killer who had no other family. Sucking down deep gulps of air, Millie looked around the swamp to see the shadows were full of faces. Soldiers, masters, slaves, the faces of the people who she had killed, there to watch if she broke. There were others, too. The other soldiers of her company, watching silently as their last survivor struggled past.

She had to keep going. It would be a disservice to her friends if Millie gave up now. She was the last one left, so she would have to hold Fred accountable for what he did. The water grew colder with every step. Mulatiwa was hidden as he swam around her. The occasional golden coil, now the size of a tree trunk, surfaced only to dip back into the murk.

Death issss part of life, little one.

The snake's voice rumbled through the trees, making the curtains of moss tremble. This was no longer just Mulatiwa, but someone more. Millie thought of Nyembi, the lord of life and death that cycled between spirit and physical with ease. Delilah had worn a carved amulet of the great snake during the war as a reminder of what they were fighting for.

You know that.

She did. Swallowing and blinking gummy eyes, Millie kept walking. The lantern was brilliant now, far brighter than any mundane flame could be. Ahead, an answering light bloomed in the dim light of the swamp. A window, illuminated by a golden glow. There was a hut ahead, built on a stilted platform in the water. It wavered at first, like a mirage, but with every step Millie took closer to it, the hut solidified.

She'd found the Granddame.

"This is such bullshit, you know," she hiccuped between sobs. The snake god's laughter rippled through the water toward her. Slogging ahead, Millie reached the small dock that stuck out from the hut's platform and placed her axe and lantern on it. Hopping up, she pressed her palms down to push herself out of the water and onto the closest thing she'd seen to dry ground in hours. Her nose was running, and her cheeks were hot from her tears. A headache was already starting, but Millie wasn't sure if it was from crying, the tea, or the current ability to see spirits.

"Mildred Berry," a lean orcish woman opened the door to the hut. Dressed in a simple blouse and skirt, her arms were heavy with beaded bracelets. Around her neck hung amulets of all different origins and materials, from a silver wheel to a carved figure of Nyembi.

"I've been waiting years for you to show up at my door." Granddame Lavoie was all sinew and muscle under wrinkled green skin. She could have blended in with the water if she chose to, though there was an undeniable ashen tint to her that reminded Millie the woman was long-dead. Surprisingly, the Granddame didn't stink any more than the rest of the swamp.

"I hope that didn't actually take years," Millie mumbled. She felt scrubbed raw, every part of her heart bared after the memories she had walked through. All she wanted to do was sit down and cry, but she needed the answers she had come for. "I won't accidentally undo... you, will I?" Millie asked instead, pushing herself up to her feet. She tucked her axe back into her belt and hesitated over the lantern.

"You will," Lavoie said with a dry chuckle. "But I can repair myself once you're gone. The magic always returns eventually." The Granddame was taller than Delilah had been, her tusks worn from age until their ivory tips had become round. Her eyes were milky, but there was no doubt in Millie's mind that they could see her perfectly. "Come in. I have some tea that will help soothe your heart and a story you will want to hear. Leave the lantern there. It has served its purpose."

Millie followed the orc inside, finding the interior of the hut to be warm and inviting. A kettle bubbled over the fireplace, a few eastern salamanders soaking up the heat of the flames. They were skinnier than their cousins out west, and less prone to setting themselves on fire, but the sight of them made Millie homesick. She missed her girls, and the cool nights and dry days out on the Prairie.

Herbs and fungus hung in garlands around the hut, and a bedroll was neatly folded in one corner. Lavoie lowered herself into a wooden rocking chair in front of the fire and motioned for Millie to take the other seat, a cushioned stool that was just the right height for a short elf. Wiping off the worst of the muck from her feet at the door, Millie joined the other woman at the fire and accepted an earthenware cup of tea.

It smelled familiar, of roots and fungus, the liquid a deep amber. The warm mug grounded Millie, soothing her frayed nerves in the way only tea can.

"Normally I would speak in riddles," Lavoie said, ladling herself a cup of tea as well. "Truths are always the strongest when we come to them on our own, after all. But we do not have the luxury of time, little ghost, and the very soul of Marigot is at stake."

The Granddame took a sip of her tea and cleared her throat.

"A gris-gris meant to enslave a freedwoman, a second butcher killing those the first meant to protect, and a would-be master hides in plain sight. Three things that should be separate but are each just one side of a ternaire built to catch one very slippery elf."

Millie blinked, the cup hovering a half-inch from her lip.

"A ternaire, like back in Wyndford?" she asked, "But why me? And who?"

Lavoie smiled, her tusks gleaming in the hearth fire's light.

"Drink your tea, Mildred. It gets bitter once it cools," she chided. Only when Millie took a sip did the Grand-dame continue.

"Why? Revenge, power, control. Everything about this mess falls into threes, I'm afraid. It is a brilliantly crafted spell, and one that is a hair's breadth from snapping shut around you. Three tools, three perpetrators, and three sacrifices. Three sets of three, a ternaire of ternaires that should be impossible to escape."

Millie listened, dutifully sipping her tea. She'd thought the ternaire spells had to be physical, but the way the Granddame was talking about them, it sounded like these were metaphorical.

"Those who are behind such a foul plot are a lover, an enemy, and a shadow. The first two may be obvious. Who would hate you the most in Marigot? Who have you taken the most from?"

The lover was Fred. Lavoie said the enemy was obvious as well. Who had she taken the most from? She had killed countless soldiers and freedmen over the years, but who had she done something even worse to?

"O'Leary," Millie said. She'd killed his heir in a duel, she'd crippled his army for years, and finally, she had caught him about to perform heretical magic that would have destroyed his family's reputation. Millie had embarrassed him, a crime worse than murder to the old families who took pride in how fancy they were. O'Leary had been outsmarted by an elf, and he could never forgive that. Could his surviving family?

Lavoie's eyes crinkled.

"That is the correct question. Could they?" Granddame Lavoie asked to the question that Millie hadn't voiced.

"The shadow's truth will be up to you to uncover, I'm afraid. Only you can catch them out, but they are the most dangerous of the three. Keep your wits about you and remember who you are." Lavoie rested a hand on Mille's shoulder. "Who you *really* are."

Without warning, the orc yanked Millie backward, off the stool. Instead of landing on the floor, the elf plunged into swamp water. The brackish water flooded her mouth and nose, and Millie pushed off the muddy bottom to the surface, coughing up dark water as she got her feet under her.

"Well, that was a dramatic return," Ghat said, seated calmly in her canoe, a dozen paces away. Millie looked at her, wide-eyed, then back into the swamp. There was no trace of the watery trail she had followed, just a normal-sized Mulatiwa, who swam past her to Ghat's canoe. Reaching down, Ghat scooped him up and set him down on the thwart in front of her.

Millie stared at the snake, unsure of what had just happened.

"Come on," Ghat said. "It's started raining and since you got back, my magic won't keep us dry." She sighed, watching as Millie waded over to the canoe. "You lost my lantern."

"She didn't send it back with me," Millie sputtered, spitting muck from her mouth. "She's your grandmother. If you want your lantern back, go ask her."

Ghat leaned hard towards the opposite side of the canoe to keep it balanced as Millie levered herself up into it, using the gunwale. Looking at the water around them, Millie saw raindrops splattering the surface. Already soaked, she hadn't noticed it was raining. The rain was light now, but if the storm was about to hit, the rain would start in earnest.

Picking up her paddle, Millie dug it in deep. Storms in Marigot made the stormbirds out on the prairies look like turkeys. If they didn't reach shelter before it hit, she and Ghat were in trouble.

32

BUTCHERED

NATHALIE

RUTH HAD HELPED NATHIE haul out the old Wolfe family genealogy records, including all the correspondence about suitors from before the war. Now the two were sitting at the dining table, with the letters spread out before being sorted into slowly growing piles. Ruth wasn't a strong reader, but she knew the family crests nearly as well as Nathie did, making her a quick study on which letters went with which house.

"I knew the O'Leary family were remarkably fecund, but this is ridiculous," Nathie muttered, setting aside yet another letter about the birth of an O'Leary son. So far she had six who were old enough to fight in the war, but young enough to be grandchildren of the general who led the Marigot Rebels. The women born during the same period hadn't got the same attention, with only mentions in the birth announcements of their brothers.

That didn't eliminate a woman from being behind the plot to lure Mildred back to Marigot, though it was difficult to imagine the men involved would follow a woman

very far. Nathie squeezed her eyes shut and tried to remember when she was young. She had daydreamed endlessly about who she would end up marrying.

Someone knocked at the door, and the sharp rap jolted
Nathie nearly out of her skin. By the time she glanced at
her maid, Ruth was already halfway to the door. Gilbert
hadn't been gone long. Had he forgotten something? Curious, Nathie stood and crept over to the hall, peeking
down it to see what the banker wanted.

But it was not the banker at her door, it was Pierre.

"Hello Ruth, I'm -wait-I'm-here-to-apologise," Pierre
said, shoving himself into the doorway just as the maid
tried to shut the door again. Pierre grunted as the door
thudded into him. Nathie winced, and the moment must
have drawn Pierre's attention. Spotting her down the hall,
he waved with the hand that was inside the home.

"Nathie, please," he said. "You deserved to know long
before now. I'm sorry. I can't fix that, but I can make sure
that you know all my other secrets before anyone else can
tell you."

The embittered shard of Nathie's mind whispered to let
him tell his secrets, then kick him back out onto the street.
He had made her feel hope for her future, only to prove
himself as terrible as his brother. Hope was a dangerous
thing. It cut far deeper than hatred or jealousy. When hope
shattered, it cut to the bone.

"Fine," Nathie said, steeling herself. She had let Pierre
hurt her once. She would not leave herself so vulnerable a
second time. "Ruth, let the coward in."

The maid opened the door abruptly, letting Pierre
stumble into the house. He dusted himself off and hurried
over to Nathie, his cheeks pink.

"Frederic killed my mother," he blurted out. "She was our father's second wife and protected me as best as she could. I was away at school for most of the year, so I wouldn't need to be near Fred or our father except on holidays. One autumn she fell pregnant again. Fred didn't want another sibling, so he pushed her down the front steps. I was away at school. They only told me when I returned home that midwinter."

Nathie had expected more brutality. She had to bite back her knee-jerk response of 'that's all?'. Compared to what Mildred had been through, what she herself had suffered, losing a parent and being away at school sounded like a normal upbringing.

"Is that why you've been so afraid of him?" she asked. "Because he killed your mother?"

Pierre had the grace to look ashamed, but there was a sharpness to him now. He scowled down at his hands and flexed them. They were the hands of a concert musician, Nathie thought. Not the brutish paws of a killer like his brother. Yet, what use were hands when all one did was sit on them?

"He used to make Mildred and I fight," he continued. "She beat me every time, and I thought it was his way of telling me he could get rid of me without so much as lifting a finger. A way of humiliating me, making me lose to this tiny scrap of an elf." Pierre frowned down at his hands. Nathie waited, crossing her arms impatiently.

"After the war, I realised he was punishing her, too. Every time we fought, she had to break the law by striking me. If she didn't, he would beat her. I didn't realise until later that if she ever tried to leave, he could drag my sorry self to the courts and have me tell them about all the times she'd fought me. She would have been hunted down. Fred knew both of us well enough to play us off each other, and I was too terrified of him to see that until he had left for Wyndford."

Pierre walked over to where she sat and knelt in front of her.

"I am no warrior, Nathalie," he said, those blue eyes earnest and pleading. "But I would fight to make you proud, even though I'm rather terrible at it." He reached into his waistcoat and pulled out a small sheaf of papers bound along one edge with neat stitching.

"But I am good at law, and I will do everything I can to make sure we find out who took Fred and drag them to face justice." He held out the papers, face going beet red.

"These are the last of my secrets," he said, pressing the sheaf into her hands. "I have loved you from the moment I first saw you. I am a restless sleeper and prefer tea to coffee. And last, I write horrendously embarrassing poems about things I couldn't say otherwise."

Nathalie wasn't sure whether to laugh or cry, or both. She gingerly took the papers he offered and glanced at the first poem. She stopped reading as she felt her resolve waver.

"I trusted you," she said, her voice sharp and cold. "I told you about where they put me after Ted died, what it was like. I told you how bad my other marriages were, how they ended. You knew my sins, but you kept me at arm's length."

"I'd hoped they were both dead," Pierre admitted, red with shame. Good.

"Well, they aren't," Nathie snapped. "I want to believe you're different from Frederic, but you'll need to prove it.

You hurt me once. I'll be damned if I give you another opportunity."

Ruth, bless her, cleared her throat loudly from the hall.

"Apologies, Madam, but you wanted to be informed if there was another Butcher murder?"

The rest of the conversation would have to wait. Nathalie tucked the sheaf of papers under the family history book for safekeeping. She knew Ruth wouldn't read them, but the Goldmans and mages were a different matter.

"Come with me," she said to Pierre, rising out of her chair. "You're the only other one who has seen the elf's work in person. I'd like to know your thoughts on what we find." She levelled a cool stare at him. "Let's see if you really mean what you said."

THEY FOUND A BLOODBATH.

The murder had taken place close to the river, a few blocks out of the Bakimban quarter. The apartment was perched atop a bakery, owned by the murdered family inside. Locals weren't happy about Nathalie and Pierre's arrival, but a few bribes went a long way into soothing hurt feelings, as did a promise that they were there to help find out who was killing all these people. It was a sad truth that the city guard would not be investigating the murders of an inhuman family, no matter how brutal.

The bakery itself was tidy and empty, the ovens unlit and the usual scent of freshly baked bread was absent. A small shrine to the Messiah sat on the counter, with offerings for prosperity and happiness. Nathalie glanced at it on the way by, noting that the usual token dollar was missing. How odd.

They climbed the steps to find a burly orc with elven features standing at the top, arms crossed. He narrowed his eyes and stepped aside, looking pointedly at Pierre.

"Oh merciful Messiah," Pierre said the moment Nathalie opened the curtain that closed off the single bedroom. "I didn't think the bodies would still be in here."

The smell was overpowering. The dead did not fare well in the Marigot heat, and the bodies had been waiting for nearly half a day in it. Someone had pulled sheets over the corpses to keep the flies away, but that helped little with the smell.

Pressing her handkerchief over her mouth and nose, Nathalie walked into the room, careful to avoid any patches of blood that were still sticky. It was splattered all over, and she counted four bodies in the room. Two, the baker and his wife, lay in bed together, while the remaining bodies were smaller. Children.

Nathie pulled a hatpin from her hair and used the tip to lift the sheet. She was no stranger to death, but she was not used to seeing it delivered in such a brutal manner. Feeling ill, she forced herself to look at where the poor man had been hit. A glancing blow had caught his temple before a second killed him. She lowered the sheet and turned toward where Pierre stood at the exit.

She froze, her hand holding the handkerchief fell away as she stared at the doorway in shock.

There was a bloody handprint placed above the doorway. It was deliberate, too perfect an impression to be accidental. There was no way that Mildred could have left it. She was far too short to reach, unless she'd dragged over a crate to stand on. But a quick look at the bloody floor told Nathie that no furniture had been moved.

A bloody handprint. Was that what the splotch on the note had been before Nathalie's solution had dissolved it? It would have been made using a stamp, but it was possible.

"What is it?" Pierre asked, reluctantly following Nathalie into the room. He turned and followed her pointed finger to spot the handprint. He edged back toward the doorway and lifted his hand, holding his fingers together and his thumb apart, just as it was on the print. His own hand was larger, but not by much. Whoever had made the mark would have been significantly taller than Mildred, or even most elves.

"This wasn't her," Pierre said, choking on the stench of the room. He shook his hand and stepped back into the hall, trying not to vomit. Nathalie followed, closing the door behind her. But the smell of death was in her nose, now, and the door did little to help clear it.

"There was magic there," Pierre said. "I could feel it. I don't know what it was, but it made the bones in my hand buzz."

The guard in the hall's ears perked, and he looked over at them from under glowering eyebrows.

"Send for Madame Lavoie," Nathalie told the man. "I'll cover her payment, but I believe that whoever did this was not the same Butcher as the one who was around during the war."

"No shit," the de facto guard rumbled. "The old one didn't kill kids this young." He shook his head.

"Have there been handprints at every recent Butcher killing?" Nathalie pressed. When the green elf looked away, she bit her lip. "Please, this is very important."

"Yes. Now, please, leave." The 'please' was mere formality, and Nathalie nodded before grabbing Pierre and dragging him down the stairs and out of the bakery before the man lost the last shred of patience with them.

"The murderer missed one swing," she whispered to him as they emerged into fresher air. A cool breeze cut through the street, promising rain before evening. "It nearly took the poor man's ear off, but it wasn't a killing blow. It glanced off to the side."

Huddled close together, the humans moved away from the crowd gathered in front of the bakery. A few ears swivelled to follow them, but soon the residents resumed talking amongst themselves. Nathie and Pierre were not the only ones who wanted to figure out what happened.

"Well, Mildred isn't perfect, but she rarely missed," Pierre whispered back. "I haven't seen her fight recently, but she wasn't one to kill kids in their sleep, either."

"Whatever magic was left in that handprint would have been washed away if she had been in that room." Nathalie added. "I think we need to ask Madame Ghat to help." She sighed, remembering who Mildred said she was travelling with that day. "But she's gone until Mildred returns."

Pierre groaned.

"Back to the finances, I suppose."

Nathalie looked back at the gathered neighbours and tamped down the urge to march over and start asking questions. It was frustrating to know that non-humans kept secrets from people like her, but after what she'd learned since meeting Mildred, Nathalie could hardly blame them.

"Actually, I think I have an idea," Nathalie said to Pierre. "But I'll need your help in Ruth's place while I send her on an 'errand'. If Annie is free, maybe she could join her." She reached for Pierre's arm and caught herself. A fresh pang of heartbreak struck her. Nathie shoved her hands into the pockets of her jacket in a very unladylike manner and strode back toward the main road of the quarter. It would be easiest to hail a cab from there. With any luck, Ruth could sniff out the information that Nathalie was after.

33

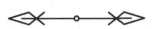

OLD MONEY, OLDER POWER

RHIANNON

RHIANNON WAS BACK IN her study, the portrait of her father looking over her shoulder as she studied the pile of letters she'd been ignoring since her return to Wyndford. Sorting through them, she placed each into one of three piles. Names that she knew were tied to Marigot: Gallois, Flaubert, O'Leary; names she wasn't certain about, and then the individuals she knew had no ties to the city.

The third pile was her wastebasket, which had filled with alarming speed. Fyodor lay next to it, no longer reacting when she dropped in a new envelope.

It was exhausting to read letter after letter praising her survival, as though she had done something remarkable instead of being a scared girl that Millie had dragged out of the manor in tears. All Rhiannon had done for the first two years was follow her friend's lead, as the elf taught her how to survive among the common people.

The state of the world had shocked Rhiannon. Down pillows were a luxury instead of commonplace, and meat was a treat instead of a staple until Millie could get her hands on a gun. She hadn't complained much, doing her best to rise to the circumstances she found herself in. Mostly, she'd just been scared. First, scared that Rousseau would find them, then scared she would lose the family she'd found in Scorched Bluffs.

A family she'd barely written to since arriving. Rhiannon frowned at the letter in front of her. No wonder Millie felt like she was choosing the company over their friendship. Did Sweetpea and Annie feel the same way?

Guilt twisted in Rhiannon's stomach. As soon as they had a lead on who took Fred, she was going to Marigot. The company would be fine for a week or two, and she'd sent Millie back into the personal Hell the elf had spent years trying to heal from.

Rhiannon blinked back hot tears and crumpled the letter in her hands, tossing it into the basket next to Fyo. The dog groaned without opening his eyes. With a heavy sigh, he rolled over and rested his head on her foot.

"I made a mess of it," she told him, wiping her eyes with the heel of her hand. Her calluses had softened and started to peel. Even her hands were forgetting what life was like outside the Manor. Rhiannon rubbed the water off onto her skirt and reached into her desk, pulling out the second letter Millie had sent before she left.

'For when you know the truth.'

Rhiannon wasn't sure if she did yet, but she'd damaged things by waiting. Waiting for evidence, waiting for the trial. She would not waste any more time.

Pulling the letter out, she immediately noticed the thin parchment had puckered from old tears that blurred some of the carefully inked letters.

Ry,

I don't know what your cousin told you. I don't know how I hurt you, but I'm sure I did. It's the only thing I'm good at: hurting people. That's the Marigot way, whether it's sharp words in fancy dresses, or blood in the streets. Marigot's mother tongue is violence.

When we first went west, you asked me how I could kill someone. I didn't have an answer back then, and I still don't because I don't know how to explain something that's been a part of me since I was born.

I'm a killer, and I've hurt a lot of people in my life. In the end, I was too brutal, even for Marigot. There's no fixing what I've done, but this will be a start.

I'm sorry, I never meant to hurt you.

Please, watch over the girls. They're the only good thing I've done in my life.

M

It was a goodbye letter.

Now the note about Allan made more sense. Millie hadn't planned on coming back from Marigot, so she wanted Rhiannon to build a new family to help her navigate the world. Her friend didn't trust high society, but she trusted Allan, who was more comfortable in prairie dust than he was in fancy houses. Rhiannon wasn't a girl anymore. She might have lost some of Millie's trust, but by the messiahs, she was going to go get it back.

Rhiannon grabbed the letter and stood upending Fyodor's nap. He rolled to bleary alertness, his ears perked as he hauled himself to his feet.

"C'mon, boy," she said, crossing to the door of her office. Just as she placed her hand on the knob, it turned and pulled open, out of her grasp. Murphy jumped, startled that she was already at the door.

"My, that's a fierce look today, Miss," he said with a breathless chuckle. "A Corporal Plackitt is here to see you. Shall I show her in?"

"To the parlour, please," Rhiannon said, shoving Millie's letter into her pocket. "Can you send for Allan and Hal? Tell them to bring whatever they might need for a week away."

Murphy nodded and Rhiannon headed to the parlour, absently picking at one of the loose bits of callus on her palm. If Plackitt was here, that meant something had happened. Hopefully, Harrold had reconsidered the offer. It fit that he'd want to draw the answer out to make her sweat.

"Miss Colfield," Plackitt said, entering the parlour, removing her cap in respect. "I'm afraid I bring bad news. Your uncle was found dead this morning." Plackitt looked over their shoulder and stepped closer to Rhiannon, pulling a slip of paper out of their cap.

"The overnight guard said Mister Colfield died in his sleep, but I—" Plackitt cleared their throat. They awkwardly ran a hand through blond curls. "Well, you would recognise my name, I'm sure. I never had the knack for ironwork, but I spent some time around the mine when I was little. When someone suffocates, their eyes get bloodshot. Doesn't matter if they suffocated on gas in a mine or by a pillow while in bed."

Plackitt held out the slip of paper to Rhiannon with solemn eyes.

"I found this in the front pocket of his nightshirt. The cantankerous old bastard knew this was coming. I thought it would be best if I brought it straight to you."

Rhiannon took the note and opened it, smoothing the parchment between her fingers. A single name was written on it.

Charles Whistenhowler.

"Did you tell anyone about this?" Rhiannon asked, heart missing a beat. If there was a single family in Wyndford who had almost as much money as the Colfields, it was the Whistenhowlers. The two families once had a long-standing friendship, though the advent of the railroad had launched the Colfields well beyond the wealth of their former friends. The Whistenhowlers had never quite forgiven them for it, but there had never been a history of violence between the two.

"No Miss," Plackitt said, frowning. "Something isn't right with the police. I don't know who I can trust there, but your family has always done right by mine. I figured you'd know what this meant."

Rhiannon pressed her lips together, unsure what to feel. Harrold was dead. There would be no trial and no public sentencing of guilt. Justice had died with him, and she hated him for it, escaping the consequences of what he'd done to her.

But with his last breaths, he had given her a clue that might save her friend's life.

"Thank you, Corporal," Rhiannon said. "For your own safety, I think it would be best for you to take leave for a week or two. Maybe go visit your family up by the mines."

Plackitt nodded, square jaw set in a grim line. The corporal placed their hat back atop their curls and excused themself, leaving the parlour.

Rhiannon looked down at the paper in her hand, her thumb running over the name written there. The Whistenhowlers were a northern family, but their family tree spread across all of Amelior. It wouldn't be improbable that they held interests in Marigot. The question was: what were they?

Placing the slip into her pocket with Millie's letter, Rhiannon whistled for Fyodor to heel. Time was of the essence.

"Murphy?" she called out, crossing the front hall with quick steps that made her skirts swish noisily behind her. "Prepare a private train for Marigot, ready to leave at once. I'll have a telegram to be sent in just a moment."

Hurrying out of the foyer where he had been seeing off the corporal, Murphy nodded. To her great relief, he didn't start asking questions about where she was going.

"Miss?" he said, catching her up in surprise. "Whoever it is you're after, I hope you get them."

A smile of surprise pulled at Rhiannon's mouth.

"I didn't know you were so bloodthirsty, Murphy," she said. "I will. I've lost enough family, so I'm going to go bring back what's left."

"Very good, Miss," Murphy said, his moustache twitching into a pleased smile. "I took the liberty of commissioning some fresh adventuring clothes for you from the dressmaker. I believe the maid has placed them in the trunk at the foot of your bed."

Rhiannon stepped over to him and pulled him into a hug. She'd been so devastated, mourning the family she had lost, she'd not noticed the new one she was making. Murphy stiffened for a moment before he returned the hug.

"You are very dear to us, you know," he said, his voice shaking ever so slightly. "Please don't make us wait another five years to see you again."

"I'm coming home the moment I can," Rhiannon promised.

RHIANNON STOOD ON THE platform for the personal express she had commandeered, arms crossed as she studied the locomotive. It seemed to be 'Penny', the same machine that had carried her to Wyndford from Plainsfield, little more than a month ago. Rhiannon was back in a duster coat, her old boots re-shod and polished, but as comfortable as ever. At her hip rested a revolver, while her trusty rifle was strapped to her back. Fyodor pranced back and forth in excitement, eager to go on an adventure after what must have felt like a long holiday.

For the first time since she'd returned, Rhiannon felt comfortable in her own skin. She was confident that going after Millie and Nathie was the right decision. Millie had called Marigot a city that spoke only in violence, and the memory of their last conversation twisted in Rhiannon's belly.

She had said some terribly stupid things, and only the Messiahs knew if Millie could forgive her.

"This feels familiar," Hal said as he and Allan walked down the platform to meet her. "Is Gervais driving?"

"Who?" Allan asked, dressed in his old clothes. They'd been laundered and repaired, and seeing him out of his police uniform made Rhiannon feel a rush of relief. This was the same Allan that used to sneak her news about silly things with the mail deliveries.

Rhiannon, emboldened by her earlier success with Murphy, stepped forward and pulled both men into a hug one by one.

"Thank you both for coming," she said, reluctantly letting go of Allan. "I've been a bit of a mess lately, but I can explain everything that's happened on the train. The short of it is that we have the name we were after."

Allan's face had gone bright, and Rhiannon felt her cheeks grow warm in equal measure. Hal lifted his eyebrows in surprise.

"Harrold changed his mind?" He asked, mouth open. "Well, I guess I was wrong about him."

"Not exactly," Rhiannon said, taking a deep breath to help compose herself. The severity of the situation helped push the thought of how good that hug had felt from her mind, but only just. "But his pettiness meant we got what we needed in the end." She reached for the passenger car's door.

Hal climbed on first, and Allan made as if to follow, but he stopped next to Rhiannon, face flushed.

"Are ladies allowed to hug police officers?" he asked. "Will I have to arrest myself?"

"Maybe not," Rhiannon said, feeling that smile return to her face. "But I don't think I'm interested in becoming a proper lady again. I'd much rather be there for my friends than eat tiny sandwiches."

"Allan, get on the damn train," Hal shouted from inside. "You two can flirt once we're underway."

34

NUMBERS NEVER LIE

GILBERT

THE SECRET LEDGER WAS hidden behind a collection of hunting memoirs by various wealthy humans that wanted to kill dangerous things after their non-human servants did most of the work. Gilbert had to admit it was clever. Pierre was clearly not made from the same mould as his brother, and likely had no interest in reading about shooting animals. Out of morbid curiosity, Gilbert had flipped through one memoir to find that it was exactly what he expected it to be. Self-aggrandising bullshit.

Maybe as a boy, he might have been impressed, but Gilbert had watched two short women take down a greater blue dragon on their own. Hunting boasts would always pale compared to watching his wife punch a dragon in the face. There was just no contest.

The ledger was far more interesting. It matched the others, bound in leather and full of financial secrets. Gil ran his hand over its cover as he limped back to the desk. Easing himself back into the chair with a grunt of pain, Gil moved the official ledgers aside to make room. Opening the hidden one, Gil scanned the first page. It was from several decades ago, when Fred was just a boy. The loans were primarily outgoing with interest rates carefully noted, along with the initials of who the money had been loaned to.

Flipping ahead to the years just before the war, Gil raised his eyebrows. Gone were the outgoing loans, replaced by incoming ones. The interest rates ballooned from loan to loan, a detail that might have been put down to increasing economic uncertainty. But Gil knew better. The interest rates increased because whoever was loaning Fred the money was growing less confident he would pay it back.

There were bribes, too. Bribes to the court, to lawyers, to merchants. What was missing was the constant stream of gambling debt that Gilbert was familiar with. In Wyndford, most of Fred's money had gone toward his vices. Gambling, cigars, whiskey. Here, the merchants listed were none that Gil recognised. One set of initials looked suspiciously like those of the gunsmith that Gilbert had bought for Fred before the drunkard tried to kill him.

Had Fred been building his own army? The idea would have been funny, if not for some conversations Gil had with Millie. She'd mentioned that she had been responsible for creating a militia of slaves, but slaves couldn't fight with only farm tools. They would need firearms to hold their own against the Marigot army.

Gilbert sat back and scratched at his beard. He needed a local's help with this, but he wasn't sure if he could trust Pierre yet. He'd need to smuggle the ledger back to Nathalie's house and ask Millie when she got back. She would be the most likely of them to know what companies these payments had been to.

Flipping the page, Gil scanned the entries until he found the year of the war. All payments on previous loans stopped, though the payments to the mysterious companies increased. Bribes, too. Gil turned the page and found the entries ended abruptly, one month before the official declaration of war. Pasted on the empty page was a note in Fred's handwriting. It took Gilbert a moment to recognise it. He was used to seeing it in scrawling loops and splattered with ink. But this Frederic Rousseau had not crawled into a whiskey bottle, and his writing was school-boy perfect.

P. O. dead, via duel with M.

Cease all payments to O'Leary family and other anti-abolitionists.

- F

Gilbert clucked his tongue. He knew exactly who 'M' was. Whoever 'P' was, they must have been one of the significant lenders, otherwise, why mention their death in a debts ledger? Stretching his bad leg out, Gil felt something in his hip pop, and he sighed in relief.

He needed to talk to his wife. He just hoped she would make it back from the swamp in a good mood. She hated banking, but she was his best bet for answers. Gil sighed again, resting his chin in his hand. Perhaps it would be prudent to procure a bribe of his own before his wife returned.

Gilbert sat on the second-story porch of Nathalie's home, watching the rain fall on Marigot. The storm cut through the unbearable heat of the city, but the storm was only getting stronger, and Millie had yet to return from her trip to the swamp.

She'd lived out in the wilderness for years during the war, but it had been almost a decade since then. What if a tree fell on her? Or a snake bit her? Or... the possibilities were endless and all equally unlikely. Still, he wasn't able to stop thinking about them, or how he might have to explain to their daughters that their mama wouldn't be coming home.

Instead of pacing, he sat outside and watched the rain. The fact he could see the street from his seat was simply coincidence, and he certainly didn't lean forward every time he saw someone hurrying past.

Finally, just as the day dimmed from grey to darkness, he spotted a familiar pale figure walking down the street with a lanky companion, both completely soaked from the rain. Gilbert got to his feet and stepped back inside. He grabbed one of the towels left for them in their room and limped downstairs to meet his wife. Nathalie and Pierre had disappeared before he'd returned from the Rousseau house, but Gilbert was glad to see that the maid, Ruth, had returned from her own errands. Annie was at the dining table, reading a hardbound booklet.

When he'd first returned from Pierre's, he'd asked about arranging a bath for Millie once she got back. Ruth, looking harried, pulled out a small copper tub, inscribed with an enchantment to keep the water warm. Nathalie had an emergency request that Ruth had to fulfil, so Gilbert thanked the woman and said he'd fill it himself. He neglected to mention that his wife would strip the enchantment from the tub the moment she climbed in, but the tub kept the water hot for her until Millie's arrival.

"Mildred and Madame Lavoie will be back in a moment. Could you please put on some tea?" he asked. Ruth didn't even answer. She just bobbed in place and disappeared into the back of the house where the kitchen had to be.

After years of living with Arnaud, who always had some complaint or other, Gilbert found the silent obedience unsettling.

"They're back?" Annie asked, standing up and joining Gil in the hall. She looked at the towel in his hand, and Gilbert caught a small smile on her face before she rolled her eyes.

"You're making me look like a bad niece," she muttered, heading deeper into the house to get a towel for Ghat.

The front door opened, and Gilbert headed to the foyer to intercept Millie before she could drip on something important.

She looked like a soaked kitten, all her bluster and fluff washed away by the rain, leaving a gaunt little elf with ears and eyes that seemed too big for her head. She looked up from wringing out her braid at the doorstep, and he smiled at the look of surprise on her face.

"I thought you might have got caught in the rain," he said, wrapping the towel around her. He touched her hand and found it cold, the tips of her fingers red. "Tsk, I need to get you something to keep you warm that you'll actually wear."

Millie threw herself into his arms, hugging him tight, her face pressed against the cotton of his shirt, immediately soaking it. Gilbert wrapped his arms around her, rubbing the towel over her arms to help warm her up.

Ghat staggered inside, her snake coiled around her neck to stay warm in the downpour. She tilted her chin up at him, a silent acknowledgement of approval. She looked to be in better shape than his wife, but only just.

"You don't need to say anything," Gil murmured to Millie. "Ruth is putting on some tea and I've got a bath waiting upstairs for you." He made to kiss her hair but stopped, realising it was a different shade than usual and smelled like rotting leaves.

"Darling, your hair seems to have some green in it," he muttered, plucking a stray bit of leaf matter from her braid and tossing it onto the doorstep. That done, he reached past her to pull the front door closed. Nathalie might be busy arguing with Pierre, but he was certain she would be upset if the rain got into the house.

"I ended up in the swamp," Millie mumbled, relaxing into his arms so much Gil was worried she might fall if he let her go. "Tea and a bath sound wonderful right now."

Annie reappeared and tossed the towel she'd found to Ghat, who caught it one-handed.

"Tsk, no respect," the conjure queen muttered, gratefully wrapping the towel around her shoulders. "Go on, Gilly boy," she said. "She'll need to rest."

Gil wished he could scoop Millie up and carry her up to the bedroom, but he knew his hip wouldn't hold after all the trips he'd made up and down the stairs earlier to fill the tub. Keeping one arm around her, he walked back to their room with her tucked into his side.

The copper tub waited in front of the room's fireplace, along with the other bribes he had picked up for her. He'd carved a few slivers of lavender and lemon soap into the steaming water, and a white paper bag held beignets for later. He'd found the shop with the longest line for them, and bought a half dozen to share. The smell of them was heavenly, and it had been a test of willpower not to take one out and try it.

"Spirits, that smells good," Millie said as she stepped inside. "Did you get-"

"I had to guess on the soap, I'm afraid. But I figured you could use something relaxing after the hell you've been dealing with since you came back here," Gilbert said, removing the towel from her shoulders. He helped her peel off her belt and axe, followed by the mud-stained vest and shirt.

"You didn't have to do all this," she protested, turning to look at him over one horribly scarred shoulder. Gilbert smiled.

"I know, but I wanted to," he said, kissing her shoulder lightly. The extent of Millie's scars had shocked him the first time he'd seen them. Now, they were just part of her, as much as the ghostly stretch marks on her belly. "I also need your help later, but it can wait. I'd rather you enjoy yourself than worry over banking talk."

She wrinkled her nose, but turned to kiss his cheek all the same.

"Thank you."

Once her wet clothes were peeled off and set upon the dirty towel, Gilbert helped Millie into the tub and perched on a stool next to it as she settled into the hot water with a small groan of pleasure. The moment she touched the copper, the glowing inscription winked out. No matter, Gil would pay to have it re-enchanted before they left Marigot.

"Let me help," he murmured, undoing her braid. Making a small face, he plucked bits of leaf and twigs from her hair as he went, tossing them into the fireplace. Millie handed him a sliver of soap from the water and he gently scrubbed the mud from her scalp. He was pleased to see her ears flick in pleasure, the way her daughters' did when she gave them baths back at Wyndford. Like mother, like daughters.

"I had to drink some kind of tea before I went to see Ghat's grandmother," Millie murmured, eyes closing as Gilbert worked on her hair. "It made me see things out there."

"Real things?" Gilbert asked, using his hand to scoop water from the tub to rinse out her hair, leaving it pristine and white again, the mud turning the tub water murky.

"Real enough," she said with a sigh. "I saw my friends from the war. I watched them die, one by one, and I never forgave myself for not saving them." Her voice shook slightly at her confession. Millie could admit to murder, but Gil knew admitting to being vulnerable was far harder for her. He didn't interrupt her, picking up her comb to untangle her hair instead.

"I had to watch them die all over again, out there," she whispered, curling up in the tub to hug her knees. "But they told me..." she took a shaky breath. "They told me they didn't blame me. Do you think that was really them?" She asked, looking up at him over her shoulder. He could see the tears in her eyes, and Gilbert set the comb back down. Her hair could wait.

"I think it was. They knew what war meant, and so did you." He moved his stool over so she could face him without craning her neck. Reaching out, he took her hand

and lifted it to his lips, kissing the warm, soapy skin. "I saw you at work in Scorched Bluffs. You care about your soldiers and you love your friends, Mildred Berry. They adore you right back, you know. These friends may have died, but they died knowing it meant the rest of you would get a little closer to what you were all fighting for."

Her lip trembled, and she leaned forward, resting her cheek on his knee. Gilbert wrapped his arm around her shoulders, gently rubbing her arm.

"It's bullshit, you know?" she said, the tears finally escaping her lashes. "The whole idea of a 'war hero', it's bullshit. It's just a way to make the last ones standing feel like maybe they deserved to be there instead of surviving because of blind luck. They had families, they had futures, and I had nothing to live for. It's so wrong that I'm still here."

"I would agree with you, but I've watched you take on a dragon and punch it in the face," Gilbert said, holding her. "So I have to argue that some of your survival is due to how stubborn you are."

She laughed, but it ended in a cry that she stifled into her hand. The tea and beignets would have to wait. Gilbert reached down into the tub and scooped her up, pulling her into his lap. Wrapping the clean towel around her, Gilbert held his wife close as she finally broke into sobs. He closed his eyes and pressed his lips to her hair, murmuring soft assurances that she was safe with him. He held her like that until the sobs subsided into the quiet, deep breaths of sleep. And then he held her a little longer, not wanting to let go.

35

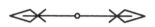

THE FAMILY LEGACY

CHARLIE

CHARLES WHISTENHOWLER STOOD IN his late grand-father's study, hands tucked behind his back as he looked up at the portrait of the last male conjure worker in their family. With an impressive silver beard and moustache waxed at the tips, General O'Leary stared back with fierce determination. Wearing the green uniform of the Marigot Rebel Army.

Yet, for as brilliant a strategist as the General was, he'd proven less capable than Fred and the elf. He had made a crucial mistake that Charlie would not: elves were not simpletons who waited slack-jawed for a human to come and lead them. Mildred Berry proved elves could be as canny, crafty, and cunning as any human. What they needed was to be trained, the way bad habits were trained out of a dog.

Someone knocked at the door, and Charlie told them to enter, his eyes still fixed on his grandfather's portrait. The door opened and the gentle tap of his grandmother's cane announced Georgette O'Leary before the cloying smell of powder could reach Charlie's nose.

"He would have been so proud of the man you've become, Charlie," his grandmother said. "I wish he could have lived to see it."

Charlie looked over at her and smiled. She was the perfect southern lady, hair in precisely curled, dainty gloves covering her arthritic hands, and always dressed for the occasion. She reminded him of his mother, who had so many of the same traits. The O'Leary women were more powerful than anyone gave them credit for. They kept the social ties among the old families strong, and could destroy a reputation with a well-placed whisper. Too often, Charlie's uncles had bought into the story presented to the public: that the men were the leaders of the family. It had been their downfall, and not a mistake that Charlie was interested in repeating.

"His spirit knows," Charlie said, walking over to kiss his grandmother's hand. "It won't be long before we restore society to its proper place."

Georgette smiled and patted Charlie's cheek.

"Your friend, the Gallois boy, is downstairs. Shall I send for him?"

"No," Charlie said, shaking his head. "I'll go speak with him. I know it's late. Go rest, Grandmother. Tomorrow we recover what we've lost."

Once she nodded and patted Charlie's hand, he left the study and jogged down the townhome's stairs. Gallois stood by the window, peering out into the evening through the curtains. The orange trees gave their home privacy, but the eyesore that was Rousseau House was easily watched from where Gallois stood.

"Anyone there?" Charlie asked, walking over to the drink cart and pouring himself and Gallois a glass of whiskey.

"Pierre returned a while ago, looking like a kicked dog," the large man said. He accepted the drink with a nod of thanks. "So nothing new there. My scout says the elf and Madame Lavoie have returned from the swamp, and that the elf looked exhausted."

Charlie nodded, taking a sip of his drink before he answered.

"Excellent. Prepare everyone for tomorrow and keep a close eye on where she is at all times."

"Not tonight?" Gallois asked, his glass halfway to his lips.

Charlie smiled.

"No, not tonight. Tonight, we allow the spirits to wear her out. I won't underestimate her again."

36

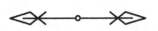

THE SHADOW

MILLIE

MILLIE WAS BACK IN the swamp, which was bullshit. It was especially bullshit because the usual reeds had grown into tall sugar cane stalks that shook under the heavy rain. Sugar cane didn't grow naturally in the swamp. The canes meant she was dreaming, or that Ghat had drugged her with that tea again.

Looking around, she spotted the red glint of vishap eyes in the water, their gator-like snouts poking out of the surface, looking like just a half-sunken log. Millie tried to wade forward into the sugar cane for cover, but the silty bottom sucked at her legs and feet, slowing her to a painfully slow slog.

"Ghat?" she shouted over the rain, lifting a hand to block the water from running into her eyes. The sugar cane rustled and the dead body of Clem staggered out. She was burnt along one side of her, her dark eyes filmy white.

"Mildred," dead-Clem rattled. "You killed me."

Ah, it was this kind of dream. Normally, it tore her up, leaving her a sobbing mess until she woke up in a cold sweat.

Instead, Millie was utterly spent. The grief was still there, a great hollow thing in her chest that ate away at her, but all the acidic self-hatred she usually carried there had been emptied, leaving her with nothing.

Akhun lumbered out of the cane stalks to her right, missing giant chunks of himself from vishap bites. One still stalked him, a juvenile that didn't know better. It lunged at the giant man, latching onto his calf. Dead Akhun didn't even blink.

"I get it," Millie said, resting her hands on her knees and squinting at the third figure that emerged from the sugar cane. "You're the shadow, right? The third side of the ternaire?" Whoever it was must have figured out regular magic didn't work if they were coming after her dreams.

Mildred's ghosts laughed, and the dead Delilah was leaking swamp water from the bullet holes that riddled her body. The absurd corner of Millie's mind wanted to shout that made no sense, unless Delilah had been hollowed out specifically to hold water.

"The Butcher is back," the trio chanted in unison. "The Butcher is back. She'll give you a whack! She'll cut you up and leave her mark, then use your blood for summoning dark."

The vishaps had crept closer, but in a flash they turned and darted away like minnows before a pike. The murk shivered underfoot, and Millie fell backward into the water as mud lifted around her, washing off brilliant scales that shone like sunlight in the storm's gloom.

The dead bodies fell apart into clumps of mud and leaves as Mulatiwa raised his head from the water and flicked a tongue as thick as Millie's wrist into the air. Scrambling forward and over one of his giant coils, Millie dug through the dissolving clump that was Clementine. Her fingers closed around something squishy, but firm. She pulled it out and rubbed it under the surface of the water to remove what mud she could.

A dark gris-gris, sewn shut with red string.

"You were not afraid," the snake rumbled, lowering his head to stare into Millie's eyes.

"I'm still afraid, but I'm so tired of this. Of all of this," she admitted. She lifted her arms up to gesture at where the sugarcane had been and let them fall uselessly back to her sides. The cane was gone, leaving only the familiar twisted trees and curtain moss of the swamp.

"I watched the people who'd become my family die, and I thought I'd never recover. Now that I have people I love again, I'm scared the same thing will happen. That I won't be able to save them and that I'll be the last one left alive. That I'll have to bury my daughters, my friends, or Gilbert. I don't think I can do that, not again."

Around her, Mulatiwa coiled, creating a protective wall between her and the rest of the wilderness. He lowered his head to rest on the back of one loop, tongue flicking out as he spoke.

"You could, if you had to," he said. "Because, Mildred, you will always see the potential for a light in the darkness. You know as deeply and instinctively as I do that there will always be balance. For all the death you've seen, you have seen new life spring forth. For every evil, a kindness. Nature will always self-correct to seek that balance."

Her limbs felt like lead, and she was so tired. Millie wanted to argue, but the snake was right. In the cellar's darkness, it had been the memories of Clem, Akhun and Delilah that kept her sane. It had been their collective promise to each *other to die free men and women that kept her from giving up. It had been the hope that there was some better life out there that stopped her from killing the scared young woman in the Colfield manor all those years ago.*

"Are you really him? Nyembi?" she asked. "Why give a shit about an elf who didn't even believe in you?"

"I am a facet of him, which issss enough," the snake said. "All life is precioussss. As is all death. But the shadow you spoke of, it would seek to disrupt thissss balance. Not just for you, but all of Marigot."

"And I'm supposed to stop it?" Millie asked. "Isn't there some younger hero out there that could do this? I'm tired, I'm a mother, I don't want to keep fighting wars."

She swore the snake's mouth curled up into a smile.

"No, Mildred. You are sssupposed to choose which path to take when the time issss right. Nature will always sssself correct, but you will always have a choice. That issss the beautiful thing about being alive. You are the sssshaper of your future. But it issss important you know the truth when you face that choice."

"And what's that? What's the truth?" She asked, frustrated.

This time she was certain the snake smiled.

"Every aspect of life issss based on a choice we make. Inaction is a choice. Sssubjugating the weak is a choice. Death in the face of defeat issss a choice."

Mulatiwa slithered forward, his snout a hand's breadth from Millie's face, turning to watch her with one of his black, unblinking eyes.

"The question will be, Mildred, what choice will you make when the time comessss?"

Millie twitched in her sleep, her body reacting to a misstep she'd never taken. Gilbert grunted in his sleep, lifting his head groggily and looking around the room. He'd moved them to the bed, though she was still wrapped up in the soft cotton towel he'd bundled her up in after the bath.

"What is it?" he asked, voice still thick with sleep as he pushed himself up onto an elbow and looked around the room with bleary eyes. It was morning, though the usual sunshine was missing, replaced by a dull grey light that announced the storm had truly begun.

"Just a dream," she said, resting a hand on his arm. "I'm sorry I woke you up." She looked up at him, the snake's words still ringing in her mind. She had married this man, a near stranger, when he'd made the offer, just as she had come back to this hellish city to save the legacy of her friend's family.

"It's alright," Gilbert said, rubbing his eyes. "I still need your help with something, if you're willing."

"I'll do my best." Millie yawned and stretched her legs out as straight as they would go, toes pointed. "You bought me beignets and had a bath ready, which earned you a lot of goodwill." She rolled over, wrapping her arms around him once again.

"Thank you," she said, pressing her ear against his chest. "I'm sorry I—"

He shushed her, running his fingers along her scalp. Her hair had grown since they'd left Wyndford, and the fuzz along her scalp felt wonderful as he played his fingertips over it.

"You're the strongest woman I know," he said. "Thank you for trusting me enough to see more than just your spiky shell."

Millie pulled back just far enough to look at him. "You make me feel safe," she admitted. "Safe enough to just be myself. Please don't take advantage of that. I don't know if I'd be able to survive it a second time."

He pulled her close, sealing the unspoken promise with a kiss.

THE PROBLEM WITH COFFEE was that it was only accessible in the kitchen, which meant she and Gilbert eventually had to dress and head down to the dining room where the others were eating breakfast. The tension was palpable between the humans. Pierre looked like a kicked puppy who kept sneaking glances at Nathie, who frostily ignored each and every one. The dog barrelled down the stairs and trotted over to Ruth, begging shamelessly for a bit of bacon. Annie and Ghat looked up from their eggs and toast, both looking relieved that they were no longer left alone with the fighting humans.

"It's one of the O'Learys," Millie announced, setting down the paper bag of beignets next to her plate and immediately reaching for the coffee cup and carafe. Nathalie reached out and swatted the back of Millie's hand with a spoon.

"Let someone else pour," Nathalie snapped. "I'm already going to have to re-enchant my bathtub. Leave my poor carafe in peace." Gilbert smiled and picked up the coffee, pouring Millie a full cup. He set down the ledger next to his own place setting and poured himself a cup to equal hers.

"Rude," Millie muttered, rubbing the back of her hand.

"I found Fred's debt book yesterday," Gilbert said, and Millie blinked in surprise. She'd never thought banking would be helpful, but it turned out Fred was even more of an idiot than she'd expected. Every loan, every interest payment, was logged in that book Gilbert had found.

"His what?" Pierre asked with a small frown. Millie and the rest of the table ignored him.

"Fred had been racking up unheard-of amounts of debt as the war got closer," Gilbert continued, flipping through the book until he reached the last page where the note had been pasted. Millie had confirmed it was Fred's writing upstairs. "I thought at first it would be the usual vices. But he was spending all this money on preparing for the war. Buying weapons and bullets for his slaves, who were training to fight and become his personal army."

Millie made a face at that. It was true, but she'd been certain that it was proof Fred was one of 'the good ones'. He was arming his people, promising them freedom and preparing them for the fight that would earn everyone in Amelior the same. Instead, he'd looked at the two sides of the conflict and correctly guessed the Union would come out the victor. The bastard had been rewriting his history even before the war started.

A glance toward Ghat told her the conjure queen felt similarly conflicted. She had been old enough to remember the hushed conversations held in the slave dormitories, debating the value of freedom when paired with the risk of war. Eventually, and with Clem and Delilah's help, Millie had convinced most of the able-bodied slaves to join the militia. Now they were all dead. All of them.

Millie pulled out a beignet and tapped the excess powdered sugar off onto her plate, wishing she could shake off her guilt so easily. The pastries were a day old, but delicious when dipped into fresh coffee.

"The question is," she said, around a nibble of the pastry, "Which O'Leary is it? The General died in prison shortly after he was tried for treason. I killed his eldest son, Paul—"

"You what?" Nathalie said, dropping her spoon onto her eggs. "When? Why didn't you tell us?"

Millie shrugged, glancing at Pierre. He'd known, hadn't he? Or had he been up North by that point? It was all fuzzy and hard to remember.

"It was a duel. He insisted on fighting me himself. Technically, it was legal. Old Man O'Leary couldn't come after Fred officially, but war was declared within the week and Fred and the Irregulars evacuated Marigot to head north for orders from the main Union forces." She took a sip of coffee and another bite of the beignet.

"My guess is it's a direct relative of Paul," Gilbert said. "Though that is just a guess at the moment. I'll need Pierre's help today to go to the city archives and see what we can find for who is still alive and who isn't."

Pierre straightened in his seat, nodding eagerly. Whatever was going on between him and Nathalie seemed to make him eager to help. Millie would wait to see if Pierre was still eager when the scary men with guns showed up.

"Excellent. Mildred, I was hoping I could borrow you for a personal errand today," Nathalie said, spots of colour appearing on her pale cheeks. "I would very much like to show you my family's home and see what you can remember. If that's alright."

The warmth in Millie's belly from the morning faded. She nodded, swallowing her mouthful of beignet. Nathalie was dressed in reasonable clothing this morning, which should have clued Millie in that the other woman had plans to go out into the storm. Millie hoped she wouldn't need to walk through the swamp barefoot and drunk on tea again, but she would if it meant giving Nathalie some measure of closure.

"It's the very least I can do," Millie said. "I hope I can find the answers you need." Under the table, Gilbert rested his hand on her knee and gave a gentle squeeze. She slipped her hand over his and gave a gentle squeeze back. Hopefully, her swamp clothes were dry from yesterday. It wouldn't make sense to stain another shirt.

"Excellent, we'll set out once we've finished eating," Nathalie said with a firm voice, despite the grief lurking in her eyes. Annie shot Millie a questioning look, but a swift blow from Ghat's elbow stopped questions before they could be spoken.

Ruth returned from the kitchen with a fresh pot of coffee and a telegram card in hand. She handed the card to Nathalie and topped up Millie's cup.

The colour drained from Nathalie's face as she read the telegram and, wordlessly; she held it out to Millie. Taking it, the elf skimmed the block letters.

Coming to Marigot. W behind F, dangerous to share who. Will arrive Thurs eve. -R

Millie frowned. Annie leaned over and Millie handed her the telegram.

"It's Wednesday today," she said, looking up at Gilbert. She wasn't entirely sure how long she'd spent in the swamp. "Right?"

"Thursday," he said, grim. He'd read the telegram over her shoulder. "They're going to arrive in the middle of the storm."

Nathalie stood, tossing aside her napkin. Millie wracked her brain for who 'W' could be. She knew people who had names that started with the letter, but they were as dead as everyone else she'd known in Marigot.

"Ruth, I need you to send a reply immediately," Nathalie said, panic creeping into her voice. "Tell them to stay in St-Makir's."

"They'll be on the boat already," Millie said, biting her lip. "Annie, can you find the boat and tell them to turn around before it's too late? Please, I know the storm is bad, but—"

"But it's Ryan," Annie said, grim. "Yeah, I can. It's tough flying in this weather, but it's Ryan." She shovelled the last bit of egg onto her toast and shoved it into her mouth. She stood, brushing off the crumbs onto her pants, and slipped out of the room to get ready.

Nathalie nodded, chewing on the cuticle of her thumb. She paced, and Millie got up and walked over to her. Rhiannon was Millie's friend, but she'd seen how much Nathalie cared about her cousin. Millie knew she was not the only one who saw Rhiannon as a sister.

"Annie will find them," she said, catching Nathalie by the arms. "You heard her. She cares as much for Rhiannon as we do. She'll make sure Rhiannon gets to safety. It'll be okay."

Nathie took a deep breath and nodded. Millie watched her repeat the assurances to herself under her breath.

"Do you still want to go to the farm?" she asked the human woman. Nathalie nodded again, visibly pulling herself together. As much as the two clashed, Millie recognised how difficult this was going to be for Nathalie. That she was still determined to go, in a storm, made the elf see Rhiannon's grit shine through her cousin's glamorous exterior. It was comforting.

"Yes," Nathie said. "It's up river. If anything happens, we'll be closer to help the ferry. Please be ready within the hour. I'd like to get there before the storm gets much worse."

Millie nodded. The dog heaved himself to his feet with a yawn and trotted over to lean into her leg. Having him come with them might help soothe Nathie's worries. Rhiannon's family liked dogs, right?

"I'll be ready in fifteen minutes."

37

RECLAMATIONS

NATHALIE

THE RAIN WAS FITTING for the day's work and suited Nathie's penchant for the dramatic, but it made for a miserable trip upriver to the Wolfe farm. The wind had picked up, blowing hard at their backs, which made for less work paddling their canoe, but it meant they would have to face the wind on their return. Already, the normally placid river was choppy, and Nathie knew it would get worse as the storm intensified.

"Tell me about him," Mildred said, seated at the front of the canoe, with the dog lying down right behind her. She'd borrowed an oilcloth cape from Ruth. All of Nathie's had been far too large and all of Owen's were too small. "Your father, you said he was a good man. I'd like to hear about him, if you're willing to share."

The request shook Nathie out of her grim thoughts.

"Why?" she asked, digging in her paddle hard against the current. The fingertips of her hand at the base of the paddle brushed the top of a wave. The water was still warm, but it had already cooled from the rain. By the time the storm had passed, the river would be the same temperature as a rain barrel.

"I'd like to apologise properly," Mildred said, having to raise her voice to be heard over the rain. "Knowing more about who he is might help me remember. But if not, it still helps me understand what he meant to you, how much I took from you. If you don't want to talk about him to me, I'll understand."

Nathie thought about that, and for once, Mildred didn't press the issue. They paddled in silence for a while, but as they neared the farm, the memories choked out the rest of Nathalie's thoughts.

"He worshipped my mother while she was still alive," Nathie said, feeling her throat grow tight. "After she died, he focused on me. We visited Wyndford every summer, but for the rest of the year, we lived in Marigot and on the farm. He preferred being out here to the city."

The river curved ahead of them, winding to their left. The farm was behind the bend, Nathie knew. It still produced sugar, but at a reduced capacity compared to during her childhood. She was afraid to learn the reason, but that was part of why she'd asked Mildred to come.

"He used to tell me," Nathie continued. "He used to tell me that as the landowners, it was our role to keep our workers safe, fed, and sheltered. The work was hard, but that was so important to him. He loved this farm, and he wanted to make sure I loved it too."

Mildred glanced over her shoulder, but only for a moment.

"I ruined that for you," Millie said. Nathie knew it wasn't a question, but felt the need to answer it, regardless.

"Yes." She took a shaky breath and forced it out, blowing away a drop of rain from the tip of her nose. "But it was more than just you. It was the war. It was watching husband after husband try to work our farm hands into the dirt. I think, mostly, it was me growing up."

Rounding the bend, Nathalie steered them toward the left bank. There was a simple dock there, used mostly for cargo barges to carry equipment in from the city, and sugar out to it. Next to the dock was a sloping bank that would work better for the canoe.

"I can understand that much," Mildred said, her voice almost lost in the rain's din. "I lost my father when I was very young. Old enough to remember it happening, but too young to remember much else about him other than glimpses." Nathie watched the elf's shoulders sag slightly.

"How did he die?"

"I don't know," Mildred answered, hopping out of the canoe into the water as they reached the riverbank. The dog followed, splashing ahead onto the grassy bank. The elf grabbed onto the front of the canoe and pulled it up to rest partially on the grass. "He might have been stabbed, or might have been shot. I just remember a lot of blood, and that my mother never recovered after."

It was odd. Nathie had never really considered if Mildred had a family before. She'd been a slave.

"What about her?" Nathie asked, climbing out of the canoe. She stowed her paddle in the bottom and helped the elf haul it up the grass so the rising water wouldn't pull it away. The dog immediately trotted ahead, sniffing at the ground intensely.

"She sold me to Rousseau for half a barrel of wine," Millie said, her voice flat. She turned the canoe over, so the rain wouldn't fill it, and tucked her own paddle into the space underneath. "Then she kept trying to take my earnings until she died."

Nathie watched as the elf looked around them, desperate for any sign of recognition on that pale face. Surely Mildred would remember, she just needed to be here.

"How did she die?" Nathie asked, unable to resist pressing the issue. "Was she killed, too?"

Mildred's face was impassive as she turned to look at Nathie. Her lilac eyes looked almost grey in the weather, reflecting the miserable day with a stoniness that Nathie was familiar with. She'd seen it in the mirror often enough when discussing the death of some unwanted husbands.

"In a way. I found her in a ditch near the Rousseau Plantation. She was drunk, and had somehow made it out there from the city, probably to beg for more money."

"You left her there."

"I did. It rained, she drowned. I don't think she ever woke up," Mildred said. "There are deaths on my hands that I regret, but she was the one who killed herself. I just didn't reach out to save her that night."

Nathie nodded as if she understood. There were plenty of people she would leave to drown, but she'd always taken a more proactive approach to people who were in her way.

"Well, this is it," she said, changing the topic. "There used to be a barn over that way, up that little incline by the far side of the cane field. It burnt down after the war and we stopped breeding horses at this location, so I chose not to rebuild."

The women trudged along the access path, each walking in a wheel rut left by carts used to load the barges with sugar while the dog ranged nearby, unbothered by the weather. The rain grew louder the closer they got to the sugarcane field; leaves rustling with every raindrop.

"Up ahead was the house, though it's empty now. The workers live in the dormitory off to the right..."

Mildred had slowed and was staring back over at the hill where the barn used to be. A thrill of nervousness ran through Nathie, and she swallowed hard to keep the hope out of her voice.

"Do you remember something?" She asked.

"Can we head that way?" Mildred asked. "I remember a barn. There was a storm, worse than now, and we needed shelter. We were starving."

Nathie bit the inside of her lip. She nodded, leading the way around the sugar cane to the stone foundation of the old barn. In the years since, grasses had overtaken the ruin. An apple tree had grown in the old manure pile, and now green fruit hung from its branches. It was still too early in the year for them to be ripe.

Mildred climbed up onto one pile of rock, lifting a hand to shield her eyes from the rain.

"We were starving," she said again, sounding like her thoughts were far away. "We hadn't eaten proper rations in weeks, and we were desperate for supplies. If we didn't find something to eat, we would be forced to risk the vishaps and go diving for catfish."

Nathie held her breath, a hand pressed to her mouth.

"We'd lost two soldiers to the river trying just that, earlier in the week. The vishaps got used to the taste of dead bodies from the fighting, and they'd started stalking any encampment we made. Most of the farms were heavily fortified or were burnt."

She said nothing for a while, then turned to Nathie with sad eyes.

"Our scout had said the house was empty," the elf said. "I'm so sorry. He said it was completely empty."

38

THE FOG OF WAR

MILLIE

THE PLANTATION HAD LOOKED like any other, until Nathalie pointed out where the barn used to be. Now, standing on a pile of rocks that had once been the building's foundation, Millie was catching glimpses of a memory. She closed her eyes and slipped the hood of her cape back to feel the rain on her face, the way she had that night.

"His name was Remi," she said. "He was one of the few human soldiers in our company, and by then he was the only one left other than Fred." She took a deep breath, and she was certain she could smell the lingering smoke from the other plantations that had been burnt down. "Remi was awful, but he didn't lie to Fred, so when he reported that the house ahead looked abandoned but intact, I led the sortie to find out."

Rain pounded down, flooding out the low-lying sugarcane field that stretched between the scouting party and the landowner's manor. It turned the dirt to mud underfoot, leaving the footpaths between sugarcane rows treacherous despite the traction that fallen leaves provided. The cane was almost ready for harvest, the stalks taller than Akhun by a head, giving even the eight-foot-tall orc full cover. In a few weeks, whoever remained to work the fields would burn off the leaves to make harvesting the cane easier.

Harvests were brutal: slaves worked until they died on their feet. The bodies were moved aside until the crop had been collected, then buried in the fields over winter to fertilise the soil for the next year. Orcish spell-singers sang of decay to speed the process along, while human overseers stood carefully out of range of the spell. It was a wonder the field workers didn't trip over bones more often.

Mildred led the pack, water sloshing around her thighs as she waded through the field. Her ears perked to catch any strange sounds, but the din of rain on leaves overhead made that nearly impossible.

A tap on her shoulder drew her attention, and she looked back to see Akhun tap his nose, then lift his hand with his middle and ring fingers pressed to his thumb, pinky and index raised. He smelled dogs. Mildred had yet to catch the scent, but she trusted him. It figured Remi had fucked up the initial reconnaissance. If there were dogs, there were people. The master's house was hardly abandoned.

Mildred raised her hand, curling her fingers into a fist to signal a halt. Remi, already useless in the dark, would stay put, more of a liability in the darkness than he usually was. Slipping her rifle off her shoulders, she passed her gun down to the human to hold clear of the mud and water.

Mildred gestured to La Paz to join Akhun, and motioned for Lavoie to follow as she stepped through the gap between clusters of sugar cane. She and Lavoie were slight enough to pass through the rows of cane, circling around toward the boundary of the cane field where the lawns of the plantation began. There would be less cover there, but unless some of this plantation's slaves remained loyal, Millie and her squad could sneak over without being spotted. The rain would cover their footsteps, and hide their scent from the dogs.

Nearing the edge of the field, Mildred eased into a crouch, partially submerging in the cold floodwater to keep from being seen. The field had been built in a hollow of the land to help with irrigation, and the land rose steadily up from where she crouched to the small hill where the manor was built. Earthen berms had been built up around it to keep the flood at bay, but the water had yet to extend beyond the lowest third of the lawns.

The dirt berms wouldn't cause a problem for them. They were only about three feet tall and built to keep floodwater at bay, not soldiers.

Millie opened her eyes and looked out over the 'farm'. It was a plantation, but if Nathalie's father had wanted it to seem like something less cruel to a daughter he loved, Millie wasn't about to ruin that illusion just yet.

"It was a little later into storm season," she said, stepping down from the rocks. "The cane was taller, nine feet, maybe."

Millie looked at Nathalie, unsure if this was helping, but the human woman nodded. Her eyes were over-bright, and Millie hoped it was grief that gave them that gleam, rather than hatred.

"I don't remember much else yet, but I can tell you what we would have done," Millie said. She started for the cane fields, circling around to enter them near the riverside. "The cane was an ideal cover, especially when we weren't sure what we were walking into. Some homesteads were sympathetic, others were hoping to kill us to claim the bounties O'Leary established."

"Bounties on the company?" Nathalie asked, following behind. Millie tried to ignore the itch between her shoulder blades. Something was off, but she wasn't able to pin down what it was just yet. If Nathalie had wanted to kill her, she could have done it on the river.

"On escaped slaves," she answered. "Akhun's was the highest. He—" Her throat caught on the memory. Millie forced the emotions down with a deep breath. "He was my friend. Akhun had escaped before and been caught, and before the Rousseaus bought him, he had been owned by one of the other families. Gallois, I think."

Glancing to the side, Millie caught herself expecting to see his hulking shadow moving silently through the cane, one row away. But he'd been dead for nearly ten years. Akhun was gone, even though he felt so much closer out in the field than at any other time since the war. Millie had to stop herself from reaching out into the rain, hoping to find her friend's massive hand.

"What happened to him?" Nathalie asked. "Was he caught?"

"He died," Millie said bluntly. "He died fighting at the battle of Chasseurville." The battle wasn't as famous as the one for Marigot. It had been a victory, but both sides suffered heavy losses because of the muddy terrain. And as far as Millie could tell, once she'd escaped Fred, no one wanted to talk about the vishaps and what had happened the night after.

"Ghat's older sister was here," Millie said. "Annie's mother, too. The three of them were my regular squad. If I had to go look for food, I would have brought them." The wisp of Clem's laugh caught Millie's ear, nearly lost in the rustling of sugarcane leaves.

"Did you hear that?" She asked, looking back at Nathalie. The human shook her head slowly.

"Was it the dog? I didn't hear anything."

Millie had known returning to Marigot would be difficult, but she felt like her sanity was unravelling. That had been Clem's laugh, and she was certain that she'd glimpsed Akhun moments before, walking alongside them. She pinched the bridge of her nose and closed her eyes, focusing on the sound of the rain and the smell of the infamous black mud that made Marigot so fertile.

"Are you alright?" Nathalie asked, and Millie felt a gentle hand rest on her shoulder.

"Ghat didn't give you any tea to slip into my coffee, did she?" Mildred asked, letting her eyes open and her hand drop. It felt like reality was a slip of silk right now, and she couldn't quite keep her grip on it.

Nathalie frowned, the sharpness returning to her expression that had been missing since Millie had returned from the swamp.

"I didn't poison you," she said, removing her hand from Millie's shoulder. She brushed past Millie, marching up the row of sugarcane toward the edge of the field.

"I didn't mean–" Millie called after her. Swearing under her breath, the elf followed. The dog was still exploring the field and could wait.

The water was up to her thighs, cold from the storm. Millie crouched, sinking into it up to her neck as she watched a light bob along the dark lawn. The smell of wet dogs was thick in her nose, but Millie couldn't see them.

"You killed me, you know," Delilah *whispered into her ear. "I left my sister all alone in this world because you said you would keep us safe."*

Millie blinked away the memory. Delilah had died when they'd breached Marigot, nearly a year after the company had been raiding in this area. Whatever Ghat had given her seemed to still be fucking with her. Slapping her cheeks, Millie tried to shake off the intruding visions. These were *not* memories.

Squeezing her eyes shut, Millie took a few deep breaths and crouched, putting her hands on her knees. She was stronger than this, at least. She *could* be stronger than this for long enough to help Nathalie and get away from the plantation. Sometimes it was important to be realistic with yourself, and Millie was barely holding on to what was real and what wasn't. Whatever had happened in the Grand-dame's hut had left Millie seeing shadows in the corner of her vision.

"You're going to kill me too, you know."

Millie's eyes flew open, and she looked to her left to glimpse Rhiannon fading into the sugarcane.

"That's not fair," she muttered, glaring at the direction the shadow had gone in. "She's not even dead." Pushing herself to her feet, she wiped her hands on her leggings and hurried after Nathalie.

The human woman waited at the entrance to the house, arms crossed and glaring at Millie from under the hood of her cape. It was very imposing, but right now, the sight of someone solid was a blessing. Millie made it up to the top of the rise and stopped, staring at the home.

Snatches of memory were surfacing, but they were out of order, and Millie wasn't sure if it was even from the same night.

"You had dogs," she said, looking at Nathalie. "Right? They were outside."

Nathalie's scowl tightened, but she nodded. "A few were guarding the house with our groundskeeper. Who was also dead, by the way. I'm shocked you didn't kill Rufus and Philip, too."

Millie opened her mouth to ask who those men were, only to shut it when she realised Nathalie was talking about the dogs. Right.

"Akhun and Delilah made them sleep, so we didn't need to hurt them," Millie said, feeling the tips of her ears get warm.

"But you thought killing our groundskeeper was fine?" Nathalie asked. "What kind of logic is that?"

"Flawed logic," Millie admitted. "Dogs aren't cruel, but their masters can be. We didn't know who was here, just that we needed food. If there hadn't been any inside, we probably would have taken the dogs back to camp to eat them."

Nathalie recoiled from Millie, horrified.

"What kind of monster are you?" the woman hissed.

"Well, they called me the Bayou Butcher, so..." Millie trailed off. Nathalie's scowl was back, and Millie lifted her hands. "Okay, that was a tasteless joke, but I need you to understand just how desperate we were. We needed food. If you don't eat, you can't fight. In a war, if you can't fight, you die. And they weren't killing escaped slaves with bullets back then. They were making examples out of us."

While Nathalie seemed determined to remain angry, Millie saw shame soften her scowl and those dark green eyes dropped to stare at the ground.

Wordlessly, Nathalie pulled out a key and unlocked the house. She pushed the door open and stepped inside, out of the rain. Millie followed, glimpsing some other long-dead shadow slip down the entryway into a side room. It moved too quickly to see which face it wore this time, but the shape had been too small to be Akhun.

Peeling off the wet cape, Millie walked into the bare home. It had been furnished back then, she assumed. Sparsely, though, if she could trust her memory at all.

"We thought the house was empty, at first," she said. "I would have picked the lock and slipped inside to check for anyone else, but I wouldn't have let the others in if I thought more people were left. I figured maybe a maid or two. It looked like the house was closed up, the owners gone."

Nathalie's boots clicked on the wooden floor behind her, following Millie step by step.

"We were planning to leave once the storm let up," Nathie said quietly. "But Papa didn't get that chance."

Millie's ears drooped, but she didn't hang her head. More of the memory was coming back to her with every step. She had hurt Nathalie terribly, but her actions hadn't been malicious that night. Not like some of the other raids she had led.

"I led us to the pantry and kitchen, and we searched for food that we could take," she said, feeling a tug in her chest, as though the memory itself was pulling her toward the place where everything had gone wrong.

"Remi..." Millie breathed, stopping just outside the kitchen. "I'd lost track of Remi while looking for food until I heard something upstairs. A man's voice. I couldn't let Remi fuck the night up any more than he already had, so I went upstairs and threw him out of the bedroom where your father was."

Yes, this much she remembered. It was the night she'd taken Remi's eye. He'd argued with her after she had killed Nathalie's father, threatened to kill her and then blame it on the owner. Fred would never have believed him, but Remi had been a special kind of stupid, the kind that thought his plan was invulnerable.

The master's house was dark, but it offered a respite from the rain that made it easier to listen for the sound of any more dogs or servants that might be left behind to take care of the empty house. How predictable were masters that they cared more about their buildings than the lives of the people left behind to protect them?

Mildred sneered at the thought as she passed silently by sparsely furnished rooms, each item covered in a sheet to keep the dust off. She checked those on the right while Clem searched any room to the left. Akhun held the rear at the door, ready to hold off any surprise visitors. Remi and Delilah followed, the former eying the house's fixtures with greed while the latter had a hand pressed to her belly. Mildred felt it too, the slow gnaw of an empty stomach feeding on itself in the absence of food.

Millie checked the next room and smiled to herself as she discovered the kitchen. She did a quick sweep for any cooks or servants and stepped out into the hall to motion her squad over. Akhun and Delilah joined her, searching the kitchen and attached pantry for food that would last well.

Salted meat, canned vegetables, and hardtack biscuits were all carefully packed into rucksacks, wrapped in oilcloth sheets to keep them from spoiling in the rain.

There wasn't enough food to keep the whole company fed, but it was enough to give them a reprieve from starvation. Clem whistled softly, and motioned Millie over to look at a trap door that had been hidden under a braided rug. They crouched in front of it. Millie drew her revolver and held it ready as Clem lifted it to peer inside.

No surprise attackers leapt forth, so Millie turned and motioned for Delilah to join Clem in investigating what might be in the cellar. She frowned, doing a quick head-count. Akhun was still wrapping food, but Remi was missing.

"Shit," she hissed under her breath. "Keep working. I need to find the rat bastard," she whispered to Delilah, her unofficial second-in-command. The woman nodded and made a sympathetic face. She'd been right. They were babysitting tonight.

Millie stepped out of the kitchen, ears perked for the clumsy footsteps of their human compatriot. What she heard instead was a scuffle and an angry shout from upstairs. Millie broke into a run, taking the steps two at a time. Remi might be a shit soldier, but he was an enthusiastic killer. Too enthusiastic, and Millie wasn't willing to risk the screams of some poor asshole drawing the attention of anyone. The nearest homestead was a mile downriver, but the Marigot army had started to patrol the plantations after Millie had started burning them down.

"Stand down," she shouted, spotting the room that glowed with the light of Remi's stupid lantern.

A man grunted and Remi hauled him up to the doorway, a knife pressed to the man's throat. This was a master, there was no doubt about it. Kindly wrinkles at his eyes belied his soft hands and the comfortable paunch around his middle. The man was terrified. His eyes were wide, and he held his hands out to show he meant no harm.

"Did you say something?" Remi asked, grinning at Millie with those shark teeth. "I couldn't hear you over the squealing of this pig."

"Stand. Down," Millie hissed. "That's an order, soldier."

But Remi's eyes glinted. He stuck the knife into the master's belly twice before Millie reached them. He shoved his victim directly into her, and the injured man knocked Millie into the room Remi had left his lantern in. She kept her footing, shoving the master off her and to the side. It was a bedroom, probably his. Simple and expensive, the white linens of the bed staining red as the man fell against the bed before slinking to the floor.

"I don't take orders from elves," Remi spat, "Our captain said—"

Millie drew her revolver and fired. A single, neat hole appeared in the master's forehead. It was a far kinder death than the gut wound that Remi had inflicted. Then, so quiet that she almost didn't hear anything at all, Millie heard a gasp.

Shit. There was more than just the master.

"No witnesses," Mildred said, crouching next to the man she had just killed with her back to Remi. She searched his pockets and pulled out a ring of keys, surreptitiously sneaking a glance under the bed. Two large, frightened eyes stared out at her from a pale, blood-splattered face. A girl, covering her mouth with her hands. She was older than Millie had

been when she killed for the first time, but this girl didn't deserve whatever Remi would do if he found out she was there.

"Did you hear me?" The bastard strode over and kicked Millie over, laughing as she rolled through the blood slowly pooling by the dead man.

Remi didn't realise the mistake he had made until Millie launched herself at him. He jabbed forward with his knife, but she ducked under it, tackling him to the ground. He was taller and stronger than she was, but Millie was better trained. Scrambling up, she pinned his arms to the floor with her knees and grabbed each side of his face, forcing him to look up at her.

"Take a last good look at me," she snarled. "If you ever question my orders again, I will leave you blind. Do you understand?"

He didn't. Not until she dug his eye out with her fingers and crushed it in her hand in front of his face. "Don't ever look at me like you're better than me," she said, tossing the useless eye aside. "Know your place, private." She got off him, hauling him up to his feet and shoving him out of the room.

He was still screaming about his eye as he stumbled down the stairs, tripping and falling down the last few. He landed in the middle of the foyer as the other members of the squad reluctantly came out to check on him.

Millie wiped her hand clean on the bed's ruined sheets and followed at a measured pace, closing the door to the bedroom behind her.

"And you shot him." Nathalie finished. "Because he saw you."

Millie let out a slow breath, turning to face the woman she had orphaned that night.

"I shot him, and I ruined your life."

She saw the slap coming, but did nothing to dodge it. Nathalie was much stronger than she looked, and the strike made Millie stagger back a few steps. Her ear was ringing, and Millie flicked it a few times to get the sound to stop, with no luck.

"Why not just make him promise?" Nathie shouted, pointing up at the staircase that led to the bedrooms. "Why did you have to *kill* him?"

Millie rubbed her stinging cheek and looked up at the furious woman. Nathalie had every right to hate her, and if she drew a gun on Millie at that very moment, the elf wasn't sure she would try to stop her.

"I killed him because I was a soldier, and I had orders," Millie said. "Which is no excuse, even if I thought it was back then. No survivors, no witnesses." Only she hadn't held up that order either, had she?

"I want to hate you," Nathalie spat, her shoulders trembling. "I hated you for years and then you did the one thing that I thought was impossible. You brought Rhiannon back." She clenched her hand, and for a moment, Millie was certain another slap was coming. Instead, Nathalie turned and slammed her fist into the wall, shattering plaster and breaking a few of the wooden slats that held the plaster in place.

That was not the punch of a high society lady. Millie saw the way Nathalie had pivoted and threw her weight behind it. That was a punch that could break an elf's jaw.

"You trained, didn't you?" Millie whispered. "You trained since the war, so that you could kill me."

"And look where it got me," Nathalie cried, cradling her hand to her chest. "Instead of killing you, I *owe* you for saving my cousin. For telling me the truth about Pierre." Her shoulders shook and Nathalie valiantly tried to pull herself together. The hole in the wall flickered, and Clem's eye appeared behind it, peering out with a giggle. Millie tried to ignore it.

"I need to know," the human woman said, finally letting out a sob. "I need to know if my father was as good a man as I thought he was, or if he was just like all the rest. I need to know, Mildred. Please, where would he have punished our slaves?"

Millie swallowed. She didn't want to do this, but she couldn't lie to this woman about her father. Not after taking away any chance for him to explain to his daughter what running a plantation was like.

"It's in the kitchen," Millie said, defeated. "It's a cellar in the kitchen. We found it while searching for food that night."

39

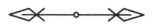

PENANCE PAID

NATHALIE

"THE CELLAR IN THE kitchen is just a food cellar," Nathie said, but her voice sounded doubtful, even to her. Her hands wouldn't stop trembling, so she crossed her arms and pinned the treacherous things down. "We kept cheeses and wine in there, not *people*."

Nathie hated the way Mildred was looking at her, those purple eyes so full of pity when she should be wracked with guilt.

"I'll show you," the elf said, leading the way to the kitchen. "I don't think your father was a bad man, Nathalie. But good people can do awful things, sometimes."

Nathie wanted to snap that there was a difference, that her father had never kept someone chained up in a cellar, but the need to know the truth made her follow. The elf's ears kept twitching, flicking up and back before repeating, like she was a cat trying to figure out where the mouse had run off to.

Belatedly, Nathie realised that while this felt like it could be a trap, she didn't think it was. Mildred was many things, among them a murderer, but she was straightforward. If she wanted Nathie dead, she would have probably said so. It was an odd comfort, one that coaxed her over to the cellar door.

The elf kicked aside the rug and knelt to pull the wooden trapdoor open. It opened soundlessly, still as well-maintained as if it was part of a thriving household. The cellar was pitch black, but Mildred descended the steps without hesitation. A moment later, a match flared to life in the darkness, and shielding her eyes, Millie lit a half-used candle that was set on the nearest shelf.

"It's back here."

Leaving the candle for Nathie, the elf walked to the far end of the cellar. A few barrels of grain stood along the far wall, and with a grunt, the elf rolled them out of the way, one by one. Unable to stand and watch any longer, Nathie descended, picking up the candle to light her way. The farm cellar was far better kept than the one at Rousseau House, with stone walls that were dusty but free of mildew. The ground was paved with wood engraved with sigils to keep the moisture out.

"Here," Mildred said, crouching by the wooden slats that had been under the barrels. Pulling out her axe, the elf stuck the spike under a wooden slat. Pushing down on the axe handle levered it up with a crack. Pulling the plank to the side, Mildred dug into the soil with the pick, loosening it until her axe struck something metal with a muffled 'clink'.

Nathie's heart sank. She nearly dropped the candle as she staggered to her knees, digging through the exposed dirt with her free hand.

"The chains," the elf was saying. "It might have been from before your father. We can't know for certain."

Did it matter? Nathie gulped down air thick with the smell of dirt, exposing more of the shackles with frantic digging. The life she'd grown up with was a lie. The Wolfes had owned slaves, yes, but she'd thought they were one of the good families. That they didn't rely on the barbaric punishments the Rousseaus had used.

A sob bubbled up in her throat, and Nathie collapsed on the ground, hot wax stinging her hand as the candle spilled. Careful hands removed the candle, setting it aside somewhere. The same hand caught her face and pulled Nathalie's head up to look at Mildred in a tender moment.

"I'm so sorry," Mildred whispered. The elf lifted her free hand and opened it, blowing a fine powder into Nathie's face. She tried not to breathe it in, but her tears drew in a ragged breath. The powder numbed her face instantly, and Nathie struggled to push the elf away, but the powdered frog was a powerful paralytic. Her hands felt like blocks of wood, and Nathie landed a single blow before her arms became too weak to do anything more than bat the elf in the face.

"I'm so sorry," Mildred whispered again through a newly split lip. She hadn't even flinched when Nathie hit her. She lowered the woman to the ground gently. "Someone has been following us, and I can't let you get hurt. I didn't save your life that night to let you die now."

Nathalie watched, unable to look away, as the elf picked the candle up from where she'd wedged it between two floorboards and blew it out.

"Take care of Rhiannon," Mildred whispered from the darkness.

The elf climbed out of the cellar and closed the trapdoor behind her, leaving Nathie in complete darkness. She tried to scream, but could do nothing but listen to the footsteps overhead.

40

A TAINTED LEGACY

GILBERT

WITH MILLIE AND NATHALIE gone to her 'farm' and Annie flying out to warn the ferry of the incoming storm, Gilbert and Pierre set out for the city's archive to get a full list of surviving O'Leary descendants.

Marigot's archives were across the street from its high court, the buildings of brick and plaster well-kept with planters of flowers that now had burlap tied over them to protect the blooms from the heavy rain. It was comfortable inside, reminding Gil of his old university's library. Large wooden desks with caged lanterns filled the main floor while archivists in white cotton gloves carried large leather-bound volumes from tables to shelves and back again.

"Where do we start?" Pierre muttered, looking around.

Someone shushed them, and Gil raised an eyebrow. The 'shh' had been twice as loud as Pierre's question. Marigot was beautiful, but Gilbert wouldn't mind if most of its population suddenly fell into the river. Turning toward the sound, Gil spotted an archivist frowning at him over her delicate spectacles.

"Excuse me," he said, walking directly over to the woman. He exaggerated the tap of his cane with each step, leaning on it more heavily than he needed to. The archivist was middle-aged, a dowdy sort that probably prided herself on keeping order within the most ordered part of the city. At the sight of his cane, her frown disappeared and was replaced by girlish embarrassment.

"I'm so sorry, sir. I didn't mean to cause any disrespect. I didn't realise you were a veteran," the lady babbled in a voice quiet from years of shushing others. She adjusted her spectacles. "I hope you got the greenskin who hurt you."

Ah.

Gilbert's smile hardened slightly.

"Actually, it was the traitor Rousseau who shot me," Gilbert said honestly. The archivist gasped, placing her gloved hands over her mouth. He had her sympathy now, so Gil turned on his schoolboy charm. "I'm looking for the birth and death records for General Robert O'Leary. He said that he was an admirer of the great man. I have a debate to settle with my friend about one of his descendants, you see."

The archivist lit up and clapped her gloved hands together like a giddy schoolgirl.

"Oh! How marvellous! Right this way, sir." She hopped off her stool and scurried ahead to a shelf with large leather-bound books. She counted her way through the alphabet and pulled the 'O' archive out, grunting under the weight. Gilbert watched, feeling no urge to help the racist little woman.

"Here," she puffed, sliding the book onto a nearby table. "Here it is. Now," she paused between words to catch a breath, "who are we looking for?" She pushed up her spectacles and smiled up at Gilbert.

"My friend here believes that there's a direct descendent of our dear General with the initial W. I've pointed out that none of his children or grandchildren had such a name."

"Oh, no," the archivist said, clasping her gloved hands to her chest in delight. She didn't even open the book. "Not by first name. There hasn't been a Wilbur O'Leary since General Robert's grandfather, but his second daughter, Shannon, married into a very wealthy family up north before the war started."

Gilbert's gut sank. They'd been looking in the wrong place. If the threat had been a northerner, why lure Millie to Marigot? If it was a matter of getting her away from Wyndford, causing a crisis at Scorched Bluffs would have been a more certain success. Besides, they had been attacked when Ghat's shop had been set on fire. They were in the right place.

"A wealthy family up north?" he prompted, scoffing at the idea. "Surely not."

"Oh yes! She married one Bartlehiem Whistenhowler and had quite a number of children with him. While it's not officially part of Marigot's history, I have a personal interest in the family, just as you do," she said, positively beaming.

Gilbert's chest collapsed around his heart, leaving him breathless. He swallowed hard, his smile gone as he struggled to maintain his pleasant demeanour. W. Of course,

Rhiannon would figure out who was behind the plot if it was a Whistenhowler.

Feeling sick, Gilbert thought back to Charlie's strange interest in Mildred. The near reverent way he'd stared at her, at Rhiannon's party. He'd been sitting right next to Gilbert, and would have had plenty of opportunity to slip a gris-gris into his pocket. He'd spilled coffee on Mildred, giving him equal chance with her, and while normally his wife was ever vigilant, the party had completely over-whelmed her. Her panic over the ruined dress had been enough to leave the party, no doubt it would have covered the act of Charlie planting the second gris-gris on her.

"Sir?" the archivist prompted.

"Is one of their sons named Charles?" Gilbert asked, clutching the handle of his cane hard enough for his knuckles to turn white.

"One of them, yes," the archivist said, blinking as she looked up at Gilbert. "Oh dear, don't feel bad that your friend bested you. The Whistenhowlers are hardly a southern family. You couldn't expect to know them."

"That's the thing," Gilbert said, turning to Pierre. "I know Charlie." Shit. Frederic had known Charlie. Gil had thought Charlie had a bit of hero worship for the disgraced 'war hero', but now that he knew Charlie was the grand-son of the general that Frederic had captured. How long had Charlie been working his way into Frederic's good graces?

"Well, isn't that a surprise!" chirped the archivist. "What's he like?"

"He's a little shit," Gilbert said, catching Pierre's arm and dragging him toward the exit. Behind them, the archivist gasped.

"If he's from Wyndford, why did he want Mildred back down here?" Pierre muttered, apparently remembering he could speak only after they had the information they needed.

"I'm supposed to be asking *you* that question," Gilbert snapped. Millie was in trouble. While Gilbert trusted that his scrappy little wife could fight her way out of almost anything, he didn't trust what Marigot had been doing to her. She'd hidden it pretty well, but he had held her while she broke down. He'd seen the damage the ghosts of this city were causing.

"Oh, right." Pierre opened the door, and a gust of wind nearly ripped it from his hand. "Well, the families down here place high importance on tradition and ritual. Maybe he wanted to have her down here so he could properly take revenge."

Gilbert stepped outside and helped Pierre push the door closed.

"What did you just say? About rituals?" he shouted over the wind.

"It's important to the old families here, tradition. Rituals, even if it's not conjure. They see it as a kind of respect for the past."

Ritual... Millie had told him she'd caught the general in the middle of some sacrificial ritual. Charlie had planted gris-gris on both her and Gilbert. Was he the conjure worker they'd been looking for?

"Let's say Grandad O'Leary had an unfinished ritual. How important would it be for one of these 'old families' to finish it?" Gil asked, flagging down one of the few cabs still out in the storm.

"Extremely," Pierre said, frowning. "What do you know? What did Mildred tell you?"

"We need to talk with Madame Lavoie." Gil shouted to the cabbie as he pulled up. His horse looked miserable, and Gil hoped after this trip the cab would take shelter. A quick glance at the sky told him the storm was only going to get worse.

"What did Mildred tell you?" Pierre asked again, shouting over the din of hard rain on the cab's canvas roof.

"Millie told me when she found O'Leary, he was in the middle of sacrificing some poor man to summon a demon," Gil said, leaning over to speak into Pierre's ear. "She stopped the ritual, but it became part of the 'Bayou Butcher' myth that the ritual was the Butcher's work."

Pierre looked at him, brow knit.

"Well, that's not good," he said.

"No shit," Gilbert said, leaning back in his seat. "That's why we need Lavoie. If anyone knows more than Millie about the ritual that night, it will be her."

It turned out that Ghat was waiting for them at Wolfe House, ready for an excursion. Mulatiwa flicked his tongue in greeting, peeking out from under the hood of her cape, and Gilbert gave the snake a gentlemanly nod in return.

"You are late," Ghat said, shooing them back out the door into the storm.

"Your injury will slow us down. Since Mildred isn't here, I'm going to cast a spell to help. It won't be permanent, even without her, I'm afraid. But it will help."

Gilbert nodded. Ghat placed her hand on his hip and murmured a small incantation in the local creole. Before she had finished speaking, the pain drained away, leaving his back and leg blessedly relaxed. This was the first time since he had been shot that his hip didn't hurt, and Gilbert was overwhelmed at how different it was.

He'd lived like this for years and taken it for granted. Now he had a reprieve, but he had to make it count. Millie and Nathalie needed to know who was after them. Well, the man who was after Millie, though Gilbert was sure Nathalie wouldn't be welcomed by Charlie after his comments at the party about her.

Shit.

Charlie had even told Gilbert that he'd known who Nathalie was, and Gilbert had never asked how. He'd never wondered why, even after Nathalie revealed she was from Marigot. God, he was an idiot, and he'd let Millie down.

"Doubts can wait until we're on the boat," Ghat said, swatting Gilbert's shoulder. "Come, it's not far. Annie told me where Mildred and Ms. Wolfe were." The conjure queen led the way directly to the levee and climbed the steps set into the earthen wall without so much as pausing for breath.

Gilbert followed, incredibly grateful that his hip was quiet. He could still feel the scar tissue pull with every step he took, but the pain always slowed him down. The difference was shocking, and Gilbert felt himself get misty-eyed as the limitation of his injury truly settled in.

"This way," Ghat motioned to the men, leading them down along the levee toward a hut built on the river. The water level was several feet higher than it had been when Gil had arrived on the steamboat, and what had been a quiet river was now swirling in eddies and whirls as the storm pulled in seawater from the ocean.

"Peter Blackwater," Ghat shouted as she made her way to the hut. The name caught Gil's attention. Blackwater, like Millie's mentor, Waya? Was he even still alive? Gil had seen that Millie had bought the man his freedom, but not how old he'd been.

"Quite a storm out there," a man said, opening the door to the hut just a crack. He was Osaugan, without a doubt. Older than Mildred, but only just. He squinted through the rain at Gilbert and Pierre. "Since when do you work for humans, Lavoie?"

"I don't. That tall one is Mildred Berry's husband," Ghat said. "We need your help to get upriver. Didn't you listen to that spirit I sent you? She needs your help."

The man huffed, muttering something over his shoulder in his language. Stepping outside, he threw on an oilcloth poncho. He stepped out and was followed by three others, a woman with her long hair pulled back into a pair of braids that reminded Gil of the Ghost Eye clan out west, while the two men wore their hair like Millie did, their scalps freshly shaved.

"Well, why didn't you say so? That spirit was so hungry it only said you were on the way," Peter said. He walked up to Gilbert and pulled him into a hug. "Your wife is beloved among our family, no matter what the rumours were. Uncle Waya was gone for a long time. She brought him home for us. He got to see his grandkids before he moved on."

Peter clapped Gilbert on the back, knocking off a shower of water from Gil's coat. "That was an honourable thing she did. If we can help, we will."

The rest of the family nodded, solemn-faced.

"Canoe's this way," Pete said, leading them around the hut to the floating dock attached to their stilted platform. The osaugan men lowered the canoe from where it had been lashed next to the hut down to the dock and then settled it in the water. Ghat climbed in immediately, and Gilbert followed, taking care not to tip the boat.

Once they were all in, the four Blackwaters dug their paddles into the swirling river. The canoe launched forward, cutting through the muddy water with an ease that Gilbert was certain was due entirely to the canoeists paddling for them.

"What'd Ghostie go and do this time?" Pete asked, over the rain. "Aside from getting married? Last we'd heard, she was up in Six Fires territory."

"She was," Gilbert said, twisting to answer the man. "Rousseau found her." Pierre flinched and Gilbert shot him an apologetic look. "The Captain Rousseau found her," he corrected. "Then someone kidnapped the captain, who was supposed to stand trial."

"Ah," Pete said, nodding slowly. "Men trouble."

The lady Blackwater laughed. "Any trouble is men trouble," she said. "Wives always gotta fix your trouble, isn't that right, Lavoie?" Ghat snorted.

"This is one of many reasons I will never get married," Ghat muttered.

"Don't you go falling in that water," Pete said, changing the topic. "When the current's like this, you don't know which way it'll pull ya. It'll get better upriver, still strong, but less messy. Long man river likes to dance a bit during storms. Makes him feel young again."

Gil squinted ahead, unsure if that was just a story to explain the current, or if there really was a spirit of the river. He looked down at the muddy water and decided it was safe to assume there was. Gil hoped the long man river spirit wouldn't cause them trouble.

The knot in his chest hadn't gone away, instead, it just twisted over and over on itself.

Charlie. It had been Charlie, and Gil hadn't seen any of the clues. God, he hoped Millie was safe until they arrived. She needed to know.

41

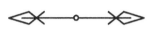

FACE TO FACE

MILLIE

MILLIE COVERED THE TRAPDOOR with the rug again, then took a deep breath. The look of betrayal in Nathalie's eyes had cut deeper than she thought it might. The shadow ghosts flitted around the edge of her vision, but the boots Millie had heard moments ago were drawing closer. A dog whimpered, nails scrabbling on the floor as someone dragged him along.

Five people, maybe six. Likely armed, and Gilbert still had the revolver. While she was a good fighter, Millie knew she wasn't good enough to take out that many people without a firearm, even with the dog's help.

She walked out of the kitchen, wiping her hands on the already stained fabric of her leggings. Millie made a show of spitting blood from her mouth and wiped her split lip on her shirt-sleeve.

"Did I keep you waiting long?" She asked, then squinted at the gathered men and women. There were six of them: one half-elf and the rest were human. The man at the front was wearing a self-satisfied grin and held the stray dog by its collar. The poor thing whined at her, pulling so hard against his collar that he wheezed.

"Who are you people?" she asked, looking from one face to another. She didn't recognize any of them, though a few had faces that resembled something familiar. They were all different ages, from the man at the front who was younger than she was to the older half-elf who had silver at his temples.

The man at the front's smile faltered, and his face turned red.

"Wh-what do you mean, 'who are you'?" he asked, chuckling nervously. "I'm Charlie. We met at Miss Colfield's party. Don't you remember?"

Millie blinked, trying to remember any interaction with the man. He was medium height for a human, with un-remarkable hair that was currently slicked back from the rain and a bland face that was rapidly losing what was left of his smile.

"Coffee?" she said, sounding out the word in a sort-of question. "You were the one who made me ruin that dress." The smile was back, and the man was beaming, as though she had just confirmed he was someone worth remembering instead of being someone who had ruined a perfectly good cup of coffee and an expensive silk dress.

"Charlie," he repeated. "Charlie Whistenhowler. I asked Gilbert to introduce us, but you left the party before he could. You're a flighty one, Miss Argent. I had to follow you all the way—"

"That is not my name," Millie said slowly, enunciating every word so they cut through the air. First Pierre had used it, now this asshole. "My name is Berry."

"Apologies, Ms. Berry," Charlie said, bowing with one hand over his heart. "Though I must say, 'Argent' sounds far more refined. We can discuss all of this later, however. I'm afraid you're going to have to come with me. I *insist*."

His lackeys moved forward, two on either side. For a moment, Millie debated reaching for her axe, but the half-elf had a repeater rifle trained on her and the human man was built like Fred used to be. She might get one or two of them, but she'd be riddled with so many holes that it wouldn't matter.

Someone grabbed her arms while another took off her belt, removing her axe. Millie didn't blink, keeping her eyes focused on this 'Charlie'. Her wrists were lashed together behind her back with some thin rope that bit into her still-fresh burn. The hemp scratched over her blistered skin, and the sensation of liquid dripping from bust blisters that ran down her fingers brought up memories of her years in the cellar. Wrists rubbed raw by the metal shackles in Fred's cellar, and the blisters often grew infected when no one checked on her for days... Millie forced down her rising panic and took slow, even breaths to force her body to relax. She was not in Fred's cellar and rope was much easier to break than iron.

"There was another woman with you when you arrived," the half-elf said, keeping the rifle trained on her. "Where is she?"

"We fought, I killed her," Millie lied, and pointed at her bruised face and split lip. "You can check if you want." She squinted at the half-elf. "Were you the second one on the boat?" She asked, ears perking forward.

The man clenched his jaw, and the rifle trembled ever so slightly.

"And the other one was..." Millie trailed off, leaving the question hanging.

"My sister." The half-elf's face grew pinched, and he glared at her. "You dumped her for the vishaps. They should have taken you instead. Why didn't they?"

Millie shrugged. What else were you supposed to do with a body on the Eyatsi? Just leave it on the boat to bloat in the heat? At least they seemed to have forgotten about Nathalie or believed that the other woman was dead. Had it been anyone other than Rhiannon's cousin, maybe Millie really would have killed her.

"I apologize for the incident on the ferry," Charlie said, pushing down the half-elf's rifle. "What was supposed to be a simple abduction turned into an unsanctioned assassination attempt." He shot a frown at the half-elf, cowing the other man. Shouldering the rifle, the half-elf stepped away, waiting by the abandoned manor's doorway.

"Are you an O'Leary?" Millie asked. She had seen the note on the assassin. 'The woman who killed your parents will be on the next ferry. Take her, and the chattel debt is gone.' Millie herself might have thought 'take' meant 'kill'. That was why marching orders had to be precise, leaving room for interpretation was leaving room for disaster. "You're missing the jowls they get."

Jowls or not, General O'Leary had been a shark of a man: if you showed any weakness, he'd lunge for it. He had before the war started, and it was what kept the Union army at bay for so many years. This 'Charlie' looked to be soft, but that didn't mean he hadn't inherited his grandfather's instinct.

"My mother," Charlie said, motioning her forward. "His daughter, though I don't think you two directly crossed paths. She had quite a lot of stories about you, you know. How you must have been a brilliant fencer to kill Uncle Paul, how you were the real brilliance behind Frederic's army."

He smiled at her, a face full of even teeth.

The powdered frog would only keep Nathalie quiet for a short time, so Millie followed, eager to get the group outside of the house. She'd already wasted enough time with questions. As she listened to what was supposed to be glowing praise, her ears turned red, and she stared at Charlie in naked confusion. She'd expected to be hated, but the way he was talking, this man looked *up* to her old self.

"Your mother didn't hate me for killing her brother?" Millie asked, stepping outside into the rain. More armed men waited outside, confirming to Millie that surrendering herself had been the smart decision. Charlie pulled his hood up, his cape nearly ripped off his shoulders by a gust of wind. Millie felt the wind and rain cut through her clothing, leaving her instantly drenched. She glanced up at the clouds, noticing how dark the sky had become.

"Hardly. Paul was an excellent fencer, but a terrible brother. He was quite like Frederic, actually. Drinking and gambling away too much of the family fortune," Charlie shouted over the howling wind. "When I finally met Frederic, I expected to find that Mother had been wrong about it all. It was Frederic Rousseau. How could he not be the war hero everyone claimed him to be?"

Charlie slipped his arm through hers, and Millie stiffened at the unexpected contact.

"But Mother was right. Frederic was a hopeless drunk. Whenever I asked about the war, he'd change the topic instead of telling me how he breached Marigot all those years ago. Eventually, I realised he didn't know what had happened that night, because he hadn't been on the front line."

To borrow a phrase from Gilbert, good God, this man talked a lot. Millie wanted to ignore him, but she also needed to know what the hell this was about. Keeping him talking meant she could get more information about what was happening. She tried to think about what Gilbert would do, what he would say. He'd always been so good at getting information out of her. Maybe she could try that on this 'Charlie' asshole.

"Not everyone wants to talk about the war," she said to Charlie, but kept her eyes on the move. The sugarcane trembled under the rain, but there was a slight movement among their stalks that was perpendicular to the wind. A glimpse of gleaming green eyes within the stalks buoyed Millie's spirit. That was a panther, and hopefully, it was Annie, though Millie would have been just as pleased with a regular big cat if it attacked one of the men surrounding her.

"Why is that?" Charlie asked, leading them down to the water.

Millie waited, only to realise the question was in earnest.

"Because war is horrible," she said, a little bewildered. "It's different when you're fighting instead of just giving orders. Fred, for all his bullshit, was a captain that suffered right alongside us. He starved, he froze on nights we had to sleep in the rain, he saw our wounded. He wasn't on the front line at Marigot, but he was still there. If he's forgotten what happened that night, it's because he wanted to."

She flicked rainwater from her ears and then tucked them back down to keep the wind from blowing into them.

At the farm's dock, a long rowboat waited under the guard of two burly half-orc men. No doubt the rowers, judging from Charlie's manicured hand holding onto her arm. Charlie helped Millie into the centre of the boat and sat next to her. His entourage took seats around them, the two half-orcs manning the oars as expected. The dog cowered at their feet, looking up at Millie with sad eyes. He knew what was coming; she realised. This was Charlie's dog, and she bet the scars on it didn't come from dog fights.

Some things never changed.

"Did Fred fight next to you?" Charlie asked with a smile that told Millie he already knew the answer. No, Fred had not fought on the front lines. That wasn't uncommon, though. Officers were the strategists, the planners.

"Did your grandfather fight alongside his army?" Millie asked, expecting the smile to disappear, replaced by a fit of rage. Instead, Charlie laughed.

"No, Miss Berry, no he didn't. But he didn't have you on his side, did he? The Ghost of Marigot, the Bayou Butcher, Mildred fucking Berry, who took Marigot right out from under him." Charlie's eyes were uncomfortably bright as he looked at her, flicking back and forth to take in as much detail about her as he could.

"No, you were the deciding factor in the war. My grandfather was an idiot to think Frederic was the real threat. No, you are something else, Mildred Berry. Something special."

42

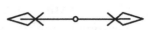

SINKING HOPES

RHIANNON

THE TRAIN MADE EXCELLENT time, shaving off a full day from the usual travel time to St-Makir's Rest. Rhiannon was torn between being proud of her family's company and disgusted that it was her uncle's success that got her there. Now that Harrold was dead, Rhiannon's control over West-Colfield Rail would be uncontested. It'd been what she wanted, but Rhiannon couldn't help but feel cheated out of a trial. She'd wanted to hold him accountable in the eyes of history and the public.

The dead weren't able to be prosecuted for the same reason they couldn't testify. You could never really be sure who it was in the body, at least to the degree required by the court. So Harrold was gone. Technically, he would never be a murderer, just a man accused of it. Rhiannon wasn't sure she'd be able to stomach it if history made him out to be anything but a murderer.

She had told Hal and Allan everything she'd learned, from Corporal Plackitt's visit to the slip of paper they had handed her. Hal, ever the detective, had asked if the handwriting was Harrold's. It was. When she'd evicted her uncle from the family home at gunpoint, Harrold had left behind most of his correspondence. Over the last few weeks, Rhiannon had read through all of it in the search for any evidence against him. By now, she knew her uncle's penmanship better than she knew her own father's.

It started raining the day they reached St-Makir's Rest, cutting through the heat that had been increasing with every mile further south. In Wyndford and on the prairie, the rain was cold even during the hottest days of summer. The rain that greeted Rhiannon as she stepped off the train was lukewarm, a welcome respite from the stifling humidity.

"Do we need any last-minute supplies?" Hal asked as they disembarked. The platform was empty of people and shuttered stalls ran along it. In better weather, the train station would have been a marketplace, but it seemed like the town had all retreated inside to avoid the weather. "There should be a trading post. They're kind of like the general stores of the south."

"Food, maybe," Rhiannon said, shouldering her light pack. "I'll go see about hiring the ferry. I'll meet you at the dock."

"I'll go with Ry," Allan said, squinting up at the sky. The rain clouds weren't too dark. Rhiannon didn't see any thunderheads on the horizon. "It doesn't look too bad," he said, echoing her own thoughts. "Boats still work in the rain, right?"

"I hope so." Waving to Hal, Rhiannon stepped out from under the shelter of the train platform and into the rain. It was much warmer than the rain in Wyndford ever got, making it far more comfortable to be caught in.

"I don't actually know much about boats," she admitted as they picked their way down the muddy road toward the river. Rivulets of water made it easy to find, running downhill through the mud until they joined the Eyatsi over by the docks.

The boats Rhiannon was familiar with were the ones that sailed the cascade lakes, steamers with a paddle wheel on the side and large masts for sails should the engines break down. They were modified ocean vessels; she remembered her mother telling her. With sharply angled hulls designed to cut through whitecap waves and rough water.

The ferry waiting at the dock was none of that. It looked like someone had nailed a building to a barge, and the boat's hull sat so low in the water that Rhiannon wondered if it had already started to sink. There was less than half a foot clearance from the lowest part of the deck to the river's surface.

"That's a boat?" Allan asked her under his breath.

"Apparently," she answered. "It looks like a cake." She wasn't familiar with ship design, but this one looked awfully top-heavy. Two stories of windows perched on top of the main deck, and the whole thing was painted white and red. Weren't boats supposed to have round portholes? Rhiannon wished Nathie was there. Her cousin knew boats.

"No cake I've ever seen," Allan muttered, eying the boat with suspicion.

"The fancy ones never taste as good," Rhiannon said, realising too late that, of course, Allan would never have seen the ornate buttercream art pieces that socialites loved to show off at parties. The more impractical the better.

Walking down the dock, Rhiannon cupped her hands around her mouth and called out. She couldn't see any crew, but they would probably be inside, out of the rain.

"Hello? Is the captain on board?"

The door to the main level of the boat's 'building' opened, and a young, dark-skinned man poked his head out. He was wearing a sailor's uniform. The bib collar was Rhiannon's strongest clue, though the straw hat that sat on his tightly coiled curls was a close second.

"Why're you looking for the captain?" he asked, blinking at the sight of Rhiannon and Allan standing in the rain. "Why're you standing out in the rain?"

"I thought it would be rude to just board a ship without asking," Rhiannon said, suddenly aware of how quickly the rain had soaked through her clothing. The water was warm, but she would need to dry out her outer layers once they were on the boat, or risk catching a chill overnight. "I need to get to Marigot and I'm willing to pay to get there."

The sailor looked over Rhianon's gear, then doubtfully at Allan. He pursed his lips and squinted up at the rain clouds.

"Yeah, alright. We've sailed in worse weather than this," the man said, and motioned them aboard.

"Excuse me," Rhiannon said, confused. "Are... *you* the captain?" He looked to be younger than she was. She'd always assumed that all boat captains had saltpetre beards and round bellies. It was silly now that she thought about it. Not all sheriffs were the heroes that had lived in the books Rhiannon read as a girl.

"Yes ma'am," the sailor said, tipping his hat. "Captain Sandu Mattie, at your service. Been sailing since I was six.

If you're willing to pay for a third of my tickets, we can leave on the hour."

"Done," Rhiannon said, stepping on board. She noticed both Allan and the captain were looking at her strangely. "What?" she asked, looking between the two. "I told you it was urgent."

"Ry," Allan said, gingerly climbing up after her. "Most people don't just agree to pay something without knowing the amount those things cost."

The tips of her ears grew warm, and Rhiannon busied herself with wringing out her braid. She hadn't made a slip like that in years. Under a month back in a life of luxury, and already she had forgotten how the vast majority of people lived.

"We're waiting on a third, then we'll be ready to leave," she said, pretending the mistake hadn't happened. She whistled for Fyodor and he hesitantly jumped onto the boat, immediately spreading his weight and lowering himself to keep his balance. "We can discuss payment on the way."

Captain Mattie shrugged. He opened the door to the cabin for them and pointed up the flight of stairs.

"Sure thing, berths are up there. Fewer mosquitoes in there, too."

THEY GATHERED IN THE common room, draping waterlogged clothing over the backs of chairs in a vain hope that they might dry in the soup-like air. A fire would have helped, but given the wooden structure of the boat, Rhiannon thought better of asking if there were any fireplaces aboard.

Hal seemed to be the only one in their group comfortable with the boat's design. Allan sat with his feet spread apart, ready for ocean swells that were found in the Cascading Lakes, but not the Eyatsi. Fyodor had got over his earlier fear and lay at Rhiannon's feet, chin resting on his front legs. Rhiannon tried to ignore every creak and groan of the boat, taking reassurance from the steady chug of the paddle wheel driving them forward.

"Where do you think we'll find Nathalie, Miss Rhiannon?" Hal asked, chewing on a bit of fried bread. He'd brought back some for all of them from the trading post, along with dried meat for Fyodor and for them the next day. Allan hadn't touched his food yet, but the smell was making Rhiannon's belly growl.

"It depends on when we arrive," she said, lifting the paper-wrapped bread to her mouth. She took a delicate bite from it and sighed. They'd been on the river for a few hours by now, so the bread had cooled hours ago, but it was still soft when she bit into it.

Hal chuckled at her reaction and nodded in agreement. Swayed by Rhiannon's approval, Allan gingerly took a bite of his own bread. She watched as his face lit up and laughed as he devoured the loaf as soon as he realised it tasted good.

"Whassat called again?" he asked, picking crumbs out of the paper wrap it had come in.

"Fry bread, Osaugan traders brought it over from inland. I was hoping you'd have some out in the Bluffs when I arrived," Hal admitted, wiping crumbs from his hands onto the wooden deck below.

"Well, maybe the Six Fires make it," Rhiannon said, wondering if Eyota knew the recipe. If they did, would they teach Sweetpea how to make it? The thought of their town left her heartsick. She'd left it in literal smoking ruins, and while she'd sent money and supplies to rebuild, she hadn't so much as written to ask if they needed anything else.

"So, your cousin," Hal prompted. "Where would our first stop be once we arrive in town?"

"If she's not already at the docks waiting, her town-home," Rhiannon said, finishing off her bread. "Her family has a lot of property in Marigot, but she only lives in two places. The family farm on the river, or the townhome."

Hal winced.

"What?" Rhiannon asked. "I know people don't all have ten properties. What did I say this time?"

"That's... probably not a farm," Hal said delicately. "But a plantation. Which is similar to a farm but with added slavery and suffering."

She sighed, brushing crumbs from her lap. A few landed on Fyodor, who lifted his head and twisted to lick them off, smacking his chops noisily.

"I know," she said. "Nathie doesn't go there if she can avoid it, though." She knew her cousin's life was her own, but they were well beyond the point of having any secrets. "Millie killed Nathalie's father there. It holds a lot of bad—"

"*Excuse me*," Allan said, his mouth falling open. "Wait, Ry. Please, what do you *mean* the scary elf lady killed your cousin's father?"

"You didn't think that was important?" Hal asked, frowning at the revelation. "Does Mildred know?"

Rhiannon frowned, ears hot again. She felt like she was getting chastised in school, only she'd always been a well-behaved student. She'd prided herself on being an obedient daughter, and then a lawful Sheriff. This was a new and unwelcome feeling.

"It wasn't my story to tell," she said, crossing her arms. "Nathalie promised she would set that aside to help find Rousseau." She levelled her eyes at Hal. "And yes, I trust my cousin. She's sharp-tongued, yes, but she's not like Harrold."

The Stratton lifted his hands in defeat and he leaned back in his chair.

"Berry's gonna be real mad at you when she finds out," Allan said, concerned. "But I guess I understand. Your cousin might want to talk to her first. Tell Berry herself." His brow knit, and Allan looked down at Fyodor for a moment before he lifted his eyes back to hers. "How do you feel about that? You and your cousin seem close."

"Millie told me some of what she'd done in the war. She only spoke about it when I asked," Rhiannon said, thinking back to the elf's letter. "I never asked for details." She looked away from Allan, shame creeping up her throat. "I didn't want to know, to be honest. Millie didn't know she killed my uncle, of that I'm certain."

"She would have told you," Allan said. Reaching over, he gently took her hand.

Rhiannon nodded, folding her fingers around his. Allan's hand was warm, and the rough calluses on his fingers were comforting somehow. Anchoring her when everything in her life felt like it was floating away.

The steady chug of the engine caught mid-cycle, groaning and sending a deep shudder through the boat. A loud clunk was the last sound they heard before it died, leaving the sound of heavy rain and howling winds in its place. The boat felt different under them, loose on the river now that it didn't have the paddle wheel steadily pushing it forward.

Allan turned white, and now it was Rhiannon's turn to squeeze his hand to show her support. Hal was already on his feet, heading for the back of the boat, a deep frown on his face. Rhiannon almost followed him, but what did she know about boats?

"Do you know what that was?" Allan asked.

She shook her head.

"I know it's not the boiler, which is a good sign," she said with an encouraging smile. "Otherwise the boat would explode." Allan looked at her in horror, and Rhiannon cleared her throat. "Which is why it's a good thing it's not a problem with the boiler."

"Great," Allan muttered. "So we either die by explosion or drowning."

Rhiannon gave his hand a squeeze, then let go, pulling on her coat from where it hung over the back of another wicker chair next to them. It was still damp, and it clung to her arms as she pulled it on over her equally damp shirt.

"Where are you going?" Allan asked, panic creeping into his voice.

"Just to the outside part of the deck," she said, pointing at the door that led outside. The windows of the boat reflected the light of the lanterns that hung in the common room, making it difficult to see where they were on the river.

"I'm coming with you," he said, standing. Under their feet, the boat bucked and pivoted, the stern pushing ahead until they were broadside to the wind. The boat listed to their right as its tall decks caught the full force of the wind that howled up the river.

Rhiannon whistled for Fyodor to heel. She grabbed onto Allan's hand and picked her way across the inclined floor toward the door to the outside deck. She knew the boat had looked top-heavy, and she didn't trust it to last long before it capsized. Why, in all the Messiah's grace, would anyone design a boat to be so blocky and sit so low? It was asking to sink.

"Where do we go?" Allan asked, his voice carrying an edge of panic. "I can't swim, Ry."

Hearing that, Rhiannon's heart dropped. She could swim a bit, but it had been a long time since she had, and Allan was a large man. She wasn't sure she'd be able to carry him to shore if they didn't get any closer to either riverbank.

"Listen to me," she said, catching his face in her hands. "If we go in the water, you grab onto Fyodor. He's strong enough he'll be able to bring you to shore. Until then, I'm not letting go of you, alright?" His eyes were still wide, but he nodded, resting his hand on top of hers.

The door in front of them banged open, and a drenched Hal leaned into the room, one hand outstretched to help them get out.

"We need to get to the edge of the boat," he said. "When it rolls over, we climb onto the hull." He looked from Rhiannon to Allan, jaw set. "Take your jackets off," he added. "They'll just weigh you down in the water."

Rhiannon nodded and helped Allan pull his coat off, tossing it aside. It landed on the floor with a splat and slid down the incline of the rapidly tilting room. Hers followed, and they climbed out into the storm. The rain was colder here, hitting her skin so hard that each drop hurt. Through the haze of water, she saw they were almost dead centre in the river, having just emerged from the relative cover of the forest into a wide plain of tall grass fields that did nothing to slow the wind.

"Come on, this way," Hal said, helping them toward the edge of the boat. "If you fall into the water, you need to get out as soon as you can. This river's current is stronger than it looks, and it's full of vishaps ready to take you."

"Take me where?" Allan asked.

"They eat you, Allan," Hal said with a pained groan. "They eat you."

With a creak, the boat tipped the rest of the way onto its side, its upper decks slapping into the water. Rhiannon held on to the railing and to Fyodor, who scrabbled for purchase on the now vertical deck. Reaching down, Allan grabbed the dog around the waist and lifted him up to the side of the hull that had risen from the water.

Rhiannon hauled herself up over the railing and helped pull Fyodor the rest of the way up, his frantic whines breaking her heart.

"You two stay close," she whispered into the dog's ear. "I can't lose either of you."

43

A Born Killer

Millie

THE O'LEARY PLANTATION HAD been rebuilt since the war, and it stood as grand as it had been the day before Millie and the Irregulars burned it down. Spotless white plaster walls glowed in the rain, and two tiers of matching wooden porches featured perfect gingerbread trim that would typically be covered in blooming flowers, perfectly spilling colour over the white porch railings in the O'Leary family colours.

Today, it had been storm-proofed, with wood planks placed over the windows and the planters removed so as not to lose them to the powerful gusts of wind. The house was surrounded by a wide lawn that was equally man-icured, with topiaries wrapped up in burlap to prevent their perfectly unnatural shapes from being ruined by ac-tual nature.

"Oh, you rebuilt it," she said dryly as Charlie walked her up the long driveway to the house. The two half-orcs were evidently not invited to whatever was about to happen, as they stayed by the dock to stow the rowboat. Someone took the dog away to the kennels, where a chorus of deep barks greeted the escapee.

"Ah, yes," Charlie said with another laugh, treating the whole thing like Millie was a guest instead of a captive. "I heard it was your company who burnt it down. By the time the war began, we'd moved most of the valuables somewhere safe. Still, it was difficult to find proper labour to restore the grand old lady after abolition."

A servant opened the front door for them. The rain had grown colder, and it was a relief to step out of it, even if that meant stepping into a plantation house. Millie didn't really have another option, anyways.

It was like walking back in time, to the Rousseau manor during the early years. Cheery wallpaper and light linens brightened the darkened interior, while a massive staircase carved from oak led up to the second floor. The foyer was large enough for all nine of them without feeling crowded, though the marble floors had been covered with woven reed carpets to catch the mud and water from their feet.

The butler, a mostly-human man with the slightest point to his ears, looked Millie over and sniffed in derision.

"Shall I prepare a bath, Master Whistenhowler?" he asked in the same deferential tone that all slaves used to use when speaking to masters. Millie made a face, and it earned her a sharp glare from the butler. *Remember your place* had been a common phrase in Millie's life before the war. She recognized it in the butler's expression, and it chafed as much now as it had back then.

"No, just some towels to dry off. I'd prefer not to keep the lady waiting."

"Waiting for what?" Millie asked, and was completely ignored. Charlie finally let go of her arm, but she was quickly grabbed by the half-elf and a woman with heavy bandages on one arm. They were far less genteel about restraining her.

"Get her tidied up and bring her to the dining room," Charlie instructed, peeling off his dripping cape.

For a moment, Millie debated digging her heels into the mats and making them drag her, but both captors outweighed her, which meant the effort would be a waste of energy and time. Better continue to be the docile elf and wait for a more opportune moment.

They brought Millie to a side room where a small basin of steaming water waited with a few towels. There was also something laid out on a table that looked disturbingly familiar.

"Wash, and get dressed," the half-elf said, undoing the knots at her wrists. Water had soaked into the rope, making it swell and the knot held fast despite the man's best efforts. Every tug of the ropes scraped over Millie's still-healing burn, setting her teeth on edge. With a grunt, the woman pushed him out of the way and pulled a knife free, cutting through the swollen fibres with little care if she stuck Millie or not.

"Do they not teach thugs how to use knives anymore?" Millie hissed the second time the knife bit into her. She stepped back, snapping her head into the woman's nose. Hearing a satisfactory crunch, Millie pulled free, grabbing the knife as the woman dropped it to grab her face.

The half-elf stepped forward, but Millie dodged with an easy sidestep, sawing away at the rest of the rope with bloody hands. Finally freed, she threw the rope at their feet and slammed the knife into the tabletop next to her.

"I hate to agree with what's his name, but if you're the best he could hire, then trained workers must be really hard to find." Millie walked over to the basin, washing her hands of the blood on them. She inspected the fresh cuts, but they were shallow and had missed her ligaments and the important veins. The burn was irritated from the rope and the blisters had burst some time ago.

"You broke my node!" the woman hissed, still holding her face. "You can't hitd humand!"

"You stabbed me first," Millie said, unbothered. "And pretty sure I've hit plenty of humans, no god has reached down from the sky to stop me yet."

"Bidth."

Millie sighed. She missed Gil. She missed Annie and Ghat and even Nathalie. She even missed the dog, even though she'd only had him for about a day and a half. Millie told herself it was best that she was here alone, but her heart remained unconvinced. The gear laid out on the table where she'd planted the knife suggested that something terrible was about to happen. Drying her hands, she walked over to look at what had been prepared for her to wear.

Buckskin leggings with woven garter ties to go around her knees, a white tunic and sash that matched the knee garters, a pot of black face paint and worst of all.... A perfectly sized coat in the navy blue of the Amelior Union. She picked it up, looking over the sergeant chevrons on the shoulders and shiny brass buttons. The coat was no replica. It was a modern Amelian cavalry uniform cut a little shorter than the standard issue infantry coats during the war. The wool was woven tightly and would be warm after being out in the rain, but just looking at it made her feel ill.

There was no feeling of homecoming pulling on the war outfit, not like she'd had back in Scorched Bluffs when she had pulled out her old kit. This wasn't hers; it wasn't the clothing she'd lived in, bled in. It was a costume made by some kid who wanted to act out some fantasy with her, like she was a doll.

Like Fred used to.

Picking up her discarded shirt, Millie used her stolen knife to cut strips of the cotton into bandages. The cuts were still oozing and would continue unless she wrapped them up. The wet cloth soothed her burn as she wrapped the strips around first one wrist, then the other.

Last came the warpaint.

Saying a small apology to Waya, Millie smeared black pigment across her eyes. She had used it during the war to keep the sun from blinding her, but these assholes wouldn't understand that it was for a purpose. To them, it was just another part of the costume. War paint was only worn when you were going to war, and it felt wrong to put it on just for show. Millie made a silent promise that she'd make good on the paint's promise as soon as she was able.

Wiping her hands clean on the towel, the Butcher of the Bayou turned to her captors.

"So, now what?"

SHE SHOULDN'T HAVE ASKED. Millie was led to the dining room, which had been repurposed into what looked disturbingly like what she had stumbled into the day she caught General O'Leary. A tabletop was propped up against the wall, with straps nailed into it for holding someone suspended from it. A regular table was covered with a red cloth and had leather cuffed shackles at each of its four legs, one side locked around the table, the other set on the table.

"Oh." Millie sighed, her ears sagging in annoyance. "You're going to kill me to raise that demon thing."

Charlie and the others were now wearing black robes, except for the half-elf and the woman, who had disappeared to go tend to her broken nose.

"Kill you?" Charlie said, taken aback. He walked over to her, stopping just out of arm's reach. "My darling Butcher, you are the most lethal person Amelior has ever seen. Why would I *kill* you?" He reached up, as if to touch her face, but stopped himself. His eyes were gleaming again with what Millie now understood was fanaticism.

"No, you are almost perfect. So close, except for that incorrigible stubborn streak."

Millie's ears flattened. She'd be annoyed if she died to summon a spirit, but she didn't like where Charlie was going with this at all.

"No, my dear," Charlie said. "You are going to be its host. You'll still mostly be yourself, but just a little more..." he looked her over and bit his lip. "Tractable."

"I'm going to kill you," Millie said, feeling a chill run down her spine. Dying was one thing. She deserved to die for all the killing she'd done in her life. But forced servitude? No. Never again. Becoming a slave again would spit on the memory of every soldier who had died fighting alongside her.

"I am going to kill every last one of you," she continued. "But you, Whistenhowler, I am going to make it slow so you can understand the full weight of the mistake you are about to make and regret every second of it."

Charlie shivered, a crazed smile spreading across his face. Then he giggled, clasping his hands together in glee.

"You know, I used to think the stories about you were exaggerated," he said, completely ignoring her threat. "But then I met you and just, wow. You are everything and more, aren't you? You are a born killer." He clapped his hands and Millie felt herself grabbed by the arms.

This time she tried to wrench herself free, but not even the Bayou Butcher could overpower six able-bodied men. They lifted her onto the main table, forcing her arms and legs out to each corner. Charlie happily flitted from shackle to shackle, buckling them around her wrists and ankles tight. He was even *humming* as he did.

Only when she was secured did the cultists let her go. What else could they be called? This was cult shit, the stuff that plagued proper conjure workers who made an honest living.

"You're the conjure worker, aren't you?" She asked, watching Charlie set about placing bundles of herbs around her. Next came crystals, though Millie wasn't sure what the shiny rocks were supposed to do. What kind of connection or meaning could a rock have?

"Ah, don't tell me you thought only women could work conjure," Charlie said, clucking his tongue. He bopped her nose with a sprig of geranium flowers.

What the fuck? Millie made a face and strained her head away from the geranium.

"I walked in on your grandfather trying to do this, so no," Millie said, watching Whistenhowler take out some kind of liquid and flick it through the air. A drop landed on her cheek, and Millie wrinkled her nose. Bourbon. Disgusting.

"Bring out the drunk," Charlie ordered, setting the bourbon aside.

As if this couldn't get any worse. Millie groaned. She'd come to Marigot looking for Fred, but this was not how she'd wanted to find him. Two of Charlie's cultists dragged a very drunk Frederic Rousseau into the room. To Millie's horror, they lifted Fred's limp body up onto the vertical table, lashing him in place. They left his head hanging forward, his greasy blond hair falling into his eyes. A bead of saliva fell from his wet lips, and Fred didn't so much as stir as it fell to the floor.

"Normally, I'd be all for killing Fred," Millie said, testing the leather cuffs on her wrists. They held fast. "But I don't want that piece of shit bound to me for the rest of my life. Can't you use someone else?"

Charlie walked into view, crouching in front of her, a ritual dagger in his hand. It was simple iron, but runes were etched along its blade and the cutting edge looked as sharp as any knife's.

"I'm afraid not," Whistenhowler said with a small sigh. "His tie to you will just make this spell bind all the more tightly. He has blood on his hands, too. But if it's any consolation, his spirit will not survive the process. Yours will."

"He only has one hand. If you need someone with blood on both, you should use someone else," Millie said, no more convinced about the situation than she was a moment earlier.

Charlie didn't give her more time to complain, though. He stood and turned, plunging the ritual knife into Fred's chest. Millie watched Frederic grunt, his hand flexing to reach for the knife in his chest. The straps held him in place, and soon his saliva ran red as he coughed up blood.

For years, Millie had fantasised about killing Fred. She'd thought about doing it quickly to show how little she cared. She'd thought about drawing it out the way he'd hurt her back in the cellar. Then, when the chance presented itself in the shape of an injured, pinned Frederic on his lawn begging for mercy, she had set that desire aside for the benefit of her friend.

Rhiannon never knew how much Millie had given up so she could get that goddamn inheritance back. Now, some rich asshole took that opportunity instead, leaving her unable to exact the revenge she'd dreamt of for almost ten years.

She screamed, trying to wrench herself free in a blind rage. Strong hands grabbed her and held her down. Whistenhowler misunderstood, looking at her with surprise in his eyes.

"You'll love me just as much," he said, misunderstanding her anger. "More, even."

Millie screamed again, furious at how helpless she was. They were going to use Fred's soul to bind something to her, to make her a slave again, with a magic collar instead of an iron one. She would never be free of him now.

"Quickly." Someone poured a cup of tea into her mouth. Floral and coppery warm water caught in her throat and she coughed it out only for someone to grab her face and pour more down her throat. It tasted like Ghat's spirit tea, but less potent, the blood mixed into it overwhelming the floral taste. She coughed again, but she'd swallowed some of it.

Until now, Millie had been worried about what would happen when the spell didn't take. But now, as shadows climbed down from every corner of the room to coalesce into a single figure, Millie found herself terrified the spell would work after all.

Hello Mildred, a distorted voice said in the back of her mind. It made Millie's brain buzz and ache. *I've been waiting for such a long time for this.*

The shadow spirit crawled up onto the table on its hands and knees, its face poised directly over her own. Red eyes gleamed down at her as the shadow paled into familiar features. Her younger self smiled down at her, cheekbones carved sharp with hunger and its pale skin splattered with blood.

The doppelgänger collapsed into shadow again, splashing down into Millie's body. The darkness took her with it, carrying her down past the physical body still tied to a table, through the floor and into the spirit world below.

"Finally," the shadow-Mildred said, still perched above her. It smiled, its red eyes glowing like embers. "You've gone soft, Mildred *Berry.*"

44

Storm Surge

Nathalie

Nathie listened to as much of the muffled conversation as she could from where she lay in the dark cellar. A fitting punishment by the elf, though one that Nathie hoped never to repeat. The cellar door lifted, and a lantern shone in, light passing over her body. Then the lantern was gone, and the trapdoor closed with a bang, leaving her alone once more.

Immobilised in the dark, she tried not to think if there were snakes or rats in the cellar with her. Surely, even if there were, they would go after the stored food instead of nibbling on Nathie's nose or lips. Messiah, she hoped she would be able to move before any mouse or rat grew curious enough to try.

Left with only her thoughts, Nathie turned the elf's parting words over and over in her mind. Mildred had seen this as protecting her from whoever had arrived, choosing to face them alone instead of with support. Nathalie's first thought was that Mildred had double-crossed her, but no.

A far more likely scenario was that the elf didn't think she was going to survive.

This won't fix things. I'm sorry.

The idiot really thought that marching off to her death while leaving Nathie hidden would absolve her?

But it was the second part of what Mildred had said that kept wiggling deeper and deeper into Nathie's mind.

I can't let you get hurt. I couldn't that night, and I can't now.

All those years, Nathie had thought she'd remained undetected, a silent witness to her father's murder and the brutal punishment of the human soldier. Mildred had known she was there that night. The elf had still killed Nathie's father, but she had practically dragged out the soldier whose eye she had taken.

Had she been trying to protect Nathie? The thought made her want to laugh, but the only sound her frozen body managed was a huff of air.

How cruel was that? Killing a girl's father, then making her live through the grief of life with no protector. The elf probably thought it was a mercy, when a kinder fate would have been to die that night. Yet, the chilling question remained: if Mildred had been protecting her, what horrors would the other soldier have inflicted if he'd found her?

The cellar trap door opened a second time, the dim light filtering in from the kitchen barely enough for Nathie to see the figure who climbed down into the cellar. She blinked and twitched her foot in greeting. Messiah, she hoped this was a friend, and not a rear guard here to loot the damn house.

"Oh," a familiar voice said, spotting where Nathie lay. "Tsk, Mildred, what did you do..." Annie walked over to her and carefully picked her up. A wave of relief swept over Nathie as the elf cradled her in strong arms and carried her out of the cellar.

"She ran off into trouble again, didn't she?" Annie asked, and Nathalie blinked in reply. She was certain the profanity was lost in translation.

Annie gently lowered Nathie onto the dusty preparation table and reached into one pouch at her belt. Breaking off a piece of root, she held it up to Nathie's lips and gently tucked it into the pouch of her cheek. The root tasted a little like the black liquorice her father used to like. Nathie had tried it once, only to spit it right out, declaring her papa mustn't have any taste.

As the taste spread over Nathalie's tongue, she felt the numbness fade.

"Once you can, chew that. It'll help get rid of the paralysis," Annie said. Now that they were in the dull light of the kitchen, Nathalie could see the other woman's face was grim. "While you do, I need you to listen very closely."

Nathie tipped her chin slightly and moved her jaw to crush the root. Bitterness exploded over her tongue, and she tried to make a face at the taste. She kept chewing, swallowing the juices the root released. Warmth spread through her, chasing away the lingering paralysis.

"The ferry is taking on water upriver," Annie said, holding Nathie's head between her warm hands. "Rhiannon is onboard. I need your help to go save as many people as we can before it capsizes."

Nathie clumsily pushed herself up to her elbow and tried to roll off the table to her feet. Annie caught her, helping her sit upright and swing her feet down to the ground.

"Mill?" Nathie mumbled through the painful pins-and-needles sensation that swept over her entire body. When her feet touched the ground, the shooting pain up from her feet was enough to make Nathalie's eyes water.

"She was leaving with a large escort of guards. Eight men and two more waiting at a boat. Millie is tough. If there was a single person in Amelior who could face those odds and escape..." Annie trailed off. "Well, Millie would be one of them. Right now, Ry needs us. Can you walk?"

Nathie blinked again and nodded. Rhiannon needed her. She could mope about being abandoned another time. The mention of her cousin cleared her thoughts and gave her a purpose. She pushed herself to her feet, wobbling a little as her muscles continued to wake up. Annie looped one of Nathie's arms around her shoulders and they left the kitchen. By the time they reached the open front door, Nathie could move under her own power.

"The canoe I have won't be enough to help everyone," she slurred, the wind now howling like a living thing.

"It's fine. We're not going to use your canoe to rescue the passengers," Annie said. "Upriver, the men that took Millie have a large rowboat. We're going to steal that."

Nathie smiled lopsidedly and patted Annie on the shoulder. Every step, every word coming a little easier as the root did its work. "I like the way you think. A rowboat will be more stable in the water. Are you able to swim?"

Annie looked at her in surprise, brows lifted.

"Of course I can. The question is, can *you*?"

THE WIND WAS NEARLY strong enough to blow them up-river now, making the paddle up to the rowboat easier on Nathie. Although she had her full range of motion back, there was a deep ache in her muscles that lingered from her paralysis. When this had blown over, Nathie would have words with Mildred. Many words, and most of them at high volume. As it was, saving Rhiannon was the priority.

Nathie refused to let herself consider a situation where she didn't reach her cousin in time. Five years ago, she hadn't been there when Rhiannon had needed her. Nathie would die before she let her cousin drown when she was so close by.

In the front of the canoe, Annie held up her hand. Through the downpour, Nathie could only just make out the dock at the river's edge. The rowboat had been dragged out of the river, but only just. A canvas tarpaulin was pulled over it to keep the rain from accumulating inside.

Approaching cautiously, Nathie squinted at the shore. Two large figures stood on the road up to the master's house, hunkered against the wind, but with no protection against the storm.

Carefully crawling up the length of the canoe to where Annie sat, Nathie cupped her hands around her mouth and still had to raise her voice over the rain.

"Is this O'Leary's?" she asked.

Annie turned and nodded. She pointed her paddle at the two guards.

"Those two might cause a problem."

Nathie turned back to evaluate the situation. They could spend precious time fighting the guards, but there was another option. A faster one.

"Hide back there in the reeds," Nathie said, pointing at a cluster that they had just passed. She pulled off her boots and tucked them under the rear seat of the canoe. "I'm going to recruit more help."

"What are you—" Nathie didn't hear what else the elf said. She stepped out of the canoe and into the swollen river. As she went under, the cold water cut off whatever protests Annie might have said. Kicking out, Nathalie resurfaced and started swimming for the dock with powerful strokes. The current was stronger than usual, but Nathalie had grown up swimming in the Eyatsi. This close to shore, she'd be able to make it with little problem.

The river's currents were deceptively strong at Marigot, and drowning was a regular occurrence. Nathalie's father insisted she learn how to swim for that very reason. His younger brother drowned when they were young, caught by an undertow just off the farm's dock. It had always been a source of relaxation to her, but now it was something that would help her save Rhiannon. It had to. Any other outcome was unthinkable.

Reaching the muddy shore, Nathie hauled herself out to the water and staggered forward, audibly gasping for air.

"Help!" she screamed, waving her arms weakly at the two guards. "The ferry!" she made sure her voice hitched in desperation. She looked like a drowned rat, but a wealthy, human one. If altruism wouldn't work, hopefully, money would. The guards hurried over, and as they approached, Nathie could see they were both half-orcs, only given a measly jacket each to keep off the rain.

"Please, the ferry," she gasped, falling to her knees on the muddy ground. "It's sinking."

"Madame, are you alright?" The slightly shorter of the two asked, crouching by her to help her stand.

"My cousin," Nathie's own desperation leaked into her performance. The ferry *was* sinking, and Nathie's dearest cousin was stuck on it. She truly needed their help, and her eyes watered of their own accord. "My cousin's on the ferry, but she can't swim like I can. Please, your boat, please help me."

The two guards looked at each other, then back toward the master's house.

"How far?" the shorter man asked. He looked to be the younger of the two, barely old enough to be called a man. Nathie swallowed and shook her head, still breathless. The tears falling from her eyes were real, but were only permitted because they would help sell her ruse. Allowing strange men to see how desperate she was for their help was anathema to her, but Rhiannon's life was at stake. The men had only a handful more seconds. If they hesitated any longer, Nathie would slit their throats and row the damn boat herself.

"Not far, just upriver around the bend. Please, I can pay you for your trouble." She had said the magic words, and at the mention of payment, both men looked at her sorry state.

"Are you alright to show us where the ferry is?" the taller one asked, his voice much deeper. His tusks were larger, too.

"Absolutely," Nathie said, placing her hands on her muddy knees to 'catch her breath.' "Please, I don't know how much time we have."

"Wouldn't be right to leave those souls to go down, reward or no reward," the shorter guard muttered to his partner as they set to work untying the tarpaulin from the rowboat. Tossing it aside, the men pushed the rowboat back into the water, grunting with the effort.

Stumbling after them, Nathie climbed in at the prow. She prayed to every Messiah that had ever died on the wheel that Rhiannon was still alive and that she could hang on just a little longer. The rowboat caught more of the river's current than Annie's canoe had, but with one man on each oar, they made good time upriver.

Her heart sank as they rounded a bend and she saw the white and red paddlewheel boat had capsized, its shallow hull bright red against the muddy water. The whitewashed wood of the ferry's tall deck glowed near the surface, but the upper decks had were lost in the murky depths.

Figures stood on the hull, crouched to keep their balance. At the sight of the rowboat, one stood up to wave its arms. A sob bubbled up in Nathie's chest as she heard the deep bark of Fyodor.

Splashing in the water caught her attention, and Nathie gasped in horror as she watched a survivor trying to swim toward them, only for a flash of blue scales to take him. The vishap pulled the man under effortlessly, and when the crewmate surfaced again, he was screaming. It might as well have been a dinner bell. Nathie recoiled from the rowboat's prow as a massive vishap bull passed underneath, its crest scraping along the keel under her.

"Shit," the older man muttered. "Steph, to the right. We need to go around or risk one of those bastards climbing into the boat."

Nathalie looked back at the oarsmen, face paling. She couldn't let that happen to Rhiannon. Casting about the bottom of the boat, Nathie found a length of rope. Sliding it over her head and one shoulder, she waited until the rowboat was past the blood patch, and then dove into the water.

This wasn't like swimming to the dock. Long man river's fingers were cold and strong, the current threatening to drag her into its depths. Yet it worked in Nathie's favour as much as it worked against her. The paddleboat's tall block of upper decks was catching the force of the water flowing downstream, acting like an underwater sail. Folding her hands together ahead of her, Nathalie made herself as sleek as she could, kicking hard toward the overturned vessel. It was monumentally stupid, and as she surfaced, Nathie felt a scaly tail brush her upper thigh.

Using a breaststroke to cause as little splashing as possible while she swam, Nathie closed the distance to the steamboat. She reached up and grabbed onto the slimy hull with the flat of her hands, pressing down to give herself the most grip to haul herself up to where Rhiannon and the other passengers were waiting.

"Nathie?!" Hearing her cousin's voice again made her want to collapse into a fresh set of tears, but emotion had to wait. Nathie could feel the boat sink and shift even as she pulled herself up.

Strong arms reached down, helping her scrabble up to the keel as the steamer finally rolled to capsize completely. As soon as she was stable, Nathie threw her arms around her cousin and crushed her in a desperate hug.

"Thank the Messiah, you're safe," Nathie gasped. "Thank you, thank you."

"We're not safe yet," Rhiannon said, returning the hug just as fiercely. "I can't believe you swam over. You saw what happened to that man."

"Vishaps," Nathie gasped, genuinely out of breath. Reluctantly letting go of her cousin, she slicked her hair back from her face, and took stock of the situation. Rhiannon, her dog, the ginger officer from Wyndford were the faces she knew, but there was a handful of others, both passengers and crew.

"Who's got a good arm?" she asked, pulling the rope off of her. "To the rowboat. They can come closer, but you might have to use the rope to avoid the water." The Wyndford cop lifted a hand, and Nathie shoved the wet rope at him.

"What about Fyo?" Rhiannon asked, her eyes wide. The mastiff whined, ears low and his stub of a tail tucked down. The poor thing was right to be afraid. Fyodor wouldn't be able to use the rope to climb down to the rowboat, and a dog in the water would be easy pickings for vishaps or gators. Maybe even sharks.

"How far can he jump?" Nathalie asked.

From the corner of her eye, she saw the police officer knot a loop of rope and whirl it around over his head. He let go, launching the lasso over to land around the prow of the rowboat. One passenger, a dark-skinned man with a silver badge clipped to his suspenders, helped the police officer pull the rowboat alongside the hull.

"Far enough," Rhiannon said. She whistled and motioned for Fyodor to go to the rowboat. The mastiff whined, head low. Nathie hadn't seen him ever disobey her cousin before, but this was a terrifying new situation for everyone involved.

"You have to go first," Nathalie said, nudging her cousin. "I'll help with the rest. Go, he'll follow. We don't have time to argue."

Rhiannon looked at her, then at the cop, then nodded. Biting her lip, Nathie watched her cousin judge the distance, then leap from the sinking vessel to the rowboat. She landed awkwardly, but she landed. This time, when Rhiannon whistled, Fyodor leapt without a moment's hesitation.

Turning to the other passengers, Nathie spotted a vishap crawling up the rear of the hull, its strong claws digging into the painted wood with ease. Before she could to warn the crewmate who stood with his back to it, the beast lunged, its maw gaping open to reveal horrible, curved teeth that snapped closed around the doomed man.

"Hurry!" Nathie grabbed the nearest passenger and pushed them toward the rowboat. The woman, her pointed ears poking through her waterlogged hair, made to jump. She hesitated at the last moment, slipping from the hull and landing in the water instead of on the rowboat.

Rhiannon immediately plunged her arms into the water, searching around before hauling up the spluttering woman. The remaining crew pushed past Nathie, desperate to get to safety. They leapt without waiting for the way to be clear. Most made it, though one screamed as he landed in the boat. A bad landing, though a broken ankle was far preferable to being eaten, Nathie thought wildly.

The ferry's hull had slipped below the water's surface now, and Nathalie could feel it going down quickly. With just the police officer and her left, they were nearly saved.

"I can't swim," the police officer admitted, holding the sodden rope. He was pale, and Nathie noticed his hands were trembling, his knuckles white.

"So jump," Nathie snapped, pulling the rope free from him. If she didn't, she was worried he might never let go. "Grab the edge and the others will pull you up."

"I–" he stammered. But they didn't have time for a pep talk. Nathalie shoved him hard from behind. The officer yelped as he fell forward into the water. Nathie dove after him, dipping under and pushing him up to the surface, where hands waited to pull him up.

Something grabbed onto Nathie's foot and tugged. For an absurd moment, she thought it was someone playing a trick, tugging at her leg to make her think the river really was a grumpy old man. Then she felt the pain of its teeth as the vishap twisted, taking her with it in the water. She kicked out with her other foot. She hit the crest first, slicing open her heel. Her second strike found its eye. The jaws let go of her foot, and Nathie kicked hard for the surface.

Something large brushed against her. This time it was far wider than a vishap. Smooth scales nudged under her, lifting her up. Holding on, Nathie broke the surface and coughed up river water onto golden and white scales that seemed to shimmer in the muddy water.

"Holy shit," someone muttered from the rowboat, and someone else screamed.

Nathie clung to the snake's head as it lifted her up to the boat, nudging her into it with its snout. Falling over the gunwale into the arms of Rhiannon, Nathie turned to thank her saviour, but the snake dove back under, its large coils dwarfing the rowboat. Did Lavoie's snake like the glove it had stolen that much?

"Your leg!" Rhiannon gasped, but Nathie didn't want to let her cousin go. Clinging to her, Nathie whispered platitudes about the injury. It wasn't that bad, the bleeding would stop, it didn't hurt, all lies. But the pain in her foot was only a fraction of what her heart would feel if she had to let go of Rhiannon.

"I almost lost you again," Nathie shouted over the rain. "Why didn't you stay in St-Makir's?"

"Let me look at that," the dark-skinned man with the Stratton badge said, climbing over the fainted body of the police officer to get closer to Nathie's foot. Pulling off his shirt, he tore it into strips, wrapping each carefully around the injury. "This will help slow the bleeding, but we'll need to get you to a doctor."

"None around in this storm," one oarsman said. The shorter one, 'Steph'. "But we've got a healer back at the plantation. Best to wait out the weather before trying to go back to town."

The taller half-orc glared at his partner.

"You know the master won't be happy about more guests," he rumbled.

"I didn't say bring them to the big house," Steph argued. "The dormitory will be just as safe and dry for everyone." He turned back to Nathie and offered an embarrassed nod. "It won't be up to your usual standards, I'm sure. But it'll be dry and warmer."

Nathalie nodded, still clinging to Rhiannon. For now, that was all that mattered. Her cousin was safe.

45

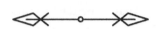

THE BUTCHERS OF THE BAYOU

MILLIE

THE SHADOW'S COLD TALONS clamped around Millie's wrists in an iron grip. Looking up at its stolen face, Millie saw flickers of shadow shaping and refining its features as she watched. It was trying to look like her, but the details were wrong. Its eyelashes were dark instead of white, the crow's feet Millie had earned around her own eyes were cracks in the shadow's skin, and its eyes couldn't form a proper pupil. Its irises kept rippling, unable to hold a solid shape.

Millie yanked herself up and forward, smashing her forehead into the thing's nose. There was no bone to break, but it let go of her wrists to grab its face all the same, giving Millie the opening she needed. Lifting her hips, she rolled the thing off her. Instead of following through to end up on top, Millie scrambled back, getting to her feet.

They were in the swamp from her dreams. Shallow water covered the muddy ground, while reeds and sugarcane stalks enclosed them in a bizarre fighting ring. She spat the remains of the ritual's tea from her mouth and wiped the wrist bandage across her lips to scrub away the taste of Fred's blood.

The demon howled, its pain dissolving into laughter.

"Okay, maybe not that soft," it said, its twisted voice no more pleasant to listen to than it was to feel. When the shadow smiled, its teeth were sharp, not like Remi's hack job but for eating meat raw from the bone. A predator's teeth.

"You've been a slippery one, elf. But it'll be over soon. The tea they gave you is weakening your spirit. Soon I'll consume it, and truly become the Butcher of the Bayou."

"You can just have that title," Millie said, bracing her hands on her knees. Her limbs felt like lead, and she didn't have any weapons on her, wherever this was. She made a face and spat again. "I don't want it. It's yours. Have fun with it."

The shadow hesitated, the smile on its face faltering. Its red eyes narrowed at her, looking for a trick.

"That is not a title you can 'give'," it hissed. "It is one that must be taken, along with your spirit. You are the Butcher, and once—"

"Yeah, but I don't really want to be the Butcher," Millie said. If she could keep it talking for a little while, she might figure out what was going on. "It's awful. Everyone says that you killed their uncle or whatever, and swears revenge on you."

The shadow smiled again. "Good, then I will hack them to pieces just like their uncle."

"The point was that you didn't kill the uncle," Millie said with an annoyed sigh. "God, was I this dumb when I was young? Or is this just a 'you' thing?"

The shadow flitted from one position in the water to another, almost too fast for her to see it move. But it left ripples behind, spreading out over the murky water as it moved. Millie's ears flicked back and forth, on high alert as she listened for where the next splash might come from.

"I know who you are under that bravado," the shadow whispered into Millie's ear from behind. "You're the Ghost of Marigot, you're Mildred Argent, now calling yourself Berry. You are my *mother*, the seed from which my spirit sprang."

Millie turned, a hand lashing out to grab the shadow, but it had flitted away again, standing on the surface of the water like it was a goddamn messiah or something. It laughed, the sound making the surface of the water shiver.

"I am *not* your mother," Millie said, gritting her teeth. While Rasha and Fenna certainly seemed like chaos spirits sometimes, they were flesh and blood and full of giggles. Just as Sarah was, though she was far better behaved. She was a mother to three wonderful little girls who were waiting for her to come back home. Millie knew she might die in this godforsaken swamp, but she also knew she could not let the spirit take control of her body. The risk it posed to her girls was unacceptable.

There is only one just war.

"But you are," the shadow said, drifting closer. It stopped just out of reach and laughed again. "Don't tell me you're ashamed of your daughter, Mildred? Your legend birthed me. The Butcher of the Bayou, they whispered about you for years before someone started feeding me such delicious tributes."

The copycat Butcher. Millie grimaced at the thought. The cult had been sacrificing families to this thing for years, fuelling its growth in power and in legend.

"You're exactly what Granddame Lavoie called you," Millie said, bristling at the suggestion that this monstrous thing was her daughter. It was only an echo of her mistakes. "Just a shadow. My shadow, trying to play dress up to become the real thing."

The shadow shrieked and leapt forward, its mouth opened supernaturally wide. Instead of flinching back, Millie stepped forward and launched a hard right hook. It connected with the shadow's jaw, knocking it to one side before the thing crashed into her, sending both of them to the ground with a splash.

"You aren't supposed to!" the shadow keened, scrabbling at Millie's face with its horrible fingers. They scratched hot lines of pain along her jaw. "You can't *hurt me*, that's not allowed!" Millie rolled them to her right, body working on muscle memory from all the wrestling matches Blackwater had put her through. The stories this spirit was born from were just that — stories. They never talked about how Millie had fought, only how she killed.

"I know who I am." Millie grunted, catching a stray elbow to her mouth. Her lip split again, immediately flooding her mouth with the taste of blood. She spat it out into the water, savouring the taste of her own blood as it overwhelmed the lingering taste of Fred's. "I know what I am." She dug her feet into the mud, using the base of the sugarcanes as leverage to push her way on top of the spirit.

"If you knew what I was, you'd be more afraid."

Millie knelt on the shadow's arm, pinning it across the demon's chest. And with a sharp jab, she broke the thing's nose, feeling the thing's newly forming bones crack under her fist. Brackish dark blood streamed out of its nostrils, staining Millie's hands and legs. It smelled like rotten corpses, left out in the heat for too long. Gross.

"You are a has-been," the shadow snarled, digging its claws into Millie's leg and shredding the meagre protection of her buckskin leggings. The elf grunted, the pain nearly causing her to lose her grip on the spirit.

"I am a survivor," Millie countered, punctuating her words with blows to the shadow's face. "I survived Fred, I survived the war, and I'll survive *you*."

The shadow lashed out, knocking Millie to the side with a backhanded swipe. Millie grabbed for her axes, but her hand found only the stupid sash Whistenhowler had given her. Seeing her disappointment, the shadow laughed and sank its claws into Millie's shoulder. It didn't need weapons, but Millie sure could use some.

The one advantage Millie had was that the shadow didn't seem to know she was a magic sink. She had to drain the spirit's magic to weaken it. The problem was that she wasn't sure how to do that, and being trapped in a swampy hellscape with the shadow who had fucking talons meant she didn't have much time to think. Spells and ambient magic didn't fight back when she drained them, but she didn't have to try. Maybe for the shadow, she had to soften it up a bit.

"Poor thing, the little elf is going to let herself bleed out in her own mind." The shadow licked its lips. "How delicious!"

Millie blinked. Wait, if this was her mind... Why the hell were they in a swamp? Why was she in the stupid costume Whistenhowler had her dress up in?

"The hell with this," Millie muttered. Taking a deep breath, she grabbed the shadow's face and threw them both sideways. They fell into deep water, sinking down as the shadow tried to tear itself free with increasing panic. Millie dug her nails into it, dragging it down deeper into the water and didn't stop until they fell out the bottom of the swamp, landing in tall, fragrant grass.

Millie sputtered, coughing up swamp water. She let go of the shadow and rolled to her feet, finding that she now wore her boots, thicker leggings and, best of all, the buckskin coat she'd meant to make from Gilbert's gift. It fit perfectly, a true second skin that hugged her and offered protection from the shadow's deadly claws.

"What *is* this?" The shadow hissed, scrabbling to its feet in the broad prairie grassland. It was still dressed like the stories of the Butcher, and it screeched when it realised Millie no longer matched its form. "You can't do this!"

"Oh?" Millie asked, pulling out her favourite axes from her belt. She gave them each a little spin to reacquaint herself with their marvellous balance. The engraving of a blueberry on the blade caught in the golden evening light and Millie smiled, brushing her thumb over it. Her favourite place, at her favourite time. At sunset, the prairie grasses turned into a sea of swaying gold. Above, nothing caged her in but open sky. If the swamp was hell, this was heaven.

"Here's the thing," Millie said, looking over at the shadow. It was trying to copy her, but its form wouldn't take, the sun burning away its shadows to leave it in the form of the Bayou Butcher. "You *are* a shadow of me, and even if you were a copy of me from back then, you'd never win this fight."

"You got old," the shadow hissed, dragging its claws over its skin, trying in vain to shed its form. "You let your friends die. You have nothing to fight for, you stupid elf!" It leapt at her with a primal scream, its long teeth bared.

Millie dove to the side, rolling to her feet. She slammed one axe into the shadow's back, the narrow blade biting deep into its flesh.

"The reason you're going to lose," Millie said, snapping her fingers. The axe was back in her hand, leaving a gaping black wound in the shadow. "Is because you're a copy of me when I had nothing left. But now I have *everything* to fight for." Daughters, friends, a better future, a husband who had wormed his way into her heart. The reasons were endless, and Millie realised that simply surviving was no longer enough. She had the rest of her life to live, and she would be damned if she let it pass without spending as much of her time as she could in the arms of her loved ones.

"Also, your strategy is shit," Millie added, darting forward to meet the latest lunge. "Rule one of engagement." she ducked a swipe and slammed her axes into the shadow's side, breaking ribs and slicing organs. "Choose your battlefield wisely." Millie twisted, using the momentum to throw the shadow. It twisted midair, landing hard on its knees.

She didn't give it time to get to its feet. Sprinting after it, she leapt forward, slamming her knee into the shadow's chin. Its head snapped back, hanging at an unnatural angle before it righted with the sound of wet bone grinding on bone.

"And you," the axes were back in her hands, chopping down to sever the tendons in the demon's arms. "Chose to fight me," she wrenched her axes free, and swung out with her backhand, the spike of her blueberry axe sinking into the shadow's head. "On my home ground."

The shadow trembled, crumbling into a fine, shimmering, black ash.

Millie closed her eyes and breathed the dust in deeply. Its power racing through her blood to every corner of herself. She refused to allow a single mote of the dead spirit to go to waste, absorbing all of it. The slashes across her leg knit closed, and the wound in her shoulder pushed out mud and tainted blood as it healed. She basked in the power as her body turned magic into life.

Gone was the warm prairie, and Millie felt the linen tablecloth under her. She smelled incense and whiskey, nearly overwhelmed by the metallic stench of fresh blood.

"Ah, here she is!" Charlie said, and Millie heard the cultists applaud. She opened her eyes and looked around. She could see motes of spiritual energy drifting around them, and at the very edge of the room, curious spirits watched in trepidation after they'd seen the demon be fully consumed by the mortal elf.

"Look at her *eyes*," Charlie marvelled. "Messiah, aren't you beau—"

The leather strips around her wrist rotted as she pulled free. Under her, the tablecloth sprouted, growing tall grassy stalks of flax that bloomed blue. Millie pushed herself up to sit on the table, noticing the oak sprouting branches from the table's legs that unfurled healthy, dark green leaves.

Lifegiver.

Oh, that's what happened to the magic Millie absorbed.

"Is... is this supposed to happen?" The large man next to Charlie asked. His eyes were wide, and he stumbled, tripping over a fresh trunk that grew up from the wood floor. She recognised his cleft chin now. A Gallois, so similar to the one who used to hang on Fred's every word.

"I think the spell might have worked too well," stammered Charlie. "Mildred, stop what you're doing." She'd heard orders for most of her life, and Millie knew the sound of a master talking to a slave when she heard it. The arrogant assumption that she would do as told with the ever-present threat that if she didn't, there would be punishment.

Millie grabbed the ritual knife, pulled it out of Fred's chest and slashed the throat of the man closest to her, his red blood splattering over Charlie and the Gallois boy. She spotted something gleaming at the larger man's hip. He had her axe.

"I said," Mildred Berry-Goldman snarled. She changed her grip on the knife and scanned the gathered cult. Most were unarmed, and fewer were fighters. This was going to be a bloodbath.

"I will *never* be a slave again. What part of that did you fuckers not understand?"

The cultists broke ranks, with most sprinting for the door, knocking into the few that stood their ground. Gallois, the large man with her axe, swung a hard right cross at Millie and she ducked under it easily to find he followed up with a left hook that crashed into her chest, knocking her back into the table. The pain was fleeting, chased off by the thrumming energy that filled every fibre of her being.

Gallois closed the distance, expecting to have her on her heels. Millie didn't bother dodging his opening cross this time. Instead, she grabbed him by the wrist and squeezed until bones popped out of place, bringing the man stumbling to his knees. She had no right to be this strong, and even as she smashed her knee up into Gallois's chin, Millie knew she would soon run out of the energy she'd gained from consuming the shadow.

With her free hand, Millie snatched her axe back from the man's belt and dispatched him with a quick strike to his temple. Pulling the axe free, she threw it into the forehead of one of the others remaining in the room. A few had been trampled, and Millie ended their suffering with ruthless efficiency.

When she blinked and found the room empty, she looked down at the bodies sprawled over the floor, staining everything red. Seedlings were sprouting up from the floor between them, unfurling beautifully bright green leaves that stood in stark contrast to the dark robes.

Following one of the taller seedlings up, Millie finally let herself look at Fred.

He hung from the table, head bowed forward like the awful figures of the messiahs being broken upon their wheels. His lips were slack, his skin ashen and his reddened eyes lifelessly staring at the table where Millie had been.

There had been a time when Millie thought Fred was the worst man on the continent. Now she knew better. There were so many of them, each hiding their awful selves while moving through the world undetected. She hadn't remembered Charlie, and he had tried to bind her as his slave in a way that not even Fred could have stomached.

Lifting his head by his chin, Millie seared his face into her memory. Once a hero, Fred had died as nothing. Not a monster, not in control, just as a means for someone else's end.

"Never again," she whispered to herself. She let his head drop and headed for the door. If Fred could die as nothing, so could Charlie.

46

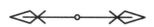

FESTERED WOUNDS

GILBERT

"THIS IS AS FAR as we go," Pete Blackwater said as they pulled the canoe up to the shore of the O'Leary plantation, anchoring their paddles among the silt and reeds to keep from being pulled back downstream.

"Hmm, someone just left," Pete said, pointing at the line left in the mud from something's keel leading directly into the muddy water. "Who else is crazy enough to go paddling in this weather?"

Gil climbed out of the canoe and scanned the open lawn ahead of him. There wasn't a guard in sight, something else that was strange.

"Do you think they took her somewhere else?" he asked, turning to Ghat. He blinked, realising her snake was gone. When did that happen? Gil glanced around the bottom of the canoe but didn't see it anywhere. Mulatiwa was too large of a snake to just 'go missing', and Gil tried to shake off the unease he felt.

"No," Ghat said, grim-faced. "She is in there. I can feel her. Something has happened... the spirits are frightened. Even Mulatiwa won't come near."

"Auntie!" The shout came from ahead, and Annie came jogging over through the shallows. "The ferry—"

"Will be fine," Ghat finished for her, her eyes fixed on the manor that loomed through the rain ahead. "Mildred will need our help, whether she knows it or not."

Gil pulled out the revolver Millie had given him and checked that it was fully loaded. It was. He sloshed ahead onto the shore, with Pierre at his side, who held a revolver of his own. Ghat and Annie followed, the latter shifting into the shape of a large panther with dark fur. When she pulled her chops back to sniff at the air, Gil caught sight of canines long enough to tear out a man's throat.

They were nearly at the porch when the front door of the manor burst open and black-robed figures spilled out, screaming.

"I see she has woken up," Ghat said, a dark smile spreading on her face. She raised a hand, and the porch erupted, vines spooling through holes in the wood and tangling around the legs of some of the fleeing humans. Gilbert tasted metal in the air.

Panther-Annie let out an unearthly scream, sprinting ahead to tackle one cultist that had broken away from the others. She rode him to the ground, her jaws clamped around his neck.

"Charlie!" Gilbert shouted. "Come out of there, you bastard. What did you do with my wife?"

One of the robed figures stumbled and looked over at him. Gilbert raised his gun, but Pierre was faster. Firing off two shots, the younger Rousseau found his mark. Charlie spun, clutching at his shoulder. The second shot caught the man behind him in the chest, and he fell, dropping a shotgun.

Throwing off the robe, Charlie raced for the sugar cane, disappearing into its tall stalks for cover.

Annie screamed again, this time her muzzle red with blood. Before the mage pursued him, the door to the master house slammed open. Mildred stood in the doorway, eyes blazing. Gilbert knew when the light caught them right, Millie's eyes seemed to glow red. Now, in the darkness of the storm, they glowed in truth. As she walked down the steps of the porch to the lawn, her eyes left twin trails of lilac smears of light, as though reality itself was struggling to contain her.

Splattered in blood and dressed up like the Butcher, Gilbert was struck by how beautiful she was. Furious, deadly, and single-minded. Good God, he loved her. He hoped that she'd survive whatever this was, so that he could tell her after all this.

"He went into the field," he shouted, pointing at the place where Charlie had bowled into the stalks.

Millie spotted him and ran over, ignoring Charlie and the other cultists. For a moment Gil wondered if there was someone behind him that she was going after. Instead, she threw herself into his arms and hugged him tight enough to pop something in his back. He returned the embrace, kissing her bloody forehead. Her touch was electric, and Gilbert felt like every single one of his nerves was waking up from a numbed sleep to feel the real world for the first time.

The rain hit his skin harder, the scent of mud and blood thick in his nose. Even his hip ached and throbbed in her presence. Though oddly, that seemed to fade the longer he held her.

"I need to go after him," Millie said, reluctantly pulling away from him. She looked up at him with those strange, ethereal eyes, and Gilbert just smiled and kissed her forehead.

"I know," he said, brushing a stray rope of white hair behind her ear. "I'll be here when you're done."

She smiled up at him and it could have brightened the whole damn bayou, as far as Gilbert was concerned.

"You're not going to tell me to be careful?" she asked.

"You wouldn't listen to me if I did." He kissed her and let go. "Make him suffer."

She lifted onto her toes and kissed him again, grabbing his hand to give it a last grateful squeeze. Turning, Millie pulled a blood-splattered axe free from her belt. Pride rippled through Gil as he saw it was the one he had given her at the very start of this mess.

He watched her break into a jog, disappearing into the sugar cane after the last of the cultists. He kept watching until someone swatted his shoulder, hard.

"Wake up," Ghat said. "If you stand there much longer, the grass will swallow you."

Blinking, Gilbert looked down at his feet to see that the neatly trimmed lawn he'd been standing on was now a tangle of prairie-like stalks up to his knees, thick with wildflowers. Carefully extracting himself, he looked up to see that everywhere Millie had stepped was now erupting into fresh growth.

"Uh," he said, pointing at it. "Is that what lifegivers do?"

"How am I supposed to know?" Ghat asked, throwing her hands up in the air. "None of the spirits that tell me things will come close to this place right now. There was a stain, earlier, of truly awful magic. But now it's just a hole."

Elf-shaped Annie hurried over to them, spitting out blood on her way.

"They're all in the field now, but I can't change into anything. There's no magic left." She looked at the path of flowers and grass and frowned. "That's weird."

"Agreed," Ghat said with a scowl. "Maybe Dee saw this before, but I sure as hell haven't."

"Baby Rousseau went into the house," Annie said. "Gilbert, can you go make sure he's not crying or something? Auntie and I will finish helping Mildred out here. Vishaps will smell the blood before long. It's best to put the bodies by the water rather than near the house."

When she put it like that, stepping into the blood-splattered plantation manor sounded like a much better option.

Gilbert trudged up the rest of the lawn to the porch. Millie's exit had left fresh shoots growing through the planks of the porch deck, along with a few branches growing from the planks themselves. Stepping over those to avoid getting caught up, Gil made his way into the house. It felt good to be out of the rain, but the smell of blood and incense was thick enough to choke him.

"Pierre?" he asked, looking around for any hidden robe-wearing assholes. The entryway of the manor was magnificent, impeccably wallpapered and decorated with vases that were now overgrown with blooms so heavy that several of the vases had fallen to one side. A wide staircase led up to the second floor, which seemed untouched.

Millie's trail of blood and blooms led Gilbert into a dining room that was mostly red. It wasn't all blood, but a lot of it was. Bodies were clustered in the doorway leading out, some with their throats cut and a few with familiar-looking wounds to the head.

Beyond them was a raised bed of flax flowers that cascaded over the edges of the bed, blue blooms splattered red with blood. It took Gilbert a moment to realise the flowers had grown from a tablecloth.

"I'm here." Pierre's voice was exhausted, and came from just out of view. "I found Fred."

Stepping over the bodies, Gilbert startled at the sight of the upended table. Frederic hung there from leather straps, his head hanging low and a gaping hole in his chest just over his heart. Blood stained his lips and had painted his front a deep red.

Pierre was standing in front of his brother, looking up at the terrible scene.

"Good God," Gil muttered, "what happened here?"

Pierre made as if to say something, then just sighed and let his hands drop uselessly against his sides.

"You know, I've dreamt of killing him for most of my life," Pierre said, staring at his brother in a daze. "I'd work myself up to do it, and every time I was too afraid to go through with it." Pierre gently lifted the curtain of oily hair from his brother's face to stare into it.

"I'd hoped she would do it," Pierre admitted. "But not like this. I don't know if even Fred deserved *this*."

Privately, Gilbert thought Frederic deserved to be torn apart by vishaps, but tactfully kept that opinion to himself. If Pierre was a devout follower of the Wheel, this sacrifice meant that Fred's soul would never recycle into another life. Again, Gilbert thought this was not necessarily a bad thing, given how shit of a man Fred had been. Tact might be less fun, but Pierre didn't need to be reminded of the horrors his brother had wrought.

"Annie said we should get the bodies to the river," Gilbert said. "Do you want something different for—"

"No," Pierre said, pulling himself together. He stared at his brother and clenched his jaw. "Let the river have him."

47

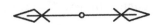

BONES OF SUGARCANE

CHARLIE

SOMETHING HAD GONE TERRIBLY wrong with the ritual. When the elf had opened her eyes, Charlie had been so certain it had worked. Her eyes were *glowing* for Messiah's sake. The power he'd felt for that moment had been intoxicating. He had the most dangerous person in Amelior as his loyal pet, but she'd stolen that from him by slitting the mage's throat.

Then fucking Gilbert had shown up before Charlie could get everything back under control, and now he was hiding like some rogue greenskin in the sugarcane, clutching his shoulder that Fred's asshole brother had shot. The men must have interfered somehow, given Mildred an antidote to the tea before Charlie'd found her.

Catching his breath, he held it as he heard splashing off to his left. The sugarcane offered cover, but it also was even darker under the canopy of leaves. It might as well have been night, and Charlie told himself that made it safer, not less.

The splashing paused, and then intensified with a scream. Charlie couldn't be sure, but he thought the scream belonged to Yves, Gallois's cousin he'd lured in with the promise of returning fortune. Shit. Yves had been a solid supporter, recruiting half the Marigot chapter of their circle.

The scream died, the heavy rain drowning out any dying words Yves might have had.

Heart in his throat, Charlie crept further down his row of cane stalks. Despite the pounding rain, he was certain his pursuers could hear every breath he took, every slosh he made in the rapidly flooding field.

A lone howl rose over the sound of the storm. Charlie could have cried. Someone had released the dogs. More loyal than slaves ever could be, they'd been trained to protect from birth and were bred from Moorlander stock with lowland shepherds to make them pure muscle. Butcher of the Bayou or not, Mildred was still just an elf. Even that one dog she'd stolen was no match for a whole pack.

The dogs would bring her down and wait for him to call them off. They'd give him time to figure out what went wrong and fix it.

Something sharp bit into the meat between his shoulder and chest, the force behind it knocking Charlie back a step. His heel caught on something, tripping him up, and Charlie went down onto his back with a grunt of surprise.

Glowing purple eyes swam down to watch him as his Butcher crouched next to him and pulled the spike of her axe from his shoulder. Messiah's grace, Charlie realised the demon was in her. It just wasn't coming to heel the way it was supposed to. The ritual couldn't have gone any worse.

"I promised I would make this slow," she told him, her voice nearly lost to the storm. "But you're making this too easy."

Charlie grabbed a handful of mud, but before he could throw it, her axe sank into his wrist. He screamed, the hot pain flooding up his arm. She yanked the axe free, and Charlie looked down to see his fingers relaxed, useless in the mud. When he tried to move them, he realised she had severed his hand from his wrist.

"Run, swine," the Butcher whispered, and then she was gone.

He didn't need to be told twice. Charlie scrambled up to his feet with a sob, picking up his hand out of the mud. He had to get to safety. Healers could reattach his hand, he was certain. Right? All he needed was to get away. He could perform a minor healing ritual and stop the bleeding.

A dog leapt out of the cane stalks ahead. Charlie recognised it as his favourite. When once it had been the most loyal pet he'd had, now its lips peeled back from its teeth in a snarl. Mildred had ruined his dog, too. All those years of careful training and it had turned on him the moment it saw her.

"She's that way," Charlie shouted, pointing with his remaining hand in the direction he'd come from. Hoping that years of care would win out over the elf's magic.

The dog took a step closer, licking its teeth between snarls. Its eyes weren't focused on the cane rows behind Charlie, but on the man himself.

This couldn't be happening. Was it because of the demon? Had it driven the animals mad?

Charlie pushed through the cane rows, running as fast as he could, the sturdy stalks slowing him every few feet as they slammed into him, their leaves cutting at his face and throat. He had to get to the river. The greenskin guards were still there with the boat. They would listen to him.

He could hear the dog at his heels, snapping its jaws at him whenever it got close.

Charlie didn't see the glow of purple until it was too late.

48

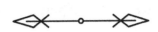

BLOOD IN THE WATER

MILLIE

WHISTENHOWLER PRACTICALLY RAN RIGHT into her in his mad rush away from the dogs. Millie swung her arm out, catching his neck in the crook of her arm. His momentum did most of the work, cutting off his air abruptly. With a choking gasp, Whistenhowler reached up for what had caught him. His remaining hand scrabbled at her arm, drawing blood as his manicured nails frantically tried to dig his way free.

"No master," Millie whispered into his ear, sinking the ritual knife into his side. It was a killing blow, but he didn't know it yet. The liver bled heavily, and even with a healer's intervention, plenty of soldiers had died in the field hospitals from blood loss.

The dog crashed through the cane stalks next to her. His short coat was marked with scars, and a white stripe down his chest was spotted with mud from running through the field. Millie smiled at him, glad to see he was alright after being taken away earlier.

"Sic," hissed Charlie. Millie twisted the knife in response. In an instant, her dog friend's snarl disappeared, and it sat, carefully arranging its front paws, licking his chops politely.

"Look at you, finding your way out. What a good boy," Millie cooed at him, using the tone of voice that Fyodor liked. The dog's mouth split into a near-grin, a pink mud-flecked tongue hanging out to one side. Charlie was still trying to tell the dog to attack, but at the small praise Millie had given it, the dog looked up at her with big brown eyes and scooted over to press his head against her leg.

"I missed you too, buddy," Millie said.

"Traitor," gurgled Charlie.

"The thing you don't get, Charlie," Millie said, pulling the knife free. "Is that cruelty doesn't earn you loyalty. Not with dogs, not with people. It just makes people afraid, and any animal that's afraid will snap when it gets to be too much." She shoved him forward, kicking him out of the row they were in. Charlie had almost made it to the edge of the field, and as he stumbled forward, he found it now.

She followed, watching how he staggered out onto the lawn and froze as he looked around at the scene in front of him. The rowboat he'd used to bring Millie to the plantation was at the dock, but it was unloading soaked strangers, some in various stages of injury. Rhiannon and Fyodor were there, with the true Moorlander bounding over to Millie to say frantic hellos. Millie's new companion growled a low warning, but allowed the much larger dog close once it was clear he wasn't a threat.

Charlie was staggering toward the rowboat, shoving injured people out of the way in his hurry to get to what he thought was safety.

"No more masters," Millie bellowed. The two half-orc guards took a single look at her and cleared out of her way. Millie stalked over, readying the stupid ass ritual knife. She wasn't going to lose her favourite axe over a man like Charlie.

"Millie don't—" Rhiannon's voice entreated her from the crowd. "You're better than this." In Wyndford, she had let Fred live so he could testify about the Colfield murders. That had been a mistake, leaving an opening for men like Charlie to use that weakness against her. Against all of them.

"No," she said in response to Rhiannon, but kept her eyes fixed on Charlie. "I'm not."

Charlie looked around, unsure of where to go. The rowboat was only useful if he had someone to row him to safety. The river was too swift to risk swimming, and Millie knew there were vishaps lurking below. She could feel them somehow, feel the slow beat of their draconid hearts as they waited for something to be stupid enough to get into the water.

"No masters, Rhiannon. No kings. Never again," she shouted and slammed her fist into his face. He reached for his nose, stepping back to teeter on the edge of the dock. Fuelling every shred of energy she had into the motion, Millie lifted a foot and kicked Charlie in the gut. He fell back, landing in the water several feet out from the dock. Charlie had just enough time to let out a shrill scream before the waiting vishaps closed in.

The electric buzz in her bones dropped away, leaving Millie completely drained. She sagged to her knees, holding herself up long enough to see the flash of blue scales as the vishaps closed in. A soft whine caught her attention, and Millie looked over to see the dog sitting next to her. Without the power she'd absorbed from the shadow, Millie couldn't feel him the way she had out in the sugarcane field.

Stretching out, he licked at her face, helping keep her awake. What a good boy.

Gilbert was pushing through the gathered crowd, and Millie smiled as he stepped up onto the dock, scooping her up into his arms. She sagged into him, managing a weak smile.

"Gil," she mumbled. "I stole the dog."

49

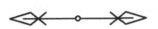

STORMY WATER

RHIANNON

RHIANNON STRUGGLED WITH HER shirt, tearing strips of the wet cotton from the hem to wrap around Nathalie's foot. Already soaked, the cotton wouldn't help contain the bleeding nearly as well as if the cotton were dry, but her options were limited. Hal's makeshift bandage hadn't been enough to cover all the gashes left from the vishap's teeth, and the rain would keep washing out the wounds, prolonging the bleeding.

"You are incredibly stupid," she huffed at Nathalie as the boat rowed the survivors downriver. "And brave, and strong, but stupid. How did you even find us?"

Pale from blood loss, Nathie smiled up at her. Completely unrepentant, the expression similar to the one Rhiannon had seen Millie wear after fighting the dragon back in Scorched Bluffs. Rhiannon thought better of mentioning the comparison. Her cousin was in no state to get worked up.

"Annie saw you were sinking and came to get me," Nathalie said, wincing as Rhiannon tied the makeshift bandage into place. "I told you Rhi, I can't lose you again." Throat tight, Rhiannon wanted to pull her cousin into a hug as much as she wanted to scream at her for risking her own life.

Fyodor rested his chin on Rhiannon's shoulder, whining into her ear. Rhiannon turned and pulled his front half into her lap, stroking the mastiff to soothe herself as much as the dog. Fyo weighed nearly as much as a grown human man. If he panicked, he could easily hurt someone by accident or knock them overboard, which was a death sentence on this river.

"Where's Gil?" Hal asked, leaning over Fyodor's rear to see Nathalie. "Why—"

Cracks of gunfire ricocheted over the water, sharp enough to cut through the roar of the storm. Rhiannon ducked on instinct, covering her and Fyodor's heads with her arms. The other surviving passenger screamed and threw herself to the bottom of the boat, hitting the man who'd hurt his leg on her way down.

"I'm guessing that's Berry?" Hal shouted, keeping his head low.

"She drugged me and left," Nathalie shouted back, carefully lifting her foot out of the way of the other passengers in the boat. "I don't know where she is."

The rowers hauled on their oars, propelling the rowboat to an impressive speed in their urgency. Rhiannon couldn't help but notice they were headed toward the gunfire. Her rifle was back on the boat, but she had the revolver she'd strapped to her belt. Pulling it out, she checked that the bullets she'd loaded it with had all survived the ship's sinking.

"Where are we going?" she asked her cousin, bending over to speak into her ear. It was hard to hear anything over the sound of the storm, and the cracks of gunfire only made it worse.

"O'Leary's plantation," Nathie answered. She made a face as Rhiannon pulled back to look at her in shock. "They were the ones with a boat," her cousin said with a shrug.

The shape of a long canoe emerged from the grey wall of rain. As the rowboat approached the shore, Rhiannon made out a few featureless figures that headed deeper into the plantation, nearly disappearing from view. Rhiannon slicked the water from her face with one hand and squinted inland. A few people lay dead on the grass lawn closer to the water, the rain washing the red from their bodies.

"Who are you?" One oarsman shouted to the canoe, "What's going on?"

"Pete Blackwater," the man sitting at the stern said, lifting his hand, empty palm facing out to show that he held no weapon. His hair was braided as Millie wore hers, and he was wearing a reed poncho that shed the rain. A few other humans were in the canoe, similarly dressed. "Was just delivering something, but I'd wait at the water's edge for a few minutes if I were you. The Butcher's hunting up there. Best let her finish her work."

Rhiannon bolted upright at the mention of Millie.

"Why aren't you helping her?" she asked, her voice shrill. She should never have let Millie and Nathie leave without her. Both ran headlong into danger and the thought of losing either was enough to make Rhiannon breathless with panic.

Pete looked at her, and then chuckled, a wide smile on his face that squished his eyes into slits.

"Best not to step on tainted land," he said, still laughing to himself. Someone screamed from the shore, and Rhiannon readied herself to jump out of the water and wade to shore on her own. "The plantations are full of suffering. The Butcher's cleaning it out. Once she has, it will be safe for all of us."

Rhiannon pulled her revolver up and pointed it at the oarsmen. One looked at the gun and sighed, while the other's eyes flew wide open.

"Row," she ordered. "Get us to shore."

Neither argued, and Rhiannon lowered her gun the moment they complied. She felt sick with guilt, but she hadn't cocked the hammer on the revolver, making her threat an empty one. Not that the half-orc men knew that.

"You know the Butcher?" the older man asked as the rowboat slid onto the grassy riverbank with a whisper of resistance.

"Yes," Rhiannon said, hopping out to help haul the boat up onto the grass. Allan joined her, and with a grunt, they got the front half of the rowboat out of the water far enough that the injured could climb out without getting in the water.

"Is that a problem?" Hal asked. He reached down to lift Nathalie out, setting her down carefully on the slippery grass.

The two oarsmen looked at each other.

"You'll tell her we helped you, right?" the younger one asked. Another scream ripped across the lawn from a field. A man came stumbling out from the tall plants, wearing a waterlogged cloak that kept tangling around his legs. Cradling one arm, he ran toward them, calling for help.

It took Rhiannon a moment to recognise him. Charlie Whistenhowler, a middle son with middling looks who had obviously picked the wrong fight.

"Of course," Rhiannon said, holding out a hand to the half-orc pair. "Apologies about the gun."

The older one snorted.

"Wasn't cocked," he said. "You could have just fucking asked." He turned and spat onto the ground, walking past her to crouch out of the way of the screaming man and the ferry's survivors.

Rhiannon's apology died on her lips as she saw Millie emerge from the field. Her eyes glowed lilac in the storm, and she was dressed in something like what she'd worn when Fred attacked the town. Something was wrong. Rhiannon could feel it in her bones, and she started forward, only to be caught by the muscular arm of Allan.

"I don't think now is the time, Ry," he said, pulling her back gently. "Let her calm down first."

Hal swore and helped Nathalie limp out of the elf's trajectory.

"Millie, don't!" Rhiannon called out. "You're better than this."

Glowing eyes fixed on Whistenhowler, Millie stalked forward without so much as flicking an ear in Rhiannon's direction.

"No," the elf said, her voice cutting through the storm like gunfire. "I'm not. No masters, Rhiannon." She backed Whistenhowler onto the dock. "No kings. Never again."

50

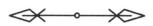

THE EYE OF THE STORM

NATHALIE

THERE WASN'T MUCH THAT shook Nathie anymore, but what she'd seen emerge from the sugarcane had shocked her. Minor possessions were common in Marigot, an agreement between a conjure worker and a spirit to trade the pleasures of the physical world for a favour. Nathie had even seen one or two, with the conjure worker taking on the posture of an old man while they were still young, or smoking cigars relentlessly despite hating the things.

The glowing-eyed elf who moved in inhumanly quick bursts and left a trail of overgrown grasses and wildflowers in her wake was nothing like the conjure Nathalie had seen before. Rhiannon had started forward, trying to stop Mildred from killing Whistenhowler. Nathie and the policeman held her back, watching the execution in silence. It was a relief when Mildred collapsed on the dock, her terrible eyes closed and no longer smearing reality.

Nathie didn't regret choosing to save her cousin over chasing Mildred, but a pang of deep guilt was growing in her belly. What had she left the elf to face?

Pierre found her trying to hobble up the path while leaning on Rhiannon's shoulder. The wind had eased, though the heavy rain continued and showed no signs of stopping.

"Would you like help? The ground is muddy and you should keep your injuries clean," he said, appealing to the only practical shred of her personality. "Mildred seems to have drained the area of magic. Neither Ghat nor Annie can do any healing until we leave."

Nathie pursed her lips, but if she was stuck with mundane healing, he was right. The mud could cause a nasty infection that might require amputation. She'd seen gangrenous limbs and the amputation process at the field hospital. A nasty process, especially when they'd run out of laudanum. Besides, she was rather fond of her leg.

"Fine," she said. "But don't think I've forgiven you. Did you find Frederic?"

Pierre's face darkened. Bending, he scooped her up in his arms, careful not to jostle her bloody foot.

"Yes." For a moment, Nathie was certain he would explain where his brother was. Pierre's silence was answer enough.

"Where is he?" Rhiannon asked, following along at Nathie's shoulder. Fyodor had trotted off to say hello to the plantation dogs, but the cop was close on her heels in his place.

They passed a pile of robed bodies, and Pierre stopped next to it, letting her see that one corpse was missing a hand.

"Did you—" Nathie asked, looking at him. Pierre shook his head. "Whistenhowler did. Mildred will know more, but when Gil and I arrived, Fred was already dead."

Rhiannon stared at the pile of bodies, a delicate frown touching her brow. She took a deep breath and set her shoulders. Losing Rousseau meant losing a key witness in the trial against Harrold, but what could they do? Undead weren't allowed to testify in court. It was too difficult to prove the soul reanimating the body was the right one.

"Let's go inside and get your injuries cleaned, then we can talk about what happens next," Pierre said, continuing up the porch and stepping around the branches that had sprouted up from the wooden planks.

"I've never seen this before," Rhiannon said, looking around at the path of life that marked Mildred's path through the manor. She followed it into what looked like a dining room, but Pierre stayed in the hall. He gently set Nathie down on her good foot. Rhiannon gasped, and Nathie's curiosity got the better of her. Bracing herself on the walls, she hopped over to peer into the room her cousin had found and her breath rushed out of her all in one go.

A bed of flax flowers stood in the centre, its blue blooms in sharp contrast to the sticky red mess on the floor and walls. A table had been set on its end; leather restraints fixed at the top to hold someone in place. Painted on its surface were a series of magic runes, every one of them dead.

"What did they do to her?" Rhiannon whispered, a hand to her mouth.

"I don't know," Nathie admitted. She had a suspicion but wanted to speak with Lavoie before sharing her suspicion with Rhiannon. Rhi, for all her grit and composure, wasn't familiar with Marigot and its customs. Nathie didn't want to worry her more than necessary. "But I think it's clear that whatever they tried didn't work."

"They tried to summon a demon," Annie said, leaning in the doorway. She was drenched but seemed to be in a better state than the rest of them. "Spirits aren't good or bad, they just are. But when people worship a spirit, they can twist it into something evil. It looks like they tried to get it to possess Millie."

Turning at the elf's voice, Rhiannon let out a soft cry and scooped her up into a tight hug. One that Annie returned, to Nathalie's surprise. She thought Annie was all snark, but she'd been wrong about one elf. It wouldn't surprise Nathie if she'd been wrong about both.

"I'm glad you're safe, Ry," Annie said. "Come meet my aunt. She's boiling some water in the kitchen. We're going to be stuck here until the storm blows over, so might as well get some soup started for everyone."

Rhiannon took up her position at Nathalie's side again, helping her down the halls to the servant's side of the manor. There was no lavish decor back there, but it was kept tidy, and the smell of cooking made Nathie's stomach growl.

The kitchen was large and abandoned in a hurry, with half-made bread left to rise too high near the stove, and chopped vegetables scattered across the counter. Nathalie spotted a familiar coil of white and gold scales nestled next to the stove, soaking up the heat after being out in the rain.

"Auntie, this is Sheriff Ryan," Annie said. "Ry, this is my Auntie Ghat."

Ghat wiped her hands on a borrowed apron and walked over to them, looking from Nathalie to Rhiannon with a tired smile.

"I heard you kept Mildred in line out on the Frontier," Madame Ghat said. "I'd ask one of you ladies to help cook, but I know neither of you can." Crooking a finger at Pierre, Ghat motioned him over. "You though, you can learn."

Rhiannon glanced at Annie, who just shrugged.

"Let's look at that foot," the elf said to Nathie. "I'll put some water to boil and get a sewing kit."

"Do... you know how to apply stitches?" Nathalie asked, some nerves fluttering in her belly.

Annie shot Nathie a look.

"I run a ranch. If it's good enough for a horse, it'll work on your foot." Nathalie knew that was meant to reassure her, but it had the opposite effect. Sensing her concern, Annie smiled. "Relax, I've stitched up Mildred and the horses plenty of times."

"I'm relaxed," Nathalie lied.

ANNIE PROVED TO BE better with a needle and thread than most nurses were. Pierre had found some bourbon and brought it over to help wash out the wounds and to numb the pain. Nathie wasn't sure what to say to him. He'd hurt her badly, but he'd also just lost the brother who had been his tormentor for years. There was no resolution there, not for any of them. Charles had stolen their vengeance.

Rhiannon stayed with Nathie while the officer, Allan, left to help move the dead down to the water's edge. Holding her cousin's hand, listening to Ghat order Pierre around the kitchen, Nathalie almost felt content.

"I thought it rained a lot in Wyndford," Rhiannon muttered. "How do you live with storms like this all the time?"

"Rot prevention enchantments are a big business down here," Annie said, finishing the last of the wounds. Nathie's foot looked like it was a doll that had been ripped to shreds and mended again, the dark thread stark against her pale skin. It would scar, but with Annie's stitches being so neat, the marks would be minimal.

"The heat was part of why we used to come visit every summer," Nathie told Rhiannon, feeling flushed from the swigs of bourbon. "The storms are the only relief, and then the moment they're over, it's right back to being unbearably hot again."

Annie tied off the last stitch and snipped the thread. Her hands were bloody, as were the needle and the pot of warm water she'd been using to wash out Nathalie's foot. Dipping her hands in the water, the elf scrubbed them clean again.

"You should wrap those up in a bandage before long so the threads don't get caught, but letting it air out might not be the worst idea." Annie looked over at where Pierre was learning how to gut a fish for the stew and shook her head.

"A Rousseau in the kitchen, that's weird," Annie muttered.

Nathie thought Pierre looked quite fetching in an apron and doing his best to help Ghat, but she wasn't about to tell him that. Maybe, after everyone recovered, she would sit down with him and talk. But she wasn't ready for that conversation yet, and she suspected he wasn't ready yet, either.

"Where is Millie?" Rhiannon asked. "I should go check on her." Nathalie took her cousin's hand and pulled herself up to stand on her good foot. At least now that the wounds were closed, she could rest the ball of her foot on the ground for balance.

"Gil carried her upstairs," Annie said, picking up the bloody pot and setting it aside to empty later. "I... Ry, I don't know how long she'll need to rest. She might not be ready for visitors."

Rhiannon nodded, but Nathie caught how her cousin's shoulders drooped. She and Mildred had parted on bad terms. Nathie understood Rhi wanted to patch things up, but Rhi hadn't seen everything that Nathalie and Annie had.

"I still want to check on her, even if she's asleep. I—" she bit her lip, and Nathie's heart twisted as her cousin tried to find the right words. "We had an argument before she left. And then she came here... for me. I need to know that she'll be okay."

Annie pressed her lips together and looked over at the stove where Ghat was. Her ears sagged, and she rubbed the back of her hand over her nose before turning back to Rhiannon.

"She might not be okay," Annie breathed. "I don't know how she could be, Ry. She came back here and had to face the ghosts of the war. It's hard enough for me, and I barely remember what life was like before my mother got me out."

"It is hell," Ghat said, leaving Pierre to keep an eye on the stew. "For Millie and for others like her, this place is hell. She is a brave woman, just like your cousin, Sheriff. But brave does not mean unbreakable. No matter how well these two hide it, this city has left its scars on them."

Nathie wanted to bristle at the accusation, but Ghat shot her a glance that cut straight through her. The conjure queen saw the scared little girl that had hid while her father had been killed. The little girl in Nathie's heart that never went away, no matter how hard Nathie tried to bury her in silks and bravado.

"She didn't come just for Rhiannon," Nathie said, holding her cousin close. "She came to find out who was after her."

Ghat smiled, her canines just peeking out from her lips. Nathie knew the conjure queen wasn't convinced, but she didn't argue.

"Go on then, you two should look after the other passengers, too. Make sure they're drying out and warming up," Ghat said. "The stew will be ready before long."

Rhiannon was quiet as they walked (or in Nathie's case, hobbled) out of the kitchen, back to the master's part of the manor. Someone had blocked off the doorway to the dining room with a side table, and the quiet murmur of voices could be heard from the parlour directly across from it.

"You can go rest there if you'd like. If Millie is sleeping, I won't be long," Rhiannon said.

"No, I'm coming with you," Nathie said. "I want to hear how Wyndford was and what you learned."

Stairs were much more difficult than Nathie had expected, but with Rhiannon's help and the bannister on the other side, she managed to reach the second floor without tearing any of Annie's stitches.

Faintly, Nathalie heard someone reading aloud. Motioning for Rhiannon to head toward it, the cousins came across a room with its door ajar. It was a simple bedroom, a fire lit in the fireplace to keep away the damp and a small figure lying on the bed under a blanket. In a stuffed armchair next to her sat Gilbert, reading from a small book. Nathalie recognised it from her school days, a story about the third Messiah, a visionary who led her people to a prosperous and peaceful period in the Ormani Kingdom.

Rhiannon touched the door and froze as a low warning growl alerted them both to the third figure in the room. One of the plantation dogs was lying on the floor between the door and the Goldmans.

Gilbert looked up and frowned. Pushing himself out of the chair, he limped over to the door and opened it just enough to speak with them.

"She's sleeping."

"Is she okay?" Rhiannon asked. "I've never seen—"

"I don't know," Gilbert said, his voice quiet but curt. "She'll feel guilty enough that she couldn't get Frederic back for your trial, Rhiannon. I don't think she needs to be reminded of that so soon after what she went through."

Rhiannon pulled back, stung.

"We're here to apologise," Nathalie said, squaring her shoulders and looking up at the banker with as much poise as she could manage in her current state. "Also, she drugged me and left me in a cellar while she ran off to face all this alone, and I expect an apology for *that*."

Gilbert's lips twitched.

"She drugged you and left you?" he asked. The bastard was trying not to laugh, and Nathie graciously pretended not to notice. "Well, that sounds like her. Let her rest for now. When she's awake, after she's had something to eat, you can apologise."

The stray dog growled softly at his side, and Gilbert cleared his throat.

"You can apologise *if* you pass her new protector." The dog stuck its wide head past Gilbert to sniff at Nathalie, but quickly retreated again after neither cousin proved to be of interest. Nathie felt faintly insulted. Dogs had always loved her.

"Thank you," Nathalie said. "I'll be resting nearby."

Rhiannon nodded, smiling tightly at the banker before he stepped back into the room and gently shut the door behind him.

"Come," Nathalie said, giving her cousin's shoulders a squeeze. "I think both of us could use a rest."

Rhiannon nodded, blinking back tears.

"I think I hurt her quite badly," she whispered, biting her lip and looking at Nathie. "I never meant to."

Gently, Nathie reached up to brush a stray tear from her cousin's cheek.

"She loves you as much as I do, Rhi," Nathalie said, steering them down the hall to find a room that they could use. "Mildred told me she'd go to the end of the world if you needed her to. She meant it. You two are as much family as we are. Goldman just..."

"He loves her, doesn't he?" Rhiannon asked.

"I suppose someone has to," Nathalie muttered.

51

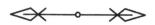

FRIENDS, FAMILY, FREEDOM

MILLIE

FOR THE FIRST TIME since setting out for Marigot, Millie did not dream of war. Instead, she dreamt of a lazy morning in bed next to Gilbert, with their daughters draped across both of them. Fenna's little girl snores complimented the sound of sparrows singing outside the window. Sarah's dark lashes fluttered against her souffle cheeks as she dreamt of something that made her smile. Rasha lay on Gilbert's chest, mouth hanging open as she slept soundly.

Looking over at her husband, Millie smiled. Gil was awake, rubbing Rasha's back gently. His hand was so large compared to hers, but instead of worrying that he might accidentally hurt her daughter, Millie felt deeply at peace. This man loved her daughters as much as she did. He would keep them safe.

"Let's go home," she whispered.

Millie rose into consciousness slowly, feeling herself float up from the depths of sleep into her body. She was warm, and a soothing voice was speaking, backed by the crackle of a fire. She lay there, listening for a while, relishing the soft sensations. Her eyelids felt heavy, and it took effort to open them. Every muscle ached, as did the joints connecting them. Even Millie's skin hurt, just from the weight of the blanket pulled over her.

"There you are."

Millie looked up at the speaker and smiled at Gilbert. He was sitting in an armchair next to her. The room was unfamiliar, but as long as he was with her, she wasn't worried. He reached out and brushed some loose strands of hair from her face, tucking them behind her ear.

"Where are we?" she mumbled, catching his hand and holding it against her cheek. The touch helped anchor her in the waking world, and slowly Millie noticed other sounds. A soft canine whine, the sound of rain beating on the closed shutters. People moving about somewhere beyond the room.

"Somewhere safe, which is the important thing," Gil said. He set aside a book and shifted from the chair to sit on the bed with her, gently pulling her into his lap. He was warm, his clothes dry. How long had she been asleep? "We're still at the O'Leary plantation, but you, Ghat, and Annie took care of anyone who might want to hurt us."

Millie blinked, looking up at him in bleary confusion.

"Ghat and Annie are pacifists," she said. "It's why Annie didn't fight at Scorched Bluffs."

Gilbert raised his eyebrows.

"Well, they could have fooled me. Annie turned into a big cat and tore out someone's throat."

Millie yawned and closed her eyes, resting against Gilbert's chest. She could hear his heartbeat like this, just as she had when she'd been overflowing with the demon's energy. It was better this way, Gil's heart beat slowly, and she didn't feel like a hive of wasps was trying to crawl out of her skin.

"I'm sad I didn't get to see that," she admitted. Something rested on her leg and Millie opened an eye to see the dog had rested his head on the bed, big brown eyes watching her. Seeing that she was awake, his stubby tail wagged, and he stretched forward to lick at her hand.

"I've decided to allow this dog theft," Gilbert teased, reaching out to pat the dog's head. "He's been guarding you since you collapsed."

"How long have I been asleep?" Millie asked, reaching out to stroke the dog's head. She remembered how scared it had felt out in the field, its heart racing from the sound of the wind. Then, as it had approached, the dog's heart slowed, and he had relaxed. Millie had felt it in the other animals, too. The mice hiding in their dens below ground, the snake that had coiled up in a furrow to wait out the hibernation, its heart so slow that Millie thought it might be hibernating.

Now it seemed she had made a friend, though Millie wondered what the fluffy puppy left back home would think of it. Freckle didn't seem territorial at all, and she wasn't about to leave another scarred veteran behind in Marigot.

"A day, maybe." Gil kissed the top of her head and stroked her hair. It had grown out from the close crop to her skull, to brush against her ears. "Not that long. The storm is only letting up now, so we've all been stuck in place."

"Once it does, do you need to stay?" she asked, looking up at him. There would be reports to make to the city guard and the governor, explaining why a quarter of the young masters had been slaughtered and why it wasn't really Millie's fault. She didn't want to deal with any of that, she just wanted to go home to her daughters.

The dog lifted his head and looked at the door a moment before someone knocked. He froze, his docked ears perked. Then he licked his chops noisily.

"I heard voices," Rhiannon said softly. "I brought soup."

Gilbert grunted under his breath. "I told her to let you rest," he murmured into Millie's ear.

"Come in," Millie said. Gil grunted again but didn't protest. Instead, he gently freed her hair from its messy braid and started untangling knots with his fingers.

The door opened slowly, with Fyodor's snout appearing first as he opened the door for Rhiannon. It was a relief to see her dressed simply again. It made the gulf between them feel just a little smaller without all the silks and ruffles. Rhiannon's cheeks went pink as she saw Millie sitting on Gilbert's lap.

Fyodor immediately went to introduce himself to the other dog in the room, while Rhiannon carried in a tray with a bowl of steaming, spicy fish stew carefully balanced on it.

"Annie's aunt said this is your favourite," Rhiannon said, setting the tray down on the bedside table. She gingerly sat in the chair Gilbert had been in earlier and tucked her hands between her knees. "I didn't know you had a favourite food. I thought it was coffee," Ryan said with a sad little smile.

"Well, coffee is my favourite thing to drink," Millie said, savouring the smell. "I didn't talk about the stew because—"

"You didn't want to talk about Marigot," Rhiannon said, nodding. "Millie, I'm so sorry. I never meant to hurt you, what I said before you left—"

"Was true," Millie said, finishing Rhiannon's sentence for her. "Almost. Almost everyone I knew here was dead. Ghat wasn't. But I was always closer to Delilah than to her. She was still just a kid when the war ended." Delilah's name caught in her throat, and Millie closed her eyes. She wondered if it would ever hurt less to say their names.

"Delilah and Clem were the older sisters I'd always wanted. And they died. I blamed myself for a long time," Millie whispered. "But it wasn't my fault. It was just sheer, stupid luck that I happened to be the one left standing. The same way it was luck that I walked into your room that night, instead of your brother's. That doesn't make it hurt any less. Not for me, and not for you. But... I wish you could have met them."

She opened her eyes to see Rhiannon reach for her hand. Millie didn't pull away.

"If I'd known how difficult this would be for you, we could have found another way. Nathie could have gone with someone else," Rhiannon said, giving Millie's hand a squeeze.

"Ry," Millie said gently. "You're family. I would do whatever it took to make you happy. But this nearly killed me, and it wasn't for *you*, it was for a company. I can't do that again."

"But it doesn't matter anymore," Rhiannon said. "Harrold is dead, Frederic is dead, there's no one left to hurt us." Rhiannon pulled back, and Millie saw her beautiful hazel eyes fill with tears.

"I know it's hard for you to understand, but hundreds of people depend on that company for work, Millie. It feeds their families and puts a solid roof over their heads. I have a duty to them, as much as I did to Scorched Bluffs. I can't abandon them."

Millie sighed, suddenly too tired to argue anymore. She didn't see how having a different owner of the company would be 'abandoning' the workers, but that was just how life had been in Marigot. If you were a slave, you could be sold or traded to another owner with no warning. Maybe the rail workers held more loyalty, but Millie doubted it. As for there not being anyone left, it was like Rhiannon had ignored everything that had happened with Nathalie. There would always be someone who wanted Millie to face justice for what she had done, and in most cases, she would deserve it. The thought was exhausting and made Millie's chest ache.

"I think that's enough for now," Gilbert said.

"You!" Nathalie hobbled to the doorway, one foot heavily bandaged. "You *drugged* me."

"Nathie," Rhiannon said gently. "Maybe now isn't the time."

"You drugged me and then you left me in that damn cellar and ran off with Whistenhowler and his cult people without so much as a thought about how dangerous it was!" Nathie hobbled a little into the room, needing to lean on the walls for support.

"The cellar was pretty safe—" Millie started.

"Not *me,* you bull-headed idiot," Nathie huffed. "Look at you! You nearly died, just when you got me to like you. You are extremely lucky that you're in as terrible shape as you are, or I'd be calling you out." She sniffed, tossing her hair over one shoulder.

"What did you fight, anyway?" Nathalie asked, finishing her lecture for the moment. "You looked like a woman possessed."

"Demon," Millie said, a small smile touching her face. "What got your foot?"

"Vishap," Nathalie answered, preening. "I'll have you know I staged a dashing rescue of our dear Rhiannon and company. Also, Mister Duncan can't swim, apparently."

"Alright, everyone out," Gilbert said with a sigh. "Except for the dog."

"In a moment," Nathalie said, putting him off. "I have something to say." She cleared her throat and stood as straight as her injured foot would allow.

"Mildred Berry, or Mildred Goldman, I believe I owe you a significant finder's fee for returning my cousin safe and sound. It's all signed in a contract with the Strattons, so there'll be no getting out of it, I'm afraid. I am also hereby postponing our duel until both of us can stand without requiring assistance."

Gilbert huffed before dissolving into laughter. Millie scowled up at him, but turned her glare back onto the human women.

"I don't want your money," she said.

"I know," Nathalie said with a dramatic sigh. "But I signed the agreement years ago and you know how the Strattons are about their contracts. Use it for something good, give it away, I don't care. But it's yours." Turning to her cousin, Nathalie motioned for Rhiannon to leave with her.

Instead of getting up right away, Rhiannon stared down at her hands.

"You called me family, but I haven't been acting like it," she said. "Being home, I was so caught up in trying to regain my old life that I left you out of it. I'd hoped, if enough things went back to normal, I'd stop missing them." Rhiannon took a shaky breath and wiped a few tears from her cheeks before smiling at Millie.

"I'm sorry. Being Rhiannon Colfield has been harder than I thought it would be. I miss being Ryan."

"So be Ryan," Millie said. "Ry, the only person whose opinion about who you are that matters is yours. And maybe Fyo's."

Rhiannon smiled, but it didn't reach her eyes. She gave Millie's hand a last squeeze before letting go. Nathalie draped her arm around Rhi's shoulders for support and from behind, they really did look like sisters. With a sigh, Millie sagged back against her husband and found herself grateful she wasn't anyone fancy. The rules they made up for themselves were so stupid that it made her head hurt.

"Don't say it," she muttered to Gil, feeling his intake of breath before he could even get a word out.

"I was just going to ask if you'd like some stew," he said, chuckling. "Good thing you know a banker to help you with that new windfall of yours."

52

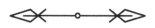

PARTNERS

GILBERT

MILLIE WAS ASLEEP AGAIN when someone opened the door just a crack to poke their head in. Gilbert was ready to tell them to fuck off until he saw Hal's face. Getting up, he limped over and opened the door to pull his friend into a wordless hug. Hal returned it, only letting go as Gil did.

"She's sleeping," Gilbert whispered, stepping out into the hall. Behind him, the dog took up guard at the door, huffing a quiet hello to Hal. Looking from the dog to Gilbert, Hal raised his eyebrows.

"Did you steal that dog, too?"

Gilbert smiled and shook his head, carefully closing the door behind him. Hal's question was a fair one after Gilbert had liberated a puppy from a cage in Plainsfield. The puppy was now named Freckle and, hopefully, was entertaining some little girls back home in Wyndford.

"This one stole himself," Gil said, stretching out his back and hip with a grimace. Something in his hip popped and instant relief flooded down the muscles of his leg. The pain wasn't nearly as bad as it had been before the storm, something that Gilbert hadn't been able to figure out. Had Ghat's spell actually healed some of the injury? Or had it been the hug Millie had given him while she was glowing?

"Have you eaten yet?" Hal asked, patting Gil on the shoulder. "There's still stew and you know I need to hear how 'Deputy Berry' turned into 'Millie' without you getting stabbed."

Gil scratched his beard, feeling his cheeks get warm. Ah, that was right. The past week and a half seemed like it was far longer. It really hadn't been that long since he'd stumbled into Millie's town and nearly got shot. They'd been through several different types of hell together since, and somehow now the woman who wanted him dead was the person he trusted the most after his father.

"Ah, well, she's not so bad," he said. "The more I see of Marigot, the more I think it's a damn miracle Millie didn't just shoot me when I showed up in town. She grew up in a barbaric society."

Hal's smile dropped, and the detective pressed his lips together grimly.

"It's why my grandad settled up north," he said, heading for the stairs. Gil followed, leaning on the balustrade to ease his hip. "We had family down here, but the week he was set to leave our home in Bakimba, rumours made it to the port that the masters of Marigot were starting to 'take on' mostly-human workers, too." Hal snorted. "Grandad was a quarter elf. Not enough for most people to care, but he thought Wyndford was a safer place to live."

"Millie said that happened," Gilbert said, frowning. "But after the war, only non-human slaves were found."

"Yeah, the fuckers killed all the mostly human slaves soon as war broke out," Hal said with a scowl. "They had no problem being traitors, but the masters couldn't stand the thought of it getting out that they were hypocrites."

"See, it'd ruin their claim that humans were better than the rest of us," Annie said, appearing at the bottom of the stairs. "Then their whole excuse for having slaves was fucked. Sooner or later they woulda just said anyone they didn't like wasn't human enough."

"Is that why you fought those cultists when we got here?" Gilbert asked Annie. "Millie said you and Madame Ghat are pacifists."

Hal raised his eyebrows and looked from Gilbert to Annie.

"There's one thing that will always be worth fighting for," Annie said. "Survival. If we let any of those wannabe cane kings get past us, they'd be right back at it, trying to stir up feelings about the 'good ol' days'. When people weren't people, but property." She sucked at her teeth and flicked her ears down and back.

"Everything else, nah. I'll protect, defend, run. But my momma died for my freedom. No way will I let some sad rich boy take that away because I don't like to hit people." Annie looked at Gil awkwardly. "Er, no offence, Gilbert."

"None taken," Gil said. "I'm neither a sad man, nor rich... compared to these people." He gestured at the manor, which was several times the size of his well-furnished, but moderately sized home in Wyndford. The elite of Marigot lived a different life, even compared to the old wealth of the Colfields. Rhiannon's family didn't *own people*.

"Now I'm sad I missed most of it," Hal said.

The sound of dog nails clicking on wood caught Gil's attention, and he looked up with concern to see his wife slowly making her way down the stairs. Hurrying up, he met her halfway. The old dog that had adopted her wagged his butt and huffed a reprimand at Millie that Gilbert agreed with.

"You should be resting," he muttered to her, helping her down the stairs. She'd found someone's shirt and pulled it on over her blood-stained leggings. It hung long on her, even belted at the waist with the sash she'd been wearing while slaughtering Whistenhowler and his followers.

"I can rest down here," Millie said, gamely holding on to Gilbert's arm to help steady herself. "Hi Hal, sorry you missed the fun."

Annie snorted and tried to cover her laughter with a cough.

"I wouldn't have minded cracking some masters' heads, but it looks like you and Gil handled yourselves pretty well," Hal said with a warm smile. Seeing his friend and his wife get along made Gilbert's chest swell. "Will I be seeing a new application at the agency soon?" He asked, arching an eyebrow.

"Me?" Millie asked, blinking in surprise. "A Stratton?" she laughed, a touch breathless. "I think I break too many laws for that."

"Don't rule it out." Hal held his hand out to the dog, letting it sniff him. "You and Gil make good partners. If banking ever falls through, the agency could use people like you."

Annie muttered something about how desperate the agency must be, but Gilbert looked at his wife. Her ears had gone pink and flicked up and down like they did when she was thinking. Catching his eye, Millie cleared her throat.

"Well. Before jumping into any new adventures, I'd like to go home for a while and spend time with my family."

"To Scorched Bluffs?" Annie asked with a smug expression on her face.

Millie's ears grew brighter, and she flicked them at the question.

"Home with my family," she said, glancing back at Gilbert. "All of them."

In his chest, Gilbert's heart thudded and tripped, skipping a beat. That sounded like she had made her decision.

"Does that mean—" he asked under his breath.

"You heard Hal, we make good partners," Millie said, giving his arm a squeeze. "I think it's worth a try. Don't you?"

"I think so, too," he whispered, stroking her cheek with his thumb. "But I think we might need a bigger house for all these dogs you keep stealing. Not to mention any more children you find along the way."

He smiled and leaned down to kiss her, ignoring the sound of disgust Annie made. Hal just laughed, ushering the other elf away to give the married couple some space. Gil was grateful, savouring the lazy kiss. After the whirlwind last few days, it felt like a luxury not to be rushing off into more danger.

"Partners," he whispered as a promise, resting his forehead against hers. Her hand was warm where it cupped his cheek, her fingertips brushing through the hair at his temple.

"Partners."

ACKNOWLEDGMENTS

Thank you to everyone who supported No Land for Heroes by buying a copy, reviewing it, or gently pointing out typos I've missed. A special thank you to Sadie, Andrew Mattocks, Lezlie, and Jamedi for taking a chance on an unknown author.

Thank you also to my wonderful beta readers K.E. Andrews, Anne N., Char M., and Tessa Hastjarjanto, and Tessa specifically for becoming a wonderful, supportive friend. Thank you to my sensitivity readers, Bookishends and Orphansnwindows for answering my questions about terms and tropes. A big thank you to Sue Bavey for proofreading and catching every incorrect capitalisation.

Thank you to everyone I spoke with about the portrayal of Indigenous culture, and the delicate issues surrounding the legacy of the American slavery system.

A special thank you to Ned Sublette for writing *The World that Made New Orleans: From Spanish Silver to Congo Square*, which provided extremely helpful context for what makes New Orleans so different from other American cities.

Thank you to *Beyond the Breakers Podcast*, for the Sultana and other paddlewheel steamer episodes, for teaching me how (easily) they sink and also to never get on one, ever.

Thank you especially to Bird the Cat, who was there for every sentence of every chapter and reminded me to take breaks when I got too engrossed in writing. Even if she deleted a third of a chapter that one time.

Made in the USA
Las Vegas, NV
19 January 2025

16654558R00288